The Pack's Doctor

The Pack Series Book 1

Cooper

Author Cooper

Dedication

I would like to dedicate this book for my fellow author, Jordan Marie. Thank you for being the kind of person who helps and encourages others. This is a difficult industry in so many ways, but it's nice to know that there are other authors out there who are willing to help those of us who are getting started and have no idea where to begin.

Thank you to my family for putting up with my crazy work schedule, even when we're on vacation.

And as always, thank you to you, my greedy readers. I wouldn't be here without you. I love your passion for reading and hope that I can continue to feed your greed for years to come.

Author's Note

First and foremost, this is a work of fiction. There is nothing in this book that is meant to represent a true emergency room or even a true medical environment for humans. In the world of supernatural shifters, there is advanced healing and an overall resistance to germs and infection (once you get your wolf). The medical scenes in this book do not, in any way, represent a true critical care or emergency room environment.

Also, in my world of werewolf shifters, gestations are five months long. I chose a middle ground between wolves (two months) and humans (nine months). So, all stages of pregnancy are advanced and occur much sooner than they would in a human pregnancy.

I'm putting a general trigger warning here. There are scenes of sexual violence, although nothing that is too detailed, and scenes of physical violence in this book. Those chapters will not have specific trigger warnings included.

I hope you enjoy this book and happy reading.

~Cooper

Contents

Chapter 1: Scent
Yara

It's been too long since I've let Annika out to run. With the number of classes that I'm taking and the heavy schedule I'm keeping, there isn't a lot of time to eat, much less let Annika run. But I have to let her out. She's becoming more and more restless.

'School is boring. Humans are boring. I want to do something fun,' she grumbles in my head.

'We're going for a run, Annika. Calm down.'

'Next time, don't wait so long.'

It's been a couple of months since I took her for a run. She's right. It's been too long. But I know how the packs fight, and I haven't wanted to risk getting in the middle of a battle or, worse, getting caught by Simon.

'I'm too smart for him to catch us. Besides, he has no idea that we're still so close to the pack.'

By 'so close' she means two hours, but it is too close. A wolf can run nearly as fast as a car, and when that wolf is on the hunt Goddess forbid that anyone gets in their way.

In the past, when I've taken Annika out to run, I've taken her in the opposite direction of Simon's pack. Well, technically, it's not his pack; it's his father's pack. Alpha Solomon has been the Alpha of my previous pack for as long as I can remember. His son, Simon,

1

is a nasty piece of work. He loves to fight, and he loves to kill. The two of us couldn't be any more different. I like to heal, and I like to save.

For whatever reason, Simon set his sights on me. I don't know why. I'm an orphan. I'm not ranked. My parents were warriors, and while I can fight, I prefer to use my biggest strength, my brain. Simon much prefers to use his strength, his Alpha strength. He doesn't have to work for it, being genetically predisposed to being larger and stronger than most wolves in the pack, so he doesn't appreciate what he has, in my opinion. I, on the other hand, have had to work for everything I've achieved in this life with the help of Alpha Solomon.

My parents were killed in a pack war when I was young. Alpha Solomon took over as my guardian and made sure that I was cared for all my life. Maybe it's because he never had a daughter, or maybe it's because I'm more like him than his own son, but he's always looked after me, even to the point of sending me away from the pack when he realized that his son had taken an interest in me. He knew Simon was no good, and he didn't want me to suffer with his son's infatuation.

When we get to the spot where we like to run, I stop, sniffing the air, making sure there are no other wolves around here.

'Annika?' I ask, making sure she's not smelling something I'm not.

'No other wolves,' she says, almost sadly. She misses the companionship of being in a pack.

I look around once more, then make my way into the forest before stripping off my clothes and tucking them onto a tree branch, high enough that someone would have to look up to see them. I have a spare set of clothes in the car, just in case anyone steals these. It doesn't happen often, but it does happen. Rather than assume that someone is being malicious, I choose to believe that they need the clothes more than I do. They're only clothes, after all.

I let Annika pull the shift, feeling my bones snapping and reshaping after so long of not shifting. It's more painful than it should be, but soon enough, Annika is shaking out her reddish-brown fur and taking off into the woods.

Even though I'm in the background while Annika runs, I can feel how good it is to stretch her legs and feel her muscles flexing in her body as she runs. It's quiet tonight, thankfully, and Annika's paws on the ground are nearly silent as she runs, giving both of us a chance to enjoy the sounds of the forest around us.

I'm not sure how long she's been running when we smell it ... blood. She slows, lifting her nose in the air.

'There was fighting nearby,' she says in our shared mind space.

'Do you hear anyone?' I ask.

'I'm not sure. I hear rustling, what sounds like a wolf in trouble. Do you hear it?' she asks as she tilts her head from one side to the other.

I do hear it. It does sound like a large animal who is struggling.

'Annika...'

'I'll be careful,' she says, knowing that, if I can, I will want to help this animal, even if it is a werewolf. It may not be possible; they may not let me get close enough to help. But I'm going to school to become a doctor for a reason. So, I can help wolves in just this type of situation.

Annika slowly and carefully makes her way to the sound of the struggling animal. As we get closer, I can tell that it is a wolf by the soft sounds that it's making. I can't figure out what it's doing, though. Maybe it's caught in a snare of some sort and trying to figure out how to get out. Or maybe it's just stuck in a hole that one of the packs dug to capture other pack members so they can interrogate them for information.

'Please be very careful, Annika. We can't afford to get caught.'

"I'll be careful, Yara.'

When we get close, she begins to belly crawl, slowly making her way closer. When the wind shifts, her whole body goes rigid, the scent of teakwood filling my nose and making my body tingle with unwanted desire.

'Mate,' she says softly.

'WHAT?'

'That's our mate, Yara. Our mate is injured.'

This is terrible. This isn't just an injured animal; it's our mate. I can't leave him out here to die, but I also can't have him trying to take me back to his pack. I have school, and I'm still in hiding from Simon.

It takes me a moment too long to realize that the wolf, my mate, has stopped moving around.

Annika barely breathes, waiting to see what he'll do.

He chuffs at us, letting us know that he knows we're here. I'm not sure how I know that he's not going to hurt us, but something in his chuff seems more like a request for help than a threat of violence.

Annika slowly and carefully makes her way through some bushes until we can see him. SHIT! He's caught in a bear trap. No wonder he's still in wolf form. If he shifts, he'll rip his leg off.

'I can't believe he's not howling in pain,' Annika says.

She's right. His leg, where it's caught in the trap, is shattered, no question.

'You have to help him, Yara. He's our mate. You have to," Annika practically begs me.

'I know. I will if he'll let me.'

As much as I hate the idea of being naked in front of this unknown man, even though he's my mate, I have no choice if I'm going to talk to him and try to help him.

I pull the shift, standing in front of the midnight black wolf who is watching me with his beautiful, intelligent green eyes.

"Hey, big guy. I see you're caught in a trap. I want to help you. I know you can't shift, or you'll rip that leg off, and that looks really painful. Your bones are probably shattered, but I want to help you if you'll let me," I say softly, keeping my tone gentle.

I slowly approach the wolf. Mate or no, this wolf must be in terrible pain and feeling vulnerable, unable to escape. I extend my hand, letting him sniff me and see that I mean no harm.

"I'm a doctor. Well, I'm studying to be a doctor to both humans and wolves. I don't want to hurt you. Will you let me see if I can help you?"

The wolf sniffs my hand, then nuzzles me. I gently run my hand through his fur, stopping when I come to stiff fur that smells like blood. I don't want to know what else is in this wolf's fur, but I can guess that guts and bones are stuck in there as well. He's obviously been fighting, and whether he got separated from his pack or he was part of a group that separated out trying to cut off the other pack's escape, he's now out here alone without anyone to help him. Anyone except me.

I look up, trying to see where the moonlight is so I can get a better look at the trap.

"Okay, big guy, are you able to move to your right a bit? I need the moonlight to help me see how I can spring this trap and set you free."

He moves to his right, keeping an eye on me as I carefully look over the trap. "Nasty piece of work," I mumble to myself. "Stupid idiots doing this to each other."

I look back up at him. "Okay, I think I've figured it out. Before I spring this trap, you need to know that when I release this, it's going to hurt really bad. But then you'll be free, and I can take a look at how badly your leg is broken," I tell him. I already know it's shattered. I can see bone splinters sticking out of his skin from above the trap.

I move my hands in position. I'm going to need Annika's strength to help me open this trap. "Try not to bite me, and if you can, try not to howl. I have no idea if there is anyone else nearby that might hear you," I tell him. He chuffs at me again, letting me know he understands.

"On three, ready? One... two ... three!" I say and push the release with all my strength, as Annika pushes with hers as well. I feel the spring give, and the trap snaps open. The wolf yelps, but it's quickly cut off as he moves away from the trap, keeping his injured leg off the ground.

He turns, looking at me a moment before his bones begin to snap as he shifts back into his human form. His ridiculously gorgeous, tall, muscular form.

Chapter 2: Mate

Warren

I can't believe that Arric and I got caught in this bear trap. Fucking Brady! I know he's the one who set this trap. We knew that he and his pack would retreat this way. I raced around, attempting to cut off their escape route, but I ended up caught in the trap.

I know my pack will come back for me, but they're in a battle, and I've been waiting for them to find me for hours. When I wasn't able to cut Brady off, they continued following his pack, hunting them like the fucking dogs they are.

I knew immediately that I couldn't shift. While I could use my hands to spring the trap, it was too risky. I wasn't willing to lose my leg and, therefore, my rank as Alpha. While the pain is significant, Arric and I are strong Alphas, and I know it is only a matter of time before the pack finds me and gets me out of here.

We'd been struggling with a way to get the damn trap off when we smelled her. I've been looking for my mate for over ten years, and now, here, in the middle of the forest, in the middle of an area covered in blood from a recent battle, I find her. Her cinnamon and nutmeg scent instantly calmed Arric.

Her wolf is a beautiful reddish-brown color, and she's obviously a very tentative little thing. Throughout her conversation with Arric, she never once gave us her name. So, as soon as she releases the trap, I step back and begin to shift so I can talk to her.

The shift hurts like a fucking bitch, my bones trying to reshape but unable to in my leg because they're in pieces. I watch her eyes go wide, and she scoots back, farther away from me.

"Easy there. You just got me out of a trap. I may be a vicious Alpha when I'm hunting my pack's attackers, but I'm not the kind of man who kills someone who just helped me," I say. Because she didn't give me her name, I'm resistant to giving her mine until I know what pack she's from.

"You said you're a doctor?"

"I'm studying to be one," she says.

"For humans and wolves?" I ask her. It's unusual, and I'm in desperate need of a good doctor in my pack. My doctor needs to retire. I need someone young, someone intelligent, someone like my little mate here, to take over my pack hospital.

"What pack are you from?" I ask, not sure I care. I'm at war with so many packs that the odds of her being from one of them are highly likely. Of course, she's out here on her own, not fighting with a pack, which is also unusual.

"I'm not from a pack. I'm a lone wolf. Did you want me to look at your leg?" I notice that she changes the subject away from her. Interesting. Or maybe not. Lone wolves are alone for a reason. It makes me wonder what happened to make my mate a lone wolf.

"Yes. I would appreciate your medical assessment," I say, wanting her closer to me. I know her touch will help with the pain.

She moves closer, and her intoxicating scent fills my nose as I take in her beautiful body. She looked shy but determined when she'd shifted. Her lean body isn't as muscular as the wolves in my pack, which makes me think she hasn't been part of the pack wars for a while. However, the softness of her only adds more allure. My fingers twitch with my desire to touch her.

"What's a lone wolf doing out here all by herself?" I ask.

"Letting my wolf out. It's not easy when you go to a human university," she says, not looking up at me. I, on the other hand, can't look away from her. She's beautiful. The reddish-brown fur of her wolf is now long reddish-brown hair on the woman. It falls over her shoulder as she looks at my leg, and I watch as she distractedly flicks it back over her shoulder and out of her way, as if this is a common occurrence in her daily life.

"You know there are pack wars going on around here," I say. She may not be mine yet, but I want her safe.

"Pack wars are going on everywhere. If I tried to find someplace where war isn't happening, I'd have to run in the human areas and risk hunters shooting Annika. You're going to need surgery on this leg. You have multiple fractures, several being compound fractures," she says, once again diverting the conversation from herself.

I already knew I was going to need surgery. I could see Arric's bones sticking out of his leg.

"Annika? Your wolf's name means merciful? How appropriate for a doctor," I say, still studying her. Her fingers on my leg are gentle. She seems to inherently know where to touch, so it only causes minor discomfort.

"Gracious or merciful, yes. And Annika is a wonderful wolf," she says proudly, still not looking up at me.

I'm about to tell her that Arric agrees when I hear my Beta's howl.

My mate's head snaps up and I smell the scent of her fear as her heart rate spikes. However, she doesn't run. She looks like she's about to take a protective stance in front of me. A perfect Luna, pushing her own fear aside to help someone in need. I smile. She's perfect for me.

"Relax, it's my pack coming back for me," I tell her.

"Oh, well then, that's good. You need to get somewhere safe. Hopefully, they won't attack me for helping you."

"I'll protect you," I say, smiling at her discomfort.

My warriors come rushing up, surrounding us as my Beta, Charlie, shifts and snarls at my mate. "Who are you?"

I snarl at him, startling him. "Stand down! She's the one who got me out of the bear trap," I command. I won't allow anyone to disrespect my mate.

He looks at her, then turns back to me, crouching to look at my leg.

"How bad is it?"

"Bad."

"Okay, let's get you back to the pack," he says, getting a couple of warriors to help me up. I wrap my arms around their shoulders and lift my bad leg, gritting my teeth against the pain.

"Ready, Alpha?" Charlie asks.

"Yeah, let's go."

Charlie shifts, taking point as guard, and the warriors holding me start to move fast.

"Wait!" I say, and everyone stops. "Bring the doctor."

"The doctor?" one of my warriors asks.

"The girl! Bring the girl," I bark, turning to look at her. I can see that she was ready to slink away. I watch her turn and look behind her as if judging whether or not she can make a run for it.

"Don't even think about it," I say to her. Charlie's wolf, Gregor, moves swiftly to her side, nudging her forward with his head. I don't like how close he is to my naked mate, and Arric growls softly.

Her eyes flash up to mine. "I should go," she says. "Like you said, there are a lot of pack wars going on around here. I probably should get home."

"Home?" I ask. I know I sound arrogant. The woman is a lone wolf going to school. Where exactly is home for her? I'm not letting her go back to wherever she wants to go. I'll never see her again. I know from the little I've learned about her that she'll never let her wolf run in these woods again. And, by the time I healed and went to find her at the university, I'm sure she'd have transferred. She's too skittish to stay where she might get caught.

"School," she says, clarifying her intended destination.

"Hmm, well, as you just reiterated, it's not safe out here, especially for a lone wolf. What kind of Alpha would I be if I left you to fend for yourself? No, I think you should come with us," I say, and my voice holds no room for argument.

She presses her lips together and stands, nodding and following behind me.

Chapter 3: Doctor
Warren

C harlie orders two wolves to flank her, keeping her safe but also making sure she follows my order.

'Alpha?' Charlie asks in the mind link.

'She's my mate.'

'Oh shit.'

'Yeah.'

'Does she know? She doesn't act like she recognizes you as her mate.'

'I'm not sure. She's a lone wolf, but she's going to school for human and veterinary medicine.'

He turns and looks at her. 'Wow. A smart one.'

'Apparently.'

'What did she say about your leg?'

'That I need surgery.'

'Well, no offense, but I could have told you that.'

'Let's see what she says when we get to the pack. And find her a shirt. I don't like her walking around our warriors with no clothes on.'

He takes off, rushing toward our pack lands. When he returns, his wolf carries a shirt to her in his mouth. I watch while she looks up at me.

"We're about to enter my pack. You're an unmarked, unknown young female. I thought you might like a shirt to put on to cover yourself," I say. If she says no, I'll insist, but I'm hoping she'll choose to put it on without me having to demand it. Thankfully, she does, looking almost relieved. Good. She's not the kind of woman who flaunts her beautiful body for all to see.

When we arrive, I'm taken straight to the pack hospital, asking Charlie about other injuries and what happened to Brady's pack. He gives me the list of injuries as we walk in, shifting and continuing to talk to me out loud as Dr. Stevens rushes up.

"Alpha, let's get you into a room so we can look at your leg. You'll need x-rays," he says.

"Yes, I will," I say. "The girl comes, too."

"The girl has a name," she mumbles. I stop and turn to look at her, her eyes going wide. She obviously hasn't been around a lot of Alphas, or it's been a long time. She keeps mumbling to herself as if I can't hear her. It's kind of cute.

"If you give me your name, I'll be happy to use it," I say to her.

"Yara."

"Yara. I'm Alpha Warren. Come with me," I say, turning back and letting the warriors help me into the x-ray room.

"Who are you? Get out!" Dr. Stevens barks at her as we walk into the room.

"She's with me," I say, ignoring his blustery attitude that a young woman is in the room with us.

She looks at him, and I'm pleased when she instinctively moves closer to me.

I get settled onto the table, and Dr. Stevens sets up the X-ray machine. While he does, I watch Yara. She has a very expressive face. Now that I can see her in the light, I can tell that she's a pretty little thing. I'm sure I'd think so even if she weren't my mate, but based on the glances my warriors keep giving her, she's a natural beauty. Yep, it's a good thing she's got that shirt on, or I'd have to rip their eyes from their sockets.

Because I'm watching her, I see her frown, her head tilting to the side as she watches Dr. Stevens. I crook my finger at her as Dr. Stevens leaves the room, beckoning her forward.

"What was that look?" I ask, realizing that my mate's eyes are a grey-green color, almost sage. My eyes are green, too, but not as dark as hers.

"What look?"

I just raise an eyebrow at her. Perhaps the pain in my leg is making me less amenable to small talk. I'm trying to ignore it, but it's not easy, and Arric can't heal me until the bones are set properly. So, I'm not as patient as I might normally be in this situation.

She turns and looks behind her to see if the doctor is there, then she leans in, her scent filling my nose.

"Why isn't he taking side views? He only took a view from the top," she whispers as Dr. Stevens walks back in. He glares at her but puts the X-ray up on the lightbox.

"Well, Alpha, your leg isn't salvageable. I'm afraid we're going to have to remove it," he says dispassionately as if he didn't just tell me that my entire world was about to collapse around me. I feel my stomach clench, and my heart skips a beat. At the same time, I hear Yara suck in air.

"Dr. Yara, what do you think?" I ask her. If she has any suggestions for me to save this leg, I'm doing it. I don't care how much pain it'll cause me or how long it will take me to recover. I've been an Alpha for twelve years. Before that, I was an Alpha in training. Without my rank, without a pack to lead and protect, I have no idea who I am.

She looks at me, then at Dr. Stevens, who is glaring at her again.

"Doctor?" he asks condescendingly. He's of an old-school mindset where women are nurses, meant to be at the beck and call of a male doctor. It's another reason he has to go. My nurses are constantly complaining and threatening to leave.

"Studying to be, but I would suggest getting x-rays of the sides of the leg before determining if the leg has to be removed," she says, more confidently than I was expecting. She may not be comfortable around me or even in the pack, but here, in this hospital room, her confidence is clear.

"You heard her, Dr. Stevens. Side x-rays," I say, seeing her glance at me appreciatively for supporting her. In truth, I'm thankful she's giving me an option, any option.

"Young lady, what are your credentials?" he demands.

"HER credentials are not what's in question, doctor. I gave you the order. Side x-rays! NOW!"

Yara jumps as I yell, but really, this asshole is going to tell me my leg needs to be removed and think that I'm not going to fight it?

He continues to glare at Yara while he does the x-rays, and when he comes back, he puts them on the lightbox and turns to her with a sneer on his face. I'm about ready to come off this table and rip that smug look off his face.

"What do you think now, doctor?" he asks, as if questioning her credentials.

Yara walks to the lightbox, looking closely at first one, then the other x-ray. "Do you have the original?" she asks, turning to Dr. Stevens. He huffs but hands it to her, and she sets it up on the lightbox, too.

She stands back, her head tilting from one side to the other.

"Yara," I ask, unable to stop the flutter of hope in my chest.

"We can salvage the leg," she says, turning to me and making me sigh in relief.

"You've got to be joking!" Dr. Stevens says. "His leg is shattered!"

"Yes, it is. And it will take a lot of time and patience. But Alpha Warren has time, and I have patience," she says, looking at me.

"Do it," I tell her, putting my future into this woman's hands and hoping I won't regret it.

Chapter 4: No Sedation
Yara

I'm not sure if Alpha Warren brought me here because he recognized me as his mate and he didn't have the strength to reject me in the woods or if he knew that his pack doctor was well past his retirement years. Either way, I'm here, and since I am, I'll help this Alpha. This is the reason I chose medicine.

"I'm assuming you want to do this now, Alpha?" I ask him.

"Yes, the sooner the better."

"Okay." I give him the list of items that I'll need to get his bones put back together properly. "Oh, and we'll need to sedate you," I say, looking around the room to see how they have their hospital rooms set up. "Is there where…"

"No," Alpha Warren says. I turn and look at him.

"No?"

"No sedation."

"Okay then, a nerve block, I'll just need…"

"No," he says again.

"Alpha, please, I'm going to have to wash the area and scrub it clean. I'm going to cut your leg open, pin your skin and muscle back so that I can get to the bones, and then slowly put them back where they belong. The pain will be excruciating. You need the nerve block."

"No," he says again, holding my gaze.

I finally look away, mumbling about stupid, stubborn Alphas. When I turn back, he's watching me with a raised eyebrow as if he heard me. I wasn't that loud, was I? Crap, I've been hanging around humans who can't hear anything for too long. How much can he hear of my mumbling?

The irritable Dr. Stevens comes in, throwing the things I asked for on the table. I jump when I hear a warning growl, looking up to see Alpha Warren glaring at him.

"Will there be anything else, doctor?" Dr. Stevens asks. He somehow makes my title, which is the same as his, sound like a dirty word.

"No, thank you, doctor. I'll take it from here."

I go to the sink and begin scrubbing my hands. I'm nervous for a lot of reasons. First, I'm in an unknown pack with an Alpha who is my mate. I have no idea what to expect from him or really why I'm here. And almost worse than that, he wants me to operate on him while he's awake! What the hell kind of crazy Alpha is he?

"You're thinking so hard that there's steam coming out of your ears, Yara. What are you so worried about?" he asks me.

I turn and look at him over my shoulder. How does he even know I'm worried? Why is he paying so much attention to me? Is this the mate bond? I've only had exposure to two Alphas in my life, Alpha Solomon and Alpha Simon. Alpha Solomon is a good Alpha, but he was never this in tune with what I was doing or thinking. And Simon...a shiver of revulsion rolls through me. He was in tune for a whole other reason. The man just gave me the creeps.

When I finish scrubbing my hands, I turn back to Alpha Warren. I see he's waiting for a response to his question. "This is going to be very painful. Can I at least give you a local anesthetic?"

"No, I need to be alert so I can protect my pack," he says.

"You can't exactly protect your pack with only one leg, Alpha."

"Warren. Call me Warren, and you said you could save my leg."

"I can, IF you were under sedation, and I'm not worried about you flinching or yanking your leg away while I'm operating."

"I have a very high tolerance to pain."

That doesn't surprise me. He wasn't even whimpering when Annika and I found him. He also has multiple, very faint scars all over his body. The man has been fighting in the

16

pack wars for a long time. He must have a very strong wolf that is able to heal him over and over.

"How strong is your wolf right now?" I ask, getting his leg prepped to wash.

"I am very strong, little one," a deep voice says, and my eyes snap up as Annika begins purring in my head. Warren smiles, once again looking as if he knows the effect his wolf is having on mine. Can he hear Annika purring?

I shake my head, trying to clear it. I need to focus my attention and NOT on Warren's incredible teakwood scent.

"If I hold the bones in place, one at a time, how long will it take for you to set them?" I ask.

"Not long, little one," he says, but it's practically a purr. "I am a very strong, powerful Alpha wolf."

The way he says it isn't bragging but more like preening. My brain flashes an image of a peacock strutting around, flaunting his feathers for his chosen mate.

"Right," I say, feeling my body responding to the deep tenor of his voice. It feels like his voice is flowing over the nerves in my body, making them all light up with a need I'm unused to feeling, especially when I'm about to do surgery.

I look up into the intense, jade-green eyes of Alpha Warren. "Are you ready, Alpha?"

"Warren," he corrects. I nod.

"Are you ready, Warren?"

"Yes, Yara."

I grit my teeth, hating that I know this is going to hurt him, but if he won't let me at least numb his leg, I can't help it.

I begin washing the blood off his leg, laying a wet cloth over the bloody area, careful that I don't tug on the bones that are still jutting out. His body is covered with caked blood, guts, and bits of bone, just like I thought it would be. Under the teakwood scent, he smells like war and death. It's good practice for me, learning how to ignore the smell of war while I work. I don't get this kind of training at the university.

"Talk to me," he says through gritted teeth.

"What do you want to talk about?" I ask, not looking up.

"You know what you are to me?" he asks, although it's more of a statement than a question. My stomach feels like it's twisting into knots.

17

"Yes," I say without looking up. "After you have healed, you can reject me. If you do it before, it could impact your healing." I don't know why the thought of this man rejecting me feels so painful. I don't even know him. I have no intention of becoming his mate and returning to the packs, not until I'm done with school anyway. And this pack is much too close to Simon for my comfort.

"Who says I'm going to reject you?" he asks, sounding offended. Now, I do look up at him.

"But I'm a lone wolf."

"What you are is my future Luna."

"You don't even know me," I say, going back to my work.

"I know that you're intelligent, you're compassionate, you're brave, and I know that you're lonely," he says.

The intelligent and compassionate parts I get. That could easily be discerned from my being a doctor and helping him; those two make sense. The brave part, I'm not sure about, but the lonely part...

"Why do you say I'm lonely?" I ask him, wiping off the blood and turning to get the scalpel. I lift it up, showing him that I'm about to cut into his leg. He nods and continues.

"The closest university with a medical school is about an hour north of here. Between here and there, there are many areas where a lone wolf could run if she wanted to. But instead," he stops, grunting as I carefully slice into his leg. "Instead, you chose to come to an area that is full of wolves."

He's partially right. Annika misses being in a pack. She misses the companionship of being with other wolves. As for me, I'd be fine living alone the rest of my life, but my wolf likes the smell of the forest, and it makes her feel more settled to smell the scent of other wolves.

Warren hisses, and I glance up at him, watching him take deep breaths to control his pain.

"How do you do that?" I ask.

"Do what?"

"Manage this level of pain?"

"Mind over matter. Physical pain will break you mentally if you let it. That's why people get tortured for information. If you can break the body, you can usually break the mind. My mind is stronger than my body, and my body is very strong."

I glance at the scars on his legs again.

"You've been fighting for a long time?" I ask, cutting and pulling the muscles away from where his bones have snapped into pieces.

"Since I became an Alpha nearly twelve years ago."

"Twelve years?" I exclaim, standing up and looking at him. He's older than I thought. That eyebrow shoots up again. It's an arrogant look, but on Warren, it's oh so sexy.

"I took over the pack when I was eighteen. I'm now thirty, that's twelve years, little wolf."

"Annika's not that little," I say, returning my attention to his leg.

"She is compared to Arric."

"Well, Arric is an Alpha wolf. Only another Alpha would be larger than an Alpha wolf," I say as I carefully pluck out the first bone. I look at it, checking to see where it goes, and then I press it against the bone it snapped off of.

"Okay, Arric, let's see what you've got," I say, carefully holding the bone in place so Arric can begin to heal the fracture. I watch as the bone begins to connect and seal in front of my eyes.

"Cool!" I say, forgetting where I am and who I'm with. I've been working with humans for so long that I forgot how quickly wolves can heal, especially Alpha wolves.

"Is it that exciting?" Warren asks me drolly.

I shrug. I know not everyone finds medicine and surgery thrilling, but I do. "It is for me."

"Then it must be my lucky day," he says, just as there is a knock at the door.

I look at the door, then at Alpha Warren, wondering who could possibly be knocking.

"I told you I would protect you," he says, smiling. His smile is so beautiful that it nearly takes my breath away. "Come in, Charlie," he says, not taking his eyes off of me.

"Alpha ... what the fuck are you doing in here?" he asks angrily, striding quickly to the table and looking at Alpha Warren's leg, filleted and open on the table.

Chapter 5: Surprising News
Warren

As much pain as I'm in, I'm enjoying watching and talking to my mate. She's unlike any woman or she-wolf I've ever met. Besides the crazy notion that I would reject her, she's funny. I love how she's constantly murmuring to herself, talking to herself as if no one else can hear her. I can hear every word, and without being marked, it's a good second to knowing what's going on inside that interesting mind of hers.

Her face is nearly as expressive as her murmurs. She hasn't learned or doesn't care about hiding her facial expressions. Once again, I find it refreshing. She isn't trying to be coy or impress me because I'm an Alpha. On the contrary, it's almost as if she's trying to get away from me BECAUSE I'm an Alpha. Not going to happen. I've searched for this little doctor too long to let her go now.

"To answer your question, Charlie, Dr. Yara here is piecing me back together, slowly and painstakingly, which is preferable to Dr. Stevens' plan to remove my leg," I say.

My Beta's eyes flash up to mine. He understands the ramifications of what I've said. And as my Beta, he's in line to take over the pack. Thankfully, I trust my Beta, and I know that he has no desire to be an Alpha. It's not an easy job, but he makes it easier by being an incredible Beta.

"Are you at least numb?" he asks, his lip curling as he looks at what Yara is doing.

"Utterly ridiculous Alpha," Yara murmurs, obviously listening in on our conversation and giving her own opinions of me that she thinks we can't hear.

Charlie looks at me, frowning. 'She knows we can hear her, right?' he asks in the mind link.

'Apparently not,' I say, smiling.

"No, no numbing," I tell him out loud.

'I might agree with her,' he says, scowling at me.

"Give me the rundown on Brady. Did you kill him?" I ask, watching my mate.

"Arric, you ready?" she asks softly, all her concentration on her work.

"Yes, mate," Arric answers, and Charlie turns to look at her again, leaning over to watch as Arric heals my bone.

"Oh shit, that's fucking awesome!" he says.

"I know, right," my mate says, smiling a huge fucking smile at my Beta. Without thinking, I snarl jealously.

Both of them jolt, and while it fucking hurts that she tugs on my newly healed bone, it doesn't break again.

"Sorry, Alpha," Charlie says, showing his neck.

She looks at Charlie submitting and then at me, and her lips press tightly together. She doesn't approve. I lean forward so she's sure that I'm talking to her.

"You're MY mate."

"What I am is your DOCTOR. Temporarily. And if you don't want me walking out of here and letting Dr. Stevens take your leg, I'd suggest that you not pull that shit while my hands are in your shattered leg again," she snaps.

I sit back, having to fight hard not to smile. Damn, I like her spunk.

I turn my head to my Beta, not looking away from Yara. "So, what happened with Brady?"

"When you couldn't cut him off, he made it back to his pack. Since we know it's booby-trapped, we didn't pass his borders."

"Booby-trapped how? Arric, again," Yara says, again not looking up at us.

I tilt my head. Does she think that she's part of this conversation? I don't care if she is. I just know that most doctors would pretend to ignore the conversation going on around them. Not my mate, though. She's not pretending anything. And somehow, she's multi-tasking, listening to us, and still working on my leg, letting Arric know when he needs to start healing a bone.

"Spring-loaded wooden stakes buried in the ground," Charlie answers her, careful now in the way he interacts with her.

"Stupid pack wars, killing for no good reason," she mumbles to herself.

Charlie's eyes snap back to mine, and I smile.

"Anywho," he says, refocusing on me. "We did get one disturbing piece of information."

"What's that?" I ask.

"Alpha Solomon is dead. Simon is Alpha now." If I hadn't been so focused on her, I'd have missed it. Her very steady hand slipped. I lift my hand, letting Charlie know to stop. I frown as her hand begins to shake.

"I'm sorry, Alpha. I need a break," she says, stepping away and not waiting for me to release her. She pulls off her gloves and rushes from the room.

"Follow her. Don't approach, but make sure she doesn't leave," I tell Charlie.

"Yes, Alpha."

When they're gone, I sit back, thinking, which is hard because my leg is throbbing and lying open on the table in front of me.

The door opens, and Dr. Stevens walks in. "I knew she wouldn't make it, Alpha. I mean..." he stops staring at my leg. "Just look at this mess! I'll get ready to remove the leg."

"The fuck you will. She's taking a break, and for your information, she's getting my bones back together. So, get the fuck out of my surgery room, doctor," I snarl.

"Alpha, I must insist..."

"What you must do is listen to your fucking Alpha. GET OUT!" I shout.

The door opens, and Yara rushes back in, seeing Dr. Stevens.

"What the hell is wrong with you? You don't leave a patient in the middle of surgery!" he barks at her.

"CHARLIE!" I growl.

"Dr. Stevens," he says, holding the door open and gesturing for him to leave.

Dr. Stevens huffs but walks out.

"My apologies, Alpha. Dr. Stevens is right. I shouldn't leave in the middle of surgery." She's not looking at me, and I look at Charlie who shrugs.

"What did you call me?" I ask, my irritation with Dr. Stevens tainting my tone.

Her head snaps up to mine. "Alpha?"

I crook my finger at her, and she walks over to me. "And what did I tell you to call me?" I ask her, forcing my tone to be gentler as I take her chin between my thumb and forefinger, forcing her to hold my gaze.

"Warren," she says, her dark green eyes nearly making me forget that I'm in a surgical room.

"Warren," I confirm, reluctantly releasing her. "Continue, Dr. Yara."

She nods and returns to my leg. I watch her take a deep breath before picking out several more bones until she finds the one she wants.

"Arric?"

"Ready, my mate," he purrs, helping her to steady her hand and her nerves. When she does, I gesture for Charlie to return.

"Any other serious injuries that Dr. Stevens is threatening to do something ridiculously over the top with?" I ask.

"Yours is the worst, Alpha. There are a couple with deep wounds that he's washing out with alcohol."

Yara sucks in air again and stands up straight, looking at us.

"Not the right course of treatment?" I ask her, starting to trust her medical knowledge much more than my current doctor.

"Why wouldn't he just stitch them up?" she asks.

"He said it would take too long, and there are too many injured," Charlie says, watching her closely. I like my Beta a lot. But until my mate is wearing my mark, I don't like all the interest he's showing in her.

Yara, however, turns to me. "Don't you have omegas in your packhouse who sew your clothing?"

"Yes," I say, frowning at her.

"It's basically the same. Yes, skin feels a bit different, it's a bit tougher than fabrics, but they could do it and not cause the pain that pouring alcohol into their wounds is causing," she says.

I look at Charlie. "Call the omegas, get them over here. Tell Dr. Stevens that he can go."

"But who is going to assess the warriors?" he asks me.

"Have the nurses give a diagnosis and recommended treatment, then bring it in here to ask Dr. Yara's opinion."

"My opinion?" she asks me, obviously surprised.

"Yes, Yara. Your opinion. I'm beginning to think that you are the perfect replacement for Dr. Stevens."

Chapter 6: Brave
Yara

Replacement? I can't be a replacement. I'm not staying. As soon as Alpha...as soon as Warren's leg is done, I'm out of here. I glance up at the broody Alpha and wonder if that's true. Is he going to let me go?

The news about Simon has me worried. If there is a paper trail from his father helping me through medical school ... he'll find me.

"Arric?" I say distractedly, holding the bones together while he heals them.

I have to get my car and my clothes. I have to get back to school. I'm a resident, I can't just up and leave.

"Tell me where your car is, and I'll have someone go get it. Same with your clothes. As far as your schooling goes, we'll have to talk about you taking classes online and working your 'residency' did you call it, here," Warren says.

I frown at him. "How did you...?"

"You were talking to yourself. It wasn't hard to hear you."

"I can't leave school, Warren," I say, looking at him like he's crazy.

"I didn't say you'd be leaving school. I said you'd be doing your residency here. You can take classes online," he says as if that settles it.

"Excuse me? You can't keep me here!"

He merely raises that damn eyebrow at me again.

"You're not my Alpha ..." I begin.

He leans forward. "What I am is your mate. Tell me truthfully, if I let you go back to school and I come to visit you in, say, a week, will you still be there?"

I look away, beginning to work on his leg again and refusing to answer him. Even if he wasn't my mate, knowing that Simon may be able to figure out where I am would have me transferring immediately.

"That's what I thought, and that, my dear mate, is why I'm not letting you leave."

He sits back, and both of us get lost in our own thoughts again. I let Arric know when I'm ready for him to heal the bones.

"Why did you say I was brave earlier?"

"What?" he snaps, and I can tell the pain is getting to him.

"Earlier, you said you knew I was intelligent, compassionate, brave, and lonely. The intelligent and compassionate I understand, the lonely part you explained, but why did you say you think I'm brave?" I ask him.

"When you heard my pack, you didn't run. You could have. You didn't know they were my pack members. You looked like you were ready to fight, to defend me. For someone who's not a fighter, that takes guts."

I look up at him, frowning. "How do you know I'm not a fighter?"

"You're not built like one," he says simply.

"Are you saying I'm fat?" I ask, insulted. I work out at the human gym. I know I need to let Annika out more often to run, but I'm not overweight, even by werewolf standards.

"You know you're not," he says, watching me. "But I saw you naked. Those of us who have been fighting in pack wars almost daily for years don't have the softness to their body that you have. And before you go jumping to any conclusions, I find your body very attractive, very sexy."

I stop what I'm doing, unsure how to respond to that.

"Sexy. That's not a word that has been used to describe me in the past," I say, and realize that once again, I spoke out loud.

I look up at him and see him smiling at me. "Some people, like me, find intelligence sexy. But I've been itching to touch you, to run my hands over the softness of your body since the moment I saw you."

"Some people, like me, find it hard to believe that someone caught in a bear trap was 'itching' to touch me," I say, rolling my eyes at him.

"Then that should tell you just how strong the pull of the mate bond is. While what you're doing hurts, just having you touch me helps with the pain. Your scent in this room, which gets stronger the longer you are in here, is helping me manage the pain. As an Alpha, it's one of the benefits of finding your Luna, your fated mate. You are the other half of my soul, and at the risk of sounding cheesy, you complete me on more than one level. Now, I have a question for you."

"Okay," I say, still focusing on his leg.

"Why didn't you run?"

I stop and look at him like he's crazy. "You were injured. If they weren't your pack, they would have killed you."

That damn eyebrow goes up again. "And they would have killed you too."

"I didn't rescue you from a bear trap to leave you to die at the hands of the assholes who set it in the first place!" I say.

"Sooo, you're more stubborn than brave?"

"Call it what you will. I wasn't going to leave you to die," I say.

"Thank you."

I wait for more, and when there isn't, I look up at him. "For what?"

"For getting me out of that bear trap, for not leaving when I could have been killed, and for not letting Dr. Stevens take my leg."

"He really needs to retire," I say.

"Which is why you're going to replace him," he says arrogantly.

"I am not going to replace him, Warren. I have school. I have ... labs and exams and things like that."

"We can talk to the school and figure out the labs. As I said, and you must know, you'll get more opportunities to practice your skills here in my pack than you will in some human school's laboratory. And exams can be taken online. People do it all the time. Any other arguments that I can negate for you?" he asks me.

"So arrogant," I mutter angrily.

"Confident," he says.

"What?" I ask, frowning.

"I'm not arrogant; I'm confident. There's a difference."

"How do you keep hearing what I'm saying?" I ask him.

"How long have you been living with humans? I think you've forgotten how sensitive a werewolf's hearing is, and I'm an Alpha; mine's more sensitive than most."

UGH! I've been living with humans long enough that I've gotten used to muttering to myself without others being able to hear me. Now, I'm going to have to start being careful what I say so I don't offend anyone.

There's a knock at the door.

"Come in," Warren calls out.

"Does no one know that this is a surgery room?" I mutter, already forgetting that he can hear me.

"Uh, excuse me, doctor. I have one of the omegas here that sews our clothing, but she says she doesn't know how to sew up a warrior," Warren's Beta, Charlie, says. I turn and see a wide-eyed young woman staring at Warren's leg on the table.

"Give me a moment. I'll be right there," I say, quickly taking a towel and covering his leg. I don't want to have to smell vomit while I work.

Charlie takes her from the room, and I turn back to Warren's leg. "Okay, I have all the small pieces underneath back in place. There are going to be some slivers that I won't be able to put back in, but hopefully, Arric can work around the small pieces of missing bone."

"I'm a strong Alpha wolf, mate. I'll make it work," he says, once again sounding like he's strutting proudly for me.

"Right. So, I'm going to put the big bone fragment against the existing bone and let you start healing it while I go check on these other warriors. When I come back, I'll finish putting the smaller pieces on top, and then we can get you sewn up and nearly back to normal, Alpha."

"Warren, Yara. Call me Warren."

I look up into his brownish-green eyes, his very expressive eyes. And right now, those eyes look exhausted. I move closer to him and put my hands on his chest, pushing him back into a lying-down position.

"Why don't you rest while I'm gone?" I say gently. "You've had a long day, and your body needs to heal." I watch as his eyes start to drift closed. I know it's a bad idea; I know I shouldn't, but my fingers have been itching to touch him since I've seen him, too. I gently run my fingers through his hair, feeling how soft it is in the places where it isn't covered in blood.

"Sleep, Warren. I'll be here when you wake up."

I'm not sure what makes me do it, but I lean in and press my lips to his, hearing him sigh as his body falls into a deep sleep.

"Sleep well, Warren," I whisper in his ear, then I cover his leg and step out of the room, letting his Beta know that someone needs to watch the room and protect their Alpha while I go help the nurses and omegas in the hospital.

Chapter 7: Car

Charlie

I can see why our Alpha is intrigued with his mate. She's a feisty little thing. I am, however, surprised that he's not putting her in line for all of the things she's muttering under her breath. On the contrary, he seems to find it amusing.

Before Dr. Yara came out and told me that Alpha Warren needed guards in his room, he had mind-linked me, telling me that I needed to send some people to get her clothes and her car.

'Make sure you scan it for trackers,' he'd said.

When she walks out of Alpha's room, she looks like she was made to be the head doctor of a pack hospital. She may lack confidence in certain things, but medical knowledge and concern for her patients aren't those things.

"Dr. Yara, Alpha Warren asked me to get your clothes and your car. If you'd tell me where they are, I'll be happy to go get them and bring them here."

"That's not necessary. As soon as I have Warren's leg put back together, I'll be leaving."

"I'm afraid I can't allow that, doctor."

"Excuse me?" she says, turning to look at me, putting her hands on her hips.

Okay, maybe I see the attraction to her spunk. Not that I would ever do anything with my future Luna. Warren would kill me, or worse, have my balls and leave me alive as a eunuch. But that doesn't mean that I don't appreciate her spirit. She's a lone wolf who isn't worried about standing up to my Alpha or me. He and I have always had similar tastes in women.

Because I'm enjoying myself, I lean over her, getting in her face. "I said, no, you're not leaving. Alpha says you stay, so you stay, even if he is unconscious."

"And here I thought I was going to like you," she mutters, turning away and stomping off. I smile, following behind her as she goes into the first room with a warrior who has deep gashes in his leg.

"What is the meaning of this?" Dr. Stevens says, scowling from the side of the room.

"Your services are no longer needed, Dr. Stevens," I say. The man is on my last nerve. If he hadn't kept so many of us alive over the years, I'd have tossed him out already.

"I beg your pardon!" he huffs, glaring at my future Luna.

I give him a warning growl. I may not be willing to toss him out because of his attitude in general, but if he keeps glaring at Yara, he's out.

"You can leave, or I can have a warrior escort you, doctor. The choice is yours."

I notice that Yara stands silently, waiting for him to make his decision. "Fine, when she kills off the pack, don't come crying to me!" he snarls before exiting the room.

When he's gone, she takes a deep breath and looks at the warrior.

"Right, so let's have a look, shall we?" she asks him. He looks at me over her shoulder, and I nod.

"Don't know why you're looking at him. He's not a doctor," she mumbles. The warrior frowns at her, then looks at me again. I shake my head, starting to see why Warren doesn't say anything. Her inner monologue, which is spoken out loud, provides some much-needed comic relief. The pack is in such a heightened state of chaos and war that having someone who is snarky yet funny is a welcome change.

She looks over his leg, assessing the injuries. "Why are these so deep?" she asks him.

"What do you mean?" he asks her.

"You're a warrior. Based on what I've heard, your pack fights all the time, so you must have more than adequate training. I'd think that you would have avoided this serious of an injury. So why are these scratch marks so deep? How did another wolf get this serious of a swipe on you? Were you fighting more than one wolf at a time? Were you cornered?" she asks him.

It's a good question – one I hadn't considered. It is a serious injury for one of our warriors.

"No, doctor," he says, looking away.

"Carson?" I ask.

"I haven't slept in four days, Beta. I was dragging and didn't get out of the way in time," he says, obviously embarrassed that he wasn't fighting up to his usual standards.

She nods and looks at him. "Well, you're about to get twenty-four hours off to catch up on sleep."

"Can't do it, doctor. We're fighting a war on multiple fronts. The pack needs me," he says.

"What the pack needs is to not lose a warrior because he's so exhausted that he can't protect himself. You'll be better after a day's worth of sleep, and so will the pack."

"No," he insists, and she turns and looks at me.

I consider for a moment, not sure what Alpha would want, but so far, he's followed her guidance, so I will, too.

"Doctor's orders are to be followed," I tell him, making him press his lips together tightly.

"Now," she says, gesturing for the omegas to come over. "Here's what you need to do."

I watch as she explains the procedure for sewing up deep gashes and then watch as the omegas carefully follow her instructions. She praises them highly, and they bask under the praise, even though they don't yet know that she's their future Luna.

I follow her to the next warrior to find out that he'd had three wolves on him at once, and that's how he'd sustained so many deep gashes. She doesn't pull him off of warrior duty.

When she's done, I pull her aside. "Dr. Yara, I need to know where your car is if you want me to retrieve it. If not, it will stay wherever you left it until such time as you tell Alpha where it is."

"Arrogant Alpha," she mutters to herself, then tells me where her car is.

"I'll have it back later. You shouldn't have any more problems with the warriors, but if you do, let me know when I return, and I'll handle it."

"Thank you, Beta Charlie."

"You're welcome, Luna," I say, making her hiss.

"I really thought I might be starting to like you," she mutters, turning to go back into Alpha's room.

35

"Keep watch on both of them. She doesn't leave the pack. I'll be back soon," I say to the guard.

"Yes, Beta."

I take a couple of warriors with me, just in case we run into problems. When we arrive, I see her car, tucked near the forest on the side of a dirt road. We get out of the car, sniffing the air around us.

"Whose scent is that?" one of my warriors asks me.

"I'm not sure," I say, not able to connect the scent of the wolves with their Alpha.

We carefully approach the car, finding that it looks untouched.

"Scan it," I tell them. Since we're constantly in pack wars, nothing comes onto our pack lands that hasn't been scanned for tracking devices and bombs. I lean down, feeling around in the wheel bed, finding the key that Yara said I'd find. I toss it to my warriors.

"Scan the inside when you're done on the outside. Give the motor an extra check," I tell them, moving to the trees. I can smell where Yara said I'd find her clothes. Her scent still lingers, but I know before I pull myself up to the tree limb that her clothes are gone. I check anyway and then return to the car.

"Anything?" I ask, looking around. When my warriors don't respond, I turn back. They're holding out five different tracking devices.

"Son of a bitch!" I say.

"Beta, who is she?"

"I have no idea, but I'm sure our Alpha will find out."

Chapter 8: Waking Up

Warren

I come awake with the scent of cinnamon and nutmeg flooding my nose. My mind is struggling to remember where I am and what happened, and then, all of a sudden, it comes flooding back. I met her, my mate. Yara.

I jolt, ready to sit up quickly to make sure she's still here, but Arric holds me steady.

'Easy, Warren. You'll wake her up,' he says, practically purring in my mind.

I open my eyes and see her with her head on the edge of my bed, fast asleep. Whether it is Arric or just my instincts, my hand is in her hair, gently rubbing her head while she sleeps.

She's sitting in a chair, and she looks terribly uncomfortable. I look down at my leg and realize that she must have finished putting my bones together while I was asleep, having also sewn my leg closed and wrapped it in bandages.

'Thanks, Arric. You're the best,' I tell my wolf, and it's true. I'd be dead, hundreds of times over, if it wasn't for the strength of my wolf.

'You can thank her this time. Being with my mate is making me stronger. The sooner she allows us to mark her, the better for both of us. We still have at least three, maybe four Alphas trying to kill us,' he says.

It's true. Brady is only one of several. I also have Quinton and Thomas fighting against me nearly once a week, and then there's Simon. Alpha Solomon wasn't the kind of man to fight a war just because he enjoyed fighting, and I had never given him a reason to fight. However, his son is a completely different story. Simon's an idiot who has more brawn than brain. He likes to fight, and he enjoys the kill. We'll have to be more careful now when we run through the general areas between the pack lands. Simon is one who will set booby traps just so he can watch someone die a slow death.

I look down at my mate. At least I have her now. The likelihood of my pack surviving, even in these war-ridden times, just increased. It's another reason I can't let her go. She's too valuable as a doctor, but as my mate, she's irreplaceable.

'Alpha, you're awake. How are you feeling?' my Beta asks in the mind link, sounding exhausted.

'Charlie, when's the last time you slept?' I ask him.

'It's been a while,' he says.

'You need to get some rest. I'm awake now. I can manage the pack.'

'Thank you, Alpha, but there's something we need to discuss first.'

'What's that?'

'I'd prefer to show you. Is our Luna still asleep?' he asks. So, he knew she was in here with me.

'She is. Was she able to get the other warriors treated?'

'Yes. I hope it's okay with you; when she gave an order, even if it was twenty-four hours down, I told the warriors they had to follow her orders.'

I look back at my mate. She seems to have an inherent ability to know what is needed and what will strengthen the pack. Or at least, that's what it seems like to me. Maybe I'm too close to see it clearly.

'Did you agree with her assessments?' I ask.

'Honestly, I think she's seeing more than I am right now. She was able to tell that Carson was too exhausted and was making mistakes. He's one that she put on recovery time for twenty-four hours. I didn't even realize he hadn't slept in days. It was affecting his performance in battle.'

I look back at my little mate, smiling proudly. Yes, she will make a fine Luna for me.

'Her orders stand,' I tell him. 'What else?'

'It might be better if I show you,' he says. Since I can hear how exhausted he is, it must be important for him to come over to the hospital for me to see it.

'Okay, don't knock, just come in. Yara is still asleep. Do you know when she came in here?' I ask him.

'Only a few hours ago. She went to see every single warrior, Alpha. Every single one. She did an assessment of them, put some on recovery time, and told others if they didn't get sleep in the next twenty-four hours, that she'd put them down officially, too. She's pretty impressive. Honestly, she makes Dr. Stevens look ... well, lazy.'

Yeah, I'd gotten that same feeling before I passed out.

'And uh, at the risk of you getting angry with me, I think I understand why you like her mumbling.'

Arric growls low in his chest. 'Why is that?'

'It's funny. I can't remember the last time I smiled, Alpha, or laughed. She's funny and witty, and even the warriors were giving her looks like they couldn't believe some of the things she mumbled.'

'They all better know that she's mine,' I say possessively.

'I told them. They're good. But as a Luna ... damn, Alpha, she's exactly what this pack has been needing, in more ways than one.'

'I couldn't agree more,' I tell him, just as I feel him outside the door. 'Quietly,' I say, not wanting him to wake my mate.

He quietly steps into the room, looking at Yara and smiling at her. I growl softly at him. He and I share a type when it comes to women. But I have no intention of sharing my mate with anyone, and if he ever tried to take her from me, I'd kill him. It doesn't matter how much I like him.

He looks away, knowing that I know he feels a pull to her. He can love her, adore her, and appreciate her as his Luna once my mark is on her. Until then, I'm feeling a bit uncomfortable with my Beta's attention toward my mate.

'You have some things to figure out with her, Alpha,' he says before laying the trackers on the bed beside me. I carefully pull my fingers from her hair and begin looking over the trackers.

'Where did you find these?' I ask, still talking in the mind link so we don't wake her.

'On her car.'

I stop, looking up at him. 'All of them?'

'Yes. Some were inside, although the key was where she told me it would be, and some were outside. One in the trunk, two in the motor, one under the driver's seat, and one shoved between the seats in the backseat of the car.'

I stare at the trackers, now deactivated. Five? Who the fuck is so desperate to get to my mate that they put five trackers on her car?

'And her clothes were gone.'

I slowly look up at my Beta.

'Scents?'

'None I recognized. I couldn't figure out which Alpha they worked for, but we could definitely smell wolves. One of the packs did this. Someone is looking for her.'

I look back down at my sleeping mate. She's been in a human university for several years. She could have gone to a werewolf university to study medicine, but she didn't. She's hiding and she's been in hiding for a very long time.

'I need you to do one more thing for me before you get some sleep. I need you to assign someone to go to the human medical school north of here. You know which one I mean?'

"Yeah, but isn't she a resident? We need to go to the local hospital or medical center, too, right? You want us to find her records and remove her from their system?' he asks.

'Yes. We need to eliminate any trace of her before whoever is looking for her finds her.'

He nods, then looks up at me. 'Alpha, if they want her this badly...'

'I know. Eventually, they'll come looking for her. Hopefully, when that day comes, she'll be wearing my mark. No one will ever take her from me. I'll kill anyone who tries,' I say.

'The pack would, too, once they know that she's our Luna,' he says.

We both get lost in our thoughts for a moment until I hear her sweet, sleepy voice.

"What are those?" my mate asks, looking at the trackers.

Chapter 9: Secrets
Yara

I'm so tired, but my body is extremely uncomfortable. I must be in some weird position. Did I fall asleep studying again?

When I open my eyes, I remember immediately where I am. I'm in Warren's pack hospital and I spent more time in one night taking care of injured warriors than I've spent in all my days of residency at the hospital.

Since my senses are full of Warren's teakwood scent, I know that I'm lying beside his bed. However, I smell Charlie as well. What's strange to me is that neither of them is talking.

I carefully open my eyes, and without moving, I look around to see that they are looking at each other. They must be using the mind link. I haven't used it in years and even before that, I barely used it, not having a family or really a lot of friends since Alpha Solomon adopted me.

When I refocus on Warren lying in front of me, I see some mechanical devices lying on his stomach.

"What are those?" I ask, pushing myself up and stretching my neck and back before looking at the two men.

"These are tracking devices, Yara," Warren says, watching me carefully.

There's something in his look that makes me think that this is significant, but for the life of me, I have no idea what I'm missing. Maybe I'm just really tired.

"What are you tracking?" I ask, picking one up and looking at it. I'm a naturally curious person. Alpha Solomon found it to be a sweet part of my personality, but many people find it irritating. I like to understand things, see them, touch them, and smell them. I don't particularly like taking someone else's word for what something is. It could just be their interpretation of what it is, which happens a lot in medicine.

"I'm not tracking anything."

When he doesn't elaborate, I look up at him, setting the tracker back down.

"Then why do you have them?"

"Charlie and my warriors found them on your car when he went to pick it up."

I look down at the trackers again, this time as if they are snakes that will lash out and bite me. I feel lightheaded as the realization hits me that this must be Simon.

"Whoa, Doc," Warren says gently, sitting up and wrapping an arm around my waist. "Take it easy. You're safe." He somehow manages to pull me onto the bed with him, but I'm so focused on the trackers that I barely notice.

"Why so many?" I whisper.

"Someone wants to know where you live, where you go," Charlie says, watching me just as intently as Warren is.

"Why do I get the feeling that you might know who did this?" Warren asks.

"I..." Shit! If he knew about Simon, he'd never let me leave. I just need to figure out how to get out of this pack and get away from here without Simon finding me. I was right. He must have tracked me to the school. I didn't notice anyone else. Annika and I didn't smell anyone else around, but that doesn't mean that they didn't show up after I went for a run.

"I have no idea why someone would be so interested in tracking me," I say, unable to look at either Warren or Charlie. I don't get the idea that either man is stupid, so I'm sure they know that I'm lying, but I need to think. I need to figure out what I'm going to do.

"I see," Warren says, and it's obvious that he does know I'm lying. "Well, someone is looking for you, and since I'm in a pack war with multiple Alphas, I'm going to let my pack and patrols know that you aren't allowed anywhere near the borders."

"WHAT? You can't do that!"

"I'm the Alpha of this pack. It's my job to keep you safe," he says. So arrogant!

"I am not your pack member. You don't have to do anything with me," I say, trying hard to be firm. I'm pretty sure it just comes across as snarky.

Warren leans in so close that I can feel his breath on my lips. Nerve endings light up all over my body at his close proximity.

"You are my mate. Your safety is my number one priority."

I can't look away from him. His brownish-green eyes are flashing with frustration and also some of the desire that I'm feeling as well.

I shove the distracting desire for this man down and narrow my eyes at him. "And just how is it that you intend to keep me safe when your leg is still healing, Alpha? Hmmm? You're in no position to protect anyone at the moment."

It's a low blow, one that I expect will anger him and cause him to lose his temper. But not Warren. If anything, he takes my words as a challenge, and he ups the ante.

"Then, I guess you'll just have to stay by my side indefinitely until I know that you're safe. I guess that's the only way that I can ensure your safety while I'm healing."

"You are insufferable!" I growl.

That sexy smile spreads across his face. "Is that why your heart rate has increased, and your cheeks are flushed, doctor? Because I'm insufferable? Or maybe it's my insufferable-ness that has you practically crawling into my lap?"

"Wha...?" I say, looking down and realizing that he has somehow managed to get me to lean over his body as if I'm about to straddle his lap. As if I was about to ... Oh, good grief! I hope he didn't mistake what I was doing ...

"I... This is very inappropriate, to be sure," I say, scrambling off the bed quickly.

"I didn't find it inappropriate at all, little mate," he purrs.

"I'm obviously tired, not thinking straight..." I gesture to the trackers still lying on this bed. "I'm overwrought with concern for who would be doing this. And you need your rest. I'll let you get some sleep," I say, taking a step toward the door. That's as far as I get before he speaks.

"I don't think so, doctor. I just told you that you'll be at my side for the foreseeable future. If you're leaving, I'll just have to hop out of bed and follow you," he says, and I turn to glare at him.

"Does that seem like an appropriate therapeutic approach to you, Beta Charlie?"

"No, Alpha. It doesn't," he says, turning to look at me and not able to hide his smile.

"Yeah, I definitely don't like you," I grumble.

"Good to know, since you're MY mate," Warren says, his smile becoming feral.

I huff at him. "I need to check on my other patients," I say to him, really needing to get out of this room with this man's incredible scent everywhere. It's making it hard to think.

"Charlie will come with you," he says.

"I don't need a chaperone, Alpha," I snap.

"Consider him a guard then. It's him or me," he says.

I turn, heading to the door. "I don't like you very much either," I grumble to myself.

"I'm an acquired taste," he says.

I yank the door open, turning to see him grinning at me as if he's won this round of word-slinging. As I step out of the room, I have to admit, he probably did.

Chapter 10: Discussion

Warren

Damn that woman! She's incredible. I can't remember the last time I've had this much fun instigating someone. Probably never.

When Charlie follows Yara out of the room, I look down at myself. I realize that I'm still covered in dried blood and gore from the battles earlier, or maybe it's yesterday now. I'm pretty sure it's morning.

While they're gone, I carefully get out of bed and wrap the sheet around my waist. I couldn't care less about walking around the pack naked, but I have a mate now. I don't want her to think that I'm flaunting myself in front of other she-wolves.

I realize quickly that while my leg is mending, I can't put my full weight on it yet.

'Those missing slivers that our mate mentioned have to be regrown, Warren. That takes time, but I'm working as fast as I can,' Arric says.

'It's okay, Buddy. You're healing me, and because of that, we'll be able to remain Alpha of our pack.'

'And claim Yara as our Luna,' he says, and I can feel his respect and admiration for her, just as I'm feeling. As usual, my wolf and I are on the same page. She's perfect for us.

'Yes, she is. And Charlie is right. She provides some much-needed humor to this pack.'

I chuckle. 'Yeah, she does.'

Normally, I'd have been offended by someone speaking their mind so frankly to me, but not her. I adore it, and Charlie and Arric are right. It's funny to listen to her mumblings because there is very little, if anything, that is ever funny in our lives anymore.

'How long do you think it will be before I'm healed?' I ask Arric.

'Another day, at least. I'll do the best I can,' he says, knowing that the longer it takes, the more likely I am to be challenged, especially if we're attacked while I'm recovering.

'Just do your best,' I say, as the door opens again.

"Oh, for crying out loud! I let Beta Charlie chaperone me. Why are you out of bed?" Yara asks, obviously perturbed.

"I'm going back to the packhouse. I need a shower. I stink, and I'm starting to itch with all this blood on me. And then, I want to eat. I'm famished. You're coming with me, though."

"I don't think so," she says, and I stop.

"Why is that?" I ask her.

"I'm leaving."

"We had this discussion. You're not leaving."

"No, YOU said I wasn't leaving. There was no discussion, and I never agreed to stay."

I look at her as if I'm trying to remember. "Charlie, help me out here. Didn't Dr. Yara agree to take on my pack hospital and move here indefinitely?" Okay, the indefinitely is a stretch, but I need Yara here to help with my warriors, and I'm pretty sure she can't walk away from that.

"She definitely agreed to take over the pack hospital since we all know Dr. Stevens is past his prime. I mean, if she backed out now, she'd basically be condemning our pack to failure and utter destitution while we wallow in Dr. Stevens' poor medical care," he says, laying it thick.

I smile at Yara as she glares at Charlie. When he looks at her, she points her finger at him. "You better hope that you never end up in this hospital under my care, or you will regret every word that has come out of your mouth this morning!"

"See, there you go again, claiming that this hospital is yours and you are the lead doctor. I'm glad we got that settled. Now, let's get going," I say, hobbling to the door.

"What are you doing?" she asks me.

I turn and look at her, giving her an exasperated look. I have no intention of staying in the pack hospital.

"I thought we'd already discussed this."

"First of all, you need to look up the definition of a 'discussion' because it's not what you think it is. Second, you can't walk. Let me get you some crutches."

"No," I say, not wanting to show weakness in front of the pack.

Unlike last night when I told Yara no, today she steps up to me, getting in my face.

"Now you listen to me, Alpha," she says, poking me in the chest. I growl softly, not liking her dominance. I mean, I kind of like it ... okay, I like it, but not when I'm incapable of giving it back to her.

"You walk into that packhouse, hobbling around like you are right now, and you're an easy target. If someone decides to test your strength, your ability to stay on your feet ..." she says, shoving my arm and knocking me off balance, "you're going down."

I growl, angry that I'm so vulnerable right now.

She sticks her finger in my face. "Don't you dare growl at me. I'm trying to protect your status in this pack. The least you can do is help me as I try to help you. Now, don't move," she says and strides from the room.

"Damn. I noticed it before, but she's a whole lot more confident as a doctor than she is as a woman," Charlie says. I agree with his assessment.

A moment later, she walks back in with a crutch. She helps me to get it set to a height that is comfortable for me.

"Now, let's try this again," she says, reaching out to shove me like she did before. This time, the crutch holds me in place.

She looks up at me, those dark green eyes flashing with her frustration. "See the difference?"

"I do, thank you," I say, surprising her.

She obviously doesn't know how to respond, so she gestures vaguely with her hand. "And the crutch can be used as a weapon if needed, too."

I stand up straight, swinging the crutch around, over my head, and behind my back, expertly showing off to my mate.

"Oh, well ... I guess you've got that down," she says before turning toward the door.

"Where are you going?" I ask her.

She sighs and turns back to me. "You can't possibly bathe yourself. I was going to go see if one of the nurses ..."

"No. You can help me."

"I'm not helping you," she says, but the blush on her cheeks lets me know this is more about her attraction to me than her unwillingness to help me.

"You just made a point of showing me that I'm vulnerable. Now, you're going to put me in a shower with a pack member who may or may not exploit that opportunity to have either themselves, their family member, or their mate try to get the upper hand on me and take over my pack? Where's the logic in that doctor?"

She looks from me to Charlie. "He can help you."

"Sorry, Luna. I've got work to do," Charlie says.

"I'm not your Luna," she grumbles.

"You're my mate. I'm the Alpha. That makes you his Luna," I tell her. "So, little mate, how about that sponge bath?" I ask, waggling my eyebrows at her.

"So arrogant," she says, beginning to walk toward the exit of the hospital.

"I thought we'd discussed that it's not arrogance; it's confidence," I say, following behind her. I feel like a stray puppy, following the nice lady who brought food, but I don't care. Maybe I'll get rewarded if I'm a good boy.

She turns and looks at me. "And I thought you were going to look up the definition of 'discussion'," she says, turning on her heel and walking out of the hospital.

"How long before she realizes she has no idea where she's going?" Charlie asks me.

"I don't know. With her, I think she'll find the packhouse by sheer force of will," I say quietly, watching Yara lift her nose in the air, trying to figure out where she's going. Then she turns to me.

"Are you coming?"

"Oh, I certainly do hope I will be soon," I murmur as I begin to follow her.

Chapter 11: Shower
Yara

I refuse to ask where the packhouse is. I'm pretty sure that arrogant Alpha, and yes, he's very arrogant, is back there laughing at me. After I painstakingly put his leg back together ... I have half a mind to break all those bones again and leave him to his own devices.

'Oh, that's not what half your mind has been focusing on,' Annika says, sending me images of Warren naked in the forest.

'I was focused on his injury,' I insist.

She changes the focus, expanding the image of Warren's penis. It's quite large, even when it's not erect.

'Gotta love big Alphas,' Annika purrs.

'You are not helping.'

'Come on, Yara. You know you're enjoying yourself. When was the last time that someone really challenged you mentally? I like him. He's ... confident," she smirks.

I roll my eyes at my wolf and continue walking.

'Tell me you know where this damn packhouse is,' I say to her.

She lifts her nose again, and I catch multiple scents, all close by.

'There you go,' she says.

I get to the packhouse and stomp up the stairs, ready to walk in ahead of Warren and Charlie, who is no better than his annoying Alpha, when Annika stops me.

'Uh, Yara. You remember that you're only wearing a T-shirt, right?' she asks me.

I look down just as I hear a growl from behind me. Charlie comes rushing up to me. "Better to wait to enter the packhouse until Alpha catches up, Luna."

I give him a look. "I am NOT your Luna."

"Whatever you say, Luna," he says, and I swear his lips twitch.

"Incorrigible," I mutter, turning to look at Warren.

I suddenly realize that he has a sheet from the pack hospital wrapped around himself as he makes his way toward me. He looks aggravated as he tries to navigate the sheet and the crutch.

"What are you doing?" I ask him, going down the steps and taking the sheet, frowning as I wrap it around him and tie it with a knot so he doesn't have to hold it.

"I'm trying to walk," he growls.

"Is that better?" I ask him with mock patience. I'm annoyed that this man thinks that I'm going to bathe him. Just because I fixed him up and just because he smells friggin' delicious doesn't mean that I'm going to bathe him.

Annika, the little hussy, sends an image of Warren naked again, making my cheeks heat.

"Oh, what I would give to know what's going on in that overactive mind of yours," Warren says softly. Because I'm so close, making sure the sheet is tied tight, I can feel his breath in my hair, sending shivers up and down my spine.

I step back quickly, not wanting him to smell what I'm sure he can, my arousal. Why does this man arouse me? He's infuriating.

'He's sexy. Look at that chest,' Annika purrs. I glance up and immediately regret it since he's watching me closely.

"I don't have an overactive mind," I say, just because I need to say something.

He chuckles at me. "If you say so. Come on, I want to introduce you to the pack."

I look at him like he's crazy. "But ..." I gesture up and down his body.

"They've seen worse, believe me," he says, and there's no humor in his tone now. I need to remember that this pack, along with most of them, is in a constant state of war.

When we walk in, the packhouse, which is buzzing with conversation, goes quiet.

"Attention everyone, this is Dr. Yara. If you haven't met her yet, you most likely will in the near future. She is the new head doctor in our hospital. When you go to see her, what she says goes. No argument or you answer to me. Understood?" he says.

"Yes, Alpha," the pack replies, and I feel everyone's gaze on me. I try to look confident, but it's hard when literally everyone is staring at me.

"Oh, and she's my mate. Fuck with her, and I'll kill you," he says seriously, making me jolt and look up at him.

"WARREN!"

"YARA!" he says in a sarcastic version of my tone. Then his lips twitch, and I just know that I'm not going to like what comes out of his mouth next.

"If you'll excuse us, my mate is going to give me a sponge bath," he says to the pack, his eyes never leaving mine.

I would growl, I want to growl at him, but instead my cheeks get so hot I feel like I'm going to burst into flames.

"You are SO arrogant," I grit through my teeth as he begins to lead me away.

"Yara, Yara, Yara, what have we discussed about this?" he says, his tone mocking.

I plaster an obviously fake smile on my face. "Does your packhouse have a library, Warren?" I ask in a sickeningly sweet tone.

"No," he drawls.

"Well, that explains a lot," I say, stomping up the stairs.

"Where are you going?" he asks me.

I turn around and frown at him. "You're the Alpha. Isn't your room on the top floor?"

"Yes, but aren't you going to help me up the stairs?"

I smile another fake smile at him. "I wouldn't want you to seem weak in front of your pack, Alpha. I'm sure you can figure out how to get up the stairs," I say sweetly.

He growls low in his chest.

"Did you want me to go find one of those nubile she-wolves to help you instead?" I ask him, still keeping my tone much too sweet.

He narrows his eyes at me.

"Then I suggest that you stop growling at me. Next time, I might just bop your nose," I say, turning and walking up the stairs.

51

I hear him making his way up the stairs, and while I probably should have helped him, the man is truly frustrating. Why in the world would he announce to his pack that I'm his mate?

I wait for him to join me at the top of the stairs. "What, you didn't go in and start my bath?" he asks, and his tone is a bit more snarky than normal. I look at him more closely and realize that he's in pain.

"Here," I say, walking to him and wrapping his arm around my shoulders.

"Now she helps me," he grumbles.

We walk to his room, and when he opens the door, I'm not prepared for the onslaught of his teakwood scent that flows out. I stop, my back arching of its own accord, my eyes falling closed, as I lift my chin, exposing my throat as my body begins to hum with desire.

"Interesting ..." he murmurs, watching me.

Before I can snap my chin back down, Warren leans in and gently nips at my throat, accepting the submission that I didn't intend to give him.

When I start to pull away, he holds me to him. "You're my mate. Submission is part of our bond," he says gently.

"Really? Are you planning to submit?" I ask him.

He tilts his head at me. "One day, when you accept your position here in this pack, yes, I will give you my submission."

I stare at him, shocked. His tone, his eyes, everything about him says he's perfectly serious.

"Surprised? You shouldn't be, but I know you don't know me well yet. But you are an intelligent, strong woman, Yara, and I have no problem treating you as my equal or submitting to your rules in the hospital."

"Says the man who insisted on walking out of the hospital tonight," I grumble, still shocked at his words. I wouldn't have expected it of a man like him, someone who is very strong and prides himself on being a strong and powerful fighter.

"My pack needed to see me after I was carried in last night. It's important, even if I'm still not one hundred percent."

That I do understand. The hierarchy of a pack that is constantly at war is always at risk of a leadership change. The fact that Warren has been Alpha for twelve years and is still leading this pack says more about his strength than anything else.

I lead him to his bathroom and let him lean against the sink while I turn to start the shower.

"Where are your clothes, and is there anything in particular you want to wear?" I ask him.

"Closet. And just shorts and a T-shirt are fine. Get some for you, too," he says.

"Thank you."

"We'll get you some new clothes," he says.

"I have clothes. At school."

"Then I'll have someone go get your clothes for you," he says, and I can see he's fading.

"Do you want to have food brought up here? Eating might perk you up a bit."

"I need the pack to see me once I'm clean."

"You need your pack to see you strong. Order some food. Have Charlie bring it up if you want, and then after you're feeling a bit better, you can go down to face your pack."

He smirks down at me as I untie the sheet. "You know what they'll think if it takes us a while to get back downstairs."

"I don't care if your pack thinks we had sex. I understand the importance of you showing a strong front to them. Come on, let's get you in the shower. You can let the water start to wash off all that blood while I go get both of us some clothes."

I get him under the water, making sure it's not too hot or cold, and then I go to get clothes. When I open the door to his closet, it's almost worse than it was when I walked into his room. The pressure in my core is nearly painful, and the man hasn't done anything except smell fantastic!

'Well, he does have quite the package on him. I bet he'd ease that ache if you'd let him,' Annika purrs.

'No!'

'Spoilsport,' she says, still purring in my head. She begins stretching like she's a damn cat lying in the sun. I roll my eyes and get some clothes before going back into the bathroom.

The moment I do, I realize my dilemma. There's no way for me to wash Warren's hair and body without getting in the shower with him. But I don't have to take off my T-shirt. I just wish it wasn't a white shirt.

Chapter 12: Truth

Warren

Whether it's the exhaustion of the battle, the broken leg that Arric is working hard to heal, or just life in general, I feel exhausted. But no matter how tired I am, I'm not going to miss my mate getting in the shower with me. I'm not even disappointed when she leaves her shirt on. Humans have wet t-shirt contests for a reason.

I stand under the water, letting it loosen the dried blood and gore in my hair. When I look down and see that the water running down the drain is bright red, I wonder how bad I look. Under any other circumstances, I wouldn't care, but I don't want my mate to think less of me. She doesn't seem surprised by the fighting, and she seems to understand the need for me to maintain a strong image in front of the pack, but that doesn't mean that she's okay with it.

"Okay, let's see what we've got," she says, walking back in and setting the clothes on the counter by the sink before stepping into the shower with me. "You're pretty tall, so I'm going to need you to bend down a bit. You'll have to close your eyes so the water doesn't wash all this gunk and soap into your eyes."

I do as she says and instantly feel myself wobbling. I feel her hands on my arms. "Hold on to me. If you start to feel like you're going to pass out, tell me. I'd rather not have you tackle me in the shower, breaking my bones on the way down."

"I won't hurt you," I say.

"If you pass out, you won't know," she says.

I open my eyes, realizing that I'm much closer to her in this position. "I won't hurt you," I say more insistently.

She nods. "Hold on to me," she says again, and I gently grab hold of her hips. Since my hands are there, I begin running my thumbs over her hip bones.

"You're too thin," I say absently as she begins to scrub soap into my hair.

"I don't have a lot of time to eat. I'm double majoring with a minor in zoology."

"Why zoology?" I ask.

"Wolves. You can learn more about them in that class, but what I needed to learn was more on the veterinary side. So, I decided to make it a minor to get the information I needed."

She pushes my head under the water and rinses the soap out before scrubbing more in. This time, I can feel her nails gently scraping against my scalp. I moan out loud, not caring if the entire pack hears me. "That feels fucking incredible, Yara."

"Can I ask you a question?" she asks.

"You can ask me anything."

"Why haven't you taken a mate?" I open my eyes, ignoring the burn of the soap so she can see the truth in them.

"I was waiting for you. I've only ever wanted my fated mate."

She looks at me, her eyebrow rising in disbelief. "You're telling me that you've never had sex before, Alpha? I'm not buying it."

"I didn't say I'd never had sex. I said I never once considered taking anyone as my mate except you, my fated mate."

"Why?" she asks, looking adorably confused.

"My parents were fated mates. As hard as my father's life was, as filled with war as it had been, he always had my mother. They loved each other in a way that chosen mates never can. He adored her, and she adored him. She made the life he lived bearable ... enjoyable. I knew from a young age that I wanted that and that I needed that in my life. No one else would do except you, Yara."

I watch the surprise flicker over her face, watch her mouth open and close as if she doesn't know what to say before she refocuses on my hair. I close my eyes again, but not before looking at the wet T-shirt clinging to her body. She's thin but with gentle curves.

Her round breasts are outlined against the shirt, and her nipples are hardened nubs, just begging to be sucked.

"Can I ask you a question?" I ask her as she pushes my head back under the water.

"Yes."

"What do you want in a mate, in a relationship?"

She thinks for a moment. "Peace and quiet."

I shake my head. "I can't offer you that. That's not the life that the packs live."

"Monogamy," she says as if this will be a deal breaker for me. Actually, I'm thrilled.

"That I can offer you. I will never be with another woman again. You're it for me, Yara."

She frowns, staring at my hair, so I dip it, and she begins washing it for a third time. "I want someone who respects me, who recognizes the value that I bring to the relationship, that I'm an intelligent woman and doctor, someone who will allow me to do the job that I love."

"Well, that I've already given you. Thankfully, you've agreed to be my lead doctor, so I can check that box off," I say, smiling at her because I know I'm about to get her sass.

"I am not your lead doctor," she says firmly.

I put my face right up to hers. "You're as much my lead doctor as you are my mate and this pack's Luna. And to speak to the other things you said, if I didn't respect you and your knowledge, I wouldn't have told my pack that your word goes in the hospital. As far as the value that you bring to this pack, you're not only my mate, but as you could see, we were desperate for a doctor...and now I have you."

"I can't stay," she whispers.

"You can't leave. I've been searching for you for twelve long years. I never gave up, even though the odds were terrible that I would find you, I never gave up. I've always wanted you, Yara. Only you."

She looks away from me. Maybe I'm giving her too much truth, but I'd rather she knows where I stand.

"What about pups? Do you want them?" I ask her.

She frowns again, turning to get a washcloth and putting soap on it.

"I ... I haven't really given it much thought. I've been focusing on my career, and ... with the pack wars, it doesn't seem very safe to bring a pup into this world."

"I would keep our pups safe, just like I'll keep you safe."

"You can't guarantee that," she says softly.

I reach up, stroking her cheek. "I would die for you. I can guarantee you that. I would die for our family. I want a family with you, Yara."

She licks her lips, and my eyes snap to her mouth. Her pink lips look positively delicious, and I growl softly. The scent of cinnamon and nutmeg begins to increase in the small space, making my head spin, this time not from fatigue.

Yara looks down, seeing my body's response to her scent and her proximity to me.

"You're getting awfully frisky, Alpha," she says breathily.

"My sweet Yara, frisky would be me ripping that shirt open and sucking your pert little nipple into my mouth. This," I say, gesturing to my erection, "is just my body's response to you."

She's been stepping back, trying to get space from me, and I've slowly been moving closer to her. Now, she's pressed against the wall.

"And I've been desperate to taste you since the moment I laid eyes on you," I say, leaning in and pressing my lips to hers.

The sweet scent of her arousal swirls around the steamy shower, and I growl possessively, wrapping my arms around her waist and deepening the kiss. Her body responds immediately, and she tastes sweet, like a Snickerdoodle cookie. I begin to lose myself in the kiss, loving the sounds of her whimpers and how her body is pressing against mine.

"Alpha, you're food's out here," Charlie yells from my bedroom.

Regretfully, I pull back from the kiss.

"I'm going to kill him for interrupting our first kiss," I growl softly so Charlie can't hear me.

I watch as the embarrassed look on her face turns to surprise at my words, and then her lips begin to twitch.

"You can't kill your Beta."

"For interrupting this, I might," I say, watching as she loses the battle and begins giggling in my arms, pressing her face against my chest so she stays quiet.

It's one of the sweetest sounds I've ever heard, right up there with her whimpers and moans of desire.

Chapter 13: Killing

Yara

I laugh when I'm embarrassed. It's a completely inappropriate response, but I can't seem to help myself. So, when Warren pulls away from our kiss, a kiss that I totally got swept away in, I'm mortified. He's naked, and I'm practically naked, and I was pressing my body against his. If Charlie hadn't interrupted us, there's no telling what would have happened. And Warren is still recovering. At least, that's what I tell myself.

Of course, the only way for me to hide my inappropriate response is to press my face against Warren's bare chest, his rock-hard chest. Wow! My fingers twitch to touch him, to see if every muscle in his body is this hard and strong. As a doctor who worked in human hospitals, I know what a 'muscular' man feels like. Compared to them, Warren feels like granite.

So now I'm even more embarrassed. I have no idea how to get out of this gracefully, but when I look up, ready to make some snarky comment, Warren's face, usually so fierce and intense, is soft, and there's a hint of a smile on his face. Shit! If I thought the man was sexy before, putting a smile on his face makes him panty-dropping sexy. And wow, his eyes may be soft, but they are no less intense.

"I love the sound of your laugh. You should laugh more," he says, his deep voice making my core clench. I swear I can feel my arousal dripping down my thighs, and based on the way his nostrils flare, I'm pretty sure it is.

"Right, well, you should smile more," I say, quickly ducking under his arm and away from him. I can barely breathe when he's looking at me like that.

"Here's a towel," I say, handing it to him without looking at him. When he doesn't take it, I start to turn, only to feel his hands pushing my T-shirt over my head, making me yelp in surprise.

"What are you doing?" I exclaim.

"You're dripping water all over my floor. You wouldn't want me to slip and fall, would you?"

I open my mouth to say something, realizing again that I feel caught in the trap of this man's eyes. However, when his eyes begin drinking me in, I snatch the other towel I brought for me and quickly wrap it around my body.

Once again, my cheeks are so hot that I feel like they're on fire. But when I look back at him, he's smiling.

"You're beautiful, but I was right. You're too thin. Come on, let's go eat," he says, finally wrapping his towel around his waist.

"I'll meet you out there. I need to put some clothes on."

He stares at me for a moment, but I don't look at him, waiting for him to walk out as I clutch the towel to my body. Finally, he begins to hobble past me, and at the last minute, he grabs the corner of the towel and yanks it off my body.

"If you need a towel, you know where to find me," he smirks before walking out.

I stare at him a moment, my mouth hanging wide open before I snap it shut and begin pulling on his clothes.

"Of all the arrogant Alpha things to do..." I mumble as I pull on his shorts. I got these because they have a drawstring. Thankfully, Warren has a narrow waist and hips, with the most incredible Adonis belt I've ever seen. His broad shoulders give him a deep V, and the line of hair from his belly button to his...

"What is wrong with me? Get your head out of the clouds, Yar," I tell myself. When I pull the shirt on over my head, I realize that I probably didn't need the shorts. The man is so broad and already being taller than I am that his shirt falls just above my knees. I pull it up, tying it in a knot to keep it out of my way. This shirt is black, so I don't have to worry about getting wet again.

When I step out into Warren's bedroom, I see that he's set up a place to eat. There are two plates.

"Are you expecting company?" I ask him.

He turns and raises that damn eyebrow at me. "I have company, and I'm very interested to know what you were thinking about when your head was in the clouds," he says, smiling in a way that makes me think he already knows. Damn the man.

I ignore that, looking around the room. "Where's Charlie?"

"Gone. I had no intention of letting him see what's mine, especially after I snagged your towel. I was really hoping you'd come get it," he says, smirking.

However, one part of his sentence stands out to me. "I don't belong to you. I'm not a possession."

"No, you're not a possession; that would imply that I own you. What you are is precious to me. You are mine to love, mine to protect. That's what I mean when I say you are mine. Well, that and I have no intention of ever letting another man have you, so in that instance, I guess it is rather possessive. But I'm an Alpha. You'll have to get used to it."

"Get used to it?" I ask as if he's lost his mind.

He walks over to me and leans down, capturing me with his intense gaze. "Yes, Yara. Get used to it. You are MY mate; you will share MY bed. If you ever take another man to bed, I'll kill him. I will not share your kisses, your love, or our body with anyone except with our pups," he shrugs as he says the last part.

"You don't even know me! What if I have a boyfriend?"

It's the wrong question to ask, and I realize it instantly as his face darkens and his eyes go black. I feel the angry aura rolling off of him.

"Who is he? I will kill him," he snarls viciously.

"Easy, Alpha. I said, 'What if' not that I do," I say carefully.

He wraps an arm around me, tugging me against him. "You are mine, Yara. And I don't share."

He leans down, kissing me thoroughly before stepping back. "Let's eat."

"Geez, overreact much? You can't just go around killing people," I mutter.

"I can, I have, and I will again, Yara. I protect what's mine. This pack is mine, you are mine, and someday soon, our pups will be mine."

I think about what he said as I follow him to the makeshift table he's set up. He pulls out a chair for me in an unexpectedly gentlemanly fashion before sitting across from me.

I pick at my food, still thinking about his words.

"You may as well just tell me. Eventually, you'll mutter it, and I'll know anyway," he says, taking a bite of food and smiling as I look up at him.

"Do you like killing?" I ask him seriously.

Simon does. I despise that about him. I know other Alphas enjoy the fighting and the killing that the wars allow. It's probably why they've lasted so long. I don't know Warren well enough to know if he does or doesn't enjoy the kill, but I know it will make a big difference in how I feel about him.

The smile drops from his face, and he sets his fork down, clasping his hands over his plate and giving me his full attention.

"No, Yara. I don't like killing. For the most part, it's senseless. I love my pack. I'm their leader and meant to protect them. Sending them out to die because someone thinks they can take what's mine is pointless. I've lost good men and women because of these wars. I kill because I have to, but I find no joy in it."

Something inside me relaxes at his words and at the honesty that I see in his eyes.

"I imagine you hate these wars almost as much as I do," he says astutely, watching me closely.

"These wars took my parents and left me an orphan. I've seen good men and women lose their lives because of these wars. I guess that's why I decided to go into medicine. I mean, we're obviously short on doctors with the number of injured that are constantly coming through the door, but I wanted to do something, something important, to try and help save at least some of these warriors."

When I look back up at him, I see that he's smiling that dangerous smile again. "Spoken like a true Luna," he says softly. He points to my plate. "Eat. Don't let this conversation destroy your appetite. You still have quite a few patients in your hospital to take care of."

"It's not my hospital," I mumble as I take a bite.

"As the lead doctor, it most definitely is," he says, the taunting smile back in place.

I roll my eyes and finish the food, which is surprisingly delicious, or maybe I'm just hungrier than I realized.

When we're done, Warren drops the towel, walking naked to the bathroom to get the clothes I brought in for him.

"We need to get downstairs. I need the pack to see that I'm perfectly fine. After that, we'll come back up here and get some sleep."

I turn, looking at the room. There's only one bed in here...

Chapter 14: Infection

Warren

While I had hoped that my invitation to come and get her towel and, therefore me, would have worked, I didn't expect it to. My mate isn't the type of woman to jump on an Alpha just because she can. Actually, she's pretty much the opposite, more likely to run from me because I'm an Alpha. And while I wouldn't say no if she did offer herself to me, I'm kind of thankful that she didn't. I'm exhausted, and when I say we're going to sleep, I truly mean it.

I watch her eyes go wide when I say we'll be sleeping in here, but I meant what I said about her sharing my bed. Besides wanting my mate, I also know that having her close will help me to heal, and I need to heal fast.

I grab the crutch with one hand and Yara's hand with the other before leading her back down the stairs. When we get to the dining hall, the room goes silent again. I can feel Yara getting nervous. The palm of her hand against mine gets sweaty. She doesn't like being the center of so much attention.

I know we just ate, but I'm going to get some more food. Charlie didn't bring enough to fill me up, which is good. I need to spend a little time with the pack and see how they are feeling about me and things in general. One important thing that I always have to do is keep my finger on the pulse of the pack. If they start to turn against me, worried that

I'm not strong enough to lead them, I have to nip it in the bud quickly. It doesn't happen often, but it does happen, usually when I'm injured, like I am now.

I've just turned to go get food when Yara's nose goes up in the air. I watch as the skittish woman of a moment ago transforms in front of my eyes into the exceedingly confident and sexy woman from the hospital.

"Yara?" I ask as she begins to move through the pack members, still sniffing the air. If I didn't already recognize this as her doctor mode, I'd be worried that she was sniffing someone that smelled good to her. Since she's my mate, it shouldn't happen, but she's not wearing my mark, so I'm uncomfortable having her around so many unmarked males.

I watch her as she approaches one of my warriors. I follow her, wondering what she's doing, what she's smelling. She leans over him, sniffing him. He pulls away from her, looking at her like she's crazy.

"What are you doing?" he asks her gruffly.

Without answering, she reaches out to put her hand on his face, but he slaps her hand away, and that's all it takes for me to be in his face.

"Haynes, you lay a fucking hand on my mate again, and it will be the last thing you do," I tell him. One of the other warriors gets up as if to support Haynes, and I swing the crutch around, jamming it into his throat and pressing him against the wall.

"Don't fuck with me," I snarl, staring the two of them down. "Yara, what is this about?"

"Haynes, is it?" she asks as Charlie moves into a position to fight if my warriors turn on me.

"Yeah," he says, watching me.

"Where's your infection, Haynes?"

"What the fuck are you talking about?" he growls. As quick as a viper, I have him by the throat and on his feet.

"Did you not hear me earlier say that this is my mate and the new lead doctor at our pack hospital? Do you have wax in your ears, Haynes?" I snarl, getting in his face. However, I realize that his body temperature is too hot. Yara's right; he's got an infection, and now that I've pulled him closer, I can smell it, too.

"Warren," Yara says softly, putting her hand on my arm and calming me instantly.

"Answer her question, Haynes."

He looks pissed that he's been caught. What the fuck, do my warriors really think they need to fight until they die?

"It's nothing," he says, but he looks away. I let go of his neck but growl a warning to him to behave himself.

"Your arm, right?" she asks him. "May I?"

"Do I have a choice?"

"No, you fucking don't," I growl.

He holds still, and Yara pushes his shirt up to his shoulder.

"What the fuck?" I say, seeing the festering wound on his arm that he tried to hide by covering it with gauze and cloths.

"How long has this been infected?" Yara asks, much calmer than I am.

"A while," he grumbles.

"Why haven't you had it cleaned? Been to the pack hospital?"

"No offense, doctor," he sneers at her, "but I've been a bit busy fighting a war."

I'm about to snarl at him again, but Yara snaps before I can.

"Now you listen to me, warrior," she says in the same sneering tone he used with her. "That infection, if not treated, will kill you. You aren't any good to this pack or your Alpha, much less your friends and fellow warriors if you're dead."

She surprises me by turning to warriors in the dining hall and addressing them. "None of you are. If you really want to help your pack, stay alive. The only way to do that is to stay healthy. Waiting until you get this bad means I'm pulling you off active duty until the infection is gone," she says, turning back to Haynes, putting her hands on her hips and getting in his face. "And since your wolf is so weak that he's not healing you, I'm guessing that's going to be a minimum of three days."

"You can't," Haynes exclaims.

"Want to rethink that comment?" I ask. This time, I keep my cool. He's sick. I'm sure his fever and probably his fear of not healing are impacting his interactions with Yara. If she's staying calm, I will follow her lead.

"Fine, I'll go in the morning."

"You'll go right now," she tells him. "I'll be there shortly, and we'll clean that out and stitch up those wounds."

He looks up at me. "You heard your Luna, go."

He growls but stomps off. I look at Charlie and nod for him to follow Haynes, then I turn to the other warrior.

"You ever threaten me again, Gael, I'll take it out of your hide. You got me?"

"Yes, Alpha."

I nod, pulling the crutch from his throat.

"If anyone else has a concern about a wound that isn't healing or doesn't smell right, come see me. I have a nose for infection. Believe me, I'll sniff you out. It would be better all-around if you come to me before I find you. Understood?" she demands.

"Yes, Luna," they all say.

She turns, giving me a look, and walks out of the room. I turn and follow her, already knowing what she's going to say. I can feel my lips twitching as I walk up to her, and she turns on me, getting in my face this time. Damn, she's sexy.

'Did you see how she faced our entire pack, not backing down?' Arric asks proudly.

'Yeah, I did.'

"I am not their Luna," she whisper-yells at me.

I lean down, getting in her face ... loving her ferocity. "Then you shouldn't be acting like you are."

Chapter 15: Concern

Yara

Oh, that man is so frustrating! Why the hell is he telling his pack that I'm their Luna? And now, they're all calling me Luna. It's infuriating!

He walks me to the pack hospital, basically handing me off to Charlie.

"Everything okay?" Charlie asks him.

"Yeah, thanks. I need to get back and show my face. Can I leave Yara with you?"

"I've got your back, Alpha," he says and begins leading me to a room where I find Haynes already seated on a bed.

"Okay, let's take a closer look at what we've got," I say to him, getting some scissors and cutting away the shirt.

I wet the bandages that are covered in dried pus and blood. Then, I carefully begin pulling them away to see the massive infection underneath.

"UGH!" Charlie says, and I turn to see that he's covered his mouth and nose. "What the fuck, Haynes?"

Haynes just looks down. There's no way he's not feeling terrible if the infection is this bad.

"I'm going to have to debride this, which means I have to scrub all the infection out of the wound. I need to see the flesh underneath and make sure it's healthy."

"Okay," he says.

"It's going to hurt. Would you allow me to give you something to numb the area as best I can? It won't numb it all; the infection will block it, but it will help."

"No," he says, still not looking at me. I stare at him in disbelief. What is with these guys?

"There's no shame in letting me numb this area. I won't be knocking you out or anything," I say, trying again.

"No," he says more firmly.

I turn back to the tray of things that I need to clean the wound.

"The whole friggin pack is as arrogant as their Alpha. No one feels pain anymore? What the hell kind of pack is this?" I mumble as I get my things together.

"She's not expecting an answer. She keeps forgetting we can hear her," Charlie says, and I turn to see Haynes frowning at me.

As I get ready to start, Haynes speaks.

"I do feel pain, Luna. But I'm a warrior. Pain is a part of my life. I've just accepted that," he says, and he sounds so defeated. I hate it. I hate that this is the only life that he sees in his future.

"Well, I don't accept it, just so you know," I say intensely. I take a deep breath and look at him. "I'm going to get started. If at any time you change your mind, let me know."

He nods, and I begin to wash out the wound. "Why didn't you come and see Dr. Stevens when this first got infected?" I ask him.

"I did. He said my wolf would heal me, but he hasn't."

I stop, looking over at Charlie before turning back to the wound. "Did he have you come back to check and make sure your wolf was healing you?"

"No, he just said to give it a few days. By then, we were fighting again, and I didn't have time to do anything else about it."

"How is your wolf? He must be pretty weak if he hasn't healed you," I say. I have to give the guy credit. He really is used to pain. I know what I'm doing is painful, but he hasn't flinched once.

When I realize he hasn't answered, I stop, moving so I can look him in the eye. "Warrior, when was the last time you heard your wolf?"

"It's been at least a day," he finally says, and I can see that this, more than anything, is upsetting him. Not for the right reasons, in my opinion. He's sad his wolf is gone. I'm mad that he's going to die because he didn't get proper medical treatment.

"The infection has moved up into your shoulder and down your arm. I'm guessing you don't have a lot of use of this arm now?" I ask him.

"No, Luna."

I ignore the title and look at Charlie. "Charlie, come look at this."

He walks over, still covering his nose and mouth. "Do you see this black area here?"

"Yeah, what am I looking at?"

"That's gangrene," I say, then tilt my head to look at Haynes. "Do you know what gangrene is?"

"No."

"It means your flesh is dying. You are literally rotting to death. And without your wolf, I'd guess you had about three days to live."

"What?" he asks. "How?"

"Your infection is rampant. We'll be lucky if it hasn't gotten into your bloodstream. Remember what I said in the dining hall? You're no good to your pack if you're dead. Well, you would have been dead, and they would have been down a warrior, a good one."

"But Luna, I asked Dr. Stevens," he says defensively.

"Well, I'm the lead doctor here now, and what I say goes, and what I'm saying is that you've earned yourself a couple of days in the hospital. So make yourself comfortable. I'm going to have to cut this dead area out. Blood is healing, so I have to cut until I get to healthy, bleeding flesh. And I'm going to tell you now, you've lost a lot of muscle, muscle that you won't get back. This arm will always be weaker than your other arm. You're going to have to readjust your fighting style to account for that. Do you understand?"

"Yes, Luna."

"Good. Okay, lie back. Let's get this done, and then I'm going to get you started on some heavy-duty antibiotics to help heal your body since your wolf has gone silent. When he's back, and you're as healed as you're going to get, I'll release you, but not until then."

When I'm done, I order the nurses to start an IV fluid bag and some strong antibiotics to ward off any additional infection.

"I'll be back to see you in the morning. I'll let them know that if anything changes, they need to call me. Don't give my nurses a hard time, do you hear me?" I say to him, seeing the two nurses in the room look at me out of the corner of their eyes and then at each other. I'm hoping that's a good sign.

When we step out of the room, another nurse comes up to us.

"Luna, there are several warriors in the waiting room. They said you told them to come."

"Put them in a room, triage them, and I'll start with the most critical."

"Yes, Luna," she says, smiling as she turns away.

When she steps away, I turn to Charlie. "I have a question for you. This pack, several warriors, more probably since we got to the hospital, are challenging Warren, testing his ability to lead this pack. But when a fight nearly broke out, you were ready to fight with him. You're his Beta, the most likely person to take over if Warren isn't capable of doing so. I want to know why you're fighting to keep him in his Alpha position when everyone else seems willing to knock him down?"

"You don't miss much, do you?" he asks me, giving me an appreciative look. "He's my Alpha. I'm his Beta because I respect him and because I have no desire to be in charge. His job sucks all the time. Everyone constantly tests him. In the world we live in, that's the way it is. The packs need someone strong to lead them. The moment he's not that person, the pack will remove him and put someone that they feel is stronger in his place. Personally, I think it's about more than strength, physical strength anyway. Alpha Warren is strong mentally, not just physically, and I think the pack forgets how important mental strength is, especially in times like these."

I look at him for a long moment. "Hmmm, I think I like you again," I say.

"One more thing, and this is important. I don't know why Dr. Stevens didn't treat Haynes when his infection started, but that's not being lazy, tired, or old. That's medical neglect; it's malpractice. I showed you that gangrene because you're going to have others who have it. If he neglected one of your pack members, he'll have neglected others. I don't know what the reason is, but I'd suggest you and Warren figure it out."

I turn and head to the nurse's station to see what's happening with the others. Seven warriors have come in, wanting to be seen. I'm surprised but glad. Maybe word will get around quickly, and more will start to come in. This pack will be stronger and fight harder if they're healthy.

It's several hours later before I finally finish. I'm exhausted but happy that I was able to catch so many problems before they became the infected mess that Haynes has.

"We'll see you tomorrow, Luna?" one of the nurses asks me.

"Yes. Please make sure you check on Warrior Haynes regularly, and I want to know if anything changes for the worse overnight."

"Yes, Luna."

Charlie is waiting to take me back to the packhouse. When we arrive, I turn to him. "I'm sure Warren is asleep. Is there somewhere else that I can sleep for the night," I ask, hoping that Charlie will put me in my own room.

"I've already linked him, Luna. He's waiting up for you."

"Oh. Great," I say, smiling a fake smile.

Charlie snorts and gestures for me to precede him up the stairs. He walks me to Warren's door.

"Good night, Luna."

He walks to the top of the stairs and turns to look at me.

"He's not leaving until you come in, Yara," I hear Warren say from inside the room.

I take a deep breath, open the door, and step inside.

Chapter 16: Found and Betrayed

Simon

"Alpha, we found her," my warriors say.

I'd tracked her to the university where my father had been hiding her for years. He knew I wanted her and he helped her escape from me. And then, he'd lied to me about it. He told me she left, renounced him as her Alpha, and that no one had been able to find her.

At first, I had believed him. I'd searched on my own, of course, needing to find that pretty little thing, that sweet-smelling, seductive little woman that I intend to take as my mate. She's smart, I like that. And while she doesn't say much, I can tell by the way she looks at me and others that she's got a smart mouth. On the rare occasion that she actually opened her mouth, she proved me right. I love the idea of taming that smart mouth of hers, of wielding her to my will, of making her mine in all ways. When I'm done killing, I always need a sweet pussy to fuck, and I just know that hers will be sweet. And since I know she's never been with any of my warriors, I know it'll be sweet and tight. The thought has me going hard, as I always do when I think of her.

"Where is she?" I ask. I'd been out fighting against another pack when I came across her clothing for the first time. I hadn't been prepared to follow her then, but I'd watched her get into her car, and I'd chased her as far as I could before I'd lost her. That was when I realized that she wasn't far away, and I began searching again. It wasn't until I'd searched my father's office that I'd found the truth. He'd been funding her education all these years. He'd lied to me, and for that, he had to die.

I'd confronted him. "You lied to me!"

"She is not meant for you. She's too good for you!" he snarled.

"I am your son!" I shouted.

"An embarrassment, more like. I have no intention of handing this pack over to you. You're greedy and bloodthirsty. That girl is kind and loving, and you would destroy her."

"Oh, father, she will be mine."

"Over my dead body," he snarled.

"So be it."

The old man wasn't even that much of a challenge. After I killed him and took over the pack, I'd gone through all of my father's things and eventually tracked Yara to the university. I'd watched her, prepared this time, and when she'd gotten into her car, a handful of my warriors and I followed her.

She was smart, going farther away from my pack. But I watched as she'd stripped in the forest, then shifted into her reddish-brown wolf and taken off. I had my warriors put trackers on her car while I'd gotten her clothing. Their scent nearly made me explode right there. It had been so long since I'd seen her, and now that we're both adults and my father is gone, nothing is keeping me from making her mine.

"You're not going to like it, Alpha," my warriors say. My attention snaps back to them.

I'm not sure what they see on my face, but almost as one, they step back. "We tracked her scent to a bear trap. It looks like she released an Alpha who was caught in the trap," they say.

I begin growling possessively.

"Which. Alpha," I snarl, standing. They take another step back, knowing how explosive my temper can be.

"Alpha Warren. And Alpha, we're hearing rumors that he's calling her his mate."

They run from the room as I explode with fury. When the red in my vision finally begins to fade, I realize I've once again destroyed the office. I look around, panting heavily.

'TRENA!' I bark in the mind link.

'Yes, Alpha?'

'Get in here. I need my cock sucked.'

'Yes, Alpha,' she says. I go to where I keep Yara's clothing packed in a tight package to hold her scent until I want to smell it. It's not as strong as it was when I got it, but it will do.

As Trena unzips my pants and takes me in her mouth, I breathe deeply of Yara's scent and let it bring me to the release I need.

~ ~ ~

Dr. Stevens POV

"Why the fuck is he still standing? I set that trap just for him. I literally handed him to you on a platter!" the Alpha growls at me.

"Because he found some bitch that has some medical training, and he's made her his lead doctor. He says she's his mate and the future Luna of the pack. She literally put his leg back together. I was ready to cut it off, but he refused, and she was willing to piece him back together."

"I've paid you very well to destroy this pack from the inside, doctor."

"And I have done exactly what you have asked. I have done the bare minimum to heal his pack members so that the pack would be weakened. It's not my fault that you and your pack can't defeat a pack that isn't at full strength," I snap.

Faster than I can track, the Alpha has me by the throat and lifts me off the ground. "Be very careful, doctor. Your usefulness seems to be coming to an end. I wouldn't want you to find yourself in an unfortunate position that might end your life prematurely," he says, the threat apparent.

I have no doubt that this vicious Alpha would kill me and probably enjoy doing it slowly. While I may not care for Alpha Warren, I have no desire to die a slow death at the hands of this Alpha.

Alpha Warren never appreciated my knowledge or skill. He just took it for granted that I would put his pack back together time after time. The least he could have done was to give me a ranked position. As a lead doctor, I think I deserved at least a Gamma position. But what I always wanted was the Beta position. Instead of giving it to me, he gave it to that pup, Charlie. I deserved to be Beta! I'm the one that kept this pack together for so many years!

It wasn't long after that that I came across one of this Alpha's warriors who had offered me money to serve his Alpha. I readily agreed, and I've been saving up to leave when the time comes. However, the time was never right before. Now, as I hang from this Alpha's hand, barely able to breathe, I realize that the time may be now.

He pulls me to his face, his eyes nearly black with rage. All of these Alphas are so used to fighting and killing that it doesn't even faze them anymore.

"Find a way to bring Warren down, or I'll kill you."

"You should attack now. His leg isn't healed. It's your best chance," I say, gasping for air.

He stares at me for a moment, then drops me on the ground. I land in a heap, clutching my throat and sucking in large lungfuls of air.

He turns to his warriors. "Get back to the pack. Prepare for battle," he growls before shifting and racing off.

Chapter 17: Sleep
Warren

As much as I didn't want to leave Yara, I knew I needed the pack to see me. Haynes and Gael aren't the only warriors who will test me. However, rather than pushing me to show my strength, the pack surprises me. Everyone is interested in Yara.

"Is she really your mate, Alpha?"

"Yes, she's my fated mate," I say, sitting at a centrally located table, making sure everyone can see me eating and functioning. For now, my fatigue is pushed aside.

"Where did you find her?"

I chuckle. "She found me. I was caught in the bear trap; some of you found me there with Beta Charlie. She heard Arric rustling around, trying to find a way out of the trap. Maybe Annika, her wolf, smelled us; I'm not sure. She came and got me out."

"She's a doctor?"

"She is. A resident, but she's majoring in human medicine, veterinary medicine, and zoology."

"Why zoology?"

I explain what Yara told me and I'm happy that I know enough about my mate to be able to answer the pack's questions.

"Is she really taking Dr. Steven's place?" someone asks.

77

"Yes. I've already found her to be a much better doctor than he is. It's past time he retired, but we all know that doctors are hard to come by. The Moon Goddess has seen fit to bless me with a mate who is also a doctor."

I answer some more questions while I eat, getting an update from Charlie about just how bad Haynes is. Thank the goddess that Yara smelled that infection. According to Charlie, I was days away from losing another warrior.

After dinner, I head back upstairs, only to get another link from Charlie that more warriors have gone to the hospital to be looked at.

'How many?' I ask him, surprised.

'Seven.'

I'm surprised but pleased that my mate's address to the pack was as impactful as it was. If she's able to make an impact fast with some of these warriors, the word will spread around the pack like wildfire. Maybe then the pack can get healthy, and we can start taking out some of these assholes who keep attacking me.

He then tells me about Yara's concerns about Dr. Stevens.

'I'll talk to her and get a clearer understanding of why she thinks he's being negligent,' I tell Charlie.

I shower again, feeling like I didn't quite get clean since I got distracted by Yara's scent and then her mouth. Just thinking of our first kiss has me going hard. Even though I'm still in pain, I'm able to find my release thinking of her sweet taste and the soft sounds she made while I kissed her. I know she's not ready for me to mark and mate her yet, and honestly, when the time comes, I want to take my time, so it's better if I don't have a hard-on all night long since I intend to have her pressed up against me.

By the time I get in bed and begin going through normal pack work, I'm exhausted again, but I refuse to go to sleep until Yara arrives. I know she'll try to get Charlie to put her somewhere else tonight, so I let him know that I'm staying awake waiting for her.

It isn't long before I hear him saying goodnight to her and then nothing.

'Charlie? Where is she?' I ask in the mind link.

'Standing outside your door, looking like she's going to run.'

"He's not leaving until you come in, Yara," I say, watching the door.

I hear her take a deep breath before she steps in, closing the door before finally looking at me. When she does, her eyes go wide. I sleep in the nude. I have for as long as I can remember. Since I'm not embarrassed about nudity, I didn't think to cover myself. And since my leg is throbbing, I have it elevated on a pillow, so covering myself didn't even cross my mind.

However, as my mate's eyes look over my body, I can see her assessing me. I've become so used to the scars on my body that I forget that I have them. However, Yara's eyes on me suddenly remind me of just how scarred I am.

"I left a T-shirt out for you in case you prefer to sleep with something on. I don't, and I would be happy if you didn't either, but I know you may be more comfortable being covered tonight," I tell her.

That jolts her out of whatever thoughts she was having about my body.

"I'm not sleeping with you!"

"Of course you are. You're my mate. Where else would you sleep? Remember that conversation about having you in my bed earlier?" I tap the bed. "This is that bed. So, go get ready. The shirt is there if you want it. Change or strip and then come join me. I'm tired, and I need some sleep. You do, too. You've had a long couple of days," I tell her.

"Who does he think he is, ordering me around like this? Like I'm just some fangirl fawning over an Alpha," she mutters as she grabs the shirt and heads to the bathroom.

Oh, my little mate, I have no doubt that you've never fawned over anyone in your life. Because of that, when you do finally give me your submission, it's going to taste so very sweet.

Unlike my mate, I keep those thoughts to myself.

"What if he's a rowdy sleeper? What if he accidentally backhands me in the middle of the night? What if he ... Oh, he better not do that," she continues muttering from the bathroom. I set my work aside, smiling as I listen to the running commentary of my mate's thoughts.

I hear her run the water, probably brushing her teeth, then pull on the T-shirt before stepping out of the bathroom.

"What had I better not do?" I ask her. I'm pretty sure I already know, but seeing the blush on her cheeks is so worth it.

She points her finger at me. "I am NOT having sex with you."

I narrow my eyes at her. "It's true that sometimes saying that you're sleeping with someone means that you're having sex. However, in tonight's context, I truly am exhausted, and I need sleep. I need to heal so I can be back on top and ready for the next attack. And believe me when I tell you, when I touch you, taste you, and slide inside you for the first time, I want to be completely healed. Because I will take my time, I will enjoy every one of your whimpers and moans, and I will have you screaming my name in pleasure before I'm done with you," I say, my voice getting deeper with my desire to have her.

I watch her pupils dilate, and her cheeks flush as her mouth drops open. Damn, I can't wait to have her. She's already so responsive to me.

I tap the bed. "But tonight, we're sleeping. Come on. I know you're exhausted and tomorrow, I want to talk about your impressions of Dr. Stevens. Charlie said you have concerns."

"A lot of them," she says, walking to the bed. "He isn't fit to provide medical care any longer, in my opinion."

"Since you're my lead doctor, your opinion is the only one that matters to me," I say, pulling back the covers. "Come on. Let's get some sleep."

She gets into the bed, laying as close to the edge and taking up as little space as possible with her back facing me. I smile as I lay down, then wrap my arm around her waist and tug her against my body.

She yelps, but I hold her steady. "Much better," I say, breathing in her cinnamon and nutmeg scent.

"I'm not a rowdy sleeper," I say, her scent already lulling me to sleep. "And I'll never lay a hand on you, not even in my sleep." It's the last thought I have before I finally fall asleep.

I have no idea how long I've been asleep when the howls of alarm go up that we're under attack. I'm up and out of bed in an instant, running for the door.

"WARREN! You can't shift! Your leg isn't healed!" Yara says.

"I have no choice, Yara. My pack is under attack, and I'm their Alpha. I have to fight. Get to a safe room," I say before leaping over the banister and shifting, biting off the scream of pain when my leg doesn't shift exactly right.

'Arric?' I ask my wolf.

'It's good enough for now,' he growls as we race into battle.

Chapter 18: Hospital
Yara

I race to the banister, watching as Warren gracefully shifts into Arric. If I wasn't looking for it, wasn't paying attention, I wouldn't have seen him flinch. Dammit! I knew that leg wasn't healed enough to shift.

"I'll have to start all over again," I mumble as I grab a pair of shorts and put them on as I race down the stairs. I quickly pull my hair up into a ponytail, tying it in a knot which will have to do for now.

"Luna, this way!" a pregnant she-wolf says to me.

"I'm not going to a safe room," I say, turning as nearly everyone in the room stops to look at me.

I turn and look at them. "I'm a doctor! Your pack members will need me. GO! If you're part of the medical team and you're not pregnant and don't have young pups, get your ass to the hospital. NOW!"

I watch as the pack jolts with my command, but I don't have time to wonder about it. I race out of the front of the packhouse and down the cobblestone drive to the hospital.

"Luna, there are only a couple of us who can assist. We've never been in the hospital during a battle before," Savannah, one of the nurses I worked with earlier, says, running up beside me. "Here, you'll need this more than I will," she says, pulling a hair tie out of her hair and handing it to me.

"Thank you, and what do you mean you've never been in the hospital during a battle?" I ask as we rush into the hospital, and I quickly wrap my hair in the hair tie.

"Dr. Stevens said it wasn't safe. That we were to report immediately after we were let out of the safe rooms."

"Then who was helping these warriors?" I ask, stopping to stare at her incredulously.

"No one. They waited until we were let out for help."

"No one died waiting for treatment?" I ask.

She looks away. "Several died, Luna. Some probably could have been saved, but ... it took us too long."

"Okay, well, that stops now," I say as two more nurses rush in, looking completely lost.

"Triage kits, crash kits, do you know what is needed and what to put together?" I ask, and all three shake their heads.

I begin moving again, walking to the storage room and beginning to pull things off the shelves.

"Triage, crash, triage," I say as I hand off what I need.

"Luna, someone's here," one of the nurses says.

"What's your name? I didn't catch it earlier," I say.

"Anna, Luna," she says.

"And you?" I ask the other nurse.

"I'm Piper, Luna."

"Who's the most senior nurse here?" I ask.

"I am, Luna," Savannah says.

"Savannah, you're with me. Anna, Piper, do you see what we need for each of these?"

They nod, looking like deer in headlights. What the hell? This is a fucking hospital, for goddess' sake!

"Keep making them until I call you. Put triage on one side and crash on the other. Add anything else you think we'll need," I say, rushing out the door and back to the main area.

"Luna! Why aren't you in a safe room?"

"Because I'm a doctor, stand aside," I say to the warrior who is holding the man I need to see.

"Does Alpha know you're not in a safe room?" he asks me.

I turn and get in his face. "I am a doctor. Would you rather I let this man die while we argue about it?" I growl.

"No, Luna," he says.

"Savannah," I say, turning to see that she's already getting soap and water to wash off the wound.

When the two warriors continue to huddle around me, I look at them. "You don't need to stay."

"We kind of do, Luna. Alpha will kill us if something happens to you, and we knew you weren't in a safe room."

I stop and look at them. "Fine. Then guard the hospital doors. No one gets in who doesn't belong to this pack."

"Yes, Luna," they say, seeming relieved to have orders.

"Why isn't your wolf healing you?" Savannah asks him.

"Too weak," the warrior says. I look over her shoulder. He has nasty slashes on his thigh, and he's bleeding heavily.

"PIPER! I NEED AN IV BAG!" I shout, turning and nearly running into Haynes.

"What the hell are you doing out of bed? Stop making my job more difficult!" I bark at him.

"I can help, Luna."

"Haynes ..."

"Please, Luna. I can't fight, but I can help you," he says.

I press my lips together and put my hand on his forehead, then his cheek, then his neck. His fever has come down.

"Your wolf?" I ask him, but he shakes his head.

I point my finger at him. "You feel any dizziness, feel faint in any way, you stop. You hear me? If I have to drag your sorry ass off the floor because you didn't listen to me, I will make your ears bleed when you wake up again, got it?"

I watch his lips twitch. "Yes, Luna."

I turn just as more wolves are carried in. "Savannah, you got him?"

"Piper's going to stitch him up. Anna, we need triage kits!" she yells.

"Haynes, you're a runner. Go get those kits from Anna so she can keep making them. Bring them out here to us."

"On it," he says.

I turn, and as one, Savannah and I begin triaging the injured as they come in. There are too many of them, too many for just the four of us. I end up having Haynes help with triage so I can at least get to the worst of the groups.

"How many more of you have weak wolves? Seriously, what the fuck is wrong with this pack?" I mutter as I debride yet another pack member with massive gashes that aren't healing. My frustration and fatigue have me cursing.

"I heard that about you, Luna," the warrior who I'm cleaning says to me. Not one of these men and women has flinched as I've scrubbed their wounds clean. It makes me think back to when I saw Warren's chest earlier. As muscular as he is, he was riddled with scars. They all are. There's only so much that a wolf can heal before the wounds heal and scar on their own. This pack's scars are a testament to their courage, their fearlessness, and their constant fighting.

"What's that," I ask, not looking away from the nasty wound I'm cleaning.

"You mumble to yourself. It's cute," he says, and I look up at him. Is he seriously flirting with me right now?

"Cute?" I ask, incensed.

"We don't get a lot of cute around here, Luna. When we do, we appreciate it," another warrior says, holding a bandage to his head.

The others sitting around all nod and mumble their agreement.

"Don't let the cute fool you. Our Luna's an incredible doctor," Haynes says, walking up with another triage kit.

I turn and look at him, surprised and a bit humbled by his praise. I'm not sure what I would have said but at that moment, warriors come rushing in carrying another warrior, this one covered in blood.

"LUNA!" the warriors yell. I rush over, putting my fingers on the man's neck and not finding a pulse.

"I NEED A CRASH KIT!" I yell as Savannah grabs a gurney and swings it over to us.

"Get him on the gurney," I yell, then jump on top of him and begin doing compressions.

"What happened?" I ask, looking up as Savannah puts a resuscitator mask over the warrior's face. I realize that this is Beta Charlie, and my stomach drops.

"Don't you dare think you're coming into MY hospital and dying on MY watch, Beta! No one fucking dies in MY hospital," I say, continuing to do compressions.

"Luna, here's the defibrillator," Savannah says.

"Get it ready," I say as Piper comes over and hooks Charlie up to a machine so we can see if he has any heart activity. Normally, we'd be able to hear it, but right now, there are too many people in the room, too much adrenaline, and too much blood pumping in my ears for me to hear it.

When they're both ready, I look at Savannah. "On three, ready?"

She frowns at me but nods. "One, two, three!" I say, and I leap up into the air above the gurney as she hits Charlie with the paddles. His body jumps from the electric shock, and Savannah pulls away quickly before I land, still straddling his body. I look at the machine. Nothing.

"What part of no one dies on my watch, didn't you understand, Beta," I growl, continuing my compressions. "Don't you dare make me chase you into the Moon Goddess' realm, Beta, because I swear to all that is good and holy in this world I will, and I'll drag your sorry ass back down here. This isn't your time, and I'm not letting you die," I snarl.

"Ready, Luna," Savannah says again.

"On three," I say, and this time she's ready. When I leap, she slams the paddle against his chest, moving quickly before I land again.

I watch the machine, and then I see it: a blip, then another, then another.

"About time you listened to your Luna, Beta," I say, getting off his gurney. "Get him to a room and prep him for surgery," I say, suddenly realizing that the room around me is silent.

I turn, looking around at the awed faces in the room. I'm about to follow Savannah when I see him, Arric, standing in the doorway, watching. He's covered in blood, too, but I'd know his scent anywhere.

I point at him, "You are also on my shitlist. Don't you dare shift until I've had a chance to look at that leg. Haynes, are you strong enough to lift your Alpha onto a gurney?" I ask.

Before he can answer, Arric growls. He isn't willing to show weakness in front of his warriors.

I stomp over to him, taking his furry face in my hand. "Now you listen to me, Alpha. You put me in charge of this hospital. I don't care if you're in human form or wolf form. You are not in charge here. I am. You will not shift until I can look at that leg, and you will get on a gurney and let my nurses put you in a room until I can make sure Charlie is stable. Are we clear?" I ask him, my eyes holding his. He pushes his nose forward and licks my face.

"Unbelievable!" I say to him, wiping my face and grabbing a gurney. "Up you go," I say, and he leaps onto the gurney as I hold it. I quickly look him over, not seeing anything terrible, before nodding to Haynes to take him into a room.

"Piper! You're in charge until I've got Beta Charlie stable. Any one of you gives my nurses a hard time and you'll answer to me," I say, staring down the room of warriors.

"Yes, Luna," they answer, and I rush into the surgery room to make sure Charlie survives to fight another day.

Chapter 19: Respect

Warren

Fucking Brady is attacking again. His warriors have to be as exhausted as mine are, but here he is, attacking again. The asshole.

I'm not sure how he knows that I'm injured, but I'm definitely the target of this attack. While my warriors each have one wolf attacking them, I have multiple wolves constantly attacking me, trying to take me down. Each time one of my warriors goes out, the attacking wolf joins the attack on me.

At first, I was able to keep up, killing them as fast as they were attacking me. But my warriors are too exhausted, rundown, and now, I'm sure, not healing as they should because of my previous fucking doctor.

As I face off against Brady, I feel a wolf bite down on my broken leg that hasn't healed and was reinjured when I shifted. Arric howls in pain before turning and ripping off half the face of the wolf that bit us. That's when Charlie entered the fight with me. He'd leaped over me, putting himself between me and the other wolves, including Brady.

'CHARLIE, NO!' I yelled in the mind link, but it was too late. The group attacked him viciously. I struggled to get them off of him, especially since more kept coming. Finally, other warriors jumped in, but by then, Charlie was unconscious, his wolf pulling the shift back to his human form. He was covered with blood, more his own than others.

'Get him to the hospital!' I command, and several warriors shift and begin racing my Beta to the hospital. Unfortunately, I know it's too late for Charlie. No one will be in the hospital because the battle isn't over yet.

As I continue to fight, I feel a change in my pack. I have no idea where the awe or pride is coming from, but I don't have time to worry about it. Brady finally calls a retreat of what's left of his pack. This time, I don't follow him. I can't afford to lose any more of my warriors, and I can't afford to go down. With Charlie out, I'm going to struggle as it is to keep the pack whole. I'm honestly surprised that I haven't felt his tether break yet.

I order the patrols to make sure all of Brady's wolves are off our pack lands, and as the sun begins to rise, I run to the pack hospital to see if I can save Charlie.

When I get there, I understand immediately where the awe and pride are coming from. My mate is something to behold. I watch her on the gurney, pumping Charlie's heart, yelling at him that he's not allowed to die on her, and giving commands to the others. I watch her leap into the air as Savannah shocks Charlie's heart. I turn and see everyone watching her, watching her fight to save their Beta. The feeling of pride that I felt before is blossoming now. No one has ever seen Dr. Stevens fight this hard to save us. And this is their Luna. Whether she accepts it or not, it's exactly what she is.

I turn back to her when I hear the paddle thump again and I watch as Charlie's heart begins to beat. My heart soars when I hear her tell him that it's about time he listened to her, his Luna. It may not be conscious, but she's accepting her place and role in this pack, and she's doing it in front of everyone. It's nearly as powerful as if she'd claimed me publicly.

"She's magnificent,' Arric purrs.

'Yes, she is,' I say as she turns and sees us. I watch her eyes narrow, and I just know I'm about to get some of the fire I see in her eyes. Damn, I can't wait until I see that fire in the bedroom. Magnificent indeed.

I don't even care that she's berating me in front of the pack members. She's our Luna, my mate, the only one who I'll allow to do it. When Arric refuses to allow Haynes to pick him up, that fire flashes in her eyes, and she stalks toward us. It's such a contrast to the woman who came into our bedroom last night that I can do nothing but marvel at her. I'm so desperate to kiss her that Arric does it for me, licking her face and taking some of the ire out of her. I hear some of the warriors snicker, but it cuts off before she can catch them.

I know she's right about my leg, so I don't argue about getting on the gurney, but I can't show weakness in front of the warriors. I may have several injuries, but the worst is my leg, and Arric is strong enough to leap with three legs.

As she orders my pack to behave and turns to go save my Beta, I turn to look at Haynes.

'I'm staying here,' I tell him in the mind link.

"Yes, Alpha."

'Who can give me a report?' I ask, opening the mind link to the group.

"Which report do you want, Alpha? The one about how many of us our Luna probably saved today, or the one about the litany of things she had to say about us and her pack?" one of my warriors says, and as I watch, the entire group of them smiles. I'm not sure I've ever seen my pack smile. Maybe one or two, like at the birth of their child or when someone finds their mate. But as I look around, my entire pack is smiling, chuckling at their Luna's mutterings.

'Injury report first, then I want to hear what our Luna has to say about us,' I tell them in the mind link, settling onto the gurney. I turn one ear to the room with Charlie, listening to Yara muttering to herself and giving Savannah instructions about where and how to stitch Charlie up. It's Haynes who gives me the report.

"I didn't realize how many of us were losing our wolves, Alpha. I thought it was only me. But most of us are getting injured so much because our wolves are weak. I can tell you, in just the twelve hours since our Luna treated me, I feel stronger than I have in weeks, months even," he says.

"I was one of the first to come in today, Alpha, and if it wasn't for our Luna, I'm not sure I'd be ready to fight again right now. But because of her assistance, my wolf was able to heal me, and I'm ready to go back out. And because he didn't have to expend all his energy healing me, even he feels stronger," another warrior says.

"I just came in before Beta Charlie, Alpha, but I'm already starting to heal. It's the fastest I can ever remember healing," another warrior says.

I look around the room, and every one of my warriors is nodding, showing me their wounds that have already or are in the process of healing - healing cleanly, with no jagged edges, no openings that may cause infection. If they scar at all, it will be minimal.

I'm just about to ask them to tell me of Yara's mutterings when Dr. Stevens walks in as if he owns the place. Everyone goes quiet, and he looks around before zeroing in on Piper.

"I'll take over from here, young lady." Does he not even know her name?

"I'm sorry, Dr. Stevens. Dr. Yara left me in charge while she operates on Beta Charlie," she says, standing her ground. I'm impressed, but I also think that this has something to do with Yara empowering her nurses in a way that Dr. Stevens never did.

"Excuse me? You have no authority in this hospital..." he begins, but I leap off the gurney and begin stalking toward him with a menacing growl. I'm not sure if he didn't notice me on the gurney against the wall or if he thought I wouldn't intervene. Either way, he was foolish.

'Dr. Stevens, I've told you that Yara is the lead doctor in this hospital. Not only are you not welcome here, but I have serious doubts about your ability to provide medical care to my warriors. Somehow, in just one day, your Luna has made more of an impact on these wolves than you have in years,' I say, keeping the mind link open so everyone can hear me. They need to know that I'm serious about Yara being in charge here.

"Don't be ridiculous. That child is barely out of undergraduate school ..."

Arric's snarl is so loud that he shakes the walls of the hospital. I hear the door behind me slam open, and I smell Yara's cinnamon and nutmeg scent.

'Tell her to go take care of Charlie. I've got this,' I say to Haynes. Yara obviously put him to work for her, so he can be my translator. I need to mark her so I can talk to her when I'm in this form.

I hear Haynes speaking quietly to Yara while Dr. Stevens watches. I growl again when he stares at her rather than facing me.

'You will not speak of my mate and your Luna like that again, or it will be the last thing you do, Dr. Stevens. Your assistance is no longer needed in this hospital. Leave before I have the warriors escort you out.'

Almost as one, the warriors push forward. Yara's made enough of an impression that they're ready to back her as their lead doctor and their Luna rather than Dr. Stevens.

"This is a big mistake. As I said before, don't come crying to me when you lose someone," he snaps.

"Actually, doctor, if we'd had to wait for you, some of us would already be dead. While you were hiding in a safe room, our Luna was here, fighting for us," one of my warriors says.

"Yeah, Doc, so when it comes to feeling safe in the hands of one of our doctors, I'll take that child who is barely out of undergraduate school, who already has me patched up and ready to fight again, over you, who would be pouring alcohol over my wounds because it takes too long to stitch me up," another says.

I watch as Dr. Stevens looks around, realizing that everyone here is ready to fight for Yara.

"Fine. I guess I'll go then," he says, stomping out of the hospital.

"Follow him. Make sure he doesn't do anything stupid," I say to two of the warriors who look the healthiest.

They nod and walk out. I look around, waiting for everyone else to relax before chuffing at Piper to continue.

"Alpha. You'll want to get back on this gurney before our Luna catches you standing around. She already warned me that she'd make my ears bleed if I didn't listen to her. I have no doubt that she'll do the same to you," Haynes says.

I chuckle, hearing others chuckling behind me as Arric leaps back up onto the gurney.

'Now, tell me about our Luna,' I say, focusing in on Yara's work in the surgery room while letting the pack regale me with Yara's snarky commentary about my pack.

Chapter 20: Taking Charge
Yara

I have no idea what Dr. Stevens is doing here. Well, actually, I'm pretty sure he thought he was going to come in and take over the hospital. What I don't understand is why he tried to do that in front of Arric. Warren was clear with him that the hospital is mine.

I must be muttering out loud again because Savannah keeps glancing up at me and smiling as she helps me close off Charlie's internal bleeding. That's why his heart was struggling. He was losing blood as fast as his heart was pumping it.

"Okay," I say, stepping back. "Close him up. Let's keep a close eye on him. If Dr. Stevens is back, how many more nurses can we expect?"

"Only two more Luna. That's all we have."

"One doctor and five nurses for a huge pack of fighting warriors?" I ask, shaking my head. "Okay, we'll make it work. Also, who orders the medical supplies?"

"I do, Luna."

"Let's talk sooner rather than later. We're missing some things that we need in the supply room."

"Yes, Luna. I'll tell you, I'm pretty sure I know what's missing. Dr. Stevens told me we didn't need those items and that they were a waste of money."

"Right, just like stitching up wounds is a waste of time," I growl, walking out.

"Piper," I call, glancing around the room to make sure no one else looks bad. I glance at Arric, who is lounging on the gurney as if he's a lion surveying his kingdom.

I hear some chuckles from the warriors, and I frown. Did I just say that out loud?

"Yes, Luna?" Piper asks, walking up to me.

"I need a report. Did any other serious injuries come in that I need to take care of before I take Alpha Warren in for surgery?" I ask.

"No, Luna."

I focus on her. "Nothing happened with Dr. Stevens, did it?"

"No, Luna. Alpha made sure he left."

"Good. And no one else caused you any problems?"

"No, Luna. I think they're all in awe of you," she says, whispering the last part.

"Well, they'll be in awe of my anger if they mess with you. Where's Anna?"

"I'm here, Luna. I made some extra triage kits just in case more warriors come in."

I turn and look at Arric.

"Are there more coming?" I ask. I wouldn't think that Warren would leave warriors out there if they needed help.

"Alpha says there are some minor injuries to the patrols, but he was just getting ready to switch them out with some of the healthier warriors here that you've healed."

"It wasn't me; it was my nurses. Thank them," I say, looking around, wondering which warriors he's going to send out.

"Alpha says he believes that every warrior in this room, as well as the nurses, would probably disagree with that statement," Haynes says. I turn and look at him, but he refuses to look at me as his lips twitch. I narrow my eyes at Arric, but the bastard begins purring at me.

I turn and look at the room. "He's right, Luna, or Dr. Luna, whatever you want us to call you. All these nurses have been working in the hospital for years. It's not them that has us healing, although now that you're here, they're being allowed to treat us as they've wanted to," one warrior says.

"He's right, Luna. Dr. Stevens always restricted what we could do to help the warriors. You being here, empowering us like you have in such a short time, is already making a huge impact on the warriors' healing," Piper says.

"I haven't done anything," I murmur, feeling completely inadequate in the face of so much injury, but I'm glad I've helped some.

"Alright, Warren, who are you sending? I want to check them out and give my approval before you do," I say.

The warriors begin stepping up to me. I'm assuming he's telling them in the mind link to come get my approval.

"You're good," I say to the first and second warriors who approach me.

"Not you, you're not ready yet," I say to the third.

He isn't happy and begins to argue with me. "Luna, I..."

"I said no. Have a seat, warrior."

"Yes, Luna."

I clear the others that Warren sends over to me before turning to look at him.

"Are you ready, Alpha?" I ask him.

He chuffs.

"Piper, Savannah is finishing up with Beta Charlie. When she's done, she can help triage. If you need me, let me know. I'm guessing our stubborn Alpha here won't let me put him under again," I say, turning to look at him. He shakes his head no. He won't let me sedate him.

I sigh and turn back to her. "So, if you need me, I can come quickly."

I step up to Haynes and reach out to touch his face. Arric growls softly behind me.

"Knock it off, Arric. Haynes was near death less than a day ago. He's been running non-stop since your warriors started coming into the hospital," I say, touching his forehead, then his cheek, then his neck.

"How are you feeling?"

He glances at the other warriors in the room. "A bit weak," he says softly.

"Have you eaten?"

"No, Luna."

"Anna, can we get some food sent over here for our warriors?"

"Yes, Luna, I'll get right on that."

"Eat something," I say to him quietly. "Why don't you grab a chair and sit outside Charlie's room. No one but me and the nurses go in and out without my say-so, and that includes Dr. Stevens."

"Yes, Luna."

He grabs the chair, and I can tell he's fading. I look over at Piper as I move to the gurney on which Arric is lying. She glances at Haynes and nods at me. She'll keep an eye on him.

"Alright, Alpha, let's get you put back together," I say, pushing his gurney into a room. When I get there, I look around, not having everything that I need.

I'm about to go get it when there's a knock at the door. I open it to Anna with a wheeled tray that has what I need on it.

"Thanks, Anna."

"You're welcome, Luna. Food is on its way," she says, her head snapping to Arric.

"What did he say?" I ask, aggravated that I need an interpreter. This would be easier if he was in human form.

"He said to make sure I set some aside for you since he's pretty sure you haven't eaten yet today."

"Set some aside for your Alpha, too. I'm not the only one who hasn't eaten."

"Yes, Luna," she says, walking out.

"Well, since you can't speak, this will be a fun, one-sided conversation," I say sarcastically. I grab the hair sheers and begin to carefully shave the fur off his leg.

"Are you sure you don't want something for the pain?" I ask, looking up at him.

He shakes his head again.

"Fine. I'm not surprised. Your entire pack seems to be mostly immune to pain. I guess, over time, you get used to it. But I don't like them getting used to it, Warren. From what I've seen today, your pack has been suffering needlessly. Dr. Stevens is a problem. One that you need to handle sooner rather than later," I say, looking over the wound.

"Did you get bit?" I ask, appalled. When I look up, his big wolf's head nods at me. "Someone wants you to lose this leg."

He chuffs at me, but since I have no idea what he's trying to tell me, I show him the scalpel, and I open his leg. As I slice into his leg, Arric moves to watch what I'm doing.

"Big guy, I can't see. You need to sit back," I tell him, gently nudging him out of my light.

I growl when I see the snapped bones in his leg again. Without warning, Arric leans over and nuzzles my cheek, his tongue gently licking me.

"Tell me you aren't trying to calm me down when you're the one who is injured," I say, looking up at him.

Arric whines at me, and I can almost see the war in his eyes as Warren tries to get his wolf under control.

"I need you focused, Arric. I'm going to have you heal a couple of these bones, then I'm going to have you shift. It's going to hurt; there's no way around that. But I need to be able to talk to Warren and learn what's going on with you two since you refuse to accept any sedatives."

He chuffs softly, watching me intently. Where the man terrifies me as a mate and a woman, the wolf is charming. I lean forward and kiss his nose. "Behave. Are you ready?"

He chuffs again, and I take the snapped bone and hold it to the intact bone, just like I did before. Arric watches intently as he heals the bone, just enough that it's set.

"Nice. One more, big guy," I tell him. I pull the other broken bone out of his leg and show it to him. "Ready?" I ask.

He chuffs again, then watches as I hold the bone, and he begins healing it. He chuffs again, leaning forward to lick my face.

"Yeah, we do make a good team. Okay, are you ready to shift? I'm going to hold your leg so that you don't jerk it and snap more bones during your shift."

I set my hands on his leg and foot, above and below the injury, and then look at Arric. "Whenever you're ready."

He begins to shift, and I feel his body jerk with the pain of it. He clenches his teeth together as Warren pulls the shift, a low moan of pain the only sound that he makes. It's soft enough that I don't think the warriors in the main room can hear it.

When he's done, Warren is lying on his side, panting heavily. I walk up to his face. Once again, he's covered in grime and guts. I ignore it, putting my hands on his cheeks. "Are you okay?"

He looks up at me, and I can see the pain in his eyes. "Do I get a kiss since I behaved?" he asks.

I shake my head. I can't believe the man is thinking about kissing me while he's in so much pain. Maybe it's because he is, or maybe it's because I like the way he kisses me, but I lean down and touch my lips to his.

Before I even know what's happening, he sits up, pulling me across his lap as he deepens the kiss, growling possessively in a way that has my body and my wolf humming with pleasure.

Chapter 21: Adjectives
Warren

Once again, I can't resist this woman. She's incredible. I knew my instincts were right to trust that the Moon Goddess would one day send me the woman that was meant for me, but I had no idea that I would be worthy of such a woman as Yara. She's everything I've ever wanted in a mate and so much more.

I know I'm covered in blood and guts, but in truth, so is she. I don't love that she smells like nearly every warrior in my pack, but I also know why she does. One day, hopefully very, very soon, my scent will be stronger than any of theirs because it will be my mark on her neck.

Tasting her, having her in my arms, smelling her sweet cinnamon and nutmeg scent relaxes me, calms me, and heals me in ways that nothing else in this world has ever done. When I pull her into my arms, it isn't a conscious decision. Well, maybe it was for Arric. My wolf is nearly as desperate for our mate as I am. I'd felt her body tense and then relax as her arms slid around my neck. I let myself get lost in the kiss, knowing that as soon as she regains her thoughts, she'll pull away since my leg is still open and broken on the table behind her.

The kiss doesn't last nearly long enough before reality slams into her, and she quickly pulls away, moving to sit back.

"Careful. You don't want to undo all that hard work," I say softly. I'd suffer the pain for the kiss, but I know she'll be upset with herself if she does hurt me.

"You are incorrigible!" she says.

"Arrogant, insufferable, unbelievable, leonine, incorrigible ... what other interesting adjectives do you have for me, my mate?"

I see her glance up at me as she leans back over my leg. I was pretty sure she hadn't realized she'd spoken out loud about me looking like a lion surveying my kingdom. Arric had nearly barked his laugh out loud like some of my warriors did. The woman isn't just healing my pack's bodies, although that is something incredible to see. But she's also healing their minds, giving them something they haven't had in a long time. Hope.

"Stubborn, there's an apt description of you," she says, tugging a bone back into place. "Arric," she says more quietly.

I narrow my eyes at her. It didn't escape my notice that she is much more inclined to love up on my wolf than with me.

'That's because I'm better looking,' Arric says, proudly watching our mate put us back together.

I snort, and Yara looks up at me, raising an eyebrow.

"Arric says you like him better than me because he's better looking."

"Well, he is magnificent," she says without hesitation. Arric, the bastard, begins purring loudly, making Yara smile.

"So, you do like him better than me?" I ask, feeling almost jealous of my wolf.

"Wolves are easier, simpler than humans. They love, they mate, they eat, they fight for their families, they die for their families. They don't waver, and they don't judge based on stupid things. They set up a hierarchy in their packs so everyone knows their place and can feel comfortable with their role within that pack. They don't look down on their omegas, they accept their role within the pack, and the stronger wolves protect them as they should. Arric accepts Annika for the wolf she is, not just as his mate, but as a strong wolf that can help strengthen his pack," she says.

"And you don't think that I accept you as the woman you are?" I ask as she quietly says Arric's name again, and he begins healing another bone.

She glances up at me. "I think you want more than a mate."

"What do you think I want?" I ask, curious about what's going on in her head. The woman is incredibly intelligent when it comes to the hospital, but I'm beginning to realize that she's ignorant when it comes to relationships, which makes me happy.

"You want someone to come home to after you've been fighting, someone to warm your bed and give you pups," she says and then stops as if all she would be to me is a baby-making machine.

"That's part of it, but that's not all of it," I say to her, making her look up at me again.

"Why don't you tell me what you want from me," she says, and it's almost a challenge – as if she doesn't think that I'd be honest with her about what I want. I may not tell others, but she's my mate, and I want to share everything with her.

"I told you before that I want love. Yes, I want you in my bed every night. EVERY night. Yes, I would love nothing more than to bury myself inside your sweet heat every night. And yes, I want pups with you, just so we're clear. But I also want a woman who challenges me, someone who can make me laugh, someone who can calm the fury and torment inside me after a battle. I want someone I can be completely open and honest with in a way that I can't be with anyone else in the pack, not even Charlie. I want someone who leads this pack beside me, someone who earns the respect of the pack and their allegiance, not just because she's their Luna but because she deserves it. I want a woman who loves me as much as I love her, who wants me as much as I want her. I want everything. I want it all. I want your love, your passion, your tears, your children, your ire, your intelligence ... everything, Yara. I want every damn thing you have to give me."

She stops and stares at me while I speak. "The fact that you're a damn fantastic doctor is just the cherry on top for me."

"I think I'll add demanding to the list of adjectives for you," she says, getting back to her work.

"What do you want in a mate, Yara? You said you wanted someone who respects you and who recognizes the value you bring to the pack, but those are things that anyone can give. What do you want from a mate? What do you want from me besides monogamy, which I've already agreed to."

She frowns, looking back down at my leg. "Love and respect, kindness, compassion, honesty ... I don't know. I've never really given it much thought."

"Think about it. Other than the peace and quiet that I already told you I can't provide, I want to give you everything that you want in a mate and in life. And honesty ... that's an interesting one since you have yet to be honest with me," I say.

"What haven't I been honest with you about?" she asks me.

"Why did Alpha Solomon's death upset you so much? Was he your Alpha? Was he your father?" I ask, and when she looks up again, I see the sadness in her eyes, and right behind it, there's fear.

"Trust is earned, Warren," she says, looking away quickly.

"Have I done something that makes you think I'm not worthy of being trusted, Yara?" I ask.

She sighs a heavy sigh. "No. Well, other than holding me captive in your pack," she says, glancing up at me.

"Keeping you safe. Someone is after you, Yara. Five trackers don't lie," I say, watching her closely. "So, if losing Alpha Solomon isn't what scares you, then perhaps having his son, Simon, as Alpha is what makes you so nervous."

Once again, if I wasn't watching so closely, I wouldn't have seen her flinch when I said Simon's name. But I was, and I did, and now I know who is after my mate.

Chapter 22: Pack's Response

Yara

Damn. This Alpha is too smart for his own good. It's probably why he's still alive, and most of his pack members are, too. It's also why he's still the Alpha of this pack after twelve long years of fighting.

"What if it is Simon that I'm afraid of? What difference does it make?" I ask him.

"You're not just afraid of him, Yara. You've been hiding from him for a very long time. Years. And the difference is that now, I know who I'm protecting you from. I'll protect you from anyone who attacks us, but I'll put a separate focus on Simon. I've also sent a warrior to collect your things from the university and erase your presence there ..."

"WHAT?!" I ask, appalled. "No, Warren! I've worked too hard, too long for you to erase it! Do you even understand what you've done?" I ask as tears prick my eyes. All my hard work, all my studies, gone.

"I'm keeping you safe, Yara!" he says as if this is supposed to make it okay that he's erased seven of the most grueling years of my life.

And this is exactly why I didn't want to tell him. I drop the instruments on the table and turn. "Find a new doctor," I growl, walking out of the room.

"YARA!" he yells, but I keep going. I refuse to let the man see me cry. I pass Haynes as he stands from the chair he's sitting in.

"Luna? Is everything okay?" he asks as I pass.

"Do NOT let her walk out of this hospital!" Warren commands and I see his warriors stand. They look like they aren't happy to be put in the middle of this argument, but he's their Alpha, and they may call me Luna, but I'm not officially their Luna, so they will answer to Warren.

I glare at all of them, and surprisingly, I watch them all raise their necks in submission to me as if they are apologizing for acting on their Alpha's command.

"Yara, let's talk about this," Warren says, hobbling up behind me.

"Talk about it! Talk about it!" I yell, whirling around to face him. "We should have talked about this before you decided to wipe my educational history off the face of the earth. Do you even realize what you've done, Warren? You did what you told me you wouldn't do. Your mark isn't even on my neck, and you're stripping me of everything that I've worked so hard to achieve in my life. Do you get that? It's no different than if I'd let Dr. Stevens take your leg, stripping you of everything that you've worked so hard to achieve. The difference is, I gave you a choice, and you took mine," I say angrily as hot tears begin to stream down my cheeks.

He takes a hobbled step towards me. "Yara..."

"Don't you dare lay a fucking hand on me," I snarl, swiping the tears off my face.

"What did you do, Alpha?" I hear a warrior ask behind me.

"I kept your Luna safe from the Alpha who is hunting her."

"Is that what you're going with? Keeping me safe? You had to erase seven years of medical school to keep me safe?" I yell. "News flash, Warren! If he knows where my car was and he knows that the trackers have been disabled, then he would have sent warriors out to hunt for me. What would he have found, Warren? Hmmm? He'd have found your scent and mine on that fucking bear trap. And then they'd have followed your pack's scent and mine back here. I'm guessing Simon already knows I'm here."

I feel heat at my back. I expect Warren's warriors to grab me and keep me from leaving, but instead, Warren's gaze tracks to them, and his eyes narrow.

"I think our Luna needs a break from you, Alpha," a warrior says, making Warren growl.

"Now really isn't the time for you to pick a fight with us, Alpha," another warrior says. It's a clear threat. Warren's leg is still open, his bones still healing. It's the perfect time for one of his warriors to overthrow him, especially with Charlie down.

"We'll take her to the packhouse. We'll keep her safe while you and Beta Charlie recover," another warrior says, basically wrapping me in the protection of the pack.

"Savannah, close Alpha Warren's leg for me, please," I say, then turn to the warriors. "I'm going to the packhouse, but I will be very disappointed if you take this opportunity to try and overthrow your Alpha. Just because he's a terrible mate doesn't mean he isn't a good Alpha."

"Yes, Luna," they say.

I turn and walk out, not surprised when I hear Warren call out to me. I ignore the conversations behind me, just needing to get away before I completely break down. Thankfully, the warriors who escort me back to the packhouse don't say anything. I walk up to the Alpha floor, not knowing where else to go. I stop outside of Warren's door, then move down the hall, unwilling to sleep in his bed. When I choose a door, one of the warriors opens it, checking it to make sure it's safe before letting me in.

"If you need anything, Luna, let us know. We'll be right outside your door," one of the warriors says.

I stop just long enough to look them all over and make sure they're medically stable enough to be on guard duty before nodding and walking into the room. I close the door and collapse on the bed, burying my face in a pillow as I begin sobbing.

~ ~ ~

Simon POV

"Alpha, Alpha Brady's pack attacked Alpha Warren last night," my warriors tell me over breakfast.

"Who won?"

"Alpha Warren, but I heard that he might be injured. His Beta is most likely dead. They had a lot of casualties from what we could see," he says.

I stand, beginning to pace.

"Do we know what type of injury Alpha Warren has?"

"I believe it's still related to the bear trap that we found, Alpha."

So, the Alpha is down, and the Beta is out. "What about a Gamma?"

"I'd heard that his Gamma was killed in a battle a while ago, but he hasn't had time to replace him."

"So, no healthy ranked members? Is that what I'm hearing?"

"Yes, Alpha."

"Well then, perhaps it's time for me to go get my Luna. I wouldn't want Alpha Warren to have a chance to put his mark on her neck and ruin everything. And we don't want some other Alpha to get there and kill her before I can claim her. Gather the troops. Our goal is Yara, but if we can kill Alpha Warren in the process, that will just be a bonus."

"Yes, Alpha."

Chapter 23: Apology

Warren

I watch as Yara walks out of the hospital. I take another step to follow her, but a wall of warriors steps in my way.

I snarl, ready to fight my way to her.

"Alpha, give her some space. If you push her now, you could lose her forever," Savannah says. "The warriors will watch over her. We've all obviously learned to love our Luna in a very short amount of time."

That's the understatement of the fucking millennium. I can't believe my pack just basically turned on me to protect Yara. Shit, if she were so inclined, they'd probably take her as their fucking Alpha. However, it didn't escape me that she told them that she'd be disappointed in them if they tried to fight me in my current state. Disappointed, not angry. A true Luna.

"Come on, Alpha. Let's get you stitched up. It looks like our Luna got your bones all reset, but I'll take a look."

When we get back to the room, I look at her. "Savannah, I need a phone."

"I'll find one after I finish this."

"No, I need it now. If I'm going to fix things with my mate, I need to do it before it can't be undone."

"Yes, Alpha," she says, going to get me a phone.

Her words ring in my ears. 'He's a terrible mate.' FUCK! Yara's right. While my intentions had been purely to protect Yara, erasing her from the school would cause a lot of problems that I'm not sure even I could fix.

As soon as she's back, I call the warrior that Charlie sent to the university.

"Alpha, is everything alright? I heard we were attacked again last night. Do you need me to come back?"

"Archie, where are you at with erasing Yara's presence from the school?"

"I've cleaned out her dorm room, Alpha. I'm just about to wipe her records from the system."

"Don't. Leave them."

"Are you sure, Alpha?"

"Yes but make a copy. She may have to transfer to a werewolf university," I say and hang up.

'He's a terrible mate.' Her words keep playing in my mind. I've wanted nothing more than her my entire adult life, and now, I find out I'm terrible at being a mate. I probably am. I don't know the first thing about being compassionate or loving. I know about fighting and war. But I'm willing to learn – for her. I can become whatever she needs me to be. She just needs to give me a chance.

"How is Beta Charlie?" I ask Savannah as she finishes closing up my leg.

"He's stable, Alpha," Savannah says. "If that changes, I'll let Luna know."

"Thank you for this," I tell her, pulling my leg off the bed.

"Alpha, you should stay the night. Let Alpha Arric heal your bones."

"Savannah, I need to go make amends with my mate. I need to apologize, and I need her to understand that I wasn't trying to take her life or her title away from her."

I stand, and she hands me the crutch. "Anna has food for both of you. Our Luna never ate today."

"Thank you, Savannah."

"She really is special, Alpha. It says a lot that the Moon Goddess gave you such a mate. Don't blow it," she says, but it's not unkind.

"I'm going to do my very best not to," I tell her.

I walk out of the room and see Haynes still sitting outside Charlie's room. "Switch out with someone, Haynes. You're still recovering. You wouldn't want to disappoint your Luna."

"No, Alpha, I wouldn't."

When I walk to the waiting room, I see most of my warriors are still there.

"What are you going to do, Alpha?" they ask.

"I'm going to go make things right with Yara. Charlie is down. Do I need to make a patrol schedule?" I ask.

"We'll rotate out, Alpha. Get some sleep. We don't know when we'll be attacked again, but most of us are already healing and getting stronger. We can manage the patrols until you wake up. Just ... just make things right with our Luna," a warrior says.

"Yeah, she's the best thing that's happened to this pack in most of our lifetimes," another warrior says.

"We don't want to lose her, so figure it out, Alpha. We're already stronger because of her, and she hasn't even been here two days yet. Imagine what she'll do to strengthen this pack over time."

"I intend to do whatever it takes to keep Yara here with us," I tell them.

That seems to calm them for the moment. Now, I just need to make it happen.

As I walk back to the packhouse, I think about what I can do to make Yara happy. The respect and honesty that she wants are easy, and those are things I've already given her. The love part is easy in concept. I already love Yara, but how do I show her that? My parents made it look easy, but I'm sure there was more to it that I never saw, just like there will be things between Yara and I that the pack and our future children will never s ee.

The kindness and compassion that she wants will be the hardest. Kindness and compassion in times of war don't come easy.

As I'm walking back to the packhouse, I see some wildflowers growing beside the cobblestone drive from the hospital to the packhouse. I stop, picking several of them, wondering what her favorite color might be. Rather than dwell on the fact that I have no clue what her favorite color is, I decide to pick as many colors as I can, making the bouquet bright and cheerful looking. At least, I hope she'll think it is.

When I walk into the packhouse, everyone goes quiet. I'm not sure if that's a good thing or not, but at the moment, I don't care. I'm exhausted and sick at the idea that Yara may try to leave me.

I go to the kitchen and find a glass, filling it with water. I'm pretty confident that we don't have any vases in the packhouse, but I can get some if Yara seems to like the flowers.

Then, I carefully make my way up the stairs, following her scent. I'm happy that she at least went back to our room, but that happiness wanes when I get to the top of the stairs and see that she's not in our bedroom.

"Alpha, the others said you're here to make amends with our Luna," one of my warriors says.

"That's correct."

"See that you do. I don't like hearing my Luna cry herself to sleep," he says, and they step away from the door to allow me entry. I don't like knowing that she did, either.

When I step inside the room, I see that she's on top of the bed, clutching a pillow to her body. I set the flowers down on the nightstand and quietly move around the bed before sliding beside her and wrapping myself around her.

I feel her shift, and I know the moment that she realizes that I'm behind her because her body goes rigid in my arms.

"Please don't leave," I say, pressing my lips to her shoulder. "I'm sorry. You were right. I didn't think through the decision and the impact it would have on you. I didn't do it to hurt you. I did it to keep you safe. But I understand that it was the wrong move to make, and I've fixed it," I tell her.

She scoffs. "How did you fix it?"

"My warrior hadn't wiped you from the educational system yet, so I told him to leave your information. However, he's cleaned out your dorm room and is bringing your things here. It's not safe for you to be there; you must know that. But you're right. Seven years of hard work shouldn't be erased. You're too good of a doctor to have to start all over. Please forgive me for my oversight. I know it was a big one, but I truly am sorry, and I've fixed it so you can maintain your title and continue your studies," I say quietly, hoping my words are enough.

She's quiet for a long time, and I feel cold fear, unlike anything I've ever felt, sliding through my veins as I wait for her verdict.

"What are those?" she asks, pointing to the flowers.

"I picked those on the way over here. I didn't know if you liked flowers, and we don't have any vases for them since I can't remember ever having flowers around the packhouse, and I'm not really good at knowing how to show you that I love you, but ... I wanted to try. I know you said you wanted respect and honesty, and those things are easy for me to give you. I love you already. I love you with everything in me, but I don't know how to show you love in a way that lets you know that I mean it. I don't know how to show kindness and compassion like you want. I think ... I think that's why the Moon Goddess paired you with me, Yara. You are the other half of my soul. You are the softness and gentleness that I need in my life. I am willing to give you anything and everything that you desire in this world, but I need your help. I don't know how to be all of the things that you want ... not yet, anyway. But I will. If you can be patient and help teach me, I will."

I kiss her shoulder again, waiting a really long time again while she thinks.

"You make it really hard to deny you," she finally murmurs.

I have no idea if she meant for me to hear it or not, and I don't care. Something inside me relaxes, and I wrap my arm more tightly around her.

"How's your leg?" she asks.

"Better thanks to my amazing doctor, Luna, and mate."

I close my eyes, and I'm nearly asleep when I hear her again.

"I like flowers."

I smile, knowing my mate will be getting flowers from me everyday for the rest of her life.

Chapter 24: Healing

Yara

No one's ever gotten me flowers before. I don't know why seeing the bright, colorful bunch of wildflowers makes me feel special, but it does. Maybe it's because of the man who got them for me or because I know that it's so far out of his wheelhouse that I know it was a conscious effort on his part to try and make up with me.

I'm also surprised that he put a stop to eliminating my school records. I just assumed that he wouldn't care ... that he would do what he wanted because he's an Alpha and assumes he knows best. But he didn't. He seemed to understand the importance of my education, and he made sure to keep my records intact.

I'm not upset about him getting my things from my room. He's right that it's not safe for me there any longer, and I'm glad I won't have to go back and possibly run into Simon. The only other option for me was to leave everything behind, and I hated that. It may not be much, but my entire life was in that dorm room.

Warren falls asleep before I do, but I follow closely behind him, which is good because, once again, we are awoken by the sounds of howls alerting us to an attack.

"Warren!" I yell again as he leaps out of bed.

"I'm better than I was last night," he says, rushing back to me. "Get to a safe room," he says before taking my mouth in a quick, fiery kiss.

"No," I say as he starts to turn away.

"Yara ..."

"I'm a doctor, Warren. You need me in the hospital."

He looks at me for a long moment. "Fine. Be careful," he says before rushing out and once again leaping over the banister. I grab a pair of shorts and the hair tie from yesterday that is sitting beside the flowers and rush out the door and down the stairs.

I see Savannah, Piper, and Anna rushing up to me. "Let's go," I say, turning to see some warriors standing behind us.

"What are you doing?"

"Alpha's orders, we're on hospital guard duty."

"Fine," I say, ready to go, when more warriors come rushing up.

"Luna! Alpha says you have to give us clearance to fight since you put us on downtime," the warriors say. I look behind them and see a line forming. SHIT!

"How many warriors are on guard duty?" I ask the warrior behind me.

"Three Luna."

"Two of you go with Anna and Piper. Start getting the triage and crash kits ready. Savannah ..."

"On it."

"Make two lines. If you were injured, in my line. If you needed rest, in Savannah's line," I shout above the noise, hearing the safe room doors slamming shut and locking nearby.

"How's your wolf?" I ask the first warrior as I look over his injuries. They're healed.

"I'm good, Luna," the wolf says. I look up and nod.

"You're good to go," I say, and he turns, shifting and racing into the fight.

The next two are the same. When someone begins arguing with Savannah, I step over.

"How's your wolf?" I ask him, looking him over. I narrow my eyes, seeing that he has an injury. He should have been in my line.

"He's good, Luna," the warrior says.

"I need to hear him say it," I say, remembering that this warrior got slashed across the stomach. I yank his shirt up and see that it's still healing.

"You're out," I say, then grab his chin in my hand. "And don't you dare fucking lie to me ever again."

"But Luna ..."

"Quit wasting time, Nick," the warrior guard says and yanks him out of the line. "Luna's orders stand."

I quickly get through the group, pulling only five out and letting the others go.

"You five," I say as we begin to make our way to the pack hospital. "You will be the second line of defense in the hospital."

"Yes, Luna." It's not ideal, but I know that they need to feel useful while the battle is going on.

"Umm, Luna. Piper says that Beta Charlie is awake and trying to leave the hospital."

"Tell the warriors that he is to remain in the hospital on my orders," I say, running faster. I'm not sure how much my order will override their Beta's, but I guess I'm about to find out.

When I get there, I see him standing unsteadily on his feet, trying to get past the warriors I told to hold him.

"Charlie, what are you doing? Why are you out of bed?" I ask, grabbing the triage kit that is already put together and walking up to Charlie to check his pupils. They respond normally, but he pulls away as if the light is painful.

"There's a war going on, Luna. I need to get out there."

"You're in no shape to fight, Beta," I tell him.

"You are not in charge here," he snaps.

"On the contrary, I am very much in charge here. This is a hospital, and I override everyone here, including your Alpha. So, sit your ass down and get comfy. I don't have time to fight with you, and I didn't bring you back from the dead yesterday just so you could go kill yourself today," I say, snarling by the time I'm done.

What is with this pack?

"I believe her words were that she would follow you into the Moon Goddess' realm," one of the warriors says.

"And drag your sorry ass back down here," another pipes in.

"Because she wasn't going to let you die, and no one dies in her hospital," a third says.

"Okay, peanut gallery, your commentary is unnecessary," I say to the group.

"And let's not forget that if you do something stupid that makes you pass out, when you wake up, she'll give you a tongue lashing that will make your ears bleed," Haynes says, walking out. "Am I good to go, Luna? I waited for you to arrive, but I feel much better."

"Your wolf?"

"I'm back, Luna. I'm not at full strength, but I'm much better, thanks to you," his wolf says to me.

"Okay, but if you get injured again today, you don't go back out until you get back to full strength, got me?"

"Got you, Luna," Haynes says, rushing out the door and shifting. I smile when I hear his wolf howl happily at being back, even if we are in the middle of a war.

"So, what do you want me to do?" Charlie grumbles as he sits.

"Tell me what's happening on the battlefield. Last night, we already had people coming in. Where are they?" I ask.

I look around as all of the warriors' eyes go unfocused.

"They're healthy," one warrior says in awe.

"They're fighting hard and well," Charlie says.

"One coming in now," one of my guards says.

I get ready, but it's a simple gash. I wash it and let Savannah stitch it up. It's so quiet that she uses the time to show Piper how to stitch deep wounds.

"How is it out there?" one of the warriors that I kept from fighting asks the injured warrior.

"Luna, I don't know how you did it, but the pack is already stronger. One day and we all feel it. Even with this many of us not in the fight, we're fighting so much better than we have in ... I don't even know how long. Years, maybe."

I only have a moment to smile before another group comes in, chased by attacking wolves. The guards leap into action, and the other warriors stand, ready to attack.

I quickly get to work, taking the worst injuries and washing them and stitching them up so their wolves can heal them faster, but there's nothing as severe as yesterday. I'm nearly done, and the fighting is continuing outside when I see several heads snap to the storage room behind me. Charlie, who is standing between me and the entryway to the hospital, snarls, taking a step toward me, his eyes focused over my head.

I turn to see what's going on, and my heart sinks. Simon has Piper by the throat, and he's holding her in front of him like a shield.

"Hello, Yara. Time for you to come home."

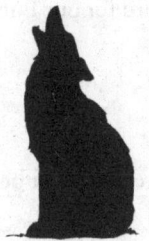

Chapter 25: Attack

Warren

This time, when we're attacked, I'm surprised. This is Alpha Solomon's old pack, and I guess his son really is the asshole that I thought he was. Not only do I now have another pack attacking mine, but the asshole isn't even here in the fight.

Solomon wasn't a bad Alpha, but he was older and tired, and it shows in his warriors' lack of fighting ability. Add to that, Yara has already strengthened our pack significantly in the very short amount of time that she's been here, and this battle is much easier than any of the recent battles we've had.

'Does anyone have eyes on Alpha Simon?' I ask, ripping another one of Simon's warriors apart.

'No, Alpha,' I hear my warriors reply.

Most of them are still fighting. Only a small number had to go to the hospital. I'm not surprised that Charlie isn't out here. I know he wanted to be, and I can feel him focusing on the fight, but I'm sure Yara refused to let him leave. I'm in total agreement. This battle may not be the worst we've ever fought, but Charlie was practically dead yesterday. No, he WAS dead yesterday. Yara brought him back to life.

I don't like it that Simon isn't here. If he knows that Yara is here, that's the most logical reason why he sent his warriors to attack, but where is he? Is he standing back, searching for her?

'Charlie, is everything alright in the hospital?' I ask him.

'The guards you put on are fighting some wolves who got through. Our injured are starting to jump in. I'm standing guard for our Luna.'

'Is Simon there?'

'Not that I can see.'

Where the fuck is Simon?!

'Keep vigilant. He's got to be here, and he'll be coming for Yara,' I say, just as I feel Charlie's mind link close.

'Charlie?' I ask, pushing his mind link open again.

'He's here, Alpha. He's here in the hospital, and he's after Luna Yara,' he says softly. Through the bond, I can feel him going into fighting mode. I can feel his body coiling to pounce.

I snarl, turning and howling to the pack.

'Kill them and get to the hospital! Alpha Simon is after your Luna!'

I'm not sure what I expected from my pack, but it wasn't the rush of adrenaline and fury that I just felt. Where the battle was being won more slowly, now my warriors begin thrashing and killing like wild, feral animals, turning to head to the hospital.

I push the mind link with Charlie open again.

"Let her go, Simon. There's no way you leave here alive," Charlie says to him.

"Yara won't let this little girl die, will you, Yara?" I can hear Simon's sickeningly syrupy voice as he purrs at my mate.

Arric pushes harder, trying to reach her. I refuse to let him take her from me.

"Just come with me, Yara, and I'll let her go," he purrs.

I quickly filter through my pack's minds and realize that he has Piper.

'Stay strong, Piper. I'm on my way,' I say to her.

'He has me by the throat, Alpha. His claws are touching my voice box. If he moves, I'll never be able to speak again, or it could kill me,' she says, and I can feel her fear through the bond.

'Just hold on. Yara and Charlie won't let you die.'

I'm nearly there when I hear a howl in the distance. Because I'm connected to Piper, I feel Simon jerk in response, making Piper whimper in pain.

"Time to go now, Yara. Last chance before I kill her," he snarls.

'Do NOT let Yara give herself to him to save Piper,' I snarl at Charlie.

He doesn't respond and I know it's because he's ready to leap and protect our pack member.

"You're out of time, Simon. You'll never get out of this pack alive. Warren will kill you. He will hunt you down and kill you for coming after me," she says, making my heart soar. She's basically telling Simon that she's mine.

"You were meant for me, Yara," he snarls.

I feel pain rip through Piper just as Arric bursts through the front doors of the hospital. It's chaos inside, blood everywhere. Charlie, unable to shift, is rushing to the back of the hospital.

'He's going out the back! Simon is going out the back of the hospital!' he yells in the mind link.

Arric rushes over to where Yara is kneeling on the floor.

"Savannah, I need a crash kit!" she yells as Arric pushes against her, guarding her with his body.

"Arric, I need space. Simon is gone," she says, not looking at us.

Piper is jerking on the floor as blood pumps out of her neck. Arric moves as Savannah rushes over.

"Here, hold your finger here. Keep pressure on that artery," Yara says to Savannah, her voice calm but urgent.

I turn and look at Piper. Her throat is hanging open on one side. That asshole tried to rip her throat out.

'Stay with me, Piper. Yara won't let you die. I know it hurts,' I say in the mind link. I feel more than hear her whimper. She's not able to make a sound with her throat torn open.

'Can you put her out? She's terrified,' I say to Savannah.

"Not yet. We have to stabilize her first," Savannah says out loud.

"What?" Yara asks.

'Alpha, do you want us to chase Alpha Simon past our pack borders?' one of my warriors asks me.

'No. I'm not there to assist, and neither is Charlie. Protect the borders; don't let him back onto our lands. Make sure he doesn't sneak back. He's after Yara,' I say.

Savannah has been telling Yara what I asked.

119

"We can't risk putting her under while she's losing so much blood, Warren. It's too dangerous. As soon as I have her stable, we'll get her into surgery," Yara says.

'Charlie, make sure the pack is secure,' I tell him, turning to look at the other warriors that have been fighting around the hospital.

Charlie begins having our warriors sound off that each area of the pack is secure, making sure that Simon's wolves are either dead or retreating off our pack lands.

Arric moves to lay over Piper's legs, helping to hold her still and warm her. I can feel that she's in shock, and her body feels cold to her. Yara glances at me but doesn't say anything as she continues to fight for Piper's life.

'She's fading,' I say to Savannah.

"Luna, Alpha says she's fading," she tells Yara.

"Not today, Piper. I need you too much. You don't die today. You hold on. You fight. That bastard doesn't get to take you from me. Do you hear me?" she asks, barely glancing up at Piper. "Anna, I need a gurney!"

"Here, Luna," one of the warriors says. They had all been on their way here to fight. The ones who didn't chase Simon away stayed to watch Yara try to save Piper.

"Warren, I need you to shift. Savannah and I can't take our hands out of her throat, or she'll bleed out."

Arric steps back, and I pull the shift. "What do you need?"

"If you'll take her head, one of you take her lower body and lift her gently but quickly."

We get into position, and several warriors step up to help. "On three, ready?"

She counts, and we lift Piper onto the gurney. Anna begins pushing her toward a room while I stand there, feeling completely useless. I'm not sure if she just needs the help or if she realizes that I hate feeling useless, but she glances at me.

"Warren, grab that tray beside you and I need another one just like it," she says.

I grab the tray, and Haynes steps up. "I'll get the other one. I know where they are."

I turn, following my mate into the surgery room, just as I hear Charlie give the all-clear on the pack lands.

As much as I want to help her, listening to Yara take charge and begin working on Piper is like listening to a foreign language. I have no idea what to do and I stand there until the two nurses in the safe rooms rush in and begin helping.

"Warren, check the others. Find out if anyone else is in bad shape," she says, looking over at me. I nod but can't tear my eyes away from Piper. That could have been Yara. If it were her lying on the table, she'd be dead. There would be no one to stitch her back together.

"Warren!" she says, her tone sharp, making me look up at her. "Go check your warriors. Let me know if any of them are in need of immediate medical attention."

I nod, this time turning around and walking toward the door as anger and fury begin welling up inside me.

Yara was right. Simon will die for coming after what's mine.

Chapter 26: Exhaustion

Yara

I've never encountered this type of injury before. In humans, someone with this type of throat injury would be dead. So, I'm terrified that I'm going to do something wrong. While it's not out of the realm of possibility that she could still die on me, even if I save her life, I can't guarantee that she'll be able to swallow like normal or even speak again.

"You're doing great, Luna," Savannah says to me.

I glance at her, and I don't know what she sees on my face, but she nods. "You're doing great."

I refocus on Piper's throat. I'm using every little bit of knowledge I have about anatomy to try and stitch her up properly. The throat isn't an easy place to stitch.

"Luna, the other warriors are stitched up. Alpha Warren sent them back to the packhouse to get cleaned up and get some rest," Anna says, coming in and looking at Piper.

"You should go get some sleep too, Anna."

"I can stay, Luna. Katie, Erica, and I are going to rotate to keep watch on Beta Charlie and Piper today while you get some rest. If anything happens to either of them, we'll let you know," she says, including the other two nurses that I've barely had a chance to work with. I know that they are doing a pretty good job, though, because Haynes was healing nicely when I saw him earlier, so I feel comfortable that they can look after Charlie. I'm not confident about Piper, though. She will be in critical condition for a while.

"I'll need to speak with them, Anna. I haven't spent any time with them, and all three of you need to understand how critical Piper is. Even after she wakes up, she's going to need time to heal," I say as I finally finish with the last stitch.

"I'll bandage her, Luna," Savannah says.

I nod and turn to Anna. "Are they here? I can give instructions to all of you at one time."

Anna goes to get the other two, and after formally introducing myself to them, I explain what they need to look for with Piper, that if she wakes up, she's only allowed liquids and she's not allowed to speak out loud.

"Yes, Luna. We'll look after her," Katie says.

"We'll come get you if anything changes," Erica says.

I look at them and realize that Katie is the one who is pregnant. "Katie, how is your pregnancy going?"

"It's going well, I think, Luna. One day, when we aren't in the aftermath of a battle, I'd like you to take a look at this little one."

"Maybe I can do that later today," I say, feeling the adrenaline rush from before flowing out of me as if someone uncorked a bottle and dumped it upside down.

"Whenever you get a chance, Luna," she says.

"When's the last time you ate?" Savannah asks, coming up to join our group.

"I don't even know what time it is," I say.

"Mid-afternoon, Luna. You've been in surgery for hours."

I nod. The days have blended together since I've been here. I honestly don't know what day it is or what time it is, much less when I last ate.

"I'm going to go get some sleep," I say, feeling the exhaustion hitting me hard, making it feel like I'm walking through concrete. "You need some, too, Savannah."

"Yes, Luna," she says. I look at Piper one more time before stepping out of the room.

All I want to do is crawl into bed. I'm so tired that I don't even have the strength to wash the blood off of me. I pull my gloves off, tossing them in a bin as I walk into the hospital waiting room. I look up and see Warren. He's waiting for me. He stands, looking at me intently. Without saying a word, he opens his arms for me.

I feel my lips begin to tremble as everything from the last few days begins crashing down on me: my fear for Piper, my anger at Simon, my hunger, my lack of sleep, my worry about the warriors in this pack, my fight with Warren ... all of it hits me as the adrenaline that has kept me going dissipates. I lose the battle with my tears, and a moment later, I feel Warren's strong arms wrap around me, embracing me as if he knows that I'll shatter into pieces unless he holds me together. I cling to him like he's a life preserver in a stormy sea, and without him, I'll drown in my emotions.

"Come on, baby. Let's get you to our room," he says gently, scooping me into his arms.

"Get back in bed. You can argue with your Luna about coming off the injured reserve list when she's stronger," he says. I'm assuming he's talking to Charlie, but I don't look. I lay my head on his shoulder, tucking my face against his throat as he begins walking back to the packhouse.

As we walk, I take deep breaths of his teakwood scent, letting the mate bond calm me. I've heard of the power of the mate bond, but this is the first time that I think I've had a chance to truly test it. I hear Arric begin purring, the sound rumbling in his chest and against my ear, lulling me into something like a trance. I'm aware but not fully awake.

I know the moment we step into the packhouse as the murmuring stops. Still, I don't look up, and Warren doesn't stop. I feel him climbing the stairs to our bedroom, and when we walk in, I take gulping breaths of his scent in our room.

He doesn't lay me on the bed, instead going into the bathroom. He stands a moment, then sits on the side of the bathtub and turns on the water, keeping me in his arms.

"I'm going to take your clothes off, Yara, and then I'm going to bathe you. You're covered in blood. I know you're tired, but you'll be happy to be clean when you wake up."

I nod, too tired to speak.

He sits me on the sink and pulls the shirt, his shirt, over my head. "Hold on to me," he says softly, putting me on my feet and pushing his shorts off me. I feel him removing his, too, and then he carefully pulls his shirt off while still holding me up.

Then he picks me up and steps into the bathtub, sitting and putting me in between his legs.

"Just lean back against me," he says.

I do, and he begins running the warm water over my tired body.

"When's the last time you ate, Yara?" he asks softly as he continues to rinse me off.

"I don't know."

He kisses the side of my head and begins pouring warm water over my hair. We're quiet as he washes my hair, rinsing it and replacing the soapy water in the tub before beginning to wash my body.

I feel my fear for Piper pushing forward again.

"What if she doesn't make it, Warren?" I whisper, choking back a sob.

I feel the washcloth pause before he continues. "Then you'll know you did everything you could to save her, and Simon will die an even slower death for killing that sweet girl."

I feel my lips trembling. "What if ..." I hiccup, trying to hold back my tears. "What if she survives but can't speak? What if she can't swallow? What if surviving is worse than dying because I wasn't able to stitch her throat properly?"

I feel him rubbing his face against my head, kissing me as he thinks.

"We'll figure it out, Yara. If there's a specialist that we can bring in to work with her, I'll do it. But let's not get ahead of ourselves. You're an incredible doctor and Piper, while young, is strong with a strong wolf. It may take her some time to fully heal, so let's not rush it. Let's wait and see how she is tomorrow."

I nod, then sigh as I feel him gently washing my body. I can't remember the last time someone took care of me. Definitely not like this. Alpha Solomon was kind, but he was a busy man.

"Just so you know, this feels an awful lot like kindness and compassion," I tell him.

I feel Arric's purr, which hasn't stopped, increase in intensity.

"I consider this taking care of my mate. But if this counts as kindness and compassion, maybe it won't be as hard for me as I thought," he says, kissing the side of my head again. "Sleep, Yara. I'll take care of you."

If you had asked me if I'd ever be able to fall asleep in a bathtub with a naked Alpha washing my body, I'd have probably laughed in your face. But between my own exhaustion, Arric's purring, and Warren's assurance that I'm safe, I fall into a deep, deep sleep.

Chapter 27: Plan of Attack

Quinton

"What the fuck do you mean he's still alive, Brady?" I yell into the phone. Brady had one job. Eliminate Warren. He swore he had it under control, but now, rather than Warren getting killed, Brady has put his pack out of commission.

"Look, I had the doctor! He was destroying the pack from the inside. But Warren found his mate, and she's supposedly some doctor. I'm telling you, Quinton, we attacked him two days in a row. I don't know what the fuck that lady doctor is doing, but his pack was stronger the second day than they were the first. They should have at least been as weak as we were, but they weren't. It was uncanny."

I sit back, thinking. Brady is a good fighter, and he loves his booby traps, but he's not that smart. That's why I'm the brains of the operation.

"His mate, you say?" I ask.

"Yeah, and if she's this good at healing people, I want her in my fucking pack," he growls. "I could use some TLC from a lady doctor."

"Was Warren marked?" I ask, ignoring the rest of his comments.

"I don't think so. His scent was the same as it always is."

"Do you know what Simon's doing?" I ask.

"Nah, he's a loose cannon. Although, I'm pretty sure he attacked Warren's pack last night. Do you really think he killed his father?" Brady asks.

"Sure do. I don't think Solomon ever intended to give him the pack. Simon's only chance of getting it was to overthrow his father."

"You thinking of bringing him into this group?" he asks. 'This group' includes me, Brady, and Thomas. We've been targeting Warren's pack for years, trying to bring him down. He's got the largest pack lands that just happen to be situated in an area that makes getting supplies, water, and electricity easy compared to the rest of us. His father was unwilling to give it up to my father, so we've been at war ever since.

Over time, I pulled Brady and Thomas onto my side of the war against his pack. It should have made taking Warren and his pack out easier, but so far, we've been unable to kill off that damn Alpha.

I don't truly need the pack lands now, but I want them. My mate, my chosen mate, gave me an heir, and my son deserves to have the largest pack lands in the region. He's getting older, but he's not old enough to take over from me yet. Before I hand the pack off to him, I want Warren gone.

"No. Simon, as you said, is a loose cannon. What we need to do is give Warren time to mark his mate. Then, we can go for her. If she's a doctor, killing her will severely weaken Warren, and if what you said is true, it will severely weaken the pack, too. Then, we swoop in and take over."

"You sure we can't keep her?" Brady asks. "What if we snatch her out from under his nose, and one of us marks her? Then he loses his doctor and his mate, and I gain a doctor."

"You?" I ask. Brady has been looking to take a mate, but he doesn't want any of the she-wolves in his pack. Since we're all at war so often, our only option for taking a mate is within our own pack. My own mate is fine, but maybe I want someone younger. If this lady doctor is Warren's fated mate, she'd be around his age, and I'm older than he is.

"Well, yeah. You have a mate, and I'm older than Thomas, so she should come to me," he says. And this is why he's not the brains of the operation. Any intelligent Alpha would realize that if this lady doctor is able to strengthen a pack that quickly, every Alpha is going to want her. Even if he already has a mate.

"You really think she's the reason that his pack became strong so quickly?" I ask him.

"Nothing else changed, Quin. The only difference is her."

"The old doctor is a loose end. Tie it off," I say, letting Brady know that I want the doctor dead. "I'll send Thomas to attack Warren next. If he agrees with your assessment of his pack's strength, then we'll come up with a plan to get this lady doctor."

"Do it fast. If he has time to mark her, he won't let her go," he says.

"If he marks her, then he's signing her death warrant. Because once his mark is on her, killing her will be the fastest, easiest way to kill him."

~ ~ ~

Warren POV

I finish bathing my mate, careful to hold her up after she falls asleep in my arms. Arric's purring turns down to a low rumble once she's asleep, keeping her in the deep sleep she's in. My mate is exhausted, and it's obvious that her concern for Piper and the rest of my pack has taken a toll on her.

If she's been in a university for the last seven years, she hasn't been around the fighting that the packs have. For her, this constant level of heightened awareness must be physically and mentally grueling. In addition, she's healing my pack faster than anything I've ever seen before, me included. I'm a bit surprised she didn't ask me about my leg, but that just tells me how exhausted she is.

'The leg is healed,' Arric says, watching as I pull her into my arms and stand. I grab a towel, wrapping it around her and grabbing two more as I walk her into the bedroom. I lay a towel over her pillow before laying her down. Then, I quickly dry myself off.

When I'm done, I carefully dry Yara's hair as much as I can before drying off the rest of her body. I was right about her body; it's soft compared to every other warrior in my pack. I look over her body, her gentle curves and her perky breasts, then up to her unmarked neck.

Arric growls in my head. 'We need to mark her before Simon comes for her again.'

'Agreed, but not until she's slept and eaten. And let's hope we don't get attacked again. Even for us, this is excessive.'

'We need a plan to kill Simon,' he growls.

While Yara was in surgery, I'd had the patrols take me on the path that Simon had run to escape my warriors. This time, I'd followed his scent past our pack borders, and I hadn't gone far when I smelled the metallic scent that I'll never forget. After being caught in a trap, you don't forget the scent of one.

So, Simon had a plan to get away with Yara. I had my warriors spring the traps. There were five of them. He definitely knows she's here.

'I'd love to go on the attack, but when can we? We've barely had a moment to breathe, much less attack. Our mate hasn't eaten in over a day because we've been so busy.'

'Brady attacking twice was probably because he thought you'd still be too injured to win. Simon was after Yara. Both of them suffered quite a few losses in warriors.'

'That still leaves Thomas, Quinton, and Harold. But you're right. We won't see Brady for a while. I'm not so sure about Simon.'

'Agreed. He's too arrogant to wait.'

I set the towels out to dry and pull the blankets out from under Yara before going around to curl up behind her. I tug her body against mine, feeling the exhaustion of the last three days of fighting and my body healing.

'We need to put more warriors in the hospital. We know Simon will be back, and if word gets out that Yara is healing our pack and making us stronger ...' I begin.

'I will never let anyone take my mate,' Arric snarls.

'They'll try though, Buddy, so we need to be prepared. Three warriors weren't enough. I need Yara focused on healing our pack, not worrying about someone sneaking in through the back.'

'Agreed.'

'And Arric?'

'Yes.'

'Thanks for healing me so quickly,' I tell him.

'Our mate deserves most of the credit. Just laying with her like this is re-energizing me. I'll be ready to fight when we're attacked again.'

'That's because you're the best fucking Alpha wolf that ever lived.'

'You got that right,' he says, making me smile before I follow my mate into sleep.

Chapter 28: Accepting the Alpha
Yara

I awaken, warm and comfortable, except for the hard pole sticking into my back. My mind is slow to wake up, so it takes me a moment to realize that there's a warm hand sliding up my thigh from my knee to my hip. Warm lips press against my shoulder, and Annika begins purring as the hand slides over my stomach.

In my brain haze, I recognize that I'm naked, and the hand makes its way up to my breast. If this is a dream, I hope it doesn't end too soon. I hate waking up just as I start to have an orgasm. They always fade away and leave me desperate for more.

I arch my back as the warm lips continue to kiss their way to my neck, the hand moving to my breast and teasing my nipple into a hard peak. I moan softly as another purring sound starts behind me, reverberating through my body and lighting up my nerve endings.

"Yara," Warren's soft, deep voice says in my ear.

I know I should probably pull away from him, but he feels so good, and I suddenly realize what's pressing into my back. Warren wants me. I'm not sure how I feel about that. I've barely had time to get to know the man, but his hands and his mouth are working magic on my body.

"I want to make love to you. I want to mark you and have you mark me. But you, my little mate, haven't eaten in much too long," he says.

I look up and see that it's dark outside. I slept all afternoon and into the night.

"When I make you mine, I want you energized and ready to take everything that I give you. I want to take hours, kissing you, tasting you, exploring your body, making your come, and then I want to hear your screams, feel that sweet pussy pulsing around my cock when I sink my teeth into your neck."

His words make heat pool in my core, and I feel him chuckle behind me.

"Based on the spike in your scent, I'd say you like that idea. Unfortunately, this is not that moment, although I do want to make you feel good, and I intend to ease that ache between your thighs, Yara. But first, I have a question for you," he says, moving his hand from one breast to the other as he gently nips my neck.

"What's that?" I ask, my voice so breathy it barely sounds like me.

"I need to be able to reach you using the mind link. Without your mark on me and mine on you, we aren't connected. Would you be willing to accept me as your Alpha, Yara, so that we can share a mind link? I need to know you're safe and I want that connection to you. It will also make it easier for you to talk to the pack members and, of course, give you access to me any time you want or need it," he says, gently tugging on my nipple and causing the ache between my thighs to increase.

I think about it for a moment. It would make everything easier, not just between me and Warren but also in healing the warriors in the pack. I think about the type of Alpha that Warren is, and I know he's nothing like Simon. He's not even like Alpha Solomon. He's a better Alpha than Solomon was.

"Yes, Warren. I'll accept you as my Alpha," I tell him.

"Mmmm," he says, sliding an arm underneath my head and pulling his hand in front of us. "Thank you, Yara. Are you ready?"

"Yes."

He reaches out to slice his hand, and I whimper at the loss of his touch. He chuckles behind me.

"As soon as you accept me, I'll return to what we were doing," he promises.

"Do you, Yara Ellis, accept me, Warren Hill, as your Alpha?" he asks, slicing his hand.

"I, Yara Ellis, accept you, Warren Hill, as my Alpha," I say, and he brings his hand to my face. I reach out and lick his blood, making the connection and sealing his wound. I feel the tether to Warren snap into place, and unlike what I felt with Alpha Solomon, Warren's power and strength as an Alpha are incredible.

Behind his power as an Alpha, I feel his emotions for me: love, possessiveness, desire, awe, and acceptance. I gasp as he lets his feelings for me flow through the bond. His feelings for me are as impactful as his hands and mouth on my body. The warmth of his feelings for me flows through my mind and into my body.

"Now you know how much I love you, Yara," he says, the hand that I just licked moving to my breast as the other slides down my stomach until it finds the heat between my thighs.

"Open your legs for me," he says.

"I ..."

"Here, lift this leg over my legs. I want to touch you. I want to feel you come undone in my arms."

I do as he suggests, lifting my top leg over his and opening myself to him. His fingers slide through my soaked lips.

"Mmm, so wet for me," he growls against my neck as his other hand teases my nipple. "Goddess, I can't wait to slide inside you, to feel your heat wrapped around my cock," he growls, his fingers beginning to make circles on my clit.

"Warren ..." I gasp.

"Yes, baby. I am going to make you come. I'm going to ease this ache for you."

He begins purring again, louder this time. "Now I know just how to touch you to make you feel good," he says, staying connected with my mind and quickly bringing me up to the peak.

I cry out as he pushes me over the edge, my body jerking as he holds me against him, forcing me to ride out the pleasure he's giving me.

"So responsive to me," he growls, gently biting on my ear and sending more heat through my body.

"Come again for me," he says, "this time, say my name."

Because we're connected, I can feel that he's also right on the edge, ready to shoot off behind me. Whether it's the jerking of my body, his enjoyment at making me come, or maybe both, when I explode the next time, I feel the warm jets of his cum shooting against my back.

This time, he slowly brings me down, kissing my shoulder again as we pant.

"Fuck we will be so good together," he says. I lean my head back, feeling his lips pressing against my head. "You need to eat so we can finish what we've started here."

"I need a minute," I say, still basking in the afterglow of two amazing orgasms.

He chuckles, and I know he's about to say something when the howls of alarm go off again.

"Son of a fucking bitch!" he snarls, leaping out of bed.

"WARREN!"

He turns quickly, taking my mouth in a possessive, fiery kiss, made more so by his emotions flowing through our bond.

'I'm okay. I'm healed. Keep in touch with me. Let me know if you're in danger. I love you, Yara. Take care of my mate,' he says in the mind link as he kisses me.

Then he turns and rushes out the door, once again leaping over the banister and shifting on his way out to fight yet another battle.

'You take care of my mate, too,' I say before rushing to get dressed and heading downstairs.

Chapter 29: Prisoners

Yara

I race downstairs and realize the warriors on injured reserve from yesterday are already lined up and waiting for me to release them. I step up to the first one, but before I can ask anything, one of the warriors guarding the hospital yesterday hands me a breakfast wrap.

"What's this?"

"Alpha's orders. He says you haven't eaten in close to two days," he says.

"I didn't catch your name yesterday," I say, taking the wrap and biting into it. It's got eggs, bacon, ham, and goddess knows what else, but it's delicious.

"It's Bradley, Luna," he says, and I swallow quickly, turning to the first warrior.

"Bradley, are you the only one guarding the hospital today?" I ask, checking the warrior's injuries that have healed.

"Your wolf?" I ask the warrior.

"I'm good, Luna," the deeper voice of the wolf says.

"Go," I say, turning to the guard.

"No, Luna. Alpha has added more guards after what happened yesterday. They are already there making sure that no one gets into the hospital."

I nod, looking over the next warrior as Savannah comes rushing up. "Luna, I ..." she stops, sniffing the air. I know Warren's scent will be strong on me. I didn't have time to shower, and he ejaculated on my back just before the alarm went up. Savannah smiles but doesn't say anything about my scent.

"What do you need from me?" she asks instead.

"You check these four. I'll check the ones from yesterday," I say, and once again, we split the group up.

"Bradley, how long have you been awake?"

"I just got up, Luna."

"Savannah?" I ask.

"Same."

"Do we know who is on at the hospital?" I ask, clearing two warriors to go fight.

I see Bradley's eyes go unfocused, and I realize that I can now reach out, too, except I'm not sure who to reach out to.

"Anna is on, Luna," he says.

I reach out in the mind link, looking for Anna, but connect with Warren.

'Yara, are you okay?' he asks, and I can tell he's fighting.

'Yes. Sorry, I'm looking for Anna.'

Warren does the mental equivalent of taking my hand and leading me to Anna, connecting me to her.

'Thanks, Warren. Be careful,' I say, holding on a moment longer to feel just how strong of a fighter he is. I can feel his pride at my assessment before I disconnect and connect with Anna.

'Anna?'

'Luna?' she asks, surprised.

'Yeah, how is Piper?'

'She's stable, Luna, but she's awake.'

'Okay. Savannah and I are checking the warriors here, and then we'll be there.'

I feel another wrap get placed in my hand, and I absently thank the person as I continue to assess warriors while I eat.

'Luna, Beta wants to get in the fight. The warriors are refusing to let him leave.'

'Tell him I'm on my way, and if he gives you any grief about waiting, he'll answer to me.'

'Yes, Luna,' she says, and I can feel her smile through the link.

When we're done, I look up and see Bradley holding a third wrap. "Still hungry?"

"Not really, but who knows when I'll get to eat again. I'll take it for later."

We begin jogging over to the hospital, and now that I have the pack link, I open my mind, carefully feeling around the pack to see who may or may not be injured. I'm pleased when I feel very few injuries.

"So, you accepted our Alpha as yours, Luna?" Bradley asks as we jog. His eyes are everywhere as he guards me and Savannah.

"Yes, so if you need me, you can link me now."

"Good to know," he says, smiling as we get to the hospital.

I walk straight up to Charlie. "Luna, I need to be out there."

"Settle down, Charlie. The longer it takes for me to look you over, the longer it takes for you to get back out there if I agree."

I quickly flash a light in his eyes, and this time, he doesn't flinch. I look over his injuries and see that they are healing.

"Your wolf?" I ask as my fingers run over the now healed gashes on his body.

"That tickles, Luna," a deeper voice says to me. I look up and see the darker eyes of Charlie's wolf.

"What's your name, Beta?"

"Gregor, Luna."

"Gregor, how is your strength?"

"Full strength, Luna, thanks to you."

I nod. "Off you go then. And Gregor!" I say, just as Charlie leaps and shifts. "No more coming into my hospital without a pulse!"

'Yes, Luna,' he says in the mind link.

I quickly push against Warren's mind, feeling him open the link instantly.

'Charlie's good. He's on his way.'

'I'm not sure we need him. I don't know what the hell you're doing for this pack, Yara, but every one of my warriors is stronger than I ever remember them being.'

'I told you. You need to talk to Dr. Stevens. Something is off there,' I tell him.

'Something definitely is if we could have been this strong all along.'

We begin working on the injuries that come in. Most of them are simple gashes that need to be cleaned and stitched, and, in some instances, the wolves are strong enough that they've started healing their humans before they even get to us.

Because we're slow, I have a chance to look over Piper, and now that I have a mind link, I'm able to talk to her and find out how she's feeling.

'You need to stay in bed. Don't talk. Liquid diet until your wolf can heal you. There's another battle, but Alpha Warren put more warriors here at the hospital, so you're safe,' I tell her.

She nods, flinching as even that movement hurts her. I leave her room, and I've just about decided to start taking inventory of the storage room so we can order supplies when I hear a commotion outside the hospital.

'We're bringing in some prisoners, Yara,' Warren says before he, Charlie, and a warrior I remember named Carson come in dragging warriors from the other pack. All three look like they're near death.

I look up and see Warren covered in blood. "Is any of that yours?" I ask him, walking over and quickly assessing the prisoners.

I see Warren look down at himself as if he's just realizing that he's a mess.

"I don't think so," he says. I let Annika sniff quickly to make sure, and not smelling Warren's blood, I turn my attention back to the prisoners.

"What are we doing with these guys?" I ask.

"How do you feel about healing them enough for us to interrogate them?" he asks me.

"Interrogate meaning torture?" I ask, not sure I like the sound of that.

He gives me a pained look. "That depends on how much they're willing to tell us."

I squat down and look at the first man. He doesn't look up, and his wolf isn't healing his open wound. Of course, he smells like he's had many open wounds, and it's possible his wolf is exhausted and unable to heal him anymore.

"What are you trying to find out?" I ask, looking up at Warren.

"These attacks are coming too fast, too close together. I want to see if any of these warriors know anything about that."

I think for a minute, then stand and step away, gesturing for Warren to follow me.

"I don't like the idea of healing these guys just so you can kill them more slowly, Warren," I begin.

"I understand, Yara. But I need to be able to protect this pack, and I need to know why we've suddenly been attacked four times in four days."

"What if I were able to give them something that would make them more amenable to telling the truth?"

"Like what?"

"Not a truth serum exactly, but something that relaxes them enough that they wouldn't be as inclined to hide their responses from you."

He smiles at me, reaching out to gently touch my face, pulling back when he realizes that his hand is covered in blood.

"We'll try it your way first, my Luna," he says. I smile, knowing that calling me Luna rather than mate is his way of telling me that I'm acting like the heart of the pack, and he's willing to listen to his heart before acting with this head.

"Thank you."

"Thank you for accepting me as your Alpha. I like knowing how you're feeling and how you're responding to me," he says, making my heart flutter as I get a flash of our night together before the battle started. His smile lets me know that he knows EXACTLY how he just made me feel.

I blush and turn away, going back to the men. "Okay, let's triage."

"I want two warriors on each of these guys at all times. Yara, you don't go into a room without either me or Charlie with you. We'll take turns cleaning up."

I watch as six warriors step forward, basically choosing their person as Savannah, and I begin doing triage.

"I'll take this guy first. Am I right that he's a Beta?" I ask Warren as Anna brings over a gurney.

"Yeah, I'm pretty sure that's Thomas' Beta," Warren tells me.

"Okay, I'll start with him," I say as they load him onto the gurney.

"Charlie, go get washed up. I'll stay with Yara," he says.

"Yes, Alpha," he says, and Warren, Thomas' Beta, two warriors, Anna, and myself walk to one of the hospital rooms so that I can begin saving this man's life.

Chapter 30: The Beta

Quinton

"He captured my fucking Beta! That's how fucking strong his pack is, Quinton! MY BETA!! Strong isn't even the right word. There's no way that pack should be as strong as they are if they've fought four days in a row! It's like they're getting stronger with each battle. What the actual fuck? How the fuck am I supposed to get my Beta back?"

"We'll get your Beta back, Thomas," I say, sitting back. "Did Warren smell like he'd marked his new mate?"

"Who the fuck cares about his mate, Quinton! He has my Beta!" he snarls at me. My answering snarl causes the walls in my office to vibrate and the pictures on the wall to shift.

"Don't you dare take that fucking tone with me, Thomas," I say, sitting forward. "I said we'd get your Beta back, and I meant it. But I need to know if we have to kill the woman or if we can capture her."

I hear him breathing heavily on the phone, presumably getting his temper in check. When he's calmer, he answers.

"I could smell her on him, but not enough that he was marked," he says. "Quin, how the fuck is his pack getting so strong so fast?"

"Brady thinks it's this lady doctor, Warren's mate."

"Then she needs to fucking die," he snarls. And this is why Thomas isn't the strategist in our group either. He's too stupid to think past the moment he's in, too stupid to realize that if she's making Warren's pack that strong, she could make any pack that strong. She could make MY pack that strong.

If I had her, my pack would become stronger. If I had her, I could become the strongest Alpha in the region. If I had her, I could take over all the packs, and everything in this region would be mine.

"I'll talk to Brady. We need to team up and attack together, go after them with everything we've got, rather than sending one pack at a time," I tell him.

"And we'll get Axel back?" he asks.

"Yes, Thomas. We'll get your Beta back."

~ ~ ~

Warren POV

"Have you eaten?" Yara asks as we walk into the room.

"No. But I'm not leaving you alone with Thomas' Beta. I don't care if he's unconscious. I don't want him waking up and hurting you."

She looks at Anna, who nods and then leaves after putting the IV into the Beta's arm. A moment later, she returns with a breakfast wrap.

"Wash your hands first, Warren. You're covered in blood," Yara says, nodding her head at the sink in the room.

"Are you taking care of me, Yara?" I ask, pleased that my mate is looking after me.

"No more than you were taking care of me earlier, Warren," she says.

When I look, I see her smiling as she begins to wash the wounds on the Beta's body. Arric and I hate her touching other men, but it's the job she does, and it's necessary.

"Have you two eaten?" I ask my warriors.

"Last night, Alpha," they both say, and I nod.

I link the kitchens to bring food to the hospital. Yara's doing a great job of healing my pack, but they need to stay healthy. I have no doubt that Thomas will be back for his Beta. If anyone captured Charlie, I'd tear down their pack to get him back.

"I take it the Alpha escaped?" Yara asks.

"Yeah, the coward ran off," one of the warriors says.

"He knew he'd lost. Honestly, I'm surprised the fight was so easy," I say which reminds me that I need to have a chat with Dr. Stevens.

'Charlie, when you're done showering, find Dr. Stevens. We need to have a heart-to-heart,' I tell my Beta.

'On it,' he says.

'Oh, and get something to eat. I have food being sent over here, but you've just gotten out of the hospital. Believe me, you don't want Yara angry at you.'

He snorts. 'You're not the first person that's said that. Our Luna has a bit of a temper, eh?'

'Only when it comes to saving our pack, apparently,' I say, watching my mate as I eat, and she begins to stitch the bleeding wound closed.

I frown, setting the food aside and stepping closer to the bed. Something feels off, but I can't figure out what it is. Arric pushes forward, feeling the same change that I do. Yara is doing her usual mumbling about how no one seems to know they're injured anymore. Anna is looking at the monitors ...

"Alpha?" one of the warriors says, just as the Beta's hand snaps out to grab Yara by the throat. I'm at her side, my claws slicing through his wrist in an instant. His breathing had changed. It had taken me a moment too long to realize that's what I sensed.

He snarls, not releasing Yara's throat. "So, you're the lady doctor everyone's so hot and bothered by."

"Let go," she says, her voice deadly calm.

"I don't think so," he says, and I'm about to rip his hand off when he begins screaming in pain, his hand pulling away from her.

"When a doctor has her hands inside your stomach, Beta, you don't want to piss her off," she says, remaining calm.

"Sedate him, Anna," I snarl, pushing Yara behind me. I'm impressed that she was able to get him to let go of her, but I'm not taking any chances with her life.

The moment he's unconscious, I turn to look at her.

"Warren ..."

"Let me see," I growl. I gently lift her chin, seeing the fingerprint bruises on her neck. I snarl viciously, and several warriors rush into the room.

"Annika is already healing me, Warren," she says, putting her hand on mine. "Let me finish treating the Beta before he dies on my table."

"Let him die," I snarl, pulling her into my arms. I don't care that I'm covered in blood. He could have killed her. I already know I don't want to live without this woman in my life. I've waited too long to find her, and she's so much more than I ever hoped to find in a mate.

"He knows about me, Warren. He's not part of Simon's pack, and he knew who I was. You're right. You need to interrogate him. Why would they even care about me?" she asks, and while her voice remains steady, I can feel the fear in her through our bond.

I look up at the warriors in the room. "Because you're making us stronger, Yara. The longer you're here, the stronger this pack becomes. Other Alphas would want that, especially ones who are greedy and want to increase the size and scope of their pack. That's my guess, and you're right. I need to see what this Beta knows, but he'll die for putting his hands on you. Don't fight me on that," I tell her.

I can feel her resistance, her unwillingness to let anyone die. However, her fear is stronger than her need to heal, so I'm thankful when I feel her nod against my chest.

"I'll protect you, Yara," I tell her.

"We all will, Luna," one of the warriors says, and the others agree.

"Thank you. Okay, let me get back to what I do well: putting broken warriors back together."

She starts working on the Beta again, and I watch her, keeping a close eye on him this time.

"How did you know how to hurt him enough that he'd let go?" I ask her, curious.

She looks up at me and then at the warriors in the room. "A doctor learns how to heal, but in the process, we learn about anatomy - what makes us strong, what makes us weak, and where a person is most vulnerable if they are injured. But aside from all that, someone squeezing your stomach and liver in their hands is going to cause excruciating pain."

She turns back to the Beta as I smile, feeling the smug satisfaction from the pack at Yara's words. My mate is one hell of a badass.

Chapter 31: Charlie's Assistance

Yara

It makes me nervous that another pack is hunting for me. I mean, I know that I'm healing Warren's pack, but it's not that hard. They really just needed to rest enough to let their wolves heal, and of course, they needed to not have Dr. Stevens, who was making it harder for them to heal.

Could he be working with them? Could he have intentionally been weakening Warren's pack? But for what purpose? It had to be for personal gain. There's no other reason to betray your own pack ... unless he has a personal vendetta against Warren.

"Who are we talking about?" Warren asks me as I check over the Beta.

"Hmmm?" I ask him.

"Who would be working with 'them' intentionally weakening my pack for personal gain or a personal vendetta?" he asks me, and I look up, seeing everyone in the room watching me. I must have been mumbling out loud again. I've really got to stop that.

"Oh, Dr. Stevens. Your pack would have been much stronger if he'd done what he should have been doing to keep you all strong. I mean, all I'm doing really is helping your wolves to heal and forcing you to get some rest, so you're stronger, and your wolves are stronger. I'm not some miracle worker. It's just common sense."

"I'm pretty sure all of us would disagree with you about being a miracle worker, Luna," one of the warriors says. I see Warren's eyes go unfocused while they talk to me.

"Truly, other than Beta Charlie and maybe finding Haynes infection, I haven't done much."

"Luna, I don't even have a scar from where you stitched me up the other day."

"Well, that's just practice," I say, turning back to the Beta when Warren snarls, startling me.

"Warren!" I scold. I can't have him doing that in my surgery rooms.

"Sorry, Yara," he growls. "Dr. Stevens seems to be missing. No one has seen him since yesterday."

"So, he's run now that he can't hurt your pack anymore. Was it a personal vendetta, Warren?" I ask, finishing my stitches.

"I don't know what personal vendetta he'd be holding on to," Warren says.

"He wanted to be your Beta, Alpha, remember?" one of the warriors says to him.

"That was twelve years ago, and he wasn't Beta material. He might have been a good doctor, which I think he was at the time, but being a good doctor doesn't make you a good Beta. They're completely different skill sets," Warren says.

"I agree. I'd make a terrible Beta," I say, looking at the warriors. "You can shackle him now. It will keep him from healing, Warren, but then I can remove the sedation from him and let him wake up," I say.

He nods, and the warriors put on gloves before putting silver handcuffs and shackles on the Beta to keep him on the bed.

"Anna, make sure you and any of the other nurses who come in here are careful. If he can burn you, he will."

"We won't need them. Once he tells us what we want to know, we'll get him out of here," Warren says distractedly. "Do you really think all of this is about not becoming my Beta?"

"It's a powerful position, Alpha. Most of us haven't had time to think about it, but being a ranked member is something most wolves dream about when they're young," one of the warriors says.

"Did you dream about being a ranked member?" Warren asks me.

"No. From the moment my parents died in battle, I've dreamt of being a doctor, hoping that I could save another child like me from losing their parents," I say quietly.

"You've done that, Luna. Many of us have pups and were worried that we'd leave our pups and our mates without anyone. It's part of why your dream is making all of us stronger."

Warren pulls me into his arms again. "Are you done here?" he asks.

"Yes, but I need to check the other two."

He nods. "Charlie's on his way back. I'm going to leave him with you while I go get washed up."

We step out of the room, leaving the Beta to wake up. I still don't even know his name. I guess it doesn't matter since I'll probably never see him again.

Savannah steps up quickly. "This one's next, Luna. I did what I could, but I'm not sure he's going to make it," she says.

I take the medical record she hands me, looking it over as I walk into the next room.

"Why do you have bruises on your neck, Luna?" Savannah asks me.

"That Beta apparently knows who I am and didn't like me working on him, I guess."

I see her glance at the others, but I don't look back. I'm sure they'll fill her in, and this guy is nearly on his deathbed.

"Warren, how much do you want me to do to save him?" I ask him.

"Do what you can, but don't overextend yourself, Yara," he says, and I nod. "I'd like to interview him, and if he doesn't touch you, he can live for now, but if you can't save him ..."

"Let me see what I can do," I say.

This guy has been bleeding out the entire time I've been working on the Beta. I get Savannah and Anna to come in and, using their fingers, stop the bleeding while I begin to stitch this guy up.

"Are Katie and Erica here?" I ask, needing more fingers. This guy, geez, if he has a wolf, I'd be shocked.

"They're still working on the third guy, Luna," Savannah says.

I turn, seeing that Charlie replaced Warren while I was busy. I look him over, assessing him quickly.

"Gregor?"

"Yes, Luna?" he purrs at me.

I shake my head at him. "Don't let Arric hear you do that. Are you still at full strength?"

"Yes, Luna," he says.

"Good, put some gloves on and come over here. I need more fingers."

"Uh ... what?" Charlie asks.

I see the other warriors in the room take a not-so-subtle step backward as if I might try to get them to help me, too. For warriors who don't mind shredding someone to pieces, they seem a bit squeamish about putting those pieces back together again.

"Put on gloves and get over here, Beta," I say a bit more forcefully.

His mouth opens and closes, but he doesn't say anything, and he doesn't move.

"CHARLIE! GET OVER HERE!" He jumps at the command but moves into action, putting on the gloves and walking over.

"Give me your left hand," I say, and he holds it out. I take his pointer finger and move it to where I need him to stop the bleeding.

"Relax your hand," I tell him, and he does. "Okay, see how the bleeding there has stopped?"

"Yes."

"Good. You have to watch that artery and make sure no blood seeps out. If it does, move your finger until it stops again. Give me your right hand," I say, and I do the same with that hand, plugging another bleeder on this guy.

"I can't believe this guy is still alive," I murmur as I begin stitching him up. I watch as his blood pressure stabilizes, even if it is really low.

I work as quickly as I can, getting Charlie's fingers out of him first, then having him squirt water onto the areas where I need to see better until Anna is able to help me. Savannah had the biggest arteries that were severed, so she's last to get released.

When I'm finally done, I stand, stretching and cracking my neck and back in the process. I feel warm hands come around my waist, and I jerk until I smell his teakwood scent.

"You're amazing," Warren says, kissing the side of my head. "I have food for you."

"What time is it?" I ask.

"Late afternoon. You've been at it for hours again."

"How's the last one?" I ask Savannah.

"Better than this guy," she says.

"Okay, let me check the last one quickly, and then I'll get something to eat," I say.

The 'last one' ends up being a female warrior. When my large group walks into the room, she looks at all of us as if expecting her torture to start.

I check her vitals and see that she's got a compound fracture in her leg. "Has this been numbed?" I ask Erica.

"Yes," the warrior answers me.

"Okay, I'll be back to fix this after I eat something," I tell her.

"Why? Aren't they just going to torture me for information?" she asks, looking from me to Warren.

"That depends on you," Warren says.

"What do you want to know?" she asks.

"We want to know what your Alpha wants with Yara," Warren says.

She looks at me. "So, it's true? You're the lady doctor who's healing this pack and making them stronger?"

I look at her, waiting for Warren to decide what he's willing to tell her.

She looks back at Warren. "I'll tell you anything you want to know on one condition."

"What's that?"

"You get my sister out of Alpha Thomas' pack."

Chapter 32: Laney

Warren

"**G**ive me something so I know that you're telling the truth," I say to the she-wolf, who has barely taken her eyes off my mate. She's studying her like she's trying to figure out what all the fuss is about. As a warrior, she's looking at my mate as a fighter. What she doesn't realize is that my mate's strengths come in different ways than normal werewolf strength.

Finally, her gaze returns to me. "I'll be honest. I don't know much. I heard a little from Alpha Thomas, but mostly what I've heard is rumors."

"What did you hear from Thomas," I press.

She looks at Yara again, that same questioning assessment in her eyes. "That both Alpha Brady and Alpha Quinton want her. Both intend to capture her and take her as their mate."

I snarl as I feel Yara's fear spike. The warrior must smell her fear because she frowns. I get it. If I didn't know Yara and what she's capable of as a doctor, I wouldn't see the draw either. Not only is she my mate, but she is also strong in ways that matter, in ways that make my pack stronger than I can as their Alpha.

"They want to share me?" Yara asks. I can feel her nausea rolling around in her gut. I step up to her, wrapping my arms around her.

"They will never get to you. They would have to get through me and this pack," I tell her.

She nods, and while I don't like that this warrior who I don't trust is seeing my mate fearful or me being protective, Yara is more important. If this woman betrays me, she's dead anyway.

"What's your name?" I ask the woman, still focusing on Yara, running my nose through her hair and purring softly to calm her. She needs to eat. I know she's tired again, and now she's found out that not one, but three Alphas are after her.

"Delaney, but everyone calls me Laney," she says.

"And why does your sister need assistance to leave Alpha Thomas' pack?" I ask her, feeling Yara starting to calm down.

"Alpha Thomas wants to take her as his mate. He's a young Alpha, and she's just turned eighteen. I'm not sure why he chose her, other than she's beautiful, but he did."

"And you think your sister is unwilling to be a Luna? Or are you jealous and trying to take that position away from her?" I ask. It isn't out of the question. This warrior isn't that old.

"My sister wouldn't mate with that useless piece of shit Alpha if he was the last man on the planet," she growls. I like her fire.

"What's your sister's name?" I ask.

"Noelle."

"And why would Noelle believe my warriors if I sent them to get her? She could raise the alarm and have my men killed. Thomas' pack is weakened significantly right now, but that doesn't mean that a few of my men couldn't easily be overpowered and captured or killed. This could be a very well-played trap on your part."

"How can I prove to you that I'm telling the truth?" she asks me.

"Accept me as your Alpha," I say, and Yara's head snaps to mine. I smile and kiss her nose before turning back to Laney.

"But I'll lose my connection to my sister," she says, and now the fear in the room is coming from her. Her love for her sister isn't being faked.

"Only until I bring her here. If you accept me, then as your Alpha, I'll know if you're lying."

"Alpha Thomas will feel the tether to my connection break."

"Correct. He'll think you died like so many others did here today."

She looks at me a moment, then at Yara. "Do you trust that he'll go get my sister?" she asks her, surprising me.

"If he says he will, he will," Yara says confidently.

"Do you know why two different Alphas want you?" she asks Yara.

"We can talk more about that after you accept me as your Alpha," I say sharply. I have no intention of giving this unknown woman any information about my mate until I know I can trust her.

"Three different Alphas, I guess," she says, looking at me thoughtfully.

"Warren is my mate. The others can go to hell," Yara says, making me smile at her willingness to claim me so easily.

"So, what will it be, Laney?" I ask, releasing Yara and stepping up to the bed.

"I'll accept you," she says.

We go through the ceremony of her accepting me as her Alpha. She licks the blood from my sliced palm, and then I push into her mind. To her credit, she doesn't fight me. I go through everything: everything that she's heard, every intention she has towards Yara, which is mostly curiosity and disbelief, and her relationship with her sister. She's the older sister with no parents, so she feels the need to protect her younger sibling.

"I'll send warriors. Should I have them use your safe word?" I ask her. I'd seen that, too. Laney had come up with a way to ensure that Noelle never did anything without Laney's agreement. In order for Noelle to know that Laney agreed, they'd created a safe word. Donut.

"Yes. She'll know I'm still alive if you do," Laney says, her voice shaking a bit with emotion.

"Okay, I'll go make the arrangements. Yara, you need to eat before you do another surgery," I say.

"Just relax. I'll be back soon. Do you want to go under for your surgery?" Yara asks her.

"No. I want to be awake when Noelle gets here," she says.

"When she gets here, let's talk. I got the information, but I want your impressions about it, and I don't have time to sift through your mind for all of that right now," I tell her.

"Yes, Alpha."

I let Yara exit the room before me. I turn back to Laney. "And, by the way, you shouldn't underestimate your future Luna. She's stronger than you realize."

"She must be for three Alphas to want her," Laney says.

"Four," I say, walking out of the room. Laney doesn't know about Simon.

I'm not sure if that's a good thing or a bad thing. It means Simon is working on his own. But because she knows about Alpha Brady and Alpha Quinton, it means the three of them are working together. Brady's pack will still be recovering, and Thomas' pack will need a couple of days to recover, so that leaves Quinton's pack.

In my estimation, Quinton is the smartest of the three. Brady is a good strategist when it comes to fighting. That's how he caught me in that bear trap. But when it comes to running a pack, he's not that bright. Thomas is young and rash, never thinking through the ramifications of his decisions until it's too late. Quinton, however, is a problem. Next to Simon, he's the biggest threat to Yara.

Without thinking too much about it, I pull Yara onto my lap at the table, pulling food over for her to eat.

"Warren! What are you doing?" she asks me.

"I'm eating, Yara. What are you doing?" I ask her.

"I can't eat while sitting on your lap!" she says.

"Of course you can. My lap is a perfectly acceptable place to sit while you eat." I tap the plate in front of her. "Do I need to scoot forward, Yara, or can you reach?" I tease.

"I can reach," she grumbles. "Bossy, possessive Alpha," she mumbles.

I lean in, nibbling on her ear. "Are you adding to my list of adjectives, little mate?" I ask her.

"Maybe," she grumbles before starting to eat.

While we eat, Charlie comes in. I called him over, wanting him to take the lead on this rescue mission.

"Yara, is Charlie fit to lead the warriors to get Laney's sister?" I ask her when he walks in.

"Gregor?" she asks.

"Yes, Luna. Did you want to tickle me again to prove that I'm healed enough to run this mission? A mission that our Alpha still hasn't told me about?" he answers.

"Your Alpha wants you to stop flirting with his Luna before I remind you why I AM the Alpha," Arric growls.

"Lift your shirt, Charlie," she says.

154

Instead, he pulls it off, strutting in front of Yara. I'm positive this is Gregor. I'm not sure whether he's truly flirting with Yara or intentionally antagonizing Arric, but Arric growls warningly at him again.

"She wants to see me, Arric. You can't deny that, as a doctor, she needs to make sure I'm healed." Definitely Gregor.

I watch as Gregor stretches out his arms, flexing as he turns slowly so Yara can see his wounds are all healed.

"Gregor, what did I tell you before?" Yara asks him.

He turns and smiles at her. "I promise I won't enter your hospital without a pulse again, Luna."

"Good," I say, pulling Arric back. He tugs Yara closer to us, nuzzling her hair while I talk. "I need you to get a small number of warriors, ones at full strength. Get Yara's approval on that before you go. Then, your group is going to go into Thomas' pack and get the sister of the female warrior that we captured. Her name is Noelle, and her safe word is 'donut'," I tell him.

"How old is she? What does she look like? What does she smell like?" Charlie asks the teasing from a moment ago gone.

"She's eighteen. If she looks like her sister, she's blond and green. The sister, Laney, is in room three. Stop in and get her scent before you go."

"When am I leaving?" he asks.

"As soon as you get your warriors together. Thomas' pack is probably reeling from their recent attack. Now is the time to get her out without too much hassle."

"Yes, Alpha," he says before turning to go get his warriors and get Laney's scent.

"Now, where were we?" I purr into Yara's ear.

"You were about to let me go so I could go sit in my own seat and finish eating," she says.

I chuckle behind her. "Oh, that is definitely NOT where we left off," I say, nipping at the back of her neck and feeling her body shiver in my arms. "But once you're done with surgery, Yara, we need to talk about me marking you. You have too many Alphas after you now, and I have no intention of losing you to any of them. And since you seem to have no problem claiming me as your mate, you shouldn't have any problem with wearing my mark, right?" I ask, waiting for her reaction.

"Warren ..." she begins.

"You've already taken over my hospital. You're in my bed. You've claimed me more than once as your mate, Yara. This is important."

She turns and looks at me. "It's permanent, Warren."

"Yeah, I know. Once you're wearing my mark, if Gregor flirts with you, I'll put him down," I say, only half-joking.

"Warren! You can't kill your Beta."

"Make no mistake, Yara. I will kill anyone, *anyone* who tries to take you from me. You are mine, and the sooner you're wearing my mark, the better."

"You're probably right," she murmurs. I'm not sure if that was meant to be heard or if it was one of her mumblings, but either way, I'm taking it as agreement. It's time to mark my mate.

Chapter 33: Rescue Mission
Charlie

I picked three of our top warriors and took them to Yara for approval that they were healthy enough to go on this rescue mission. Once she agreed, we all went to the room of this warrior, Laney, to get her smell. The woman's scent was nice ... spicy but a bit too much on the pachouli side for me. At least I have the girl's scent and confirmed that she looks like her sister.

That's the other thing; this woman is attractive. Maybe it's because we don't see too many women outside our own packs but seeing her and smelling her new scent is making Gregor antsy.

'What's up with you?'

'I don't know. Let's just go find this girl,' he says. I can feel his own frustration at not understanding his reaction to this woman.

'And what's with you and our Luna? You're going to get us killed,' I say to him as I get the warriors, and we begin running toward Thomas' pack.

'I like her. A lot. She's smart, and funny, and ...'

'And NOT ours,' I say firmly. I refuse to fight Warren for Yara. They are fated mates, and you don't fuck around with that. Even if it wasn't nearly impossible to find your fated mate these days, I wouldn't fight him for her. She obviously feels the same pull to him that

157

he does to her. So, yeah, I can appreciate her intelligence, her kindness, and her sharp wit without flirting with her in front of her mate or at all – especially since she's unmarked.

'Fine,' he says, moping. I know he wants to find our mate. I didn't always agree with Warren about waiting to find his mate, but he was adamant. He'd grown up with parents who were fated mates, unlike most of us, so he knew the level of passion and commitment that could come with that kind of bond. Over the years, I'd frequently tried to convince him to take a chosen mate, someone from our pack, but when we'd gone through the list of she-wolves, none of them seemed like the kind of woman either of us would want to bind ourselves to for the rest of our lives.

So, we'd both waited. It worked for him, and I'm a couple of years younger than he is. Now, seeing what he has with Yara, I understand a lot better why he was so insistent about waiting. No chosen mate bond could ever compete with what he has with our Luna, and they haven't even marked each other yet.

As we get closer to Thomas' pack, I slow down, opening my mind link to the other warriors.

'Keep your noses up. Not only do we have to get around the patrols, but we also need to find this girl, get her to stay quiet and agree to come with us, and then get out before they even know we've gotten in.'

I get them to spread out, hoping that someone will catch this girl's scent. I move closer to the packhouse, as close as I can without crossing the borders. I'm a bit surprised that I haven't seen or heard any patrols yet. Did they send every warrior to fight our pack? If so, then Thomas is a fool, and his pack is open to attack from anyone. He may be in an alliance of some sort with Quinton and Brady, but that doesn't mean that they wouldn't take advantage of the weaker Alpha to take over his pack, especially Quinton. The man is a greedy piece of shit, not caring who dies in his quest for power. It's another reason that I am loyal to Warren. He doesn't send us out to fight for no reason. There's always a reason if we go, but usually, we're on the receiving end of battles. Now, it seems those attacks were a strategic move by Quinton.

I close my eyes, listening to the sounds coming from the packhouse. I can hear snoring, fucking, and in a room at the end of a hallway, crying.

'I've got her,' I let my warriors know. 'Has anyone seen any patrols?'

'No, Beta,' the warriors say, heading back in my direction.

Gregor stands at attention, listening intently to the girl crying. That will be Laney's sister. She'll have felt the snap of the pack link, and she'll think her sister is dead.

When my warriors arrive, we sniff the air one more time before shifting into our human forms. I'm still amazed that there aren't any patrols. But we still make our way to the packhouse carefully. Here, we find some patrols, but it looks like these poor bastards got the raw end of the deal, or maybe they were the least injured after our battle today. Either way, my men and I make quick work of them before heading inside.

As we get closer, I can feel Gregor getting more excited. The scent of mulling spices is getting stronger in the air. I love mulling spices. It reminds me of fall and winter days, of changing leaves and the first snow of the season, all things that I love.

We quietly sneak into the packhouse, climbing the stairs that the omegas would use to bring food and laundry up to the ranked members' rooms. I didn't get the impression from Laney that she and her sister were ranked. But maybe that's why she wants her sister out of this pack. With limited options, a pretty girl like Laney and her sister would be hot commodities to an Alpha, especially if he only cared about having heirs.

The thought makes Gregor snarl in my head, and he pushes me to move faster. When we get to the Alpha floor, I can see that this girl has been put in the room beside Alpha Thomas. Well, that makes this easier. If she was in his room, it would be harder to get her out without alerting the pack. This way, it should be fairly simple.

'Guard the door. I'll get her,' I tell my warriors, who turn with their backs to the door, ready to attack if someone approaches.

I quietly open the door, and when I do, the scent of mulling spices overwhelms me, nearly bringing me to my knees.

'Mate!' Gregor says excitedly in my head.

Just then, the girl's head snaps up. I'm sure her wolf smells us entering her room. I put my finger to my lips, asking her to be quiet.

"I understand you like donuts," I say softly.

She nods. "I love them."

"I have a couple back at my pack that you may be interested in."

"A couple?" she asks, wiping her tears away.

"One in particular," I say, thrilled that I can tell her that her sister isn't dead.

She huffs a relieved sob before standing up from the floor, where she was quietly crying.

"Will you come with me?" I ask, extending my hand.

She nods, placing her hand in mine. Warm, electric tingles light up my hand, shooting up my arm. She gasps, and I know she feels it, too.

"Let's go, mate," I say to her. She smiles softly and nods her head.

We swiftly leave the packhouse, having to kill a couple more of Thomas' men as we leave. It says a lot that Thomas can sleep through his pack members dying. What a miserable Alpha he is, and if he was planning to force my mate into a mate bond, then I'll be thrilled if Alpha Warren gives us the go-ahead to take out Thomas and the rest of his pack.

But for now, my mate is safe, and I'm taking her back to her sister and into the safety of our pack.

Chapter 34: The Doctor
Laney

I really didn't have a choice but to believe this Alpha, Alpha Warren. I know Thomas hates him, but he's never been clear about his reasons for hating him. Of course, Thomas is a follower, not a leader. The only reason he's still Alpha is because he's killed anyone who has ever challenged him. Some of us, me included, have wondered if he cheated to do it. Because I've never been able to prove it, and no one else has either, he's remained our Alpha.

Well, he's no longer my Alpha. I hate that my sister thinks that I'm dead. I truly hope that they get to her quickly. Thomas was on the verge of taking her as his chosen mate, against her will, right before we were told we were attacking Alpha Warren's pack. Since I know Alpha Thomas was hell-bent on getting my sister to bed so he could mark her, I know the order came from someone else. I'd guess it was Alpha Quinton. He's no better than Alpha Thomas. He's just smarter.

When the lady doctor walks back in, she has two warriors and a nurse with her. The warriors are for me, I'm sure. I'm not going to hurt this woman. I wouldn't have anyway; she's obviously not a warrior. I don't kill others who can't defend themselves. I know we've been ordered to do it in the past, but I make sure I stay on the battlegrounds, fighting the ones who are strong enough to fight.

Even if I was that type of person, a person who kills those weaker than herself, I would never do anything to put my sister at risk. If they're going to get her, to get her out of Thomas' pack, I will do everything I can to make sure they have no reason to hold my actions against Noelle.

I watch her as she walks in. Four Alphas want this woman. Since she's not a warrior, it makes me wonder if she's really that good of a doctor. These days, just having someone who can set a bone is valuable. But this woman exudes confidence the moment she walks into the room. She didn't before when we were talking about rescuing my sister. She let her mate, Alpha Warren, do the talking. She deferred to him and even became upset when she found out that other Alphas were after her. Definitely not a warrior, but now that she's here to deal with my broken leg, it's like she's a different person.

She begins looking over my leg again. "Are you sure you don't want to be knocked out?" she asks me.

"Have they left to get my sister?"

"Yes. Our Beta, Charlie, took a few warriors to get her."

I nod. "Then no, I'll stay awake."

"How is your wolf?" she asks me.

"She's fine," I say, frowning. Why is she interested in my wolf?

"I'd like to speak with her," she says.

Haise, my wolf, pushes forward. "What do you need, doctor?"

She looks up at my wolf. "What's your name?" she asks. I've never known a doctor who cares to ask if my wolf is okay, much less what their name is.

"I'm Haise, doctor."

"Haise, are you strong enough to heal bones?"

"I believe so. I'm not at full strength. My human is a great fighter, and because of that, she gets a lot of injuries," Haise says, making me smile. I'm surprised when the doctor smiles at her, too.

"You're proud of your human?"

"I am," Haise says.

"So, Haise, what I want to do is hold your bones together while you heal them. You don't have to heal them all the way, just enough for them to set. Can you do that?" she asks.

"You're going to hold the bones while my wolf heals them?" I ask, shocked.

"Yes, if she's strong enough," she says to me.

'I'd like to try,' Haise says in our mind space. In the past, we've just had braces put on our legs, and while Haise healed me, the bones were never set properly. It's probably why they broke during the battle. I've noticed that my bones are breaking more and more, especially in places where they've broken before.

"Haise wants to try," I tell her.

She turns back to my leg. "Tell me if you can feel any of this," she says and begins poking me around the injury. I let her know where and when I can feel it and she has the nurse, Savannah, give me something that numbs my leg completely.

"How long will my leg be numb?" I ask, not wanting to be at a disadvantage. I was hoping that once Noelle is here, she and I could make a run for it. I'd find a safe place for us and get a job until we could settle somewhere.

"A few hours," she says, looking back up at me. "I intend to heal you correctly this time. I can tell that you've had multiple fractures to this bone. I'll be very unhappy if I do all this work, and you ruin it by trying to walk on this leg before I give you clearance to do so."

"Believe me, you don't want our Luna to be unhappy with you," one of the warriors says. I glance at them, frowning. Both warriors are trying to hide their smiles.

"She threatened to follow our Beta into the Moon Goddess' realm and drag his ass back," the other warrior says. While they're teasing their Luna, or future Luna, there's a huge amount of admiration and respect, even from them. It makes me even more curious about this woman.

I look back at this doctor and see her roll her eyes.

"I'm never going to live that down, am I?" she mumbles. I watch both warriors duck their heads, trying to keep from laughing.

"Okay, Haise, ready?" she asks, getting my attention again.

"Ready, Luna," Haise says. I notice that Haise had changed from calling her doctor to calling her Luna. Whether it's from the warrior's respect or from this woman speaking directly to her, Haise is gaining respect for her as well.

I watch as she pulls a broken bone from my leg, looking it over and then pressing it against the bone it must attach to.

"What a mess. What the hell kind of doctor set this bone? They shouldn't even call themselves a doctor," she murmurs.

"I don't think he was a doctor. Not this last one anyway," I tell her.

"What?" she asks, frowning as she glances up at me.

"She wasn't talking to you," one of the warriors clarifies.

"She talks to herself a lot," the other warrior confirms.

"Who is setting bones if they aren't a doctor?" she mumbles.

"Nice job, Haise. Ready for another one?" she asks, holding up another bone. This time, her voice was loud and clear, so I guess she was mumbling to herself before.

"You're a very different kind of doctor," I say to her.

"Why is that?" she asks, not looking up from her work.

"No one has ever wanted to talk to my wolf before," I tell her.

"Well, that's just stupid. The wolves are the ones that heal us. If you don't know how strong they are, then you don't know what needs to be done to heal the human," she says.

Her hands go still, and I feel her wolf push forward. "Your wolf isn't the only one who is proud of her human. MY human is an incredible woman. She may not be the warrior that you are, but believe me, she has strengths that most don't," her wolf says.

I feel Haise lift our neck, shocking me with her submission to this wolf.

"We meant no disrespect," Haise says to her.

"I've watched you assessing my human. Many underestimate her because she is not a warrior. But warriors come in all shapes and sizes. You would be wise to remember that," her wolf says before pulling back.

"Now that that's settled, perhaps we can get back to healing this woman," she murmurs again. I've just about decided that I can tell when she's talking to me and when she's talking to herself when the door bangs open and my sister's scent flows in on the rush of air.

"LANEY!" she says, rushing toward me.

A loud growl stops her in her tracks. "Do not undo the work I've done to fix your sister's leg. This is a surgery room!" she growls, glaring first at my sister and then at the man standing behind my sister. He feels like a Beta.

"Sorry, Luna. She was anxious to see her sister after thinking that she had died," the man says.

I hold out my hand, and Noelle looks at the doctor, waiting for her to nod before carefully walking over to stand beside me.

"Beta Charlie told me you were alive, but I didn't believe it until I smelled your scent, and then I smelled the blood, and ... oh, you really are fixing Laney's leg, aren't you?" she asks, leaning over to watch what Doctor, no Luna Yara, is doing.

"My sister has been trying to teach herself medicine so she could help heal our pack members," I say proudly.

Noelle moves to stand closer to Luna Yara, not releasing my hand.

"Haise is healing your leg properly, Laney!" she says excitedly. "Maybe now your leg won't break so often."

"When I'm done, if your sister listens and follows my direction, her leg will only snap with a forced break. Your bones were weak because they didn't heal properly, making you weaker, Laney. Now, you'll be stronger."

And that's when it finally clicks in my head. I look around, seeing that the warriors and the Beta in this room are all strong and healthy.

"That's why the Alphas are after you," I say, making Noelle's head snap up to me.

Luna Yara looks up at me, a sad smile on her face. "Only some of them."

Chapter 35: Interrogating the Beta

Warren

Once Yara went to work on Laney, I had Anna help me disconnect The Beta from his bed, and then several warriors and I dragged him to the cells. Since I didn't intend to keep him alive, I didn't bother being careful about how we dragged him.

Once he's in the cell, I have the warriors string him up and let him hang by his hands from silver handcuffs. I ignore the smell of burning flesh while I drag a chair over and wait for him to wake up. While I do, I keep an ear on Yara and also Laney. I don't completely trust her yet, but I do know that she won't do anything to put her sister at risk.

The Beta has just started stirring when I feel Charlie getting close enough that our mind link reconnects.

'Alpha, we got her,' he says, and something in his tone makes me focus on him.

'Problems?'

'No, but ... she's my mate, Alpha.'

I breathe a deep sigh of relief. I knew Gregor's interest in Yara was bothering Arric and me, but I didn't realize just how much until Charlie told me he'd found his mate.

'Good, now maybe you'll stop flirting with mine,' Arric growls in the mind link.

'Sorry, Arric. It won't happen again,' Charlie says contritely. 'There's something else. Thomas is literally sleeping while his pack is barely hanging on. Also, the fact that he had my mate in the room beside his room meant he planned to take her as his Luna. He deserves to die. He didn't even wake up when he killed his warriors, coming or going from the pack. There are so few of them that they weren't even running patrols, just protecting the packhouse.'

'How many warriors do you think you'd need?' I ask him, feeling his distraction as I hear another voice through Yara and Laney's minds. The sister, Noelle, just entered the room where Yara is working on Laney. I'm proud of my mate for standing her ground. My pack isn't the only one becoming stronger. She may not realize it, may not see that she's slowly taking her place as Luna of this pack, but she is.

"What the fuck are you smiling about?" The Beta asks me. I refocus on him, watching him thrash against the handcuffs. I ignore him and return to my conversation with Charlie.

'We have his Beta, who will die for putting his hands on Yara. Find out from Laney and Noelle if there is anyone else worth saving in the pack.'

'I will, and to answer your question, I doubt we'd even need half our warriors to go, but if I took that many, we'd be home before sunrise, possibly before then.'

I look back at the Beta, who tries to spit on me, but he's too far away and probably doesn't have enough saliva to make it come anywhere close to me. One of my warriors walks up and punches him in the gut for his insolence.

'Do it. That's one less Alpha we need to worry about, and I'll get what I can from this Beta before I kill him,' I tell Charlie.

'You know Thomas is the least of our worries,' he says.

'Still one less worry. Right now, I have four Alphas trying to get to my mate. You have one. Let's eliminate that threat.'

'Yes, Alpha,' he growls and cuts the mind link. I know Charlie will get whatever information he needs before he leaves, so I don't bother listening in. I disconnect from Laney but keep the link between Yara and me open to ensure she's okay while I interview this Beta.

I stand slowly, insolently, from the chair, letting this Beta know I'm in no hurry to kill him. This can be fast or slow; it depends on him. Yara needs sleep, so I have all night. And with Charlie and half of my warriors gone, I need to stay awake and aware anyway.

"What's your name, Beta?" I ask him.

"Wouldn't you like to know?" he growls, earning him a punch to the face. Word got around that he'd tried to choke Yara. This pack doesn't stand for anyone hurting their future Luna, so I let my warriors get their punches in. As I said, this could be fast or slow. It looks like it's going to be slow.

"Well, Beta, how does it feel to know that while you're here, being used as a punching bag, your Alpha is sleeping away? He apparently didn't even realize that MY Beta snuck into his pack lands and scooped up some little girl from right under his nose. You must feel SO valuable, knowing your Alpha doesn't even care enough about you to stay awake and find a way to save you," I say, taunting him.

He growls at me, but I see the flash of anger and worry cross his face. "Noelle belongs to my Alpha."

"Wow, still protecting him, even though he doesn't protect you. Maybe you were planning to overthrow him at some point and become Alpha," I say, and the moment the words are out of my mouth, I see the flash in his eyes, and I know I'm right.

I chuckle. "Well, that's never going to happen now. First, I'm pretty sure my Beta would tell you that Noelle belongs to him now," I say, watching him begin to thrash again.

"Ohhh, you weren't just planning to take his title; you were planning to take his mate, too, weren't you? Well, don't worry. She's in good hands now, and my Beta is much stronger than your Alpha, which brings me to my second point. My Beta is on his way to kill your Alpha and your pack as we speak."

It's not exactly true. Charlie is still getting the list of individuals he needs to save, but as soon as that's done, he'll get the warriors and go.

"How was that even going to work? You like sloppy seconds, Beta? You like getting someone else's cast off?" I ask, still taunting.

"Why, you looking to get rid of your lady doctor? I'd take that sweet little piece of ..." That's as far as he gets before my warriors begin pummeling him.

"Don't kill him yet," I growl, fighting Arric for control. He's ready to kill this Beta for what he just said about Yara, but I need information.

When my warriors step back, the Beta is laughing. I can tell it hurts him, but he either knows what's coming or he's used to feeling this level of pain.

"Why do they want my mate?" I ask.

"Wouldn't you like to know?" he asks, earning him another punch.

"How many Alphas are after her?" I ask.

"Enough that you won't survive. Maybe they'll pass her around ..."

My warriors go at him again. This time, I see the stitches have opened, and he's begun bleeding from the gut, which gives me an idea. I don't know anatomy like Yara does, but I'm pretty sure squeezing anything inside his body is going to hurt.

I step forward and let Arric's claws come forward. I slowly cut through the stitches down the side of his stomach. "Last chance to make this easy for yourself," I say, my voice hard.

"Fuck you," he says.

"You're not my type," I say, sliding my hand inside the wound. I watch his face as he grits his teeth, and when I find something that feels like an organ, I wrap my hand around it.

"How many?" I ask again, slowly squeezing.

He fights as long as he can before shouting out his answer.

"THREE!"

"Three, including Thomas?" I ask him.

"YES!"

"Who are the other two?" I ask, not closing my hand anymore but not releasing it either.

He tries to breathe through the pain, and it only takes a little more of a squeeze for him to answer.

"Alphas Brady and Quinton!"

"The three of them have been working together against me?"

"Yes!"

"What about Alpha Harold?" I ask.

"What about him?"

"He's not part of this alliance?" I ask.

"No. He attacks us, too."

I hear Charlie call to the warriors he intends to take with him, ready to attack Alpha Thomas' pack. The howls go up all around the pack.

"I may have lied earlier. My Beta hadn't left yet to kill your Alpha, but he's leaving now. Killing you will only weaken Thomas even more. So, as much as I'd like to let you die a slow death for touching my mate, it's time for you to die," I say.

He begins thrashing, but I grip the organ and rip it out of his body, pulling more guts than I realized as it tugs free from whatever it was attached to inside his body. It only takes a moment for his body to stop thrashing as blood and guts splatter on the floor.

"Get him out of here, burn the body. Don't let your Luna see. She may not have disagreed with me killing him, but she won't want to see this," I tell them.

"Yes, Alpha."

I step out of the cell, washing the blood off my hand and arm before heading over to the hospital to check on my mate and meet my Beta's mate.

Chapter 36: Noelle
Yara

I finished stitching Laney up while Charlie talked to her and Noelle about who was worth saving from their previous pack. In the end, Laney gave him a list, but it wasn't a very long list.

"They've collected some she-wolves from other packs when we've attacked. Some were forced into mate bonds that they didn't want. They won't be unhappy that you're killing their mates, but it will make them weak," she says.

"You didn't help them?" I ask her. I don't mean for it to sound judgmental, but she's obviously a strong warrior and a woman. She could have stood up for them.

"You underestimate the menace in our pack, Luna," Noelle says kindly. "My sister has always put my life ahead of others, including her own. Even after I became an adult. They would have killed her, or worse, used me against her, if she'd stood up to them," she says, smiling at Laney.

"Everyone wanted you. You're sweet, you're smart, and you're beautiful," Laney says to her.

'I think our Beta is a bit smitten with this young woman,' Annika says in my head. I look over and see him smiling at Noelle in a way that's very similar to how Warren smiles at me.

'Do you think...' I begin.

'Yes, she's his mate.'

'That will make Warren happy,' I say, knowing that he's been feeling grumpier about Gregor's attention to me and Annika.

'It makes me happy, too. I like Gregor, but I would never choose him over Arric,' she says, making me curious.

'Because Arric is an Alpha wolf?'

'Because he's our mate, and he's a good wolf. He's good for this pack, and he's good for us, Yara. So is Warren. I know you agree with me, or you wouldn't be seriously considering letting him mark us.'

It's true. I've never wanted to bind myself to someone, never wanted to give something so permanent because I never trusted anyone enough to agree to share my life with them. But Warren ... he's different.

"You'll need to be prepared to look over those women when they come in, Luna. They'll need your help," Laney says, redirecting my attention back to them.

"How many are we talking about?" I ask, looking over the list that Charlie is creating.

"Fifteen to twenty, Luna, and that doesn't include any omegas we come across."

"How many warriors are you taking?" I ask him.

"I was planning on a hundred if you clear them."

"Savannah, let Anna finish up here. You and I need to clear these warriors, and then we need to prep the hospital for an influx of people."

"Yes, Luna," she says, walking out to speak to Anna, Erica, and Katie.

"Luna, when's the last time you slept?" Charlie asks me.

"I don't know, Charlie, what time is it?" I ask, smiling at him. I watch Noelle tense at our casual interaction, and the gesture doesn't go unnoticed by her sister.

"It's close to midnight," he tells me. I sigh. Sleep is a hot commodity around here that barely anyone gets.

"I'll sleep when everyone is taken care of," I tell him.

I watch his eyes go unfocused before he looks back at me. "Alpha will be here soon."

I narrow my eyes at him, putting my hands on my hips. "Are you telling on me, Charlie?"

"Who puts you on downtime, Luna? After what I heard you said to me about following me into the Moon Goddess' realm, it won't be me. But if you want to go toe to toe against our Alpha, that's up to you. I'll just be sorry that I missed it," he says, smirking at me and making my eyes narrow even more.

"Why would she have to follow you to the Moon Goddess' realm?" Noelle asks, and now it's my turn to smirk.

"Because he nearly died. He came into this hospital without a pulse, isn't that right, Beta?" I ask him, casually sarcastic. Two can play this game. I'm not the only one with a mate in the pack now.

Charlie's lips press tightly together as Noelle sucks in a breath. Charlie turns to her. "I'm okay. Trust me, our Luna won't let anyone fight if they aren't strong enough," he tells her, taking hold of her arms as he holds her gaze.

"How long ago was that?" Laney asks, looking from them to me.

"Two days."

Both sisters inhale sharply.

"You almost died two days ago?" Noelle says.

At the same time, Laney says, "You got him healthy in two days?"

"Yes," both Charlie and I answer at the same time.

"I have to go, but when I return …. I'd like to talk to you more about … everything," Charlie says to Noelle.

She nods, blushing softly, as Anna walks in.

"Okay, I'm going to go get the hospital ready. Charlie …"

"The warriors are outside, Luna."

I nod.

"I can help you, Luna. I'm not well educated, but I'm not squeamish at all," Noelle says.

"How are you at following directions?" I ask her.

"I'll do whatever you tell me to do," she says.

"It will help the others to see that she's alive, Luna," Laney says. "They'll trust you if they see her helping you."

"Okay. You stay at my side, and you do everything I tell you to do," I tell her.

"Yes, Luna!" she says excitedly.

I watch Charlie hide his smile as we walk out of the room. Noelle very quickly becomes my shadow, staying right at my side.

"You warriors know the drill. If you were on the injury list, get in my line. If you were on downtime, get in Savannah's," I say.

For once, my line is extremely short, and I work through it quickly.

"The key is to make sure their wolves are strong," I say to Noelle, educating her as I go. "If they say their wolves are strong, but their wolf doesn't say it, you can't trust it. You have to hear it from their wolves. Since they all consider me their Luna, and I've told them that if they give any of my nurses a problem, they'll answer to me. They won't lie to you about it."

"You are our Luna," the warrior in front of me says.

"Just because you aren't wearing our Alpha's mark yet doesn't mean we haven't accepted you as our Luna," another warrior says.

I watch Noelle's eyes go wide as the other warriors all murmur in agreement. I've gotten used to it, but apparently, the pack's devotion to me is something unusual for her to see.

Once Charlie calls them to attack, I turn back to the hospital. "Okay, let's get this place cleaned up. How many crash kits do we have?" I ask, starting to take inventory and plan for the group coming in.

Chapter 37: Unexpected
Yara

"Luna, may I speak with you privately?" one of the female warriors asks, coming up behind us.

"I can clean. I just need to know where everything is," Noelle says eagerly.

"Stay with Savannah until I get back," I tell her, then turn to the warrior.

"I'm sorry, I don't know your name," I say.

"I'm Eva, Luna."

"Eva, come with me. Let's take you into a room so we can talk privately."

I notice that she's tentative and nervous, which makes me a bit nervous. I'm not sure why she'd be nervous unless she's injured, and I missed it, and now she's come to tell me. When we get to the room, I gesture for her to sit, and then I sit across from her.

"What can I help you with?" I ask her.

"I can't shift," she whispers, looking down at the floor.

I immediately go into doctor mode, thinking through all the reasons why someone can't shift.

"Is your wolf silent?"

"No, Luna. She's here."

"Are you injured? Did I miss an injury? I don't smell any infection on you," I tell her.

She shakes her head, and a tear rolls down her cheek. "I think I'm pregnant."

I reach out and take her hand. "I can do a very quick test to see if you are. If you're not, then I'll run some other tests. If you are, then we'll talk about what that means for you," I tell her.

She nods as more tears fall. "Give me one moment. I'll be right back."

I go to the storage room and find a specimen cup for Eva to pee into. "Luna, is everything okay?" Katie asks, walking in and looking at the cup. "Oh."

Since Katie's pregnant, she would know what this means. "Don't say a word, Katie."

"Of course not, Luna," she says.

I go back to the room and tell Eva what I need, then send her to the bathroom. While I wait, Warren comes in.

"Hey, why are you still here? I thought you'd be headed to bed?"

"Laney and Noelle seem to think that we're going to have an influx of she-wolves who are suffering from broken mate bonds. Bonds that were forced on them, you should know," I tell him.

He growls at that but pulls me into a hug. "You need sleep."

"They need help, Warren. Don't bother telling me that you were planning to sleep while Charlie is gone. You don't have a Gamma, so there's no one else to oversee the pack."

"That doesn't mean that you don't need sleep, Yara." He pulls back and looks behind me. "Eva, is everything okay?"

"She and I have some things to discuss, Warren. Why don't you go and introduce yourself to Noelle? She's with Savannah," I tell him, guessing that Eva doesn't want to say anything to Warren yet.

Warren looks at her and then at me. "Okay. If you need anything, link me."

"I will," I say, and he leans down to kiss me before turning to walk away.

I sigh, knowing that very soon, he and I are going to have to have that talk about him marking me. When I turn, Eva is smiling.

"I've never seen our Alpha in love before. It makes him seem almost human. Not the fighting machine that I'm used to seeing."

"Yeah, he's pretty sweet," I say, making her snort.

"That's not a word I've ever heard used to describe our Alpha before."

I gesture for her to return to the room, and I go test her urine. When I walk back into the room, the nervous woman from before is back.

"Well?" she asks.

"Definitely pregnant. I can do bloodwork to make absolutely sure ..."

She begins shaking her head. "No, Karly, my wolf, said I was pregnant, but I didn't want to believe it."

"Okay, let's talk about that while I examine you," I say, pulling out a gown and having her sit on the table in the room.

I begin listening to her heart and lungs, and then she explains that she and another warrior had become friendly and that they've been finding comfort in each other's arms, but they aren't mates.

"Have you talked about becoming chosen mates?" I ask her as I draw blood. She may not need to confirm that she's pregnant, but if she chooses to keep this baby, I want to know that both mom and baby are healthy.

"There hasn't been a lot of time for that. At first, it was just to burn off steam, you know? We were fighting all the time and we both just needed something good, something positive and pleasurable in our lives," she says tearfully.

"There hasn't been a lot of time for much of anything other than fighting lately," I agree. "You know I have to pull you off warrior duty, right? No matter what you decide. Even if you decide you don't want this baby..."

"I do. I ..." she puts her hands over her belly, smiling a sweet, gentle smile. "I'm not sure how you can love someone that you only just realized is alive, but I do. I want this baby, even if it means raising him or her on my own."

I put my hands over hers. "You won't be alone. You'll have me and the pack. Even if you and the father decide not to become a mated pair, you still have support."

"Thanks, Luna," she says, hugging me.

"I'll need to tell Warren so he knows why I'm pulling you off duty and that it will be longer than normal. And I'll want to see you as you start progressing in your pregnancy."

She nods, smiling, her hands going back to her stomach. "I'll have to talk to him anyway about needing some extra space. Warriors don't usually like to have young babies keeping them awake in the few hours they have to sleep," she says.

"You get dressed, and I'll let him know."

When I step out, I realize that this would become my norm if we weren't in a constant state of war. Even with the battles, she-wolves are getting pregnant. Eva won't be the only one. It makes sense that the pack finds comfort together. Finding mates is nearly impossible, so finding comfort with friends or lovers is the next best thing.

I walk back to the waiting area, looking for Warren, when Carson walks in.

"Luna. Hi."

"Carson, can I help you with something?" I ask. After putting him on a 24-hour rest, he'd come back stronger than ever.

"I was wondering if ... EVA!" he says, looking over my shoulder. He brushes past me and walks quickly toward her.

"Are you okay? Are you ill? Is something wrong? I knew I heard you throwing up this morning. Did you see Luna Yara? What did she say?" he asks in a rapid-fire interrogation sort of way.

"What's going on?" Warren asks quietly, coming up behind me and wrapping his arms around me. I lean into him, needing his strength as we watch the two individuals.

"We're about to find out if Carson is happy that he's gotten Eva pregnant," I say just as softly.

"Pregnant? Damn, she's a good warrior," he says as Carson whoops and swings Eva around in a circle. Eva begins laughing, and as the two of them walk out of the hospital, most likely to go mark each other, I wink at her.

'Thank you,' she mouths to me.

I nod and turn to look at Warren. I didn't expect that he'd have the soft, gentle look that he gives me when it's just the two of us.

"You're incredible, do you know that?" he asks, stroking my cheek.

"All I did was tell her she was pregnant, and she wasn't alone."

"You do so much more than that. You give everyone here hope."

He leans in, kissing me softly at first, then deepening the kiss. The hospital around me fades away, and all that's left is Warren and the emotions that he's stirring inside me. It isn't until we hear some of the warriors howling their return that I pull away.

"Time to get back to work."

Warren growls softly. "Very soon, I'm going to finally finish what we keep starting."

Chapter 38: Forced Mates
Warren

One day, very soon, I'm going to take the time I need to mark my mate. I'm getting really fed up with constant interruptions when I finally get a moment to enjoy her. However, I know now isn't the time. She's right. We have an influx of wolves coming in, and as the first ones arrive, I know Yara will be here for quite a while.

As they start coming in, Yara goes into doctor mode, taking Noelle with her, talking to the patients, and then explaining what and why she's doing what she's doing to Noelle. She grabs a clipboard and hands it to Noelle.

"Start marking down who has arrived and what their triage status is," she tells Noelle.

As I watch, I realize that Yara already has this hospital running like a well-oiled machine. While she makes her assessments, Katie and Erica move in to start working on the ones who are lower on the risk level while she and Savannah continue to assess and Noelle documents, still listening to Yara as she explains things. I'm impressed that Noelle can listen and take notes from Yara and Savannah at the same time. Hopefully, she'll be interested in staying with Charlie. Yara could use more hands in the hospital.

"How's she doing?" Charlie asks as if my thoughts conjured him to my side.

"I was just thinking that she'd make a great assistant for Yara," I tell him, watching him smile proudly.

"How did it go? I don't see many wounded warriors coming back."

"Honestly, it was too easy. How he ever lasted as an Alpha is beyond me," Charlie says.

"I'm guessing it was his Beta. He was vying for the Alpha position and for your mate," I tell him, making Charlie growl. The sound has Noelle's head shooting up in our direction.

"Sorry," Charlie says to her, his voice much softer.

"The Beta's dead, so no worries on that front."

"How long do you think it will be before Quinton finds out about Thomas?"

"I'm not sure, but I doubt it will be long. Depending on his next step and plan of attack, he'll find out in a day or so at the most."

"Do you think he'll attack?" Charlie says, watching our mates move through the room.

"I don't know. If we hadn't gone so long without sleep, I'd say we should hit Brady's pack, but his pack lands are full of those damn booby traps, and I'm not sending our warriors out there to die."

Because I've been watching her closely, I notice when Yara's nose starts twitching. She turns, looking around.

"Luna?" Noelle asks her, but she holds up a finger, telling her to wait.

Noelle turns and looks at Charlie, but he's focused on Yara, too. We've both seen this once before. The day she found Haynes in the middle of the dining hall.

I watch as Annika comes forward, and Yara begins moving through the group, following her nose. As she does, the room goes quiet. The warriors understand what she's doing, but the newcomers are watching and wondering why she's sniffing the air like she is. When she finds the person she's looking for, she leans over and sniffs her from head to toe.

"Where's your infection?" she asks the woman.

"Just let me die," the woman says, not even looking at Yara.

"What is your name?" Yara asks her.

She doesn't answer.

"Well, whatever your name is, that's not allowed in my hospital. It sets a bad precedent. One person dies, and then everyone coming in thinks they can die, too. So, no one dies in my hospital. Now, where's your infection?"

The woman turns her head and looks at Yara. "They killed my mate. They killed my son, and that bastard forced his mark on me. I refused to give him the pup he wanted. Let. Me. Die," she growls.

I take a step forward, but Yara leans over the woman, and I have to smile. In this hospital, my mate is the strongest member of the pack, even rivaling me. Her determination to help and protect is incredible.

"Now, you listen to me. If losing your mate and pup didn't kill you, then you need to take that up with the Moon Goddess. If you're still alive, there's a reason for it, and I'm not going to be the one who has to tell the Moon Goddess that I went against her will and let you die. So, I will ask you one more time: where is your infection?"

The woman just turns away from Yara.

"Savannah, prep her for an emergency hysterectomy," Yara says.

"NO!" the woman screams and begins thrashing. Yara moves to hold her down, and I'm beside her in an instant. I growl at the woman, pushing my Alpha aura over her.

"Calm down!" I growl.

The woman begins sobbing, and I look at Yara. She presses her lips together, but Savannah gets the IV into her arm, and it's only a couple of moments before the woman is unconscious.

"Yara, are you sure ..."

"We'll have to deal with the aftermath, Warren. But she won't survive whatever she's done. She's sick with infection. If she chooses to end her life after I save her, that's on her. I'm not letting her die on me."

I reach out, stroking her cheek. My mate is so passionate. Goddess, I can't wait for that passion to turn to me.

"Go do what you do best, Yara," I tell her.

Anna comes over with a gurney, but because of the number of people lying on the floor, she can't get close. I lift the woman who is much lighter than she looks. Yara's right. She'll die from whatever she's done without my mate's intervention.

"Noelle, you're with me. Do you know anything about assisting in a surgery?"

"No, Luna."

"Anna? Katie? Erica?" she asks.

"I can, Luna," Erica says.

"Savannah, keep triaging. Noelle, give your clipboard to Anna. Katie, do what you can until you need to stop," she says before pushing the gurney into one of the rooms.

"Wow," a woman says from where she's lying on the floor beside me.

"You have no idea," I say, watching as my mate closes the door to the surgery room. Her eyes meet mine, and I wink at her. I see a partial smile before she closes the door. Good.

I turn back to the room. "Now, what was this about being forcibly marked? I know some of you have minor injuries or are suffering from the death of your mates ..."

"Good riddance. He was no mate of mine," a woman says angrily, and several others agree.

I move to them, and Charlie walks up behind me to listen. Several other warriors do as well.

"Tell me about that," I say, squatting down next to the women as Savannah, Katie, and Anna continue moving around the room.

"They came into our pack and took us. Not all of us were mated like Farrah."

"Farrah, the woman Luna Yara took in for surgery?" Charlie asks.

"Yeah. Some of us were unmated, but when they came in, they either dragged us back to their pack with them or they forced their mark on us right there." She glances around at the group of mostly women lying on the blankets on the floor, waiting for Savannah to triage them. "Some were .... passed around."

Arric growls low in his chest. "Which pack did you come from?"

"Alpha Harold's. We were forced to accept Alpha Thomas as our Alpha, so I'm sure Alpha Harold thinks we're dead."

I turn and look up at Charlie. Maybe this is why Harold is attacking the packs. He wants retribution for his pack members, or maybe he's looking for them.

"Would you be willing to return to Alpha Harold's pack?" I ask them.

The women and some of the men around me nod. "He's not a bad Alpha. He's just an older Alpha. He lost his oldest son in a battle, so he's been waiting for his younger son to grow up to take over."

"Charlie, get the names of everyone who came from Alpha Harold's pack," I say before standing and turning back to the group. "Give your names to my Beta, and I'll call your Alpha later this morning to let him know that I have his pack members here. I'll be honest, Alpha Harold has attacked my pack along with the others, so I can't guarantee that I can get you back to him, but I'll try."

"He's not our Alpha anymore," a woman says. Even her voice sounds weak, so I know she's one whose mate was killed. Force or not, a mate's death still impacts the surviving mate, but in this instance, I'm guessing the lack of love between them is what is allowing

184

these women to survive. That makes me wonder what made Farrah survive losing her mate and her son.

"If he didn't renounce you and he's the kind of Alpha you say he is," I say to the room, "then he'll still consider himself your Alpha. Trust me. I know I would."

I feel another wave of pride from my pack warriors, and this time, I realize that it's pride in me as their Alpha. I turn and look at my pack. It's good to finally feel something from them other than pain and frustration.

I smile as I look at the door where Yara is working, and I realize that most of this change has to do with my mate walking into my life.

Chapter 39: Drastic Measures

Yara

When we enter the surgery room to look over the woman with the infection, I realize just how desperate and angry she was. I don't have a choice but to slice her open. With an infection this severe, I have to make sure I get it all. However, when I slice her, the smell is disgusting. I take a minute to steel myself against the smell. It would be bad for a human, but it's worse for a shifter since we have enhanced senses.

Noelle quickly covers her nose and mouth. "If you're going to vomit, get out of here," I tell her.

She shakes her head, and I can see her trying to get her nausea under control. "Breathe through your mouth. It doesn't take the stench away, but it helps," I tell her.

"It's like you can taste it," Erica says, looking nearly as green as Noelle. "I have a young pup, and this out stinks anything my pup produces."

"What is that?" Noelle asks, pointing to her uterus as I open her up. I realize exactly why her infection is so terrible.

"She tried to abort the fetus herself," I tell her. There are holes in the woman's uterus. I have no idea what she shoved up inside herself to get rid of this pup, but she made sure she'd never be able to carry it to term. There are multiple ruptures in her uterus, and the infection is everywhere.

'Her name is Farrah, Luna,' Savannah's voice floats into my head.

187

'Thank you, Savannah. You doing okay?'

'We're good out here. Alpha is interviewing some of the pack to see where they came from originally.'

I close the mind link, knowing that Warren will figure things out while I'm in here.

"Farrah, you sure did a number on yourself," I say, getting to work.

I walk Noelle through everything that I'm doing, seeing that Erica is just as interested. While she continues to monitor Farrah's vitals for me, she's paying attention and asking periodic questions as well.

I get another flash of what my life could be like with Warren. I could start a teaching hospital. I haven't seen the werewolf school, but I'll never get as much experience there as I am here, and thankfully, I know enough to figure out what I don't know. Maybe, if we ever get out of this constant war, I'll actually be able to continue with my studies.

"Is the infection caused by what she did?" Noelle asks.

"I think that might have started it, and that's probably what caused it to get to this point. She should have miscarried when she lost the pup, but instead, it began rotting inside her, adding to the infection."

"Wow, that's so terrible," Noelle says.

"Terrible things happen in times of war," I say sadly.

"I'm not sure I've ever realized just how much Laney protected me until this moment," she says.

"Well, when we're done here, you can go tell her how much you appreciate her. For now, you have to focus on what's in front of you," I say.

She nods, pulling herself together. It takes another couple of hours to finish, but when I'm done, I've gotten as much of the infection cleaned out as I can, and Farrah's uterus and fetus have been removed from her body.

"I'm going to order her some heavy-duty antibiotics. Do you know if we have any, Erica?" I ask.

"I can check, Luna, but we never ordered the strong stuff. Dr. Stevens ..."

"Yeah, I know. He didn't see a need for it. Okay, we'll start her on what we have. Let me know what that is, and then we need to get an order in today. I'll talk to Savannah about that."

I can see that Noelle is starting to crash. It's been a long, exhausting night for her, first thinking she lost her sister, then finding her mate, and now helping me with the surgeries.

"Why don't you go check on your sister? Then we can find you a room for tonight. I know someone who will be thrilled to at least have you sleep on his floor," I say to her, making her blush.

She looks up at me. "You seem to think highly of him, Luna."

"Charlie is a good man and a good Beta from everything I've learned about him. He's true to Warren and, therefore, true to me. I don't think that you could go wrong with a man like that," I tell her.

"She's right. Beta Charlie is a good man. I take it he's your mate?" Erica asks her.

She nods, making Erica smile. "Just like our Alpha, everyone will be glad that he's found his mate. He's waited for you, just so you know."

I see Noelle's surprise, then her happiness that her mate waited to find her.

"Go see your sister, then go see your mate."

"I don't know how to find him," she says as we make our way out of the room. I lean my head into the waiting room and nod.

"He's waiting for you," I say, glancing at Charlie before my eyes move to Warren. He's waiting for me, too.

I watch as he assesses my level of fatigue. I vaguely see Charlie pass in front of me, going to check on Noelle.

"Luna," Savannah says, walking up. She looks at Warren and then back at me. "There weren't any others who were as serious as Farrah. I've got the mates of the dead warriors in rooms. There are a few pups, and after talking to Alpha Warren, we decided to keep them here so they could go see their parents if they needed to."

"Good, that's good. You need to get some sleep, Savannah."

"You, too, Luna. Alpha sent Katie to bed hours ago. Anna is sleeping here, ready to take the first shift when I leave."

"Yeah, Erica needs to go, too," I say, yawning hugely. The adrenaline is once again draining out of me in a rush. My body is starting to feel heavy, and I watch Warren stand. Whether he was listening or he felt my body's exhaustion, I'm not sure.

"How are you still on your feet?" I ask him.

He strokes his fingers over my cheek. "I had someone very important to me who was worth staying awake for," he says softly. "Come on. Time for you and me to get some sleep."

He scoops me up into his arms, and I snuggle against him. The man really is incredibly strong. I'm not sure I could carry a baby right now, and he's carrying me back to the packhouse.

"When you love someone, they feel light as a feather in your arms," he murmurs, kissing the side of my head. I'm asleep before he even leaves the hospital.

~ ~ ~

Laney POV

I can't sleep. I've been worried about Noelle most of the night, only to find out that she's been assisting Luna Yara with patients and surgeries. Between that and finding her mate, I'm not sure I've ever seen my sister so excited.

I'm happy for her; truly, I am. I'd probably be happier if I hadn't smelled my mate, too.

I'd been on the battlefield when I'd first smelled his hops and barley scent. I love a good, cold beer when I have time. I once passed a beer processing plant, and I nearly moaned out loud at the scent coming from the packaging plant. The moment we'd passed Alpha Warren's border, I'd known my mate was here.

I avoided him on the battlefield, unwilling to fight against the person the Moon Goddess chose for me. And then, my stupid leg had snapped, and I'd gotten captured. I'm not sure if he had been avoiding me as well or if the thought of his mate fighting against his pack had disgusted him, but I haven't smelled him since I got to the hospital.

After Noelle left with Beta Charlie, I leaned back, closing my eyes and trying to relax enough to sleep. As exhausted as I am, I still feel on edge. The pack is unknown, and at some point, I'll have to face my mate.

I feel the air shift, and I know the door has opened a moment before I smell his scent. I open my eyes and see him standing there, watching me.

"Have you come to reject me?" I ask him. If so, I'd rather rip the band-aid off and get this over quickly.

"That depends," he says, his voice resonating deep inside my mind and body.

"On what?"

"Are you still going to be fighting against my pack?"

I shake my head. "I accepted Alpha Warren as my Alpha."

"I heard, but that doesn't mean that you won't renounce him."

"Well, my sister is apparently mated to your Beta, so I'm not going anywhere, and I won't do anything to hurt her."

He walks into the room, looking down at my bandaged leg. "How's the break?"

"Healing, and apparently for the first time, it's healing appropriately."

He smiles. "Yeah, our Luna's pretty awesome."

The smile fades as he turns back to me. "How do you want to do this?" he asks, and my throat gets tight.

"The rejection?" I say, trying to sound strong, but even though I never expected to find my mate, now that I have, I don't want to lose him.

"No, the getting to know each other so we can build trust and decide if we want to accept each other as mates," he says, and the knot in my stomach relaxes. I hold out my hand.

"Hi. I'm Laney," I say, introducing myself and smiling softly.

"Hi Laney. I'm Haynes," he says, shaking my hand.

My body lights up with tingles. We continue to shake hands, staring at each other for a long time as we feel the power of the mate bond flow between us.

Chapter 40: Strength and Weakness

Quinton

"I'm waiting to hear from Thomas. He isn't answering my phone calls. If he's ignoring me ..." I snarl into the phone.

"Quinton, my pack still hasn't fully recovered from our last battle with Warren. He's probably still recovering. You said he lost his Beta, right?" Brady asks me.

"Yeah, but that's no excuse. I told him we'd get his Beta back, but I can't do that unless he answers his fucking phone so we can make a plan," I growl.

"What do you want to do?" Brady asks.

"I've sent some warriors over there to encourage him to answer his phone."

"So, when we attack, we're getting the lady doctor, right?" he asks.

"Yeah. Alive. We need her," I say, scrubbing my face with my hand.

"WE need her? I thought I was getting her," he says.

I have to be careful here. If what Brady and Thomas have said is true, then ...

"FUCK! I have to go. Fucking Harold is attacking," he says, hanging up.

I sit back, thinking. I know that Brady will be busy for a couple of hours. I should send warriors to help him, but my bigger issue right now is Warren. He's too fucking strong.

Since my pack is the only one at one hundred percent, I need to keep it that way. Because there's no way in hell that I'm giving that lady doctor to Brady. He's just stupid enough to get stronger and then come after me.

There's a knock at my door, and when I look up, my son, Quirin, is watching me.

"Hey, son. Come in," I say, relaxing a bit. There's nothing and no one that I love more in this life than my son.

"Is everything okay, Dad? I heard you snarling," he says.

Quirin is the future heir of this pack. He's only thirteen, but I've been training him to be a warrior since before he got his wolf three years ago.

I gesture for him to come stand in front of me. "What do you think we should do with a pack that is getting stronger, an Alpha that is getting stronger and is threatening our livelihood?" I ask him.

"No one threatens our pack," he growls in his young wolf's growl.

"That's right. No one threatens our pack. What do we do when someone threatens our pack?" I ask him.

"We eliminate them. We protect our pack," he says confidently.

"That's right. And what do we do if we find their strength, if, say, that strength is a person, a she-wolf?"

I watch as he thinks about that. "We capture her and bring her here? Force her to make us stronger while making the other Alpha weaker?"

"That's right," I say, pulling him into hug. "That's exactly what we do. So, I'm trying to find a way to get to Alpha Warren and find his strength. I will take what is making him strong, and then I kill him."

"What about the she-wolf?" he asks me.

"I will make her mine so she can never leave me," I tell him.

"Quirin, come, let your father work," my mate says from the doorway. I look up and see her lips pressed tightly together. She heard what I said, but it doesn't matter. She gave me what I needed, an heir. For that, I'll always take care of her. But this lady doctor ... she's the one who will make me strong, powerful, the Alpha of Alphas.

"Go with your mother," I say gently to my son. He's the only one who gets this side of me. Not even my mate gets this tone from me. "I'll see you at warrior training this afternoon?"

"I'll be there, Dad!" he says excitedly, pulling out of my embrace and walking toward his mother.

I watch proudly as my son holds himself in the tall way of an Alpha. He's still working on his swagger, but it's coming. I look back at my mate, who looks away before leading my son out of the room. When they're gone, I'm about to get back to work when I hear warriors heading to my office.

"Alpha," my lead warrior says, walking in with the group he took to convince Thomas to answer my call.

"Where is he?" I ask.

"He's dead, Alpha. The entire pack is dead or gone."

Son of a fucking bitch! I turn, snarling as I swipe everything off my desk, some things smashing into the wall across the room with my anger.

"How long has he been dead," I growl, not looking at my warriors.

"For most of them, it seemed like it was in the last eight to ten hours, Alpha."

Now, I do look at them. "What do you mean 'for most of them'?"

"There were several that had been killed earlier. Their bodies were closer to the borders, probably dead for closer to twelve hours."

Fucking Thomas. Had he really been so arrogant that he slept through some of his pack members being killed, letting Warren know he was vulnerable? Because it had to be Warren. He'd have killed Thomas' Beta to make him even weaker. He'd already killed many of his warriors, so Thomas was weakened already.

I stare out the window, seething with my anger. Warren is now strong enough that he's not just fighting defensively when we attack. He and his pack have somehow gotten strong enough that they've just eliminated an entire pack, one I was allied with. I may not have thought very highly of Thomas, but he had warriors, warriors that used to be at my disposal. Now, he's not only killed Thomas, but he's also weakened me.

"What about the omegas?" I ask, looking over my shoulder at my warriors.

"We didn't find any, or very few, Alpha. The safe rooms were empty, but those we found dead were primarily warriors."

Of course, they were. I would have killed everyone and made a statement. But not Warren. He's taken the weak into his pack and made his pack even larger. And then, an even worse thought hits me. Thomas loved collecting women from the packs he attacked. He'd never gotten many from Warren's pack but from Harold's ...

"Raise the alarm. We're going to assist Alpha Brady with the attack on his pack. Send out the orders, kill Alpha Harold and all of his warriors. Take no prisoners," I command.

"Yes, Alpha!"

I need to kill Harold before Warren gets a hold of him. If he has Harold's pack members and he's willing to return them, that will give Harold a reason to ally himself with Warren, and I don't need Warren to become any stronger than he already is.

I walk out of my office, howling the howl of attack, and then I leap and race to the front of my warriors, leading the charge to Brady's pack and the battle against Harold.

~ ~ ~

Noelle POV

I thought I would sleep well. I was exhausted and felt safe for the first time in a long time. But rather than being able to sleep, I'm tossing and turning.

Beta Charlie, or Charlie as he wants me to call him, gave me a room on his floor, just like Luna Yara said he would. I showered, and he gave me one of his t-shirts, which smells deliciously of him. But it's not enough. My wolf, Beatrix, can't get settled.

'I want to be closer to him,' she whines.

'I know, Bea, but what am I supposed to do? Knock on his door and ask if I can sleep with him so you'll settle down?'

'Yes!'

'Bea, come on. We barely know him.'

'He's our mate, Noelle. He loves us. He wants us close, too. I'm guessing his wolf won't let him sleep either,' she says, trying to encourage me to go to him.

'Fine. I'll go listen at his door. If it sounds like he's sleeping, though ...'

'He won't' be. I'm sure of it,' she says excitedly.

I get up, walking softly as I get to the door and open it as quietly as I can. Then I walk down the hall, and I'm just about to put my ear to the door when the door opens.

"Are you okay? Is everything okay? Did you need something?" Charlie asks me. He's only wearing a pair of cotton shorts, and his incredible physique is on display for me. He has a lot of scars on his body, but that only means that he's a strong and powerful fighter with a strong wolf who heals him. I feel Beatrix begin purring in my mind.

"I ... I couldn't sleep," I stutter, looking down.

"Is your wolf keeping you up?" he asks me. I look up at his smiling face. He shrugs. "Gregor wouldn't let me sleep either. Do you want to come in?"

I nod, and he steps back. When I step into the room, he closes the door.

"I'm not having sex with you," I blurt out.

He doesn't bother trying to hide his smile. "Good, because I'm exhausted, and I wouldn't want you trying to keep me up by begging for my body."

It's so utterly ridiculous that I burst out laughing.

"Come on. We both need sleep and now, maybe our wolves will let us sleep."

He helps me into his bed, then goes around crawling in behind me. When he lays down, he tugs me against him, wrapping his body around mine in a cocoon of warmth and safety.

"For the record," he murmurs in my ear. "When I do make love to you, it won't be when I'm tired. It will be when I have the time and energy to worship this body properly, finding every little spot that makes you moan and whimper before sliding inside you and making you mine forever."

As tired as I am, his words send heat straight to my core. I hear him sniffing the air, and I know he can smell my arousal.

"Good, I'm glad we agree. Now get some sleep," he says. I'm not sure which of us falls asleep the fastest.

Chapter 41: New Life
Warren

Once again, I wake with the scent of cinnamon and nutmeg in my nose and a raging hard-on pressed against the soft, fleshy backside of my mate.

In my half-asleep state, I check the time and see that it's mid-afternoon. We've slept through the day once again.

I begin to rub my hands up and down her bare thigh, moving to her flat stomach and up to her breasts. I knew I'd love the feel of her soft body. She fits against me perfectly, and something about her softness feels like silk sliding over my rough and scarred skin.

I smile as her body begins to respond to me in her sleep. Her backside presses against me, making my hard length wedge between her butt cheeks. I grit my teeth against my desperate desire to slide inside her. I want us to have our time, our moment, and soon, but I know now isn't that time. I need to call Alpha Harold and let him know I have his pack members. Maybe then he'll stop attacking me.

But that can wait. Right now, I want to wake my mate up in a pleasurable way. I cup her breast, gently teasing her nipple into a hard peak before moving to the next one. She begins to moan softly, and I press my lips against her shoulder.

"Warren," she breathes my name with a moan, and it's the sexiest fucking thing I've ever heard. Her hand slides over my hip, and she pulls me tighter against her.

"Did you need something, little mate?" I whisper in her ear.

She nods, her hand gripping my ass cheek tightly.

"I know what you need, but we don't have time for that right now. I'm hoping later we can finally finish what we've started, but for now, let me ease that ache you have."

She nods again, and I lean back, nudging her to lie on her back. When she does, she looks up at me with her soft green eyes.

I look down at her body, following my hands as they caress her soft, unscarred skin. When my hand gets to the apex of her thighs, I look back up at her. "Open your legs for me. Let me touch you."

She does, spreading her legs for me so I can slide my fingers through her soaking-wet heat.

I growl as my cock twitches at the feel of her. She feels and smells even better than I imagined.

"I want to touch you, too," her sweet voice says.

I shift my body, giving her access to my aching cock. Her hand wraps around me, and this time, it's me who moans.

I lean in, taking her mouth in a gentle kiss as I start moving my fingers in circles around her clit. When she begins to moan, I lift my head, watching as I slide a finger inside her. Her mouth drops open, and her back arches as I stroke her tight pussy slowly, letting her get use to the feel of my finger inside her.

Her grip on my hard length tightens as she moans.

"Your hand feels really good, baby," I tell her.

"So, does yours," she says breathily.

I lean in, sucking her nipple into my mouth, licking and sucking until I feel her inner walls beginning to flutter around my finger. I pull off of her, watching her again as I slide a second finger into her wet heat.

Her eyes flash open, and she looks at me. Her green eyes are almost completely grey now and getting darker with her desire. I'm sure my own eyes are nearly black. Her hand feels so good that it's all I can do not to come before I bring her over the edge. If her hand feels this good, I can only imagine what it will feel like to finally be inside her. But she's so fucking tight that I'll need to be careful so I don't tear her.

"I love watching how good I make you feel. Are you going to come on my fingers, beautiful?" I ask.

"Yes," she gasps as I press the heel of my hand against her clit. "Yes!" she says more loudly.

"Good. I'm going to come, too," I say, watching as her eyes roll back and her hand begins stroking me faster. I take her hint and begin moving my fingers in and out of her more quickly, gently stretching her as I do.

When I feel her getting close, I lean in, nipping her chin. "Open your eyes, Yara. I want to see you come undone for me," I growl, right on the cusp of my own orgasm.

She opens her eyes, looking at me as she begins whimpering. When I feel her inner walls start to flutter, I hook my fingers, stroking her G-spot and pushing her body over the edge. She cries out as her back arches, but I continue to stroke her, pushing her through her orgasm just as mine rips through me, my body jerking as my cock spits cum all over her side and onto her stomach.

Slowly, we bring each other back down. When her body finally relaxes and her hand slides off my cock, I pull my fingers from her pussy and bring them to my mouth, watching her as I lick them clean.

"Mmm, you taste like everything that is delicious about fall."

I see the mischievous flash in her eyes before she takes a finger and swipes it through the cum on her stomach before sucking her finger into her mouth. I'm rock hard again in an instant.

"Mmm, you taste like everything that is delicious in the forest."

I growl as I take her mouth in a possessive, dominant kiss. Fuck, this woman is incredible. I want to take her again, but I know we both have work, so I pull away and smile down at her.

"Feel better?" I ask her.

"Yes. You?"

"For now. I will feel much better once I have my mark on your neck. But I refuse to rush that. I'll keep you safe until we have more time. Come on, I'm sure you have just as much work as I do," I say, crawling out of bed and offering her my hand.

"Umm," she reaches over and grabs the sheet, pulling it over her body.

I smile, fighting hard not to laugh. I walk over to where she's sitting on the edge of the bed, not looking at me. I can already see the blush darkening on her cheeks.

I lean in, running my nose over her jawbone to her ear. "I've already seen you naked. My fingers were just inside you. My cock was in your hand. And now, my cum is all over you. I don't think you need to be embarrassed about being naked in front of me anymore."

I can feel the heat coming off her cheeks, but I stand back, putting my hand out to her, challenging her to be daring and confident. I watch as she fights with herself before practically throwing the sheet off and taking my hand, standing in front of me, and lifting her chin.

"You're fucking beautiful," I say, kissing her lightly before leading her into the bathroom.

"We're showering together?" she squeaks.

"Yara, I already bathed you once. Maybe you were half asleep then, too, but we've basically already done this. It's not new."

"It's new to me," she mumbles.

Once again, I hold out my hand as I stand in the shower, watching her debate with herself before finally accepting that this is our new life together.

When she gets in, I push her under the water, helping her to rinse out her hair before grabbing the shampoo and beginning to massage it into her hair.

"So what do you have today?" I ask her.

When she doesn't answer, I look down and see her looking at my scarred chest. Now, it's my turn to be embarrassed.

"I know my body is scarred and ugly ..."

"No, it's not," she says, her fingers beginning to trace the scars across my chest, arms and stomach. "It's a testament to how strong you are, what an incredible fighter you are. You must think I'm weak. I barely have any scars on my body, and none from battle," she says, looking up at me.

"I already told you I love your body. I love how soft you feel against my hard, rough skin. I worry that you'll find my skin too abrasive against yours." I lean down, making sure my eyes are at her level. "And you are anything but weak, Yara. Your strengths are different than mine, but that's what makes us great together."

"I don't find your skin abrasive. It's invigorating. It makes me feel alive in a way I've never felt before," she says, making me smile.

"And your skin feels like silk flowing over my skin, soft and gentle, soothing my rough edges. So, you see, we're perfect together."

I push her head under the water, rinsing it out before taking her face in my hands. "See, we're made for each other," I say before leaning in to kiss her softly but firmly, letting her know I mean what I'm saying.

"I guess so," she says when I pull away. She grabs the soap and continues to run her hands over my body.

"Now, what did you have going on today?" I ask her again.

"I need to check in on Piper, Laney, and the other warrior. Do we know anything about him?" she asks.

"No, not yet. I can ask Laney if he's one that we should keep."

"What about you? What is Alpha Warren doing today?" she asks me, smiling up at me. I lean down and kiss her nose.

"I need to call Alpha Harold. I need to let him know that I have his pack members and see if he is willing to take them back. If he is, we need to figure out a way to do that where both of us feel safe that the other won't attack."

"Sounds like both of us have a busy day ahead of us. Are we expecting an attack?"

"I'm always prepared for one, but hopefully, my call to Alpha Harold will stop any attack from him. Thomas is dead, Brady may or may not be ready to attack again, but Quinton is still out there, and so is Simon."

When we step out of the shower, we get dried off and start getting dressed for the day. I stop, looking at my mate, and I realize that this really is our new life together and I'm loving every second of it.

Chapter 42: The Injured

Yara

Before we go our separate ways, Warren kisses me, really kisses me, in front of the entire pack. I don't know what it looked like, but it sure felt like a movie kiss.

"If we're attacked, I'll send warriors to protect the hospital. You just worry about doing what you do best," he says, his eyes soft as they look at me.

"Then you do what you do best, Alpha. Fight hard and stay strong."

"With you by my side, how can I not stay strong," he says, leaning in to kiss me again.

When I turn, I see Bradley, Savannah, and Noelle all waiting for me. Noelle isn't wearing a mate mark, but she smells strongly of Charlie. I see her look past me, trying to hide her smile. When I turn, I see Charlie winking at her.

"Morning, Luna," he says as if he wasn't just flirting with his mate.

"Morning, Beta," I say, turning back to the group.

"Okay, I guess you three are with me. Did Anna get some sleep?" I ask Savannah.

"She, Katie, and Erica all took shifts today so they could get some sleep, and Erica could spend some time with her pup."

"Who's on right now?" I ask as we walk to the pack hospital.

"I believe Katie is waiting for Anna to come and relieve her."

"We'll relieve her. The three of us got some sleep. Let them rest," I say, then turn to Noelle. "You got some sleep, right?"

"Yes, Luna," she says, blushing.

"How about you, Luna? Did you get any sleep?" Bradley asks, his tone teasing. When I look, I see him trying to hide a smile. I know, even with the shower, that Warren's scent is all over me.

"I did. Thank you very much for your concern, Bradley. How about you? Did you get any sleep?"

"I get energized in other ways, Luna," he says, giving me a full-on smile.

I shake my head, and I'm about to ask Savannah if she got enough sleep when I see her blushing.

"Savannah?"

"I slept," she says much too quickly. Interesting.

When we walk in, I see Katie sitting in a chair in the waiting room, rubbing her stomach.

"Katie?" I ask, walking up to her.

"Oh, Luna. How did you sleep?" she asks me.

"Good. How are you?" I ask, beginning to do a visual assessment of her.

"This little one is being very problematic today," she says.

"How far along are you?" I ask her.

"Oh, I'm still a couple of weeks out, Luna. I'm sure these are just Braxton-Hicks contractions," she says.

"Savannah ..." I begin.

"Come on, Katie. Better to be safe than sorry. Let's get you ready for our Luna to check you out," she says.

"Noelle, you're with me," I say to her, turning to Bradley, who is watching Savannah and Katie.

"Should I call her mate?" he asks me.

"Not yet. I'll let you know if that changes," I tell him, and Noelle and I move to check on Piper first.

When we walk in, I see that she's awake.

"Hey, Piper. This is Noelle. She came from Thomas' pack and wants to be a nurse or a doctor," I say, turning to look at her. "We never really talked about it."

"I'd really like to be a doctor," she says.

"Perfect. We need more of those," I say, turning back to Piper.

As I begin to check Piper, I tell Noelle what happened to her.

"Wow. You saved her life?" she asks.

I look at Piper. "I did, but I'm hoping I saved her voice box, too."

"How's your wolf, Piper? Answer in the mind link."

'I'm good, Luna,' I hear her wolf say.

"Good, that's good," I say out loud so Noelle can participate in the conversation.

"Does it still hurt to swallow?" I ask.

Piper nods, but she also answers in the mind link. "It does, but not as much."

"Not as much, that's good," I say for Noelle's benefit.

"I'm going to keep you on soft food," I say, and Piper silently groans.

"I know it's gross, but I said soft food, not fluids. Let's see how your throat does. It needs to work to be able to swallow. Have your wolf practice that and work to heal those muscles in your throat. Once the pain is gone and you can swallow, we'll see about talking. Is there anything else you need?"

'Friends?' she asks in the mind link.

I laugh. "Yes, you can have visitors. But no speaking, and if you get tired, rest."

'Yes, Luna.'

We leave Piper and head to Laney's room. When we walk in, I'm surprised to see Haynes sleeping in a chair, his head on the bed beside Laney and her hand laying half on his head, half on his shoulder.

"Oh," Noelle says.

"Do they know each other?" I ask quietly.

Noelle doesn't look away from her sister. "No, I don't think so. But my sister has never shown any affection to a man in our pack. I think ..."

"You think both of you found your mates in this pack?" I ask her as Laney's eyes open and Haynes begins to shift.

"How are you feeling, Laney?" I ask her, watching as Haynes' head pops up.

"Oh, I fell asleep."

"So you did," I say, walking up to look at Laney's leg.

"How is Haise feeling this morning?" I ask, referring to Laney's wolf.

"I'm good, Luna," Haise says as I pull off the bandage.

"Whoa," Noelle says, seeing that the incision has already healed. I begin to press gently on the areas that were broken.

"Any pain?" I ask her.

"Just tenderness, Luna."

"You're healing nicely, Laney. I can give you some crutches so you don't have to stay here, but you can't fight until I clear it," I tell her.

She glances at Haynes. "I don't have anywhere to stay, Luna. So, if it's okay with you ..."

"We'll find you a room, Laney. It'll be more comfortable than staying here," Haynes says.

"Haynes is right, and he'd know. Besides, spending time with your mate will strengthen your wolf faster and, therefore, heal you faster," I say, making both of their eyes go wide.

"I didn't ... we didn't ..." Laney begins.

"Our Luna is very intuitive, Laney. I'm not surprised that she figured it out."

"You sleeping in here was a pretty big clue," I tell him. "Check with Warren and see what rooms we have available unless you're ready to share a room," I say, turning and heading out. I'll let them figure out their mate bond between them.

"Noelle," I call as she stands there, staring at her sister.

"Yes, Luna."

"I need to know about this next guy. He came from Thomas' pack," I say.

"Who?" Laney asks, sitting up, instantly alert.

"I don't know, that's why I need Noelle."

"Here, I'll go with you," she says.

I point my finger at her. "Stay where you are. You are not fit or cleared to fight if that's what's needed."

"I'll come with you, Luna," Haynes says, standing and nodding at Laney.

"Bradley's coming, too. Warren wants two in the room with me, just in case," I say, stepping out and calling out to Bradley.

"Luna. Katie is in a bed. Savannah says she's in labor."

"Looks like another fun day at the hospital. Did you tell her mate?"

"I did. He's on his way."

"You and Haynes are with me," I say, walking toward the next door where the warrior is strapped to the bed.

"Travis!" Noelle says, rushing to the bed.

"Noelle?" he asks, groggily. "Where am I?"

"You know him?" I ask her, stepping up. Bradley and Haynes are a step behind me.

"He's a good guy, Luna. He wasn't part of Thomas' crew."

Travis hisses at Noelle. "Alpha Thomas, Noelle," he corrects her.

"He's dead, Travis. Alpha Warren's pack killed him."

He looks back at me. "So, I'm a rogue?"

"That depends on you. Noelle says you're one of the good ones, so my mate will want to talk to you."

"Your mate?"

"She's the Luna, but she's also a doctor, Travis. She's the one that saved your life," Noelle says to him.

"Can I get out of these restraints?" he asks me.

"That will be up to Warren," I say, looking over his injuries. "How is your wolf, Travis?"

He's quiet for a moment, and when I look up at him, I notice his lips are pressed tightly together. "Silent."

I nod. "I'm not surprised. You lost a lot of blood. You're probably only alive because of your wolf. We'll get you healed up and help your wolf get stronger."

"Wolves don't come back when they go silent," he says, looking away.

"They do in this pack," Haynes says to him. "If you're a good guy and Alpha Warren agrees, then our Luna here will have you and your wolf up and fighting in no time."

"So, it's true? You're the lady doctor that's making Alpha Warren's pack stronger?" he asks me.

"What an interesting question, warrior. One that I would be very interested in knowing more about," Warren says, walking in. "Your lifespan very much depends on whether you're willing to tell me everything you know about the plans of the other Alphas to come after my mate or not."

Travis looks from Warren to me and back again.

"I'll tell you everything you want to know."

"Good," Warren says, looking at me. "When you're done here, we need to talk."

Chapter 43: Alpha Harold

Warren

As soon as I kissed Yara goodbye, I'd gone to my office and called Alpha Harold. When I didn't get an answer, I left a message.

'Alpha Harold, this is Alpha Warren. I have something important to discuss with you. Please call me at your earliest convenience.'

While I'd waited for a return call, I'd tuned in to Yara, so I knew about Haynes and Laney's mate bond. I'd just about given up hearing back from the older Alpha when my phone rang. When I saw it was him, I answered immediately.

"Alpha Warren."

"Alpha Warren, this is Alpha Harold. What do you want?" he growls into the phone. He sounds exhausted and worn out. This is why Alphas have pups young. Being an Alpha, especially during times of war like we're in, takes a heavy toll on you.

"Alpha Harold, I wasn't sure you'd heard that I attacked Alpha Thomas' pack and killed him and most of his warriors."

"Calling me to let me know you're planning to attack me next?" he growls.

"No. On the contrary, my understanding is that you are not part of the alliance that Quinton, Brady, and Thomas have put together."

"What if I'm not? You think that makes me weak? Come see how weak I am, Alpha Warren. I may be older than you, but I have a lot of fight left in me."

"I have no doubt of that, and I have no interest in fighting you, Alpha Harold. It's always been you who has attacked me, not the other way around," I say. He goes quiet for a moment, and I hear him sigh heavily.

"What do you want, Alpha Warren?" Rather than being angry, he sounds exhausted.

"When I attacked Alpha Thomas, there were omegas, young mothers, pups ..." he begins growling again. "I don't kill the weak," I growl at him. "So, stop verbally fighting me and listen to what I have to say."

"Fine," he says.

"I brought them to my pack. Many of them are in bad shape. They were forced into mate bonds, and while they may not be healthy, they've survived the death of their mates who forced their mark on them."

"How many?" he asks me.

"I don't have an exact count, but I'd say twenty to thirty. They told me they were from your pack, and they want to come home, Alpha Harold."

I hear him sit back in his chair, and it's quiet for a moment. I let him think it through. I know I'd need to if the roles were reversed.

"I want to speak with them," he says.

"I can't do that. They're all in my pack hospital and being treated at the moment. But I can tell you that I spoke to a woman named Tanya, and there was another one, Farrah, who had to go into emergency surgery."

"They survived?" he asks, and there's a new excitement in his voice.

"They were afraid that you wouldn't consider them part of your pack any longer. I told them that if you were the kind of Alpha they told me you were, you'd always consider them part of your pack."

"Of course they're part of my pack. I never renounced them."

"And they didn't renounce you. From what they said, Alpha Thomas forced them to accept him as their Alpha."

"I'm glad that fucking prick is dead," he growls.

"As am I," I say.

"What do you propose, Alpha Warren."

"You could bring warriors and come get your pack members ..." I begin.

"I can't," he says and sighs again. "I'm putting my pack at risk by telling you this, but if you really do have my pack members, I want them back. We've just returned from attacking Alpha Brady. Him and his fucking booby traps ..."

Now it's my turn to sit back. "So, your pack is in need of medical attention," I say, my eyes drifting in the direction of the pack hospital.

"And I have no doctor."

I think it through for a moment. "I could bring them to you. They mostly need rest and to rebuild their strength. Some have injuries, but we'll treat them before we bring them back to you. I would need your assurance that you wouldn't attack me ..."

He scoffs. "You underestimate how weakened my pack is right now."

I make a split-second decision. I'll still have to talk to Yara about it, but I'm pretty sure I know what she'll want to do.

"I'll make a deal with you, Alpha. You stop attacking my pack, recognize that we have the same enemies in Quinton and Brady, and I'll bring my doctor to look over your pack."

"Are you going to leave her here? We need someone full-time."

"No, I'm not leaving her there. She's my mate, but I haven't had a chance to mark her yet. And I'll warn you right now, if you or anyone in your pack tries to hurt her, I won't hesitate to kill you and them."

"Your mate is a doctor? The Moon Goddess has blessed you, hasn't she, Alpha?"

"She's not just a doctor; she's the best fucking doctor I've ever seen. She'll get your pack up and running again. You'll be amazed at what she can do in a short period of time."

"When can I expect you? You'll need to be careful. I would anticipate that Brady will be returning the attack soon."

"I'm not so sure about that. He would have been injured from his recent attack on me," I tell him.

"Ahh, so that's why so many of us escaped. Good to know."

"But watch out for Quinton. He's been too quiet lately. Thomas' death may have thrown him for a loop, but he'll be planning some sort of revenge on me definitely, and now you possibly for attacking Brady. Let me talk to my mate, and I'll let you know when to expect us."

"Alright, and Alpha Warren?"

"Yeah?"

"Thank you. I didn't expect to ever see those pack members again. Today is a good day."

"It can only get better from here for you, Alpha Harold, especially if we start working together."

"It sounds like it," he says and when I hang up, I get a mind link from Bradley that the warrior from Thomas' pack is awake.

I hop up and begin making my way to the hospital, connecting to Yara's mind again so I can hear what's going on. It definitely sounds like Noelle trusts this guy, which goes a long way towards me trusting him. I still haven't had a chance to interview Laney fully, but now maybe I can get intel from both of them.

When I let Yara know I need to speak with her, she tells me she wants to check on Farrah first, and then we can talk. While she does, I take the time to talk to Travis, but I don't learn much more than I already did. Basically, the other Alphas have noticed our pack's strength, and now they want my mate not only to increase the strength of their pack but also to weaken me so they can take me down. Not going to happen.

When she's done, I pull Yara into a hug and just hold her for a moment. It'll be another night that I won't be able to mark her. If I wasn't worried about Harold getting attacked, I'd hold off until tomorrow morning, but he's definitely at risk, and I don't want to lose the only potential ally that I have.

"I talked to Alpha Harold. He's willing to take his pack members back, but his pack is weak. He doesn't have a doctor," I tell her.

She looks up at me, and I already know what she's going to say. "I could help them."

"I know. And I was pretty sure that you'd want to help them, so I offered to let you come with me."

I stroke my fingers down her cheek. "I hate that everything seems to be getting in the way of me putting my mark on you," I say, letting my fingers run over her marking spot. I smile as she shivers. "Maybe after this, we can finally have some time to complete our bond. Would you like that?"

She slides her hands up my chest and around my neck. "You think you can handle me for the rest of your life?" she asks, leaning into me.

I wrap my arms around her waist, holding her against me. "I don't think I'd want to live this life without you in it."

Her grey-green eyes are warm and loving, and I feel something close to contentment.

"I don't think I want to live this life without you in it either," she says, making my heart soar.

"Good, then we're in agreement. I like it when we're in agreement. Why don't you go shower and get changed while I make arrangements for warriors and vans to take the patients with us. You need an assistant. Who do you want to bring with us?"

She looks around, assessing. "If it's as bad as you think it is, I need Savannah, but that leaves us with mostly nurses here."

"We'll make it work. If we're attacked, we'll be rushing home anyway," I tell her.

I lean in and kiss her, savoring her taste and her cinnamon and nutmeg scent as it increases in the air around us. I take my time, needing and wanting to make this woman mine in so many ways. I love that she surrenders to the kiss, giving me everything that I want from her.

It's much, much too soon when I finally pull back. "Come on, I'll walk you to the packhouse. I need to start collecting warriors."

"Are you bringing Charlie with us?" she asks.

"No, I need him here to protect the pack. Plus, he hasn't marked his mate yet either, so he'd be antsy to leave her."

When we get to the packhouse, I send her upstairs while I meet with Charlie and the warriors I want to take with me.

"WARREN!" my mate yells. Gone is the sweet woman from a few moments ago. In her place is an aggravated mate.

I smile, knowing exactly what she found when she got to our bedroom.

"Where is he?" she demands of someone in the kitchen.

"In the dining hall, Luna," the omega says.

"Alpha, what did you do?" one of the warriors asks me. The last time I did something stupid, they stood up for Yara. I have no doubt that they would again, but this time, I wasn't stupid.

"Nothing bad," I say, unable to stop the huge smile on my face as I wait for her to enter the dining hall. Everyone has gone quiet, watching to see what happens.

When she walks in, her eyes zero in on me.

"Did you need something, baby?" I ask sweetly, watching her eyes narrow.

"YOU!" she says, pointing at me and stomping over to me. "What did you do?"

"What, baby? You said you liked flowers," I say, pulling her against me when she's close enough.

"I said I liked flowers! Not that I wanted you to make our bedroom into a greenhouse!"

I love that she called it OUR bedroom.

"I wasn't able to get you flowers for a couple of days, so I wanted to make it up to you," I say, still smiling.

She huffs. "Warren, what am I supposed to do with all those flowers?"

"Share them with the pack. I'm sure it will make things look much brighter around here."

"Utterly ridiculous," she murmurs.

I take her chin and tilt it up to look at me. "What was that?"

"I said, you're utterly ridiculous!"

I lean in closer to her. "What I am is utterly and ridiculously in love with you," I say before taking her mouth in a passionate, possessive kiss.

Chapter 44: Franklin
Yara

I wasn't joking when I called our bedroom a greenhouse. When I opened the door, I could barely take a step inside. There are flowers EVERYWHERE! Vases of flowers, potted flowering plants, on every surface, covering the floor, every damn where!

Warren, not surprisingly, was smug about it. But then he had to tell me he loved me and kiss me in a way that had my entire body responding to him. I completely forgot that we were right in the middle of the pack dining hall, right in the middle of dinnertime, until he pulled back, that smug look still on his face.

"Did you want me to get some warriors to help you move them out?" he asks.

Then I looked around and realized that the entire pack was watching us. My skin heats to an uncomfortable temperature, and Warren leans in, running his nose over my blush and kissing my cheek softly.

"Yes," I grumble.

"What exactly are you saying yes to," he murmurs as he moves to kiss my neck.

"Not that! Not here! Not now!" I say, jumping back.

His eyes are dark, and he doesn't seem to care that his entire pack is watching our interaction and that he's being extremely seductive with me. His warm eyes twinkle as he smiles a very sexy smile at me.

217

"Later then," he says, his voice still soft. My mouth is dry, so I can only nod at him, which makes that damn sexy smile get even bigger.

He steps up to me, kissing my forehead. "Come on, let's go make some space in our bedroom."

He wraps an arm around me, leading me out of the dining hall and gesturing for others to join us. Charlie falls into step behind us, as do several others.

"I've never known a woman to complain about getting flowers, Luna," he says.

"Have you known many women that have gotten flowers, Beta?" I ask him. I wouldn't be surprised if he was part of this.

"No, but I'm taking notes, so I know what to do and what not to do with Noelle," he says.

When we get to our room, Charlie changes his tune. He whistles low, as do several of the other warriors. "That might have been a little excessive, Alpha," he says, stepping in and looking around.

"Nothing is ever too much for my mate. I'm just glad they were finally delivered," Warren says proudly.

I start directing them, telling them which ones I want to be taken downstairs. It takes about thirty minutes with a steady flow of warriors that increases as the others go downstairs and probably tell them that they need help.

Eventually, I'm left with four vases of flowers, which still seems excessive, but it's a lot better than it was before. Two of them are vases of wildflowers, which reminds me of the first group of flowers that Warren got me.

"Go get showered. I'll call Alpha Harold and let him know we're on our way," Warren says.

When I get back downstairs, I can see that the plants have been set around the inside and outside of the packhouse.

"Ready?" Warren asks, looking around at the warriors assembling to go with us, back in work mode. I take a moment, walking up to him, watching him jolt when he realizes that my entire focus is on him.

"What?" he asks softly.

"You did good, Alpha," I say, and he stops, looking around as if he's just now paying attention to the plants all over the packhouse.

"It is nice, isn't it?" he asks, wrapping his arms around me and kissing the top of my head as we take a moment to enjoy the difference that the plants make in our packhouse. The whole packhouse feels warmer and more inviting.

"It is nice," I agree before taking a deep breath and stepping back. "Okay, let's go fix Alpha Harold and his pack," I say.

He takes my hand and leads me to a van, letting me get in before him before stepping in to sit beside me. I notice that he's by the door, ready to be the first in the fight if necessary.

"Alpha Harold said they weren't currently under attack, and I hope it stays that way. But if not, we need to be prepared to fight," he tells the warriors in the van.

We're bringing two vans, partly because Warren wanted to bring extra warriors, just in case there's a fight, but also because we don't know what medical supplies Alpha Harold's pack will have. Without a doctor, they're probably just getting by with the basics, and if they're suffering from some of the injuries from Alpha Brady's booby traps, then they'll need more than bandages and stitches, so we're bringing a bunch of medical supplies with us, too.

As we pull up to the gates at the border, Warren calls Alpha Harold.

"Alpha Harold, we've just arrived at your gates," he says. I can feel the tension in the van as Warren and the warriors prepare for a battle, in case this is a trap.

The guard waves us through, but the tension in the air only intensifies as the warriors roll down the windows and everyone's noses go up in the air.

"Oh, they're a mess," I murmur, closing my eyes and smelling infection from every direction.

"Why do you say that?" Warren asks me.

"What?" I ask, then realize I've spoken out loud again. "I can smell the infection. It's everywhere."

That seems to make Warren relax, and when we pull up to the packhouse, Warren jumps out and greets Alpha Harold.

"I've got most of my warriors at the pack hospital. Did you want to start there?" he asks. I start to step out of the van, smelling infection on the Alpha now, too, but another man comes rushing out of the packhouse, his nose in the air.

Instantly, Warren is in front of me, his claws out, ready to fight.

"Franklin! What are you doing?" Harold asks.

"Where is she?" he growls, his nose still sniffing the air. I hear the door to the other van open, and I turn to see Savannah stepping out, her eyes wide.

Franklin begins purring loudly. "Mate!"

Savannah looks at me, then back at the man. "Mate."

Warren stands up, relaxing but leaving his claws out. Harold scrubs his hands down his face. The man looks absolutely exhausted.

"Young lady, what is your name?" Harold asks Savannah.

"Savannah, Alpha."

"Savannah, this is my Beta, Franklin. Franklin, this is Savannah, who, I'm assuming, is here to assist with our medical needs?" Harold asks, looking at Warren.

"That is correct. After Yara, she's our best medical practitioner."

Something passes between the two of them that I don't quite understand. I'm guessing it has to do with one of them losing an important person in their pack, either a Beta or a medical person, if these two agree to become mates.

"I'm sure the two of you would like to get to know each other, but right now, Alpha Warren has generously brought his team here to help us, Franklin. You need to set this aside for now."

Franklin looks at his Alpha incredulously, as if the last thing he wants to do is wait to mark his mate.

"I do need to help Luna Yara," Savannah says, but I can feel her own resistance at having to put her mate bond on hold.

"Of course. I can show you to the pack hospital," Beta Franklin says, walking down the stairs and straight to Savannah. I'm not sure if they both expected it or if it just happened, but he doesn't stop until his mouth is on hers and her arms are wrapped around him.

Alpha Harold sighs. "Come on, I'll take you," he says.

As we start to follow him, the warriors getting our medical supplies out of the back, I turn.

"Savannah, I'm going to need you. I'm sorry," I say to her.

She pulls back, looking shocked that she got lost in the mate bond. I'm not. I know what it feels like when Warren kisses me.

"I'm sorry, Luna. I'm coming."

"Sorry, Alpha," Franklin says, going to help with the supplies, then taking Savannah's hand as we walk.

"Alpha, why don't you tell me about some of these injuries, starting with your own," I say.

He turns and looks at me. "What makes you think that I'm injured?"

"I can smell the infection on you," I tell him.

"I'm fine. My warriors are in worse shape than I am."

"That may be, but the body can't live without the head. The Alpha is the head of the pack, so your health is just as important as theirs."

He turns, looking from me to Warren, who shrugs.

"If I were you, Alpha, I'd plan to give Yara complete control over the hospital. It's what I've done in my pack, and we're thriving because of it."

"Well, I'm guessing that your pack wasn't in the terrible shape that mine's in," he says.

"I was caught in a bear trap just over a week ago," Warren tells him. Alpha Harold stops, turning to look at Warren's legs.

"How are you walking?"

"Yara. She's that good. Trust me, you and your warriors will be thankful that you did."

He looks at me again, then nods before we start walking again.

"So, where is your infection, Alpha?" I ask, although I'm already pretty sure I know. He's limping. He's trying to hide it, but it looks like it's on his right side.

"Hip," he says simply.

"Savannah and I will triage your injured, and I'll treat them according to the severity and significance of the wound. In Warren's pack, I've also put warriors on rest when their wolves were silent. I know it makes things a bit rough for a few days, but without their wolves, they can't fight, and you'll lose good warriors. They'll be stronger faster if you agree to let me put them on the injured reserve list," I tell him.

He looks at Warren. "This is why I say she's in charge of the hospital. What she says goes, and she hasn't let me down yet."

"And I never will," I say to him as we walk in.

"No doubt about that," he says, smiling at me.

As soon as we walk in, my smile fades. This pack is a mess.

Chapter 45: Taking Charge
Warren

Even with his 'honesty', Alpha Harold severely understated the state of his pack. My pack was in bad shape, his is on the verge of dying out. I realize immediately that it will take Yara days to care for everyone here.

"What can I do?" I ask her, knowing that she needs more than just Savannah. I step up behind her, putting my hands on her hips and pushing my energy into her. I can feel how overwhelmed she is, and knowing that she's the only doctor here, the majority of this will fall onto her.

"Do you have omegas who can sew?" she asks Alpha Harold.

"Yes," he says.

"Get them here," I say to him, looking around.

"You two start triaging. I'll start laying these warriors out for you," I say to Yara, then turn to Harold, waiting for him to finish contacting his omegas. "I would suggest that you let your pack know that what Yara says goes. Otherwise, she's going to waste valuable time arguing with your warriors."

He makes the announcement, but I can see everyone looking at Yara warily. I stay close to her, assigning two warriors to her like I have at home. One of those is Bradley, who seems to have fallen into a rhythm with her.

"I need to get this one into surgery," Yara says.

"This one needs surgery, too, Luna," Savannah says.

Yara looks around again before focusing back on Harold. "Do you have anyone with any medical assistance training at all?"

He looks around. "Rebecca is the one that's been trying to keep us patched up."

"Rebecca, you're with me," she says, going over to check on the one that Savannah said needs surgery. "Savannah, I need you to stay out here. Triage and stabilize, and I'll send Rebecca to let you know when I'm ready for the next one."

She looks around. "I need a gurney," she calls out. One of our warriors grabs one, and then two lift the warrior onto the gurney.

"If you need help, Yara, let us know," I tell her. She nods, her mind already prepping for the surgery she's about to do.

"I do need some medical supplies. Can you get them laid out so I can send Rebecca out to get what I need?"

I assign two more warriors to begin prepping the medical supplies. When Yara walks into the hospital room, I look around at the room of people in various stages of injury, partial healing, infection, which I can smell now too, and overall despair. This pack knows that they are dying, but they've continued to fight.

"What about us?" one of the pack members from Thomas' pack says. I'd completely forgotten about them. They'd come in behind us, and between Franklin, Harold, and the hideous state of the pack, I hadn't given them a second thought, but they're the primary reason we're here.

I watch as Alpha Harold looks at the group, some of them sitting down because they're still not strong enough to stay standing.

"Look at you," he says, and the warriors in the room all begin murmuring. Harold walks over and begins hugging the women and the couple of men who are part of the group. They break down into tears, but I see several of his warriors get up to help get them settled.

"What can we do, Alpha?" one of my warriors asks me.

"Help me find gurneys and medical supplies. Do whatever Savannah needs help with," I say, assigning one of the warriors to stand with her and take her instructions.

"Alpha Warren, these are my omegas. You can put them to work," he says, gesturing for the four individuals who just walked in, one looks like he's going to throw up.

I remember how Yara was about someone throwing up, and I can't imagine adding that stench to the already sickening scent in this room, so I look at the person.

"If you're going to throw up, leave. We don't have time to do more cleanup than we already need to do."

The person turns and walks outside. I gesture for the other three to come over to me. "The three of you can sew?"

"Clothes," one says, her eyes as wide as saucers.

"I can help them, Alpha. Luna trained our omegas on me," one of my warriors says.

"Okay, do it. Once Savannah says they're ready for stitching, you three will stitch them up."

"Come on, let's get what we need," my warrior says.

When I look over, I see Alpha Harold holding a mini-Alpha ceremony with his pack members, bringing them all back into the pack. He's squatting in front of them, talking softly to them while they cry and accept him as their Alpha again. Beta Franklin is standing behind him, also encouraging the group and helping to calm them. I can see that his pack is still fighting even though they expect to die. They're doing it for him because they love their Alpha, and he's still fighting for them.

I see Rebecca rush out, look at the supplies, then rush back into the room, and a few moments later, she comes out again.

"Is anyone ready to stitch for us?" she asks.

"Come on, Little Lady. I'll show you how to do this," my warrior says to the omega. Her eyes go wide, but she nods.

When Rebecca sees the omega headed her way, she turns to Savannah. "Savannah, who's next?"

"This one," Savannah says, pointing to another unconscious warrior, barely turning away from the one she's looking at.

"I've got a gurney," one of my warriors says, and I walk over, helping to lift the warrior onto the gurney as Rebecca goes back over to the medical supplies and gets more of what she needs.

I take the gurney, pushing it into the room Rebecca tells me to, and I get the table set up just as Yara walks in. Her mind is completely focused on her work, and she's mumbling to herself about what she's doing and what a mess the pack is.

I walk up to her, kissing the top of her head. "I love you," I whisper before leaving her to her work.

"Love you, too," I hear her mumble in between all the other mumblings she's doing.

When I come back out, I see Franklin standing over Savannah. "What can I do to help?" he asks her.

She smiles up at him a moment before turning back to her work. "We need someone who can clean out the infection. Got anyone like that?" she asks.

"What do they need to do?" I ask her.

She stops, her hands not leaving the bloody body of the warrior she's checking over. She looks around and juts her chin at the medical table. "See those bottles of water with the little handles coming out of them?"

"Yeah," Franklin and I say together.

"Grab one of those and start washing out the infection. If you wash it out and it's bleeding underneath, let me know," she says, turning back and putting something that looks like a clamp on the arm of the warrior she's looking over.

We get into a rhythm of treating the warriors and cleaning out their wounds. The longer Yara is in surgery, the more warriors Savannah says can be stitched up.

Yara has finally taken her last unconscious warrior into surgery. Each time, I've taken the gurney in, kissed her, told her I loved her, and pushed some of my strength into her. But my mate never wavers. I know she'll crash when it's all done, but for now, she continues to push through, so the rest of us do, too.

Harold sent his returned pack members back to the packhouse to rest. Savannah tried to get some of the other warriors to go rest as well after they were stitched up, but they refused.

"I'll tell you what my Luna says to my warriors," I say, raising my voice so the entire room can hear me. "If you mess with her nurses, you'll answer to her. You may not know it yet, but you don't want that."

"No, you don't," one of my warriors confirms.

"She threatened to follow our Beta into the Moon Goddess' realm and drag sorry ass back down here," a second warrior says.

"Yep, and knowing her like we do, I think we all agree that she'll do it," another warrior says.

"And don't get us started on how she'll make your ears bleed if you disregard her instructions," yet another warrior pipes in, shaking his head.

I look up and see Alpha Harold watching my warriors talk about their Luna.

"Well, you heard them. Apparently, answering to Alpha Warren's Luna is worse than answering to me, so if you act like fools, I'm going to let her treat you like fools. Sounds like she doesn't play with fools."

"No, she doesn't," I say proudly.

I look around, realizing that everyone who had minor injuries has been treated and released. Savannah has started treating some of the lessor injuries and is helping to stitch up the more injured warriors, explaining what she's doing to the omegas while she does it. Franklin is watching her with a proud, possessive look that I'm very familiar with.

"Alpha Warren," Alpha Harold says, walking up.

"Alpha Harold. You know that you aren't excluded from being dressed down by mate, right?" I ask, noticing that he still hasn't been treated.

He nods, looking around. "I didn't know what to expect when you offered your assistance, but it wasn't this. I thank you, but I'm guessing you want something in return," he says.

I turn and look at him. "You're right, I do."

He presses his lips together. I'm not sure what he thinks I'm going to ask for, his pack maybe, but he's obviously willing to give me what I want for helping his pack members.

"What is it that you want, Alpha?" he asks quietly.

"I want an alliance, Alpha Harold, between you and me. I want the war between us to stop, and I want to know that we will help each other and support each other as allies going forward."

He turns, looking at me incredulously. "That's what you want?"

"That's what I want," I confirm.

"Where do I sign?"

Chapter 46: Harold's Secret

Yara

I have no idea how long I've been fixing broken bones, stitching up bleeding wounds, and generally putting these parts of people back together. This pack truly was a mess, and I steel myself as I walk out of the last surgery room for the rest of what's to come. I can feel the fatigue trying to push its way in, but I can't allow that. Not yet. Not until this pack is at least back to a place where they can try to heal.

"Yara," Warren says, and just his voice soothes something deep inside me. He wraps his arms around me, and I take a moment to just breathe in his scent, drawing from the strength that I know he's pushing into me.

When I step back, he lets me go. "Where's Savannah?" I ask him.

"She got everyone here stabilized, so I sent her to get some sleep and get to know her mate," he says, smirking.

"So ... no sleep then," I say.

"Probably not. Although, if he's a good mate, he'll recognize how exhausted she is and let her sleep."

"A good mate like you, you mean?" I say, smiling up at him. I know it's beyond frustrating for him that his mark isn't on my neck yet. I've actually started to get annoyed with it myself. I'm ready for this man to be mine. I realize that in a very short time, he's shown me that he's exactly the kind of man that I want to bind myself to for the rest of my life.

"Well, not everyone is as perfect as I am, but ..." he says, making me laugh, which I know was his plan.

"So, what ..." I begin and stop. I lift my nose in the air, smelling infection.

"I thought you said Savannah stabilized everyone?" I say, frowning as I step forward.

"Don't say I didn't warn you," Warren says, stepping back. I look at him, but he's not looking at me.

I turn, seeing Alpha Harold standing on the other side of the room. I begin sniffing and making my way toward him. I notice that all of my warriors take a step back, getting out of my way. The action doesn't go unnoticed by Alpha Harold, and his frown deepens as I get closer.

"Why the hell hasn't your infection been cleaned out, Alpha?" I demand.

"Because my pack needed to be treated, Luna," he says, aggravation tainting his tone.

I turn, making a point of looking around the room. At least half, maybe more, of the warriors have been sent away. Savannah did a good job.

"Which members of your pack are still taking precedence over your treatment, Alpha?" I ask, my own tone indicating my aggravation with him.

"They weren't released yet," he grumbles.

"They no longer smell like decaying flesh," I say, turning to one woman. "Except you. You'll be staying here overnight."

"What? No, Luna!" she cries.

I turn and look at Alpha Harold.

He presses his lips together. "I told you that you will follow Luna Yara's orders in this hospital, or you'll answer to her."

I frown, looking at Warren. 'Answer to me?' I ask him in the mind link.

'Our warriors were very clear about how ... insistent you are in getting them healthy,' he says, and I can see his lips twitching. I roll my eyes and turn back.

"Fine, Luna. What do you want me to do?"

"Sit tight. Since your Alpha is in agreement, I'm sure he'll be listening to my orders as well. Won't you, Alpha? Follow me," I say, giving him a fake smile and turning on my heel. I hear Warren snort, but no one gets in my way.

I'm wondering if there's a reason that Alpha Harold is hiding his wound. Maybe it's worse than others know, or it's gotten deeper than he wants others to realize, potentially making him look weak to the pack.

When I get to the room, I hold the door open for him, surprised when Warren comes up behind him.

"I'm not leaving you alone in a room with another Alpha, Yara. And since he is an Alpha, I'll give him the courtesy of being your guard instead of having Bradley in here," he says.

"It's your right hip, correct?" I ask him as I begin pulling out what I need to look over his wound and hopefully stitch it up.

"How did you know?" he asks, pulling off his shorts and getting on the table. I see him give Warren a look as if he's expecting him to attack him if I touch him.

"The way you were limping earlier," I say, turning to Warren.

"Arric," I say, waiting for Warren's wolf to push forward.

"Yes, little mate," he purrs at me. I point my finger at him.

"I have to touch Alpha Harold to see what's wrong with him and to heal him. No snarling, no growling, no attacking. Do you hear me?"

"If I'm a good wolf, do I get rewarded later?" he purrs seductively.

"Shameless wolf," I murmur.

"A wolf who loves you," he says, and Annika begins purring at him.

"Save it, you two," I grumble, turning back to the table.

"So, is that a yes, little mate? I need some encouragement to behave. He is an Alpha, after all, and you are unmarked," Arric continues.

I narrow my eyes at him. "Fine. But only if you behave."

"Oh, I promise, I can be a very good wolf."

When I turn back to Harold's hip, all the teasing leaves me.

What the hell! How long has this injury been like this? It looks like it started small and then grew over time, the infection spreading. Does he have no sense of self-preservation? Is he so arrogant that he thinks he could survive something like this? Doesn't he have a young son? You'd think he'd want to stay alive long enough to make sure his son can take over the pack.

"Easy, Alpha. She doesn't realize she's speaking out loud," Warren says. My head snaps up and I look from Warren to Harold, who looks furious.

231

"It's true, Alpha. She's been doing it ever since we started working on the warriors. After you get used to it, it's actually kind of funny to listen to," Rebecca says, smiling shyly before looking away.

Harold isn't convinced. He looks at me. "Yes, I have a son. He's twelve. I have no intention of dying. His mother is gone, and if I died today, someone else would challenge him and win the position of Alpha, I have no doubt. Perhaps I am arrogant, but I'm Alpha. It comes with the territory."

"Well, Alpha. Let me explain something to you," I say, flushing out some of the infection in his hip and washing away the dirt and grime. I hear Rebecca inhale sharply as she sees what I am smelling.

"Do you see these red areas?" I ask him.

"Yeah, they're just tender areas that haven't healed yet," he says, looking from Rebecca to me.

"Wrong. That's blood poisoning. You've had your infection so long that it's gotten into your bloodstream, which means it's traveling throughout your body, infecting your organs. Do you feel exhausted and run down all the time, Alpha?"

"Yeah, but we're always at war," he says, looking away from me.

"Rebecca, can you step out for a minute, please?" I say, watching Alpha Harold. He turns and looks at me, and I see his lips press together. He knows that I know.

Rebecca looks between us and then moves to step out. "Rebecca, can you check the warriors who have been stitched up. If they look good, they can go."

"Yes, Luna."

When she's gone, I look back at Harold.

"How's your wolf, Alpha?"

He growls. "He's fine."

"I'd like to hear him say that," I tell him.

He refuses to look at me. "I can shift," he insists.

"That doesn't mean your wolf isn't dying, Alpha. And once your wolf can no longer keep this infection at bay, you'll die, too, leaving your young son alone in this world. Is that really what you want?" I ask him gently.

"Of course not," he says, and I can feel his embarrassment at what he perceives as weakness.

"Then, let's get you healthy, and in the future, don't let your infection get this bad," I say gently.

I look at Warren. "Can you bring me the bag of antibiotics, please?"

"Absolutely," he says, stepping out.

"I didn't have a choice. We don't have someone like you around here," Harold says quietly to me.

"You didn't before, but you'll have Savannah now, I'm sure. She's wonderful. But don't give her a hard time, or you will answer to me, Alpha," I say seriously.

"Yes, ma'am," he says, smiling as Warren walks back in.

"All settled then?" Warren asks.

"Yes, I think Alpha Harold and I have reached an understanding," I say, smiling at the Alpha as I begin to clean out the infection. When Rebecca returns, I have her start an IV drip of strong antibiotics.

"Where's your son, Alpha?" I ask him.

"He's actually in the waiting room. I just met him. He's worried about you," Warren says.

"Can he come in here?" Harold asks.

"Once I'm done. Then, I'd like for you to stay the night here, too, Alpha. You can tell your warriors that I drugged you without your knowledge if that helps. But I want these antibiotics to have a chance to take effect," I say.

"My Beta won't be happy about that," he says, smiling.

"Your Beta can get in line. I've been waiting over a week to mark my mate," Warren says.

I turn and smile at him. Soon. Hopefully, very soon, I'll be wearing his mark.

Chapter 47: Henry

Warren

I didn't know an Alpha could begin losing his wolf and still shift.

'Strong Alphas can. Or ones who used to be strong,' Arric says.

'So, once Yara is done with him, he'll be strong again?' I ask him.

'Look how much stronger we are, and not just because she healed us. We're stronger because our pack is stronger. He will be, too.'

When Harold's son walks in, he looks at us cautiously.

"Henry, come here, son," Harold says warmly.

The young Alpha does, walking over to his father's bedside, still watching me and Yara warily.

"Henry, this is Alpha Warren. He and his Luna and doctor, Yara, are helping to heal me, and Luna Yara has been healing our pack members."

"We have Rebecca," he says sharply as if Yara and I are trying to secretly infiltrate his father's pack.

"Henry," Harold says a bit sharply, "these two are basically saving our pack. Show some respect."

"It's okay. I bet you're worried that we're trying to find a way to take this pack from your father and you," I say.

"Are you?" Henry asks. He's still young, but Arric can feel his wolf. Even at a young age, he has a strong wolf, which means Arric is right about Harold's strength.

'Of course I am,' Arric says smugly.

I step up to Yara, putting my arm around her. "No, I'm not. I'm tired of fighting and losing my pack members because of others' greed. I've brought back some of your pack members that were taken by Alpha Thomas," I say.

"Why would you do that? Aren't you supposed to be the strongest Alpha in this part of the country?" he asks, his tone still sharp.

"HENRY!" Harold barks.

"It's okay, Alpha Harold. In six years, Henry will become Alpha. I think it's important for the Alpha heir to know why I want an alliance with his father so that when the time comes, we can create an alliance between us," I continue. "And, if anything were to happen to your father, it would be important for you, Henry, to know that you can turn to me."

"What are you doing to him?" Henry asks, turning to Yara.

"I'm helping his body to heal so that his wolf can regain his strength. If you are as strong as Annika, my wolf, says you are, then you know that your father's wolf is dying," she says in the confident, gentle, direct way that she has. "Or, he was until I arrived. Now, I'm forcing your father to rest so that we can help him get his wolf back."

I watch as Henry fights the strong emotions rolling through him. He knows his father is dying, and he's been trying to prepare himself to become an Alpha when he is much too young to do so. At sixteen, he might have had a chance. At twelve? No way, and he'd be lucky if the person who overpowered him didn't kill him to make a point and ensure that he never came back to challenge him again.

"So, why are you doing this?" he asks again, his tone more moderate.

He steps closer to the bed, and Alpha Harold puts a hand on his shoulder. Henry doesn't look at his father, but he does reach up and cover his father's hand with his own. It makes me yearn to have my own son and a child with Yara.

"I'm tired of fighting. I'm tired of losing good pack members for senseless reasons. I have enough land; I have enough strength. I don't need more, nor do I want it. What I want now is to end the greediness of the Alphas who continue to fight me to take what is mine."

Yara turns, smiling up at me. I know that trying to find a way to end the wars will make her happy, and I can feel her pride through our bond. Pride in me. Pride in being my mate.

I smile back at her, leaning in to kiss her nose before turning back to Henry.

"Spend the night here with your father. Yara hasn't released him to return to the packhouse."

"I'm going to unknowingly drug him unconscious so that he can tell his warriors that he had no intention of staying the night in the hospital," Yara tells him.

"Nonsense. If I'm staying in the hospital, then I can be honest with my warriors that I made that choice. I'm guessing most of them know that I've been getting weaker anyway," Harold says.

"Well, that changes now," Yara says, pulling away from me and looking over the machines that are attached to him. "Starting now, Alpha Harold, you will be getting stronger. I insist on it. Don't make me look bad," she says, making him smile at her.

"Any more like you back home?" he asks her.

"I'm one of a kind, Alpha," she says, smiling warmly at the older Alpha. If I hadn't heard her tell me over and over that she loved me, too, in the last several hours, I might have growled at their sweet interaction. But my mate doesn't give her love easily and I can feel that she's given it to me.

"Are you done now, Yara? You need to rest," I tell her.

"One more. The female warrior," she says.

"What was wrong with her?" Alpha Harold asks.

"Gangrene. I could smell the rotting flesh on her."

"I cannot thank you enough, both of you, for what you have done for me and my pack," he says earnestly.

"You can thank me by entering into that alliance we discussed," I say.

"As soon as your Luna gives me the go-ahead and I'm out of here, I'll be happy to do it," he says.

I look at Henry. "If your father agrees, you should sit in. I'm hoping that this alliance lasts for generations to come. I don't have a pup yet, so you and I will eventually be the ones entering into the alliance. I'd like for that relationship to start sooner rather than later."

Henry looks at his father, then turns back to me. "I'd like that."

"Good. Come on, Yara. Let's let Alpha Harold rest. You need to finish, too, because you've been going at this for much too long," I say to her.

"How long?" she asks me.

"Nearly twenty-four hours," I tell her.

"Well, that explains why I'm so tired."

I lead Yara out of Harold's hospital room and see that only one warrior is left, and she looks very sullen.

"Can I go now?" she snaps at Yara.

"If you want to die, help yourself. But don't come back in here when you're desperate for assistance again because no one dies in my hospital, and you are going to die unless you let me treat you."

I'm not sure if she's just tired or if she doesn't like being challenged the way this warrior just challenged her, but Yara snaps at her in a way that's harsher than normal for her.

I step up to Yara and put my arm around her. It's been a very long day for her.

"Your Alpha told you that you were to listen to what Yara has to say. If you choose to walk out that door, it will be against her wishes and his. However, that's your decision to make. We're here to help, not fight you, to help keep you alive," I say to her.

It's very subtle, but Yara leans into me, and I know the fatigue is starting to get to her.

When the warrior doesn't respond, it's my turn to get harsh. "My mate needs sleep. Make up your mind and do it now. I'm not going to risk her ability to take care of MY pack because of some sullen warrior who can't get her head out of her ass."

The Alpha tone has her snapping to attention.

"Fine. I'll get treated," she says.

"Come with me," Yara says, and I nod to Bradley to follow her. My warriors are tired, too. Some of them are sleeping in the waiting room.

Just then, Beta Franklin walks in. "Alpha Warren, Alpha Harold said that I'm in charge of the pack. I wanted to find out if there's anything I need to take care of here."

"Is there a place where my warriors can get some sleep? Yara isn't done yet, but even after she's done, I know she won't want to leave until she's able to speak with Savannah and make sure that the ones she treated today are healing."

"Absolutely. I'll get a room for you and Luna Yara as well."

"And one more warrior who's in the room with her," I say.

He nods, then looks at my warriors. "Follow me."

He's back before Yara is done.

"So, Alpha Harold?" he says, sitting beside me as I wait for her to finish.

"Is healing. Henry is with him, just so you know."

"Good."

"And Savannah?" I ask, happy to see that he isn't wearing her mark. It means he realized that she was exhausted and needed sleep.

"Sound asleep in my bed," he says smugly.

When Yara walks out, I stand, seeing and feeling her utter exhaustion. I walk up to her and scoop her up in my arms.

"I love you," I say as she curls into me. I turn, following Franklin and Bradley out of the hospital.

"I love you, too," she murmurs.

I will never get tired of hearing that.

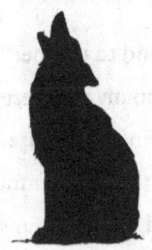

Chapter 48: Unexpected Meeting

Quinton

We'd gone to Brady's pack only to arrive after Harold had retreated back to his pack. We'd missed him by just a couple of hours.

We'd had to wait to get through Brady's booby traps. Harold and his warriors had set off some, but the biggest reason Brady doesn't get attacked is because of those booby traps. The only reason I haven't implemented them in my pack is because Brady sometimes loses one of his own pack members when they forget where they've left them. I'm not willing to lose my pack members and I don't have the knowledge of how to set and reset them like Brady does.

When we'd finally gotten inside his pack lands, I realized just how much his pack was injured.

"How much of this is from Harold?" I ask him, looking around. These warriors are in no position to attack Warren's pack with me.

He'd looked around at his pack. "Some, but most of it is still from Warren's pack."

I knew he was injured and knew he'd need time to heal, but I hadn't realized that Warren's pack was so strong that they'd caused this much damage.

"You and Thomas will have to attack without me or wait until my pack has healed," he says, checking over his injured.

"Thomas is dead," I say.

"WHAT?" he asks, spinning around to tell me. "You're just now telling me this?"

"You were a little busy and I was on my way here to help support you," I growl.

Like me, he has his warriors helping the injured warriors. Doctors are in very short supply, and the one that seems to be the best around is in Warren's pack ... for now.

"Did you ever tie up that loose end with Warren's old doctor?" I ask, reaching down to help hold a broken bone together while a warrior bandages it up. I know from experience that this bone won't heal properly and will break more easily next time.

I realize that Brady hasn't answered me, and when I finish, I turn and look at him. "Brady?"

"I needed a fucking doctor, okay. My pack would be in worse shape if I hadn't kept him."

"You're saying you have Dr. Stevens here in your pack?" I ask him.

"Yeah, that's what I'm saying," he says defensively.

"You realize that when Warren finds out that he was working for you, he'll come after both of you?" I say. Honestly, how is Brady still an Alpha if he's this stupid?

"He was coming for me anyway, right? I mean, if Thomas is dead ... At least he'll have to get through my booby traps. My pack is safe for now," he says. I'm not sure I agree with him, but I do know what I need to do.

"I'm going to go take out Harold. If he's injured, now is the time to strike. It sounded like Warren collected the she-wolves that Thomas had stolen over time. I'm worried he's going to try to give them back and create an alliance. You don't happen to have any of Harold's she-wolves stashed in your pack, do you?" I ask.

He turns and looks at me. "If you're going to eliminate Harold, it won't matter, will it?"

"Then, I'd better get going," I say.

"What about the son?" he asks.

"What about him?" I ask.

"Are you going to eliminate him, too?"

"He's an heir. Of course, I will. Unless some she-wolf there catches my eye or the eye of one of my warriors, I won't be leaving anyone alive."

My warriors and I finish helping to triage Brady's warriors, and then we head out. I'm more and more concerned about Warren's strength. He is getting much stronger, much faster than I expected, and he was already strong enough that he and his pack had been difficult to kill.

As we make our way toward Harold's pack, one of my scouts comes rushing back to us.

'Alpha, another Alpha is watching Harold's pack,' he says in the mind link.

'Who?'

'I'm not positive, but I think it's Alpha Simon.'

~ ~ ~

Simon POV

I've had scouts watching Warren's pack ever since Yara had refused to come with me, and I'd killed that girl. I don't give a shit about her, but I was pissed that Yara had refused me. I'm even more pissed that she basically said Warren would come after me as if she belonged to him. She doesn't. She belongs to me.

I hear Trena whimper as I fuck her hard, punishing Yara through her. She will be mine.

'Alpha, we spotted Yara,' one of my scouts says in the mind link. I can feel him outside my office door, and since I don't care if he or anyone else sees me fucking Trena, I tell him to come in.

When the door opens, he looks at her, then up at me. "Where did you see her?" I ask.

"She and Alpha Warren were seen leaving with a group of vans, heading out of the pack."

She's outside the protection of the pack? The thought has me shooting off, and I grab Trena's hips and grind against her as I come.

"That is very good news," I say, pulling out. "Trena, clean me off," I say, sitting in my chair.

She stands up as if going to the bathroom to get a washcloth. "With your mouth," I say and wait until she's kneeling between my legs and licking me clean before refocusing on my warrior.

"Where were they going?" I ask.

"I have scouts following them, but it looks like they were going to Alpha Harold's pack."

"Alpha Harold? Who else was in the vans?"

"Warriors and a bunch of she-wolves. A couple of males who look like omegas."

I think about what he said as I start getting hard again in Trena's warm, soft mouth.

"Do we have eyes on Brady, Quinton, and Thomas?"

"Quinton, yes. The others, no."

"Get eyes on the other two. I think we need to know what's happening in the other packs."

"Yes, Alpha."

"And find out if they get to Alpha Harold's pack. If so, I want to know immediately."

I let Trena get me off again, thoughts of finally having Yara in my grasp keeping me hard. Because I'd just come, it takes me long enough to come again that the warrior returns just as Trena is finishing up. Perfect timing.

"They're in Alpha Harold's pack, Alpha," he says.

"Let's go, then."

I bring about half of the warriors that I have left to Harold's pack. If I'm going to snatch Yara, I need to have enough warriors to fight Warren's and then some to fight Harold's warriors. I'm not as worried about Harold's warriors. If I hadn't been so focused on getting Yara back, I'd have attacked and killed Harold and his brat already. But Yara is my focus until she's mine.

I have no doubt that Warren will be guarding her. I know I won't let her out of my sight once she's mine. The thought of having Yara naked and in my sight twenty-four hours a day has me going hard again. Fuck, I want that woman.

When we arrive, my scouts tell me that she's in Harold's pack hospital. That's not surprising. What is surprising is that Warren is letting her take care of Harold's pack members. Based on the number of warriors exiting the hospital, that's exactly what she's doing. Why does he have her helping to strengthen another Alpha's pack?

"Find a way into the pack," I tell my warriors, watching to see if I can get a glimpse of Yara.

It's late in the day when a warrior comes running up to me. "Alpha, another Alpha is heading this way."

"Who?" I ask.

"We think it's Alpha Quinton."

"Be careful, but find out what he wants," I say.

If Quinton is here to kill Harold and Warren, fine. But if he wants Yara, I'll kill him.

"Alpha, Alpha Quinton wants to speak with you," my warrior says when he returns.

"Where is he?"

"This way."

I follow him, making sure I'm staying aware of the warriors in the area. I've pulled my warriors off of the search for an entrance and back to fight if necessary.

"Alpha Simon. I wasn't expecting to see you here," Quinton says. Quinton is a smart Alpha and a good strategist when it comes to battle. But so am I. I haven't survived this long because I was stupid. "I heard your father passed away. My condolences."

"It was time for a change," I say, and he nods as if I just confirmed his suspicions that I killed my father. "I wasn't expecting to see you here either, Alpha Quinton. To what do I owe the pleasure?"

"I heard Alpha Warren was here."

"He is," I say.

"He killed Alpha Thomas," Quinton says, watching me carefully. That is news. Warren doesn't usually attack.

"What did Thomas do to him?"

"Apparently, he attacked Warren's pack and made him angry."

"Funny, he didn't attack me after I attacked his pack."

"How are your warriors?" he asks shrewdly.

"Healthy," I growl.

He raises his hands. "I'm not asking because I want to fight you, Alpha Simon. I think we have a common enemy. Wouldn't you agree?"

"If you mean Alpha Warren, I'd say yes. But I'm more interested in your reasons for retaliating, and why here and not in Warren's pack?"

"I think Alpha Warren is creating an alliance with Alpha Harold. Harold just attacked Alpha Brady, and I don't want them attacking me next. Alpha Warren and his pack seem to be getting stronger very quickly, and I wanted to attack Harold before Warren and his Luna could make him stronger."

"So, you know about Yara?" I ask.

"I know she's making Warren's pack incredibly strong, and I know that's a problem for me."

"I won't allow you to kill her," I growl.

"I have no intention of killing her."

"What are your intentions with her?" I ask, watching him closely. Because I am, I see the flash of desire in his eyes.

He wants her. He wants what's mine, but he can't have her.

Chapter 49: Yara's Protection

Yara

I'm still so exhausted that I can barely open my eyes when there's a knock at the door.

"Excuse me, Alpha. Could I speak to you, please?" A voice that sounds vaguely familiar asks. Why didn't they just mind link him?

I feel warm lips press against my head. "Just a moment, Franklin," Warren says, his voice raspy and sounding just as exhausted as I feel.

Franklin? Who is ... Then it all comes rushing back to me. We must still be in Alpha Harold's pack. I open my eyes and see that we're in a room that is unfamiliar to me.

I push myself out of bed, realizing that Warren must have put me in one of his shirts, and I make my way to the door. Just as I reach it, I hear Warren growl.

"Warren?" I ask, opening the door.

He turns, pulling me against him. "Simon and Quinton are here."

"I didn't hear any howls of attack," I say, wrapping my arms around him. The thought of Simon being close after what he did to Piper makes me want to stay attached to Warren.

"The patrols saw them talking, Luna. We think they arrived here separately and are deciding if they want to attack together," Beta Franklin says.

I hear feet rushing up the stairs. "I'm here, Alpha," Bradley says.

"Yara doesn't leave your sight ... after she gets dressed," Warren says, pushing me back into our room.

247

"I'm guessing you're going to refuse a safe room?" he asks me.

"If there's not going to be fighting, I don't need to be in a safe room. If there is, I need to be in the hospital," I say, looking past Warren to Franklin. "Your mate will feel the same."

"Yeah, we've already argued a bit over that. She's already at the hospital, Luna. As soon as she woke up, she went over there."

"Alpha Harold?" I ask.

"Still asleep. I wanted to see what Alpha Warren wanted to do before I woke him."

"I'll lead this. Your Alpha is healing, and once we leave, he will only have Savannah. She's good, but not as good as Yara."

"What about Henry?" Franklin asks. "He'll want to fight, especially since his father isn't able to force him to stay behind."

"I'll talk to him. Give us two minutes," Warren says, turning to Bradley. "Get Charlie on the phone for me."

"Yes, Alpha," he says as we walk back into the room and quickly get dressed.

When we step out, Warren keeps one arm on me and takes the phone from Bradley who falls in behind us with Franklin.

"Alpha, do you need warriors?" Charlie asks. Bradley must have already filled him in.

"No. It would take you too long to get here. What I want you to do is collect half the warriors and go attack Quinton's pack. If he's here, his pack is weak. I don't know if his Beta is here or there, but I want everyone, and I mean everyone who raises a fist to any of our warriors, dead. Anyone else, bring them back to the pack. If anyone is sketchy, put them in the cells until I get back. If I don't kill Quinton, I want him going home to an empty pack."

"What about Simon?" Charlie asks and Warren looks at me as we jog down the stairs of the packhouse. It looks like they put us on the Beta floor.

"We don't have enough warriors to fight both of them. Quinton is the bigger threat since he's stronger, and we know he wants Yara, too. Take out his pack and leave the other warriors in case Brady attacks, but I doubt he will. He's recovering from attacking us and being attacked by Harold's pack."

"Who do you want me to leave in charge?" Charlie asks since Warren still doesn't have a Gamma.

Warren is quiet for a moment, thinking and probably assessing who he has here versus who is at home. "Haynes," he says. A good choice. "Call me when it's done," he says, hanging up.

When we get downstairs, I see Harold's warriors standing at attention, waiting for orders.

"Yara," Warren says, letting me know he wants me to release them to fight.

I look at Warren. He needs every one of these warriors if he's fighting two packs, but I also know that if they aren't strong enough, they'll die. I start going through them, surprised when I only have to pull ten out of formation.

"We need to fight, Alpha. Beta, you need us," they argue when they realize what I'm doing.

"You're going to protect the pack hospital. You'll only fight if the fight gets to you. Both of these Alphas want my mate, and I'm guessing every one of you can understand why," he says. They all look at me, making me self-conscious.

"Your future Beta female is in the pack hospital, too, so shut your mouths. I don't want to hear another word," Franklin growls. They nod and keep quiet as Warren begins moving again.

"Where do you want us," the warriors ask. Warren turns to Franklin.

"I'm assuming that they're somewhere near the pack hospital?"

"How did you know?"

"Simon came for Yara once. I'm guessing Quinton is here because you attacked Brady, and they have an alliance, but Simon is here for my mate. I have no doubt of that."

I feel a bit of relief when I see our warriors come jogging up.

"Wait here, I need to talk to Henry," Warren says. We walk inside with Franklin and Bradley behind us. I see Savannah getting ready, and I walk over to her to get an update on the status of our patients.

Before Warren gets to Alpha Harold's door, it opens, and Henry walks out, looking resolved, like he knows he's going to his death, but he's going to do it with his head held high.

"Alpha Warren, I think we should attack," Alpha Henry says.

"I agree, but I want you to stay here. I will lead the fight," Warren says. Henry is shaking his head before Warren finishes speaking.

"This is my pack. My father is out, so it falls to me to lead them."

"Listen to me," Warren says, putting his hands on the younger Alpha's arms and leaning down so they are eye to eye. "They will kill you. First and foremost, I won't be the one to tell your father that you died on my watch. Not happening, and I'm pretty sure your Beta doesn't want to give him that message either."

"I absolutely do not," Franklin says.

"But I have another reason for keeping you here. One that is personal to me. Both Alphas at your borders want my mate. Alpha Simon nearly killed someone to get to her the last time. That woman would be dead if it weren't for Yara. I need to know that she's safe. I'm leaving Bradley, and we have your injured warriors protecting the pack hospital, but I would feel a lot better if I knew I had an Alpha heir watching her back."

He looks over at me and I force a smile. I know he doesn't want this duty.

"It will also allow you to be here to protect your father if anyone gets past your warriors. I'm not leaving you here because I don't think you can handle yourself. I'm sure you can. But I need my Luna and your father safe. It's an important job," he tells him.

I suddenly get an image of Warren leaning down and speaking to our son like this, talking to him about why he needs or wants him to do something. Desire, unlike anything I've ever felt before, floods into my system, and I suddenly can't wait to wear this man's mark.

Warren stands, turning to look at me curiously. I shake my head at him, just enough for him to know that it's nothing for us to discuss right now.

"So, can I count on you, Alpha Henry?" he asks, turning back to Henry.

Henry looks over at me again and then at Savannah. "I'll protect your Luna, my father, and our future Beta female with my life," he says stoically.

"Thank you," Warren says before walking over to me.

"If Simon gets through, you do not give yourself up for anyone. Do you hear me, Yara? I don't care who it is. I don't care if it's me. You are too important to me."

I nod, knowing that I can't guarantee that I won't give myself up. What if it's Henry that I could save? Of course, I would do that.

Warren leans in, taking my mouth in a passionate, needy kiss before pulling back. "I love you," he says before turning to walk out.

"I love you, too," I say, needing him to know it before he goes to war with two Alphas.

He turns and smiles at me. "Is that the first time you realize you've said it to me?"

"What?" I ask. "I haven't said it before."

"You have many times, but always when you're distracted. Take care of my mate," he says before rushing out the door.

I turn, looking at Savannah and Bradley, who both nod at me.

"You've said it a lot since we've been here, Luna. Nearly everyone has heard you," Savannah says.

I shake my head. I'll think about that later. For now, I need to be ready to get Alpha Harold's pack back into fighting shape.

Chapter 50: Attack
Charlie

As soon as I got Alpha's call to attack, I did two things. I kissed Noelle, and then I contacted Haynes. Noelle has been sleeping in my room since she arrived, which means she's barely slept here at all. I was thrilled to be able to lie down with her and curl up around her. I want her to get to know me and feel comfortable before we complete our bond. And now, I feel Warren's frustration at waiting to mark his mate. I'm not sure how he can continue to wait. Gregor's going nuts, but we also know that Noelle is exhausted. She went through a lot in a very short amount of time.

But I'm going to war, and I don't want to leave without kissing my mate goodbye. Properly.

"What's going on?" she asks me when I finish waking Haynes and telling him I need to speak with him.

"Alpha Quinton and Alpha Simon are at Alpha Harold's pack. Alpha Warren wants me to attack Quinton's pack while he's away."

"Will you be okay? What can I do?" she asks, worried. It feels really good to have someone worried about me.

"Help get the hospital ready. I don't know what we'll find in Quinton's pack, but if it's anything like Thomas', we'll have mates who are suffering with the death of their other half."

"What about you?" she asks, reaching up to cup my face.

I hold it against my cheek. "What about me?" I ask, watching the worry in her eyes.

"If Alpha Warren is away, that means that you...you're in charge of this attack?"

"Yes. I'm a strong wolf. I'll be okay."

I watch as she fights her fear, fear that something will happen to me. She finally straightens her shoulders and lifts her chin, making me smile.

"Well, of course, you're going to be okay. You promised me that I could get to know you before you marked me. Well, I haven't had enough time yet, so you WILL win this fight, and you WILL return back here to me. I'm holding you to your promise, Beta," she says seriously.

I do what any smart man would do. I lean in and kiss her, taking her strength and her passion into me to carry with me and give me the strength I need to defeat Quinton's warriors. She's right. I made her a promise, and I'm not going to break it.

By the time I release her, she's clinging to me. She sways a little as I step back, making me smile.

"And I want more of THAT when you get back," she says, pointing her finger at me in much the same way that Luna Yara does to Warren.

"Yes, ma'am," I say, smiling. I know I'm going into battle. I know there's a chance that I won't survive or that I'll be badly injured. But having Noelle here, fighting for my return, warms my heart and makes me want to fight even harder. I have a bigger reason to fight now. It's not just to win for my pack and my Alpha. I have to win for her. I don't ever want to disappoint her. Ever.

We walk out of the room, and I go to find Haynes.

"Beta, what's going on?" he asks, jogging up. The warriors have started to congregate, so I can divide them into two, the ones staying and the ones going with me.

"Attention everyone. I received a call from Alpha Warren a few moments ago. Alpha Simon and Alpha Quinton are at Alpha Harold's borders."

There's general murmuring as everyone assumes what I did, that we're going to support that battle.

"Alpha Warren has said that we won't make it there in time to help fight, but instead, he wants me to take a group of warriors to attack Alpha Quinton's pack while he's gone."

No one says anything. It's basically the same as they expected, a battle, just in a different direction.

"I will be leading the attack. Haynes will remain here. He is in charge while Alpha Warren and I are gone."

"Wait, what?" Haynes asks.

I turn and look at him. "You're in charge. Alphas orders. Don't screw it up, Haynes. We need a Gamma. Make sure you continue to run patrols. Brady is still out there and could attack," I tell him, slapping him on the shoulder.

"Yes, Beta," he says, looking stunned. Personally, Haynes has been on my shortlist for Gamma for a while. Now that he's healthy, I think he has a really good chance of making the ranked member list, especially since he's found his mate. Since both are strong warriors, they would make a powerful Gamma couple. And it doesn't hurt that my mate's sister would work directly with her. They already seem to work well together, and since Yara and Noelle are both more in the medical area, it would be good to have a Gamma who is more of a warrior.

I divide up the warriors and prepare to leave.

"Charlie!" Noelle says, rushing over to me. She throws her arms around my neck and lifts up on her toes, kissing me. I take a moment to wrap my arms around her, taking her mouth in a desperate kiss, before pulling away, howling our attack, and leaping to shift into Gregor.

We run fast but quietly to Quinton's pack. When we get there, I can see that patrols are running.

'Spread out,' I say in the mind link. 'See if you can figure out who is in charge.'

As I watch, I realize that the pack is arrogant and complacent. They aren't expecting to be attacked, so the patrols are merely going through the motions.

'I think I've spotted the Beta,' one of my warriors says.

'Where?'

'Eating on the porch behind the packhouse. Several others are hanging out as if they're relaxing and partying.'

'Multiple couples in the packhouse having sex,' another warrior says.

'Don't these fucking people sleep? You'd think they'd want to be ready for an attack.'

'If they're in an alliance with two other packs and Quinton is at Harold's pack watching Warren, who's going to attack them?' I ask, realizing that this might be easier than I expected.

'We are!' my warriors say as one.

"Only fighters die. Everyone else is given a chance to prove they either didn't want to be here, or they won't fight having a new Alpha," I say.

'Yes, Beta,' they say, and I can feel the tension, their readiness to attack.

'NOW!' I say in the mind link, not giving the pack the announcement that we're attacking. We rush in, taking out the patrols quickly and easily.

'The Beta still doesn't realize anything is wrong,' a warrior says.

We spread out into an arc, and we're closing in on the packhouse.

He's not worth his title. What Beta doesn't keep tabs on his patrols, especially when his Alpha is away. The moment we break through the forest line, the Beta leaps up. Oh yeah, asshole. You're mine.

He snarls and leaps, shifting to come after me. Even from here, I can smell the alcohol on him.

'How fast should I make this?' Gregor asks me.

'Take him out,' I say, and Gregor leaps, landing on top of the tipsy Beta. Gregor slams his teeth on the back of the Beta's neck, and I hear the snap of bones as his neck breaks. He howls as his body collapses.

'Rip his head off. I want this done quickly,' I tell Gregor as my warriors begin to easily take out the warriors around us.

We race into the packhouse, and I realize that they still haven't announced our attack. Everyone is either partying or sleeping. When I burst into a room with two people having sex, the first alert finally goes up, but it's only a moment before Gregor rips the warrior's throat out and then turns to rip out the throat of his bedmate.

He's out the door before he spits the warrior's flesh from his mouth. When we get back to the hallway, I smell the strong scent of fear. Two small people are standing in the hall, pressed tightly against the wall.

"Please, please, we're omegas," the woman says. Gregor slowly walks toward her, assessing her and the male with her. The brave omega pushes the boy behind her.

'Her pup,' Gregor says, confirming my suspicion.

I shift, standing over her. "What's your name, omega?" I ask. I'm not gentle. The adrenaline of battle is still flowing through my body. She lifts her neck in submission.

"Tally, Beta."

"Tally, is that your pup?" I say, my voice still growly.

"Please! He's a good boy. He's not a warrior."

I look at the pup. He's a young teen, and I can tell he's not happy that his mother is trying to protect him, but he's also terrified.

One of my warriors comes rushing out of another room in the hallway.

"What's your name, pup?" I ask him.

"Sean, Beta," he says. His voice wavers, but he answers, lifting his neck in submission as well.

I hear snarling behind me, and I turn, putting myself between the omegas and the threat rushing up to me. A young wolf comes rushing at me. When he leaps, I grab him by the throat.

He begins thrashing in my arms, and I extend my claws. Warren and I are in agreement that we don't kill pups, but he did say that anyone who lifted a fist should die. However, this pup is ranked.

A she-wolf comes rushing into the hallway, snarling viciously when she sees me.

"Luna, no!" the woman behind me screams.

The warrior who came out of the room down the hall tackles the Luna, grabbing the back of her neck and holding her to the ground.

"Don't kill her," I say, looking at the pup in my hand.

"If that's your mom, and she's the Luna, that makes you the Alpha heir. My Alpha will want to meet you."

I reach out in the mind link and realize that my warriors have taken out Quinton's warriors. They're rounding up the omegas.

'Find a couple of vans. I'm not going to try to get these people back to our packs. Especially when we have Quinton's Luna and Alpha heir,' I tell the warriors.

'Yes, Beta.'

I look at the wolf, who is still snarling in my arms. "SHIFT!" I command, putting every bit of my Beta command behind it. He's a pup, but he's an Alpha, so it's not guaranteed that my command will work. Thankfully, it does.

"Stop fighting me and go sit with your mother," I say, nodding at the warrior who still has her pinned to the ground. When he steps back, she shifts, and as soon as I put her son back on the ground, she snatches him to her, trying to push him behind her.

"What's your name, young Alpha?" I ask him.

"Quirin, Beta. And my father will kill you for attacking us."

"Your father will be lucky if he survives attacking my Alpha," I say before raising my voice.

"Round them up! We're heading out!"

Chapter 51: Two Alphas

Yara

I'm worried about Warren. Harold's pack isn't as strong as his, and he isn't their Alpha. He won't be connected to them during the battle like he is to our pack. Our pack ... when did I start thinking of myself as his mate and Luna?

When he rushes out of the hospital, I turn and focus my attention on what I need to do. "Savannah, we need triage and crash kits. Do you know if they have the supplies here to be able to put those together?"

"I'll find out," she says.

"What can I do?" Rebecca asks, rushing in.

"Go with Savannah and help her find what she needs. Bradley, do we know how many warriors are outside the borders?" I ask him as I begin moving things around in the waiting room and grabbing gurneys to have them ready.

"No, Luna."

"What do you want me to do?" Henry asks me.

I look at him. I want to tell him to go sit with his father and basically hide, but I think about how Warren interacted with him. Henry is an Alpha, and I need to recognize and respect that, even if he is a pup.

"Simon snuck in the back last time and captured one of my nurses. I need to know that he can't do that again. Can you check all the entrances and exits and make sure they're covered by warriors or locked?"

"Yes, I can do that," he says, jogging off.

I gently push against Warren's mind, not wanting to distract him but needing to know that he's okay. He opens his mind to me, and then, realizing that I just need the connection, he does the mental equivalent of taking my hand while continuing to focus on the fight. I'm connected, but only on the periphery. I can tell that he's searching for Simon and Quinton, but he hasn't found either of them yet.

"Be on alert. Warren hasn't found Quinton or Simon yet," I say to Bradley. I look over and realize that he's focusing on the fight. I can't be positive, but it seems like he's using the senses of the pack warriors to search for Simon and Quinton as well.

"They've separated them, Luna. The packs are fighting, but not exactly fighting together. Since they don't know each other, they don't seem to realize when they're fighting against each other."

His head snaps to the left. "Incoming," he says, just as Henry comes jogging back.

"Three injured warriors coming in," he says before jogging to a different part of the hospital to check the doors.

When the warriors drag the injured in, I get them on gurneys. "Are any of you injured?" I ask the ones who brought the injured in.

"No, Luna."

"You can get back out there, but be careful," I tell them.

I call out to Savannah to join me and bring some kits with her as I get focused on doing my job.

I have no idea how long I've been working. There's a steady stream of injured people coming through the door when I hear Bradley snarl. He rips me off the warrior I'm treating, pushing me against the wall and standing in front of me.

I hear another snarl and look up to see that Henry has also taken a protective stance in front of me.

I have to look around Bradley, he's a huge man and he's purposefully blocking me. When I do, I feel my heart drop to my stomach. Both Simon and Quinton are here.

'WARREN!' I scream in the mind link.

~ ~ ~

Quinton POV

Simon wants Yara. That's a problem because I intend to make her mine. I have no intention of giving her to Simon or Brady or letting Warren have her. Simon must see that on my face because he snarls at me.

"No one gets Yara, but me."

I have a moment to wonder if this woman knows how many Alphas want her before Simon's claws come out. I'm about to shift and attack when we both hear the sound of paws rushing at us.

"ATTACK!" I yell at my warriors, all of us shifting quickly just as Harold's warriors rush at us. I separate from Simon, making sure that there are enough warriors between us that he can't sneak up on me. I saw the crazed look in his eyes when he said he wanted Yara. There will be no alliance between us, and I'm sure he'd be happy to kill me, so he knew that I couldn't go after Yara.

'Don't actively attack Simon's warriors, but if they attack you, kill them,' I say in my pack link as I begin fighting.

I feel the link to a warrior snap, and I look over, realizing that Warren is out here fighting. I haven't seen Harold yet, but I'm not sure that will matter. Warren's warriors, the few that are here, are strong enough to count as two of Harold's. I watch as one easily rips out the throat of one of Simon's warriors.

I refocus on the warrior in front of me, my wolf snapping his teeth into the warrior's flank and ripping out a chunk of flesh. I turn, ready to go for the kill, when another wolf leaps at me, ripping me off the wolf. I lift my nose, smelling Beta.

I turn, facing him to fight again, when I feel another tether snap. Warren and his pack seem to be targeting mine. Or maybe they're killing the same number of wolves in both of our packs. My warriors distract the Beta long enough for me to realize that they've separated our packs, although some of Simon's warriors are attacking mine. Idiots. My warriors are killing them. Simon may be a good fighter, but he either didn't bring his best fighters with him, or he isn't training them like his father did.

'Begin backing out slowly. I'm going for the doctor,' I tell my warriors. I don't want them to retreat, but if the focus turns to Simon's warriors, that's better for me. If we're not in an alliance, then I have no interest in protecting his back. And if he's after Yara, then he is as much of an enemy to me as Warren is.

I maim another warrior, using the gap in fighting while some warriors begin carrying their injured off the battlefield to sneak onto Harold's pack lands.

I go around, trying to find an open door in the hospital, when I see several warriors who have already been attacked lying on the ground. I can still hear some heartbeats, so I don't know if some are dead or if they've just been injured. If this is Simon, they're probably injured, as he wouldn't have wasted time killing them. When I finally find a door that is hanging open, I rush inside. Someone has already come for Yara.

I hear a snarl, and as I rush toward the scent of blood and antiseptic where I know Yara will be, I hear a second snarl, a younger one. Because of the strength behind the snarl, I know that this must be Harold's pup.

When I step into the room, Simon is already there. Warren has put a guard on Yara, and he's pinned her behind him against the wall. Surprisingly, the Alpha heir is standing in front of the warrior, protecting both of them. He's got to be close to Quirin's age and it makes me wonder if my son would do the same for someone, his mother possibly.

When Simon sees me, he snarls viciously. "She's mine!"

"Doesn't seem like it," I say, taking a step forward. We don't have a lot of time. The warrior in front of Yara is one of Warren's, so I'm sure he's on his way back here.

"Come with me, Yara, or I'll kill the pup. I don't care about him or anyone else in this room. I just want you," Simon says.

I'm about to say something when I feel the tether to several of my warriors snapping. What the fuck? Maybe Warren isn't on his way back here, but that doesn't mean I want to lose my best warriors.

I hear a howl from one of my warriors outside, and I frown. It's the howl of loss. I don't have any mates here, so what ...

Just as the thought comes to me, I start to feel tether after tether of my pack members snapping, the howls of pain going up outside increase as my warriors begin racing home. Someone is attacking my pack.

I snarl, shifting and racing out of the hospital toward home. Brady wouldn't have attacked me so that only leaves Warren. While I've been here trying to get his mate, he's sent his warriors to kill my son.

Chapter 52: Henry's Remorse
Harold

I come awake, confused. I don't immediately know where I am or why there is so much noise in my head. There's a lot of pressure in my mind.

'Wake up, Harold. Our pup needs us.'

'Conrad? You're awake?'

'Yes, but not very strong, although that lady doctor is making me stronger quickly, just like she said she would. You need to get up. Henry needs us.'

'Why? What's happening?'

'Alphas Simon and Quinton are attacking the pack. Both Alphas are here in the hospital, and our son is protecting Warren's mate.'

'Yara? Why?' I ask, trying to make both my brain and my body work. I push myself up to a sitting position and wait until the room stops spinning.

'It was Alpha Warren's way to keep him out of the battle, but I'm sure he didn't know that two Alphas would come for his Luna.'

I hear howling outside, the painful cry of a wolf losing their mate.

'What is that?' I ask my wolf as I carefully put my feet on the floor.

'I'm not sure. Those aren't our pack members,' he says. I carefully take a step, ripping the hospital gown off of me as I move toward the door.

"Come with me, Yara, or I'll kill the pup." Anger and fear, unlike anything I've felt in a long time, flow through me, burning off whatever has me sedated. No one is killing my pup today.

'Dad?'

'I'm here, son. Where are you?'

'Waiting room. There are two Alphas here.'

'I heard. What are you doing?'

'Alpha Warren left me in charge of protecting his Luna. She's here. They both want her, Dad. I'm not sure I can hold them both off.'

'I'm coming,' I say, quietly opening the door to my hospital room just as I hear several more howls of pain go up nearby.

As I step out, I see Alpha Quinton shift and race from the hospital. I've only taken a few steps when I hear the howl of the hunt. They aren't my warriors, so they must be Warren's.

I carefully make my way toward Simon, who has his back to me. He's so focused on Yara that he hasn't even realized that I'm coming up behind him. He's walking toward one of my warriors, whom Yara, Savannah, and Rebecca were treating. I see the two women huddled in a corner. They've pulled two of my injured warriors with them, but one is standing on one leg, his second leg is injured, and he is unable to hold his weight.

'I'm coming, Garrett. I won't let Alpha Simon kill you,' I tell my warrior. He's put himself in front of the other injured warriors and the nurses.

I probably could have killed Simon if Henry hadn't given me away. The moment I step into his line of sight, Henry's eyes flicker to me, and Simon spins quickly, his claws slashing down my arm.

"NO!" Henry yells.

Conrad snarls angrily as our pup rushes toward us, and Simon turns, lifting his arm to slash at him. I rake my claws down Simon's back just as we hear the howls of wolves all around us. Simon screams before shifting and racing out of the hospital.

I reach out and pull my son to me just as the hospital fills with snarling, snapping wolves.

~ ~ ~

Warren POV

264

The moment Yara's panicked voice screamed in my head, I knew she was in trouble. Arric quickly kills the wolf in front of us as I open the mind link to Bradley.

'Alpha, both Alphas are here.'

'Yara?' I ask, turning to rush back to her.

'Behind me.'

'Henry?'

'In front of me,' he growls. I know he'd pull the pup behind him, too, if he could, but Henry is an Alpha, and Bradley's job is to protect Yara.

'I'm on my way,' I say, opening the mind link to all my warriors.

'To the pack hospital! Your Luna is under attack!'

I hear wolves begin howling in pain, and I know that Charlie has reached Quinton's pack. It's only a matter of time before Quinton realizes what is happening and races home. I want him and Simon dead, but Yara is my biggest concern.

I slice through another warrior, realizing that all the warriors left around us are Simon's. I guess Quinton and Simon didn't come to any sort of agreement. That works in my favor. Divide and conquer.

I see a large wolf racing away from the hospital, and based on its size, I'm guessing it's Quinton. Since I'm still connected to Bradley, I know that Simon is still in the hospital, and I'm not willing to risk Yara to get to Quinton. I need to get Yara safe, and I need to get Charlie on the phone and tell him to get out of the pack. Quinton is heading home and I need my Beta and our warriors out of there.

I howl the attack as I rush into the hospital. I hear Simon scream a moment before he shifts and races out the back. I don't follow him; I turn, seeing Yara tucked securely behind Bradley, and I shift and rush to her, pulling her into my arms.

"Are you okay? Are you hurt?" I ask her, looking around quickly as my warriors come rushing in, snarling and ready for a fight.

"Find Simon. Kill him!" I yell, and they take off running.

I see Harold on the floor, holding on to Henry. He's got a terrible wound on his arm. I can see the bone from here.

"I'm okay, Warren. Bradley and Henry protected me," Yara says. Her heart is beating as fast as mine. "I need to check Harold. You, back on a gurney," she says to a warrior who is standing in front of Savannah and Rebecca and two gurneys.

"Get Charlie on the phone," I say to Bradley as I lead Yara to where Harold is crouched.

My eyes are everywhere, waiting for someone, anyone, to come for my mate again.

"Thank you, Henry. Thank you for protecting my mate," I say to him as he stands.

"They attacked our injured warriors outside. That's how they got in," he tells me.

"Let's get some of your warriors to get the injured inside so we can get them bandaged up," I say as Bradley hands me the phone.

"Charlie, Quinton's on his way back. Get out of there."

"We're already on our way home, Alpha. We have his pup and his Luna," he tells me.

"Perfect. Double the patrols when you get home. He'll come for them," I say before hanging up and handing the phone back to Bradley.

I look at Harold. "Yara, how is he?"

"HE can answer for himself," Harold grumbles, making me smile. "How are my warriors?" he asks.

I turn back to Henry. "Did any of them die? I don't have a link, so I wasn't sure."

"No. Some bad injuries, but no one died," he says.

"Good. Are they still fighting with Simon's warriors?" I ask. I watch as both Henry's and Harold's eyes go unfocused.

Harold looks at his son, letting him answer.

"They've killed most of Simon's warriors. Some escaped, but most are dead," he says.

"Savannah, I need you to stitch this. There aren't any broken bones, but the gashes are deep. You're lucky you didn't lose the arm, Alpha Harold," Yara says to him.

"It was my fault," Henry says.

"No, it was mine," Harold says, but I focus on Henry, and I can feel his regret. He's not going to believe his father, who is obviously injured because of something he did or didn't do.

"How so?" I ask Henry.

"I didn't stay focused on Alpha Simon. When I saw Dad coming up behind him, my eyes moved to him. It was just a moment, but ..."

"But it was enough that Simon knew someone was behind him," I say.

He nods. I crouch down in front of him. Harold has done a great job of raising his son. I already like Henry a lot, and I look forward to the day when he and I can create an alliance.

"How old are you, Henry?" I ask him.

"Twelve, Alpha."

"Twelve. That's pretty young to be protecting a Luna, a warrior, standing up to two Alphas and somehow trying to make sure that your eyes don't give you away. I think you did very well. Your father isn't going to lose his arm. I didn't lose my Luna. And you didn't lose any warriors. Today is a win. In times of war, you take every win you can get," I say, even as my warriors let me know that Simon escaped them.

'Come back. Let's make sure the borders are secure, and we need to help clean up the dead,' I tell them.

"Thanks, Alpha," Henry says.

I'm about to respond when I hear Yara mumbling behind me.

"My friggin' ovaries are working overtime to produce eggs, with you acting like the damn father of the year."

I feel hot desire and excitement run through me as I sit up straight and look at my mate over my shoulder.

"What was that?" I ask.

Chapter 53: Saying Goodbye

Yara

I look up and see Warren's dark eyes, hot with desire, burning into me.

"What?" I ask, but it comes out more like a squeak.

He turns, focusing on me more intently. I feel heat flushing my cheeks and spreading through my body.

"What did you just say?"

"I didn't say anything," I say, looking around and realizing that Savannah is focusing *very* intently on Harold's arm, her lips twitching, and Harold is smirking at me.

"Oh, Luna, you most certainly did say something. I'm beginning to understand what Rebecca meant about your murmurings being funny. Do you really not realize you said that out loud?" Harold asks me.

What had I said? I was listening to Warren, who was being the most incredible man I've ever met, acting like a surrogate father to Henry, and I thought ... oh, goddess!

I look up at Warren, and I know my eyes are wide. A smile spreads across his face.

"Yeah, that's what I heard."

"I ... I ..." I'm saved as warriors come pouring in with wounded.

"I have to work!" I squeak, standing up quickly.

"I know," he says, standing.

It suddenly occurs to me that he's naked and that he must have REALLY liked what I said. The evidence of that is standing up between us. He steps up to me, his hard length pressing against me as he cups my cheek. "I know I keep saying this, but soon, very fucking soon, my mark will be on your neck."

I nod, unable to speak with his warm, naked body so close to mine. His body isn't the only one responding.

He leans in, running his nose over my jaw before coming to my ear. "And then I'll give you as many of those pups as you want," he whispers.

Heat flows south, pooling in my core and soaking my undergarments and pants. I feel him take a deep breath, smelling my arousal.

"I see we're in agreement. Go, do what you do. I'll do what I do, and then we're heading home, my mate. It's time."

I nod again as he steps away.

Just then, Beta Franklin rushes in. "SAVANNAH!"

She pops up from where she's sitting on the floor beside Alpha Harold.

"Franklin?" she says.

He sighs in relief, then looks around. "Alphas, I have the warriors collecting the dead to burn. I just ..." he stops, looking at Savannah.

"You needed to check on your mate, Franklin. We understand that. Savannah, why don't you take a break and reassure your mate that you're okay?" Harold says.

Savannah looks at me, and I look at the wound she was dressing. "Just cover it. It'll be okay for a few minutes."

I turn back, seeing the injured coming in quickly now.

"I'm here, Luna," Rebecca says, coming up to me.

"Okay, let's do this," I say, moving into the organized chaos that is a hospital.

Several injuries were bad enough that they required surgery. After the first one, I saw that Alpha Harold was stitched and bandaged and was walking around talking to his warriors, helping to keep them calm and reassure them that all was well.

After the second surgery, Warren, Henry, and Franklin returned, all having soot on them from burning the dead. I wanted to hug Warren, but I needed to stay as sterile as possible, so after checking to make sure he hadn't sustained any injuries, I went into the third surgery.

When I came out after that surgery, Savannah had nearly cleared out the waiting room, and other than a couple of warriors, all that was left was Alpha Harold, a sleeping Henry, Beta Franklin, and Warren.

As he always does when I finish a long, grueling day in the hospital, he stands and opens his arms to me. I walk into them and let him wrap his strength and love around me. We stand there for a moment, just enjoying each other. Warren lays his head on top of mine and we both just breathe in the others' scents.

"You smell like surgery."

I nod. "I need to shower."

"Go shower. We're heading home."

"But ..." I turn, looking at where I've left the patients I've just worked on.

"I know, but Charlie captured Quinton's son and mate. He'll come for them, and I need to be there when he does. Besides that, you and I have unfinished business."

"Yes, we do."

I look up at him for the first time, ready to accept my role and place in his life and the life of his pack.

I watch a very possessive, very hungry look darken his eyes before he leans down and takes my mouth in a passionate kiss, full of the promise of what our life will be like. When he pulls back, I don't shy away from his promise. I embrace it. I am Warren's mate, I will be his Luna, and someday, I will give this incredible man a family.

He growls low in his chest as if he heard my thoughts.

"Did I say that out loud?" I ask.

"No, but I can read it on your face. You've accepted that you're mine," he says, stroking his knuckles over my cheek.

"And you're mine, Alpha. Let's not forget that part," I say.

"Never," he says softly. "Go shower. I'm ready to get home."

There is a wall of showers in this hospital, and I walk up to one, turning it on. Savannah comes in as well, also needing to shower.

"Luna, I ..."

"You're going to stay with your mate?" I ask her.

"Yes. I haven't had a chance to talk to Alpha Warren yet, but ..."

"I'm pretty sure he already knows that we're losing you. I'll leave you instructions for the injured. Once I know more about what's going on with Quinton, I'll make a plan to come back and check on them. If anything serious happens, Savannah, you know you can always call me."

I step away from the shower, wrapping a towel around me. "You're going to be in charge here now. This will be your hospital. Run it the way a hospital should be run, and if you have any questions at all, I'm a phone call away," I say, feeling sad at losing my best nurse and someone who was becoming a friend.

She wraps a towel around herself. She must be feeling as sad as I am because she pulls me into a hug. I feel the tears dripping down my cheeks. "You're going to be fantastic," I whisper to her.

"I have a great mentor," she says.

"Go back to school when you can. Get some surgical education so you can better treat the pack's warriors. Maybe you and I can start our own practical classes."

She hugs me tighter. "Thank you, Luna."

"Thank you, Beta," I say, making her laugh.

"I guess I will be a Beta, won't I?"

"Yes, you will. And you'll be a GREAT Beta."

When we walk out, our mates are waiting for us. I'm not sure if Franklin is just missing Savannah or if he knew this would be hard for her.

"I've already spoken to Alpha Warren about you staying, Savannah," he tells her.

She nods, looking at Warren.

"You're just what this pack needs, Savannah," Warren says. "But if you ever need anything ..." he begins.

"I know. Luna already told me that she'll help me."

We say goodbye and watch as Franklin leads Savannah back to the packhouse. Warren turns to me, running his thumbs over my cheeks as if he were wiping my tears from a few moments ago away.

"Are you okay?"

I nod. I know that growth sometimes means you no longer get to work with the people that you love working with. And that's okay, it's a good thing. But that doesn't make it any less difficult, especially when you have to say goodbye.

"Let's go home, Yara," Warren says, holding out his hand to me.

"Let's go home, Warren."

Chapter 54: Returning Home

Quinton

I raced home, only to find my pack dead or gone. I smelled Warren's Beta, so I know he ran this attack. Warren rarely, if ever, attacks, so it hadn't occurred to me that while I was away, he'd send his warriors to kill mine, but it should have.

He killed Thomas, and he must know that we're after his mate now, so he's gone from being defensive and reacting to attacks to becoming offensive and actually attacking, and he's doing it very effectively. I should have considered that he'd do this, but I hadn't. I've become just as complacent as Thomas, and now my son is paying the price.

I knew Quirin wasn't dead. I'd have felt the tether to him snap. But I was hoping that Yasmin would have hidden him. Since I didn't feel my tether to her snap either, I assumed that was the case. However, when I arrived home, I searched the packhouse for them. The safe rooms hadn't even been used. I saw all the chairs, cups, and alcohol outside. My Beta was having a fucking party while I was gone and hadn't bothered to protect the pack. It's a good thing he's dead, or I would have killed him myself.

When I realize my son is gone, I lift my head and howl. What's left of my warriors echoes my howls. Some of them are outside, mourning the death of their mates as they hold their lifeless bodies. The others are like me. They'd been hoping to find their mates and pups in the safe rooms. When they hadn't, they'd started searching the packhouse, but no one is here. No one that survived anyway. Warren's Beta is obviously more thorough than my previous Beta.

I mentally reach out to my pack. Nearly half of them are gone. The deaths of their mates weaken half of the ones left. Those that are left are anxious and angry, wanting to go after their mates and pups, just like I do. But I can't attack Warren's pack like this. I haven't smelled any blood that wasn't from my pack members, which means that his pack didn't even get injured in the attack. They came in, killed what was left of my warriors, and got out. Fast and, apparently, easy.

"Alpha, there are three vans gone," one of my warriors whose mate and pup are missing says to me.

"So, Warren has taken prisoners. We need eyes on his pack. I need to know what's going on."

"We need to kill him," my warrior snarls.

I turn, snarling louder and forcing his submission. "Don't think for one moment that your pup is more important than mine. He has my son, too. We will make sure they don't intend to execute them, but I don't think he will," I say, turning away.

Warren isn't like me. I'd have killed Harold's pup and not given it a second thought. But not Warren. He has my pup, and now I have to be very careful about how I attack him. I won't risk my son, and Warren knows it.

~ ~ ~

Warren POV

All the way home, I held Yara in my lap. She fell asleep almost instantly, so I leaned my head back while I held her and slept for the short drive home. Having her in my arms, even after everything that has happened in the last couple of days, makes me feel at peace. It's a feeling I'm unused to, but I never want to live without it again.

When we arrive home, I wake her up.

"We're home, baby. Why don't you go get some sleep ..."

"No, I need to go check on our patients here. Now that Savannah is gone, I'm limited in what I can leave for others to do."

I stroke my fingers down her cheeks. "Okay, let me know when you're done. I need to check in with Charlie, and then I need to talk to Quinton's mate and son. And then ... you're mine," I say, making her smile.

"And you will be all mine," she says.

I lean in, kissing her softly before moving to her ear. "I've got news for you. I was all yours from the moment I laid eyes on you in the forest," I whisper, enjoying the shiver that runs through her body at my words. I can't wait to find all the places where I can touch her to make her body respond like that to me.

I watch her as she pulls away from me, holding her hands until they tug out of mine, then waiting for her to turn and head to the hospital.

"I'll go with her, Alpha," Bradley says.

"You need sleep, Bradley. Quinton will come, and when he does, I need you to be rested and at full strength. I'm sending Archie to watch her. When the attack comes, you get to her."

"Yes, Alpha," he says before heading inside to sleep.

When I turn back, Charlie and Haynes are waiting for me.

"Haynes, report," I say, walking up. This was his first time leading the pack, and I want to know how things went and how he thinks he did as a leader.

"Alpha, all was well, except ..."

'Warren, Farrah's gone,' Yara says in the mind link.

"Except Farrah?" I ask him.

"Yes, Alpha. The patrols got her scent when they passed where she crossed our borders. I had them follow her scent for about a mile to make sure she wasn't lying dead somewhere, but I didn't want to risk leaving the pack open for attack or our warriors getting ambushed, so I pulled them back when it seemed like she was trying to get away."

I nod. "She wasn't a prisoner, so she was free to leave, although I wish she'd have stayed. I'm sure she's not completely healed yet."

'She left the pack lands, Yara. I'm sorry,' I reply to my mate. I can feel her sadness.

'She'll most likely die on her own,' she says.

'That's what she wanted. You did what you could, Yara.'

I hold the link open, wanting to know that my mate is alright. I know that for her, this feels like a failure, even though there's nothing she could have done to prevent it.

'I'm holding Piper, but I'm releasing Laney, just so you know.'

I look back at Haynes. "Your mate's being released."

He nods. "She stopped using the crutches yesterday."

"Is Farrah the only issue you had?" I ask him.

"Yes, Alpha."

"You did well, Haynes. Go celebrate with your mate," I tell him, then turn to Charlie. When Haynes doesn't move, I look at him, raising an eyebrow.

"I'd like to see how Beta Charlie reports so I can do a better job next time if you ever give me another chance to lead the pack, that is," he says.

I look back at Charlie and see his lips twitching. I know that Haynes is on his short list as a potential Gamma.

Chapter 55: Yasmin
Warren

"Charlie," I say, prompting him to report.

"I took half the warriors, as you know, and we ran quietly to Quinton's pack. His Beta was there, but they were having a party, not paying attention, and even the patrols were haphazard. We got in and killed the patrols, the Beta, and several other warriors who were partying in the back of the packhouse before anyone even raised the alarm. The omegas and pups never even made it to the safe rooms, making it easier to get out of there quickly. The only order I didn't follow was killing Quirin," he says.

I raise an eyebrow. "We don't kill pups."

"I know, but you also said to kill anyone who raised a fist, and he attacked me, as did his mother."

"What'd you think of the son?" I ask, curious.

"The son is as expected for a young Alpha. It's the Luna that has me curious," he says.

"How so?" I ask as we begin walking to the cells.

"She's protective of her son, no doubt, but there doesn't seem to be any love between her and Quinton. She didn't say that. It's just my impression."

"Your instincts are usually dead on, Beta."

I turn and look at Haynes following us.

"Oh, I can leave if you don't want me here," he says.

"No, stick around. That way, I can get Charlie's impression of you later," I say, making Charlie snort and Haynes look nervous.

When we walk into the cells, I can see that Charlie has put several individuals together in each of the cells, especially the omegas, who are hugging each other in fear. The smell of it is nearly overwhelming. However, my Beta made sure to keep pups with their parents if the number of pups clinging to adults is any indication.

"Attention!" I say loudly, making the basement room go quiet. "Is anyone here injured?"

No one responds. I look at Charlie, who shrugs.

"If they are injured, they won't tell you for fear that you'll kill them," a woman's strong voice says from the end of the cell block.

I walk slowly toward her, lifting my nose and recognizing her as Quinton's Luna.

"Well, Luna, you can tell your pack that I'm nothing like your mate. I don't kill innocents."

"My father is a good man," the young teenage Alpha says, trying to rush toward me, only to be held back by his mother.

"Your father is a murderer, young Alpha," I say, making him growl.

"Tell me, Luna, why is it that your mate wants my mate when he already has you?" I ask her, leaning against the wall. It's meant to look like I don't have a care in the world, but I very much want the answer to this question. He'd never be able to keep Yara unless he marked her, which won't be an option for him or Simon very soon.

"Is she your mate, Alpha? My understanding is that your mark isn't on her neck. And hers obviously isn't on yours," she says defiantly.

"Because my pack is continually attacked. But that's changing now. Thomas and his pack are dead, your pack is half gone, and Brady's pack is still recovering," I say, answering snark with snark.

"My father will kill you for what you did," the young Alpha says vehemently.

"He can try," I say, watching him. He's around the same age as Henry, but the differences are obvious. This young man hasn't had to face the idea of taking over his pack at a young age. He still seems to have the innocence of youth and youthful adoration of his father.

I look back at the Luna. "What's your name, Luna?"

"Why, considering a Luna trade?" she says, still snarky.

"Nope. My mate is everything I want in this world," I say, and I see the flicker in her eyes as she looks away. Interesting. "So, I'm guessing you must not be everything that Quinton wants in this world if he's looking to replace you," I say, trying to anger her to see what she might tell me.

"I gave him what he wanted," she says, glaring at me.

"Yes, a son. An heir. And now, what? You're useless to him?"

"Don't pretend like you don't know that your mate is making your pack stronger. There's no Alpha on the planet that doesn't want that," she snaps.

I push off the wall and look at her, holding her angry gaze. "The difference is, I want her because I love her, and she's mine. I don't give a fuck about how strong she's making my pack. She could be an omega, and she'd still be mine. The fact that the Moon Goddess blessed me with one hell of a doctor, someone who IS making my pack stronger than any other, says a lot about what she thinks I deserve in this life," I say. "Rest assured, NO ONE will take Yara from me."

'Warren?' Yara's sweet voice comes into my mind as if my words brought her forward.

'Yes, baby?'

'I'm done. I'm back in our room. Are you able to join me?' she asks.

'On my way.'

"If anyone is injured, we will provide you with medical care. I am aware that your Alpha and your mates will come for you. That's why you're here and not in the packhouse. You are prisoners for now, but that doesn't mean that me and my pack will mistreat you. You will have food, bedding, and medical care. My Luna takes great offense to anyone dying in her pack, so if you are injured, please let my warriors know. We will have someone look after you."

I look at Quinton's Luna and son again before turning to walk out.

"Check them. Make sure no one is injured. I don't want to face Yara's wrath if someone dies on our watch," I say to Charlie and Haynes.

"Yes, Alpha."

"And Charlie, I'm going down for a few hours. Do NOT bother me unless we're under attack," I say, jogging up the stairs.

When he doesn't answer, I turn and see him and every warrior guarding the cells smiling.

"Go get your Luna, Alpha," Charlie says.

COOPER

"I intend to," I say, jogging back into the packhouse, excited that I can finally, finally make Yara mine. Goddess, please don't let her be asleep.

When I get to our door, I listen and hear nothing. I steel myself that she might be asleep, and if so, our marking and mating will have to be put off for another day. I refuse to wake her if she's too tired for this.

I open the door and look at the bed, finding it empty. Instead, my mate is standing naked in the middle of our room.

"Time to make me yours, Alpha."

Chapter 56: *Finally*

Yara

I was completely distracted when I went to check on the patients in our hospital. As tired as I should be, I feel energized and antsy. Now that I've made my decision, I want Warren, and I want him now.

Because I need the connection to him, I reach out, letting him know about Farrah, Piper, and Laney. Piper is doing okay, but she's still not eating regular food yet, so I want to keep her while she moves into that phase of recovery in case she starts choking. Otherwise, she's good.

"Luna, are you okay?" Anne asks me.

I look at her and see her, Katie, Erica, and Noelle all looking at me.

"Yes, why?"

"You're not mumbling," Erica says.

"You always mumble," Katie says.

"We've gotten used to it, and now it's weird that you're not. It's just so unusual for you that we wanted to make sure that you're okay," Anne adds.

"Is it Savannah?" Noelle asks gently.

"No, it's not that, although that was difficult. But ..." I stop, looking around at the four of them and sigh. "When I'm done here and Warren's done checking in, we're finally going to mark each other. I guess I'm just worried that something else will get in the way."

Before all the words are out of my mouth, all four women are squealing happily.

"Oh, Luna, what are you doing here? Go get your man!" Katie says.

"Really, Luna, even I know how much the pack wants you and Alpha Warren to mark each other," Laney says, coming up behind us.

"But the patients ..." I begin.

"We'll take care of them. Ohhh, I'm so excited for you! And for our Alpha!" Anne says, rushing up and hugging me.

"Thank you. I guess ... I guess I am done here."

"Go," they say, shooing me out the door.

When I get back to the packhouse, I say hello to those who are still up and about, stopping to look at the flowers that are everywhere – flowers that Warren bought for me but are now decorating the packhouse and making it look so warm and inviting.

I go to our bedroom and look around. The flowers here make me smile, and I take a moment to smell them before looking at the bed. I don't want to wait anymore. I don't want anything keeping me from marking my mate and making that incredible man mine.

'Warren?' I call him in the mind link. I can tell that he's busy, but he answers me immediately, and when I tell him that I'm back, he says he's on his way.

Now, how do we make sure that we don't waste time just in case something else tries to keep us from completing our bond? I smile as I strip off my clothes. I know I'm not built like a warrior, but Warren has told me more than once that he likes the softness of my body. I hope he likes the way it looks, too.

I take a deep breath when I hear him walking to the door, and I lift my chin, hiding my insecurity that he may not like what he sees when he walks in.

When he does, his eyes go straight to the bed, where he must think I'm lying down. When they find me, they go from his brownish-green color to nearly black in an instant. I don't even have a moment to say hello before his mouth is on mine, and my back is on the bed, my mate over top of me.

I open myself, letting Warren in as his mouth devours mine in a hungry, desperate kiss. I begin pulling his shirt over his head, needing to feel his skin against mine. He only pulls away from my mouth long enough to pull the shirt off before he's devouring me again.

I run my hands over his arms and back, feeling the strength of his muscles and the scars of his battles. This man is so powerful, and yet, right now, as desperate as he is for me, he's careful not to crush me.

His teakwood scent surrounds me, and his hands are everywhere, touching me and caressing me as I wrap my legs around him, needing him even closer. When he pulls away from our kiss, his eyes have the most possessive look I've ever seen in them before.

"Mine!" Arric growls.

"Yes, I am," Annika purrs at her mate.

He lifts his body, shifting so he can look at mine. "So fucking beautiful, and all mine."

I watch him as he hungrily devours my body with his eyes, his hands stroking over my waist and coming up to cup my breasts. He looks at me, growling softly before leaning down to take my nipple in his mouth.

I cry out at the warmth of his tongue as he slowly begins licking and sucking my nipple into a hard peak. When he pulls off, his fingers replace his tongue as he looks up at me.

"Mine!"

I reach up and slide my fingers through his hair, grabbing on and tugging gently. "Me or my nipple?" I ask.

"Yes," he growls before moving to my other breast. I arch into his mouth, sighing and moaning with the pleasure he's sending through my body and straight to my core.

"You have too many clothes on," I pant, feeling his shorts against my leg. I want nothing but skin against skin.

He crawls off of me, and I feel the instant loss, the cold air in the room, as his heat follows him off the bed. The moment his shorts are off, he's over top of me again. He holds himself over me as he kisses me, and I wrap my legs around his waist again, feeling his very large, very hard length pressed against me.

He pulls back and nuzzles my nose with his. "I need to ask you something, Yara. I need to know if you've been with a man before. I don't care what the answer is. I just need to know how slow I need to go with you tonight."

He pulls back, looking at me. I'm twenty-five. By any normal standard, I wouldn't be a virgin, but Alpha Solomon kept others away from me in the pack, and since I started school, I haven't had time for a relationship.

"I haven't," I whisper, not sure if that answer is better or worse.

His answering growl tells me that he's very happy about that.

"Only ever mine, then," he says, moving his way down my body again.

He starts at my neck, licking and sucking on my marking spot as he makes his way down my body, stopping to suck my nipples back into hard nubs before moving farther down my body.

I watch him go, my own hands rubbing over his arms and shoulders, into his hair, and down again. As he moves, the muscles in his body expand and contract, and Annika begins purring at the strength that we feel in our mate. I don't try to hide the sound. I want Warren to know that I find him very attractive.

He looks up at me with his dark eyes before pressing my legs apart and settling himself between them. His eyes stay on me as his tongue swipes over my aching core and up to my clit. I moan loudly at the sensation just as he does the same.

"So fucking delicious," he growls before sucking my clit into his mouth, his warm tongue moving in circles around my clit.

"Warren," I cry, arching at the pleasure he's giving me. His hands slide under my ass, holding me against his face as he pushes me closer and closer to the edge.

"Warren," I whimper, looking down at him as I get to the edge. His dark eyes hold mine as he begins growling against my clit, sending my body up and over the cliff.

I scream his name as he forces my body to accept what he's giving me, the orgasm stronger than anything I've ever felt before, my body jerking against his mouth as his tongue works its magic.

When he finally brings me down, his tongue begins lapping up my arousal before he slides a finger inside me. I watch him as he slowly moves his finger in and out, getting me used to the new sensation in my body. When he adds a second finger, he sucks my clit back into his mouth, stretching me as he starts to bring me up again.

This time, I close my eyes, focusing on his scent, his warm mouth, and his sure fingers as he builds the fire inside me again.

"Warren," I moan, pressing my hips against his face and feeling his low, rumbling growl. The vibration puts me just on the edge, and when he hooks his fingers inside me, my body shoots off again.

"Warren!" I scream, this orgasm even stronger than the last. My body begins jerking with the strength of my orgasm, and Warren's strong arm lays over my stomach, holding me in place as he forces me to take the pleasure he's giving me once again.

When I finally come down again, he pulls off of me, sliding his fingers out of me and licking them clean before sliding up my body again.

"I will never get tired of hearing you say my name like that, deep and full of desire as I make you come," he says, his own voice deep with desire.

When he settles himself between my legs, he strokes my cheek. "This is going to sting."

"I don't care. I need you inside me," I say, pulling my legs up again and wrapping them around his waist.

He shifts, lining himself at my entrance. "Mine," he says softly, leaning in to kiss me as he slowly slides inside me.

I wrap my arms around him, holding on to him and whimpering at the pleasure and pain that his body is giving me. He deepens the kiss, my taste on his tongue, as he slowly pulls back and then slides in deeper.

I whimper as he stretches me, filling me in ways I never knew I needed. I tilt my hips, guiding him deeper inside me. I feel my gut clench as he presses the last of his length inside me and feel my body tear slightly from taking all of him. Rather than moving, he holds still, continuing to kiss me as if there is nothing and no one else in the world.

As the pain recedes, I begin drowning in the kiss, accepting everything that he's giving me, and when the pain is gone, another ache fills me. I begin moving my hips against him, needing more, needing him, needing his mark.

He lifts his head and begins sliding in and out of me. I reach up, cupping his face in my hands and holding his gaze as I moan my pleasure at the feel of him. I never realized what it would mean to find my fated mate, but this – this intensity, this ecstasy, is exactly why they say that fated mates are perfect for each other. I can't imagine anyone else in the world making me feel the way Warren makes me feel.

He pulls one of my legs up to his shoulder, shifting his hips and sliding even deeper inside me.

"Oh!" I moan. He kisses my inner thigh as he begins to move faster, building the heat inside me, but this time it feels even more intense. I arch against him, on the verge of falling apart.

"Mine!" he growls again, and when I look, I see that his canines are out.

"Yes, yes, I'm yours, Warren," I cry out.

"WARREN!" I scream as my body explodes around him. I can feel my inner walls contracting around his hard length, still thrusting in and out of me.

I tilt my head, exposing my neck to him. Rather than slamming his canines into my neck, he nuzzles my marking spot while I come, licking it to soften it.

"Mine," he says softly before slowly sliding his canines into my neck.

The intense wave of pleasure that I feel from Arric's venom flooding my system has me screaming much louder this time, my body shooting off again as lights flash behind my eyes. I feel my own canines come out, but unlike Warren, Annika sinks her teeth into his marking spot.

The moment his blood hits my mouth, his body explodes along with mine, and I feel the mate bond snap into place. Love, respect, admiration, adoration, desire, passion, need, and wonder flood through the bond. I realize that these are Warren's emotions, his feelings for me, and I bask in them as our bodies jerk in pleasure, the two of us wrapped around each other as our wolves push their venom into the other's marking spots, marking their mates as theirs forever.

Chapter 57: Wanting More

Warren

In a life of war, of constant struggles, of losing my parents, my warriors, omegas, and pups, I'm unaccustomed to feeling pleasure. That's not to say that I haven't had a sexual encounter now and again, but that had been a temporary release.

This, what I feel with Yara, is unlike anything I've ever experienced in my life. The pleasure of being inside her, her warm, wet heat drawing me into her body, her soft grey-green eyes begging me for more, her sweet moans, and her screams of pleasure are unlike anything I ever anticipated when I found her. I knew my parents had a special bond, but unless you experience it, you can't understand just how powerful and incredible it truly is.

I could have feasted on Yara's taste for days, the sweet taste of cinnamon and nutmeg on my tongue, listening to her soft moans or pleasure, but I needed to make her mine, needed to know that she is safe from the other Alphas who are trying to take her from me, needed to connect with her in the way that I've been desperate to connect since I met her.

When Arric slides his canines into her marking spot, the flood of emotions that I feel from her makes my throat close. If I'd been on my feet, I'd have struggled not to fall on my knees in front of her. Her softness, the gentleness of her body, is mirrored in her mind. The intelligent snarkiness is there. I know it is because of her mumblings, but behind that

287

is the most compassionate, caring, loving woman I've ever known. She has opened herself to me, letting me feel her love and pride at being my mate, for me, and for the man I am.

It's an unconditional love, unlike anything that I've ever felt from a pack member before. As an Alpha, I'm well-loved by my pack, but there are always conditions to that love. I need to be strong, to protect, to feed them, to keep them safe. Yara's love is passionate and full of fire but also slow-burning and never-ending. She loves me for the man that I am, not just as her Alpha or her mate, but for me, Warren Hill. I've never felt so seen or so understood in my life.

Arric seems to agree as he continues to flood Yara's system with his venom, pushing our scent into her as I push my love for her through the bond. Annika's venom in my system keeps me hard, so I continue thrusting, pushing both of us through the longest, most intense orgasm I've ever had.

I wrap my arms around her, holding her as tightly as she's holding me, neither of us wanting to lose this connection.

'I love you, Yara. I'm so happy that you're finally mine,' I say in the mind link.

I feel the warmth of her love wrap around me. I feel it blossoming inside me as she pushes it through the bond.

'I love you, Warren. You're never getting rid of me now.'

'I have no intention of ever letting you go, my sweet, sweet mate.'

When Arric and Annika finally release their hold on us, licking the wounds until they heal, I slowly bring us back down, laying over her and nuzzling her nose with mine.

"I didn't know how much you loved me or how important it would be to me to feel that love," I tell her honestly.

"I do love you, Warren. I love everything about you, your strength, your kindness, your intelligence, all of it," she says. I feel her possessiveness and pride in being the only one who gets to call me her mate.

Arric begins purring as I slide out of her, lying beside her and tucking her against my body.

"Did you know it would feel like this?" she asks, her fingers beginning to trace the lines of my scars.

"No. I knew you would be worth waiting for, but I had no idea it would feel like this," I say, meaning it. It's like I have someone who sees everything about me, everything that is good, everything that is bad, every nuance, every flaw, and yet loves me anyway, loves me because of or in spite of all of those things.

I move through her mind, wanting to know everything she's feeling. I kiss the top of her head. "You're not as sore as I thought you'd be."

"Annika is a strong wolf," she says smugly. "And also a demanding one," she says as she slides over my body, straddling me as she sits up. I run my hands over her thighs.

"What's on your mind, my mates?"

"You. I like the way you feel inside me. I want to feel it again, right now," she says, lifting up and shifting back, lining my already hard length at her entrance before slowly sliding me inside her.

"Fuck you feel good, and you look even better riding my cock," I say as she begins moving her hips.

She lets her head fall back as she adjusts to the different feel of this position.

"Warren," she moans.

"I will never get tired of hearing you call my name like that," I tell her, running my hands over her soft body, taking her breasts in my hands and stroking her nipples until they're hard again. Her body is so fucking responsive to me. I love it.

She begins grinding on top of me, leaning over and putting her hands on my chest. "You feel so good," she moans.

"Mmm, so do you. I love getting to watch you while you ride me," I say, teasing her nipples as she moves and finds her rhythm. She's so wet that I can feel her arousal dripping down my thighs.

She begins riding me hard, and I have the pleasure of watching her come undone. I grab her hips, forcing her to ride out her orgasm as she comes, her tight pussy clenching me and drawing me in, making it hard for me not to come. But I want to see her come again.

"You've got another one. I know you do," I say when she looks down at me. Her brown hair is hanging over me, and I push it behind her ear, wanting to see her face more clearly. "Come on, baby. I want to feel you come on my cock again. You feel fucking incredible."

"So do you," she murmurs as she begins moving again.

This time, I help her, holding her hips to help her ride me faster until she's bouncing on me, her head thrown back again, her beautiful breasts bouncing in front of me.

"Yes! Yes! Yes!" she screams, just before I feel her clamping down on me again. I force her to ride out another orgasm, pushing her to one more before I finally let myself empty inside her. This orgasm is nearly as strong as the last, and I thrust up into her, hitting her cervix as I jerk through my orgasm.

When she collapses on top of me, I wrap my arms around her. "Better?" I ask her.

"For now," she says, snuggling against me.

'I love you,' I say in the mind link.

'I love you, too,' she replies.

Arric begins purring, lulling Yara to sleep.

Just before I nod off, I hear her. I'm not sure if she mumbled out loud or in my head, but either way, I heard it.

"With a cock that big, I bet I get lots of babies."

"As many as you want," I murmur softly, and she snuggles against me. I fall asleep happier than I ever remember being in my life.

Chapter 58: Captured
Yara

I'm laughing as I watch a little boy who looks just like Warren running through the grass, laughing happily as his father chases after him.

"I'm going to get you," Warren calls.

"No, you not!" the boy squeals and tries to run faster on his chubby little legs. I smile, looking down at the baby in my arms, nursing as I rock her back and forth. She has my auburn hair, but as she looks up at me, I see her father's brownish-green eyes.

A howl of attack goes up, and I'm jerked back into a dark room.

"Yara, hurry, we're under attack!" Warren says.

"Our babies! Where are our babies?" I ask, frantic to make sure they are safe. I look around, disoriented that we're in our bedroom, and it's dark when we were just outside on a sunny, picturesque day.

Warren's hands cup my face, and he pulls my gaze to his. "Yara, we don't have babies yet. I just marked you a few hours ago. Come on, we're under attack. You need to get to the hospital!"

"I..." I turn, looking at the empty bed behind me. "It was so real."

"Baby, we'll talk about it when this is done, but right now, we both have to go. Snap out of the dream, Yara. The pack needs you!"

"Right," I say, getting up and rushing to the door.

Warren's growl stops me, and I turn. "Clothes, Yara!"

I look down at myself and realize I'm still naked from our marking and mating.
"Right!"

I turn to head to the closet.

"Baby, I have to go. I need to know that you're okay."

"I'm good. I'm good. I just..." I shake my head, pushing away the nearly overwhelming desire to have those two children in my life. "I'm good."

"I have to go. Take care of my mate," he says, kissing me hard before rushing to the door.

"Take care of mine!" I call out, hearing him leap over the banister as I pull on a shirt, then hearing Arric's paws hit the floor downstairs as I pull on pants.

The minute I'm out the door, Bradley is there. "Ready, Luna?"

"Yeah, let's go," I say and begin to jog down the stairs. I see Noelle standing at the edge of the Beta floor.

"I don't know where to go," she says, and I can hear the tremor in her voice. Being attacked is a scary thing.

"You're with me," I say to her and keep jogging, hearing her fall into step behind me.

"That's a nice mate mark, Luna," Bradley says.

My fingers fly up to my neck. "I haven't even seen it yet!" I say to him.

We collect Anna and run to the pack hospital. "Do we know who's attacking? Is it Quinton?"

"I don't think so, Luna. There are too many of them." Bradley says, just as more warriors come running up to the hospital.

"Nice mate mark, Luna," several warriors say as I rush into the hospital.

Dammit, everyone will see it before I will.

"Okay, without Savannah and Piper, who can make triage and crash kits?" I ask. I hear clapping, and I look over.

'I can make the kits, Luna,' Piper says in the mind link.

I step up to her. "Are you sure you're okay? I know this must be scary. You can go to a safe room."

She shakes her head no. 'I'm a nurse. If you need help, I can help. I just can't talk.'

"Okay, use your mind link," I turn, looking around. "Who else is assigned to the hospital, Bradley?"

292

He lists them off. "Get one of them in here. I want someone on Piper and the storage room at all times," I tell him, and I can feel Piper's relief.

When Archie rushes in, I send him and Piper off to start making the kits.

"Luna, what can I do?" Travis, the warrior from Thomas' pack, asks, limping out.

"Has my mate cleared you?" I ask, getting the waiting room organized.

"No, Luna, he hasn't had a chance."

I look at Bradley, who shrugs.

I look at Noelle. She believes in him, and so does Laney. "You do anything wrong, and Bradley here will remove your head from your body, and I won't say a thing about it," I say, making sure that Bradley knows I'm serious. I can't be worried that someone on the inside is going to start causing problems. We have enough on the outside.

"Incoming," Bradley says, his eyes unfocused.

"Do you know how to triage?" I ask Travis.

"Yes, ma'am."

"You triage. Noelle, get the clipboard and start marking each warrior's status. Anna, you're on stitching duty."

"Yes, Luna. Um, but before they get here," Anna says, holding up a small mirror. "I didn't want everyone to see it before you did."

I stop, looking in the mirror, seeing my mate's mark on my neck. I smile, my fingers going to it, caressing his mark. "It does look good, doesn't it?" I ask.

"It really does," Anna and Noelle both say as the injured start coming in.

"Okay, let's get to work."

"Luna, this is Simon's pack, but it also seems like Brady has joined the fight. Alpha is expecting to see Quinton soon," Bradley says.

"So three packs fighting us together?" I ask as I stitch up a deep wound on one of my warriors. I'm teaching Noelle as I go so she can start taking some of these harder cases.

"Technically, Simon and Brady aren't fighting together," Bradley says.

"They came in from different parts of the pack, Luna. Alpha Simon's pack first, then Brady's."

"Bradley, put another warrior on Piper. I want to make sure Simon doesn't finish what he started last time."

"Yes, Luna."

"So, Brady is probably responding to Quinton's request to attack, but Simon was already here, which is why we have more than our normal group of injured and why Warren thinks that Quinton will come," I say.

"Yes. I'd say so. Alpha is asking if we can switch out the warriors you've patched up to watch the hospital so we can send the full-strength warriors into the battle."

My connection to the pack is stronger now that Warren has marked me. I can feel all of them, and I can tell that they are divided in their battles, getting attacked on two sides by two different Alphas.

"Has he put warriors on the cells?" I ask.

"Yes, Luna," one of the warriors that's being treated asks.

"If Anna is stitching you up when she's done, you can replace one of the warriors guarding the hospital," I tell them.

I jerk, feeling pain down my thigh a moment before it cuts off. Warren just got injured, but he shut off the link, so I couldn't feel it.

"I need a status update on my mate," I say, letting Noelle finish stitching up the warrior I was working on and moving to another one.

I look around, realizing that all of the warriors are trying to connect with warriors on the battlefield to get me an answer. It's Bradley who pushes an image of Warren and Charlie fighting hard into my mind.

"He's still fighting, Luna," Bradley says.

"Of course he is. He's the strongest man I've ever met," I say proudly. "And Noelle, Charlie is fine, too."

"Thank you, Luna," she says, sighing in relief.

I feel Bradley step closer to me.

"What is it?" I ask him.

"Alpha doesn't have eyes on Alpha Simon. No one does," he says, just as a very injured warrior is brought in. I rush over to him, seeing that his gashes have cut through several arteries and he's bleeding out.

"Noelle, do you know where the surgical storage room is?" I ask, getting the warrior on a gurney and putting pressure on the bleeding wound.

"No, Luna."

"Here, put pressure here, try to stop the bleeding. Get him into a room. Anna, get an IV started on him. Fluids and antibiotics."

"Yes, Luna."

I move quickly out of the waiting room, which is my triage room during battles, past the regular storage room where Piper is still putting together triage kits. We're using them as fast as she's making them today, then farther down a hallway that isn't used very often. I walk into the storage room and begin gathering everything that I need to complete the surgery on our warrior when I hear Bradley snarl and whip around, his body filling the door and blocking whoever it is from entering.

I watch as his claws come out just before I hear a pop sound, and Bradley's body jerks backward, falling to the floor. I drop my supplies, rushing to him.

"Run, Luna," he says, and I realize he's been shot with a silver bullet.

"NO!" I start to scream, turning to see who it is when a cloth covers my mouth. I try to hold my breath, try to fight, but in this small space, there's no room. He holds me against him as I stare at Bradley, watching in horror as he struggles to breathe.

"Time to come home, Yara," I hear Simon say in my ear as I finally suck in air.

'War...' I begin to call for my mate, but I'm not sure that it went through before the darkness pulled me under.

Chapter 59: Fury
Warren

While neither pack is at the full strength that my pack is, being attacked by two packs at once, even if they aren't working together, is taking a toll on my pack. Because I'd stayed connected with Yara, I knew that I had more warriors going into the pack hospital than I had since she first arrived. And because we have Quinton's son, I'm sure he's on his way.

I'd been fighting several warriors at once when I'd felt the deep slash in my back leg, immediately followed by Yara's spike in concern. I snapped our connection closed, not only because I don't want her to feel the pain but because I don't want to distract her from caring for my pack. The sooner they see her, the sooner that they're healed and back to fighting. And without Savannah, I know she's working harder than ever.

When I'd turned, it had been Brady who had attacked me, and I'd focused on trying to kill him. However, knowing Simon was in the pack was distracting me, and rather than being able to kill him, I was only getting in good swipes every other time.

'Who has eyes on Simon?' I bark in the mind link. The silence that follows makes me even more distracted, and Arric takes a swipe to the chest from Brady's wolf. Arric snarls, swiping him across the face, leaving bloody slash marks across his cheek. He'll have scars for the rest of his life.

I'm pretty sure Brady has his Beta attacking me at the same time, along with another warrior, and I'm struggling to fight them all when I get the mind link I was waiting for.

'Alpha, Alpha Quinton is here. He and his warriors are heading straight to the cells.'

'Attack!' I yell. 'Do not let him get his son!'

My mind has been everywhere, so it takes me a moment too long to realize something's wrong. I got a very soft 'War' in my head. I slash through Brady's Beta, ripping skin and flesh off his side before I refocus, trying to figure out what Yara needs.

When I try to reconnect to her mind, I can't find her.

'BRADLEY! WHERE'S YARA?' I yell in the mind link.

'Simon...' is all he says, his voice much, much too soft.

'ALPHA!' I hear a moment later, several of my injured warriors reaching out to me at once. "Luna's missing! Bradley's been shot with a silver bullet!'

'EVERYONE! YOUR LUNA HAS BEEN TAKEN. FIND HER NOW!'

Arric turns, ripping the Beta's throat out as rage, unlike anything I've ever felt, flows through my system. Then he leaps on the warrior, biting down on the back of his neck and snapping it with one bite. I turn to take on Brady, but his wolf is backing away quickly.

I hear the howl of retreat from the other side of the pack lands.

'FIND SIMON! HE HAS YOUR LUNA!' I yell, turning away from Brady and racing to the sound of the wolf that howled the retreat. That will be Simon. He got what he wanted.

'Alpha?' Charlie asks, wanting to know where I want him.

'Find Quinton. Kill him, then get to the pack hospital. We need to try and save Bradley. Then, call Harold and see if he and his pack can cut Brady off on his way home. I'm going after Yara.'

I hear another howl of retreat, but I don't give any energy to who it is. My only focus is on finding my mate.

~ ~ ~

Brady POV

Fucking Quinton! He called me and told me to attack Warren. I told him that we were still recovering, but he said he'd join us as soon as possible. When Simon arrived, I thought for a short moment that it was Quinton, but it wasn't. That asshole Simon wants the lady doctor, too, so no way in hell I'm fighting with him. She's mine if I can ever fucking get to her.

When Quinton arrived, he barely had any warriors with him, and rather than joining the fight, he and his warriors headed straight to where I'm assuming Warren keeps his cells. Fucking bastard. I know Yara isn't down in the cells, so Warren must have captured someone important to Quinton. The only person that Alpha cares about is his son. I snarl as I realize that he was willing to destroy my pack to get to his son. Well, scratch that fucking alliance!

It's been a while since I've gone head to head with Warren, and the bastard is stronger than I remember him being. That fucking lady doctor must have healed him. I seriously need to get my hands on her.

'Focus,' Garth, my wolf, snarls at me. I'd be annoyed, but he's right. Arric is one hell of a fighter. I can't believe he's standing his ground against me, my Beta, and my Lead Warrior.

I sense the moment something happens. I swear I can see the red of fury in Arric's eyes. One moment, the three of us have Warren right where we want him, and the next, my Beta's throat has been ripped out, and my Lead Warrior's neck has been snapped.

Garth begins walking backward, knowing that we're next, when I hear the howl of retreat. It's not Quinton, which means that it's Simon. He got Yara, and that she-bitch is mine!

Warren turns, rushing in the direction of Simon's howl. I want that lady doctor, but I'm not willing to go head-to-head with Warren again right now. I was weak before. Now, I'm even weaker, thanks to that fuckhead Quinton.

I turn, howling my own howl of retreat. I need to get what's left of my pack home, and this time, we'll hole up until we're completely healed.

I can feel my pack's weariness as we run back to the pack. Thankfully, we're not being chased, so we can run at a slower pace, giving my injured warriors a bit of a break.

'Alpha, why didn't Alpha Quinton join us in the battle?' one of my warriors asks as we run.

'He did. But it was only to get a prisoner from Warren. I'm guessing Warren has his son.'

'So he used us?' one of my warriors snarls.

'Yeah, so no more alliance. Feel free to kill any of Quinton's soldiers at any time, and that includes his son.'

'What about the lady doctor? The one you said could heal us?' another asks

'Simon got her. Warren is going after him, and we'll have to see who gets her. Whoever that is, we'll be going after them next. We need her, and I want her,' I growl. 'And if Warren doesn't kill Quinton, we'll be going after him next for what he pulled today.'

The pack goes quiet after that, and I get into the rhythm of paws hitting the soft earth as I set the pace home. We're a little more than halfway there when I feel the shift around us.

'ATTACK!' one of my warriors howls. Suddenly, there's a flurry of chaos as my pack is attacked. I have a moment to wonder if Warren came after us instead of going after his mate, but then I smell him. Franklin, Harold's Beta.

He leads the charge of warriors who attack us, and I realize very quickly that Quinton didn't stop the alliance between Harold and Warren, and now, Harold's pack is much stronger than they were before.

'GET TO THE PACK!' I yell in the mind link, and my warriors begin rushing home as fast as possible.

I run as fast as I can, snapping at warriors and swiping them out of the way as I run. I feel my tethers to my warriors breaking. I've lost way too many of them by the time we reach home, and I leap over my booby traps, safe behind the barrier I've created. My weary warriors, what's left of them, come rushing into the pack behind me.

Garth turns, facing Harold's pack. I watch as Beta Franklin shifts, standing in front of me. He's covered in blood, but none of it is his, and he's wearing a very fresh mate mark.

"Come for Alpha Harold or Alpha Warren again, and we will destroy you," he snarls.

I shift, glaring at him.

"Why don't you come now?" he snarls.

"I'm not stupid enough to lose good men on whatever shit you've got buried in the ground to take me out. But if I were you, I'd stay put because the next time you step foot out of that pack, you and anyone else that joins you is dead."

Chapter 60: Taking Charge
Noelle

I'd been working on the injured warrior, trying to stop the bleeding, when there was a rush of energy, and the warriors who were able to move rushed out of the waiting room towards the back of the hospital.

Travis grabbed me and pushed me behind him as we watched the hallway, trying to figure out what happened.

"Did you join the pack?" he asks me, wanting to know if I can mind link and figure out what's going on.

"No."

He nods. Suddenly, there's shouting, and several warriors come rushing out carrying Bradley. I push past Travis and run up to him.

"Is that silver?" I ask, seeing that Bradley has been shot in the chest and is bleeding profusely.

"Yes, and Luna's missing," the warriors say as Anna pushes a gurney over to us. We hear the howl of retreat outside.

"WHAT?"

"The warriors are going after her. It smells like Simon."

I look down at our Luna's guard. Bubbles are coming out of the bloody hole in his chest. The bullet punctured his lung, and since it's silver, his wolf won't be able to heal him.

"NOELLE!" I hear Charlie's voice a moment before he pulls me to him.

"I can't stay, but I had to make sure that you were okay. Alpha's going after Yara, and Quinton is still here," he says, looking down at Bradley.

"Can you save him, Noelle?"

"I ... I don't know how," I say, terrified. This is way above my knowledge.

"You have to try, Noelle. You and Anna are his only hope of surviving," he says.

I look at Anna and see the same fear in her eyes as I'm sure is in mine.

"I'm not a surgeon. I've barely studied medicine. I'm not like Luna."

"But you've been working with her, Noelle. You're the only chance he has. I have faith in you," he says, cupping my face and kissing me quickly. "I have to go. Stay safe. Guard your Beta female," he commands the warriors in the room before rushing out.

I look back down at Bradley. His breathing is shallow. I close my eyes, trying to think. What would Yara do? What would Yara do?

"She'd triage," Anna says, making my eyes flash open.

"That's right, she would," I say, looking at Bradley and then turning to the other warrior. Travis steps up to me.

"This one is more critical," he says, pointing to Bradley.

"Yes, but this one will die while I try to treat Bradley. Anna, get Bradley set up in a room and on IVs while I finish stopping the bleeding on this one," I say.

Piper runs out, handing me two crash kits and patting her chest, asking what she can do to help.

"Can you work with Travis to triage?" I ask her, and she nods.

I turn to Travis. "She can't talk. Alpha Simon nearly ripped her throat out when he tried to get our Luna last time."

"Damn," he says, looking up at her. "It's impressive that you're on your feet."

She shrugs, then slaps her hands together, pointing to the warriors.

"Right, let's get going," Travis says.

I clamp off the warrior who's bleeding, making sure that he's not going to bleed out while I try to save Bradley. Then I rush into the room where Anna has Bradley ready to go.

"Okay, let's try to save him," I say to Anna. She nods as I grab a scalpel and slice open the wound to get to the silver bullet.

~ ~ ~

Simon POV

I know the minute Warren realizes I have his mate, that he'll be after me. I wait until I'm off his pack lands before howling the retreat to my pack members. I'll need them to help me get her out of here. I just need to get to the river. I know I can't take her back to the pack, not yet. Warren will attack there, but if I can get her away, just long enough to put my mark on her, then it won't matter if he comes for me. He won't be able to kill me without potentially killing her.

As I run with Yara over my shoulder, I can smell that bastard on her. He'll pay for fucking what's mine, and she'll pay for being with someone other than me. But that will have to wait. I have to get away from here.

I hear a howl of retreat coming from the opposite direction that I'm going. Probably Brady. Now that my warriors are gone, he doesn't stand a chance against Warren's warriors. I swear they've only gotten stronger, probably because of Yara. That's good. She can strengthen my pack, and then I'll finally be able to send Warren to the Moon Goddess' realm, but not before he sees my pup growing in her belly. I'll keep him alive just long enough for him to know that I've won.

It takes nearly an hour before I reach the river. Warren's pack is closing in on us.

'Run through the river, then circle back and head to the pack,' I instruct my pack members.

'Yes, Alpha.'

I run into the river as well, but rather than running across, I pull Yara into my arms and carefully dunk her hair underwater before lowering the two of us into the water and letting the current take us downstream. I need to hide her scent, and thankfully, the breeze is on my side. The current is taking us farther downwind. Between the water and the wind, Warren will have a hard time tracking her scent.

I turn back as I float, hearing my warriors swimming across the river, then getting out on the other side and racing towards home. I listen harder as the current carries me away, and it's only about ten minutes later when I hear the splashing of wolves as they rush across the river. When they get there, they catch the scent of my warriors and howl that the hunt continues before racing after them.

I smile, looking down at my mate.

"You will be mine very soon, Yara," I say.

As I hold her, I rub my hands over her body. She's soft and pliable, her breasts filling my hands, her nipples hard. It might be from the cold water, but I think it's that she subconsciously likes my touch. I can't wait to bury my cock inside her, fill her with my sperm. I'll have to have some control. I can't overdo it with her since I'll need her in the pack hospital. But I'm sure that I can take a day to impregnate my mate. I've waited so long for her. I deserve that.

When I'm sure that we've gone far enough, I swim back out of the river and begin making my way to the mountains I spotted long ago when I was attacking the packs. This one is between Quinton and Harold's packs but far enough away that neither of them should have wolves patrolling in this area. It's a perfect spot for me to take my time with my mate. It won't matter how much noise she makes; we won't be heard. And if she thinks about trying to get away from me, I'll have plenty of space to hunt and catch her before she can.

The thought of hunting down my mate makes me smile. Maybe I'll let her think she's getting away just so Hegir, my wolf, can hunt her down.

'I think we should. I'd love to mate with Annika. That she-wolf is feisty,' Hegir says as I climb the mountain.

I'm so fucking hard by the time I get to the cave that I've been slowly preparing that I think I might just mark my mate before she wakes up. I'm not a monster, I won't fuck her while she's sleeping, but if I mark her, then I can ease this hard-on and also make sure that she knows that she's mine when she wakes up.

I lay her down on the floor of the cave, moving her so I can see her in the moonlight. Thank the goddess that the water washed some of Warren's scent off of her, but not all of it. No matter, once it's my mark on her, it will overpower his.

I push her hair back from her face. Her skin is cool to the touch from the cold river. The scrubs she's wearing from the hospital are clinging to her body. Since I don't intend for her to wear any clothes for the next day or so, I rip open the front of her shirt, exposing her beautiful breasts to me.

I squeeze them, enjoying the feel of them in my hands as my dick begins to ache with the need to explode.

I lean over her, turning her head and pulling the shirt away from her neck as my canines come out.

I snarl. NO! NO! NO!

That fucking bastard marked my mate!

Chapter 61: The Kiss

Travis

The moment I awoke in this hospital, I knew she was here. Her smell alone helped my wolf to heal. Every time the door opened, I hoped that it would be her coming to find me, but it wasn't. I couldn't understand why her scent was so strong, but she never came to me.

That is until she'd walked out of a hospital room herself. When she clapped her hands at Luna Yara, I'd wondered about it. But then she hadn't spoken out loud, and I'd wondered if she was mute. Doesn't matter to me. Once she has my mark, we'll be able to talk using the mind link. If she wants my mark, that is.

I know we're in chaos, but she barely even glanced at me. Maybe she thinks I'm like my old Alpha. I can have Noelle and Laney assure her that I'm not if we ever get the chance.

I'm not sure that the chance I get is the one I was hoping for, but when Luna Yara is taken, and Noelle has to try and save the warrior who was protecting her, I get the opportunity I wanted to speak with her.

Of course, I'd been staring at her, my wolf, Ronyn, enamored with his mate.

"Hi, I'm Travis," I say, walking up to where she's looking over a warrior. She glances up and smiles briefly before returning to her work.

"You're Piper, right?" I ask, knowing she can't speak.

She nods, not looking up. I begin helping her look over the injured as some of the warriors who were guarding the hospital are brought in. They were attacked and are unconscious, but they are alive. I prioritize them to be stitched up over some of the others with shallower or already healing injuries.

"This one," I say, pointing out a warrior who is more injured than the others. She comes over, looks at his injuries, and nods.

"You know what you are to me, right?" I ask quietly.

She looks at me, but there is no smile this time. It's a moment before she nods.

"I'm not like my previous Alpha. I'm different. Noelle has already vouched for me, and she's your Beta female or will be if your Beta ever has a chance to mark her," I say.

She doesn't say anything, of course, so we continue working, triaging the injured.

"I mean, I'd really like for you to give me a chance. Get to know me. I never thought I'd find my fated mate, and here you are. I guess I got lucky to be captured by your pack so I could meet you," I say, wishing that I could figure out what she's thinking.

"Travis, Beta Noelle wants to know if there is anyone more critical than the warrior who was bleeding out," Anna says, walking out and pulling off bloody gloves.

I look around, making sure I haven't missed anyone, then look at Piper. "You haven't seen anyone else that critical, right?"

She shakes her head no, and I look back at Anna. I see her eyes are unfocused, and when they refocus, her eyes are sharp on mine. I guess Piper told her that I'm her mate.

"There's no one more critical," I say.

She nods, then looks at Piper again before turning back to the surgery rooms.

I work in silence for a bit, getting Piper what she needs to stitch up the most injured and talking to the warriors to hear what's going on. They've lost contact with the warriors who went after their Luna, which means they're so far away that they can't hear them.

Periodically, I see Piper mind linking the warriors, probably telling them what she's doing or going to do with them. I have no idea.

I sigh, and I must have done it several times because Piper stops, turning to look at me and giving me a look as if she wants to know what's wrong with me.

"This would just be a lot easier if I knew if you were willing to give me a chance or not. I have no idea what you're thinking, if you hate me, if you're scared of me, if you're as distracted by my scent as I am by yours. I just ..." I sigh again. "I just wish I knew how you were feeling and if you're going to give me a chance."

The room goes quiet. I'm basically professing my desire to be with this woman in front of a group of her pack members. If they didn't know that she was my mate before, they do now. If she says she doesn't want to get to know me, I'll have to suck it up and deal with her pack members' condescension and judgment while I help them, but I don't see any other way around it. It's the truth; the not knowing is killing me.

She steps up to me, and I watch her, wondering if she's going to slap me across the face. Instead, she leans in and presses her lips to mine. I close my eyes, feeling something inside me relax. The kiss doesn't last nearly long enough, but when she pulls back, her eyes are warm and kind.

"That's a good sign, right?" I ask her softly.

She smiles and nods her head at me.

"Okay. Okay, good," I say, returning her smile, my heart feeling lighter than it has in a very long time.

~ ~ ~

Warren POV

'Why can't I smell her?' I growl at Arric. We've been chasing Simon's pack for hours, slowly catching his pack members and killing them as we go. They're heading back to their pack, and I've sent some warriors to cut them off.

'It has to be the river. It must have masked her scent,' Arric says.

I hear the howl of return and attack, one after the other. We've reached Simon's pack lands. More warriors come rushing out, but my adrenaline is still pumping hard and fast in my veins. I need to find Yara. I have to get to her before that bastard hurts my mate.

'At least she's wearing our mark,' Arric says.

'That won't stop that asshole from doing other things to her,' I snarl. I will kill him, slowly and painfully, for taking my mate.

Before I'd left the pack lands, I'd heard my warriors tell me that he'd attacked some of my already injured warriors, the ones protecting the hospital. I curse myself for not leaving my strong warriors in place to protect Yara. I'd thought with that many warriors, he wouldn't get through, but Simon's a sneaky bastard.

His warriors are ready to fight, but I don't have time for them. I need to find Simon and get Yara.

'Kill them!' I snarl, seeing Simon's Beta guarding the back of the packhouse. I don't have time to waste with this asshole, so I leap on him, Arric biting and slashing him. When he pulls himself away from us, Arric rips a large chuck of flesh out of his back. We don't stop to finish him. My warriors will do that.

Arric rushes inside, his nose in the air.

'Where is she?' I growl.

I can feel Arric beginning to panic. He rushes past the women and children, screaming in fear, rushing up the stairs, and taking out anyone who tries to get in our way.

When I get to the Alpha floor, a woman is standing in the hallway.

"Are you Alpha Warren?" she asks.

Arric sniffs the air. Yara isn't here. He turns, ready to go search the rest of the pack-house.

"Because if you are, the woman you're after isn't here."

I turn back and look at her. "The lady doctor, right? Yara?"

I shift, moving fast and slamming the woman against the wall at the end of the hallway, my hand on her throat.

"What do you know about my mate?" I snarl.

"I know he wants her. He has someplace, not here, where he planned to hide her. I don't know where, but that's where he would have taken her," she says, and I can smell her fear.

"Why are you telling me this?" I growl.

"Because he hurts me, especially when he's mad at her or you. I want you to take me with you. Please."

I step back, releasing her throat, realizing that she has faint bruises on her arms and her throat.

"What's your name?"

"Trena."

"Trena, you don't know where he took her?"

"No. I just know that he wouldn't bring her here. Not yet. He knew you'd come for her."

She looks at my neck. "He won't be happy when he finds out she's marked already. He wanted to make her his Luna."

"Too bad. She's mine," I snarl, turning to go.

"Wait. Please. Take me with you. Please, don't leave me here with him."

I turn back to her. "Can you shift?"

She nods yes.

"Come on then, you're with me. If this is a trap, or you try to betray me, my mate, or my pack, I won't hesitate to kill you."

She nods again, and I leap over the banister, shifting as I go. I look up, seeing her looking at me with wide eyes. Arric barks, telling her to hurry. She rushes down the stairs as I howl the retreat. We need to get back to the river. That's where I lost her scent.

Chapter 62: Trade

Charlie

After checking on Noelle and leaving the hospital, I called Harold to tell him of Yara being taken and about Brady running home. He told me he'd send Franklin and his warriors and asked if we needed Savannah.

"Honestly, I don't think she'll make it on time. Yara's guard was shot with silver. If Noelle can't save him, he won't live long enough for Savannah to get here," I told him.

'Beta, we have Alpha Quinton and his warriors trapped in the cell block,' Haynes says in the mind link.

'Hold them there, I'm on my way.'

"Let me know if you need anything. Should we send a search party for your Luna?" Harold asks.

"Alpha Warren is out hunting Simon down now. If we need help, I'll let you know. Thank you, Alpha."

"It's what allies do, Beta. I'm glad to know that we can help."

I hang up as I get to the cells, walking down the stairs and hearing the crying of the omegas, pups, and other prisoners. I also hear the sound of their warrior mates trying to soothe them. The smell of burning flesh lets me know they've tried to reach through the cells to touch their mates and pups.

Warren and I didn't talk about it, but he told these people that they weren't prisoners. What's left of Quinton's pack will be weak, especially without their Alpha. As I go down the stairs to the cells, I make a decision that I hope Warren will agree with.

When I get to the bottom of the stairs, I look, seeing warriors pressed as close as the silver bars will allow them to be, some having taken off their shirts and wrapping them around their arms so they can touch their scared mates or pups.

At the end is Quinton, standing tall outside the cell with his son and Luna. While the son is standing as close to his father as possible, the Luna remains seated away from both of them.

I look at Quinton. "What's it going to be?"

"A trade. My son is a pup. Me for him," Quinton says immediately.

"No, Dad!" Quirin says.

"Hush, son," Quinton says, his eyes never leaving mine.

"Your son? Not your son and your Luna?"

He glances at his Luna sitting in the cell. She doesn't look surprised.

"No, of course not, because you wanted our Luna, right?" I say, making my warriors growl angrily. The scent of fear in the cells spikes, and the pups and omegas whimper.

"What I wanted or didn't want no longer matters, does it, Beta?" he asks.

"No, I guess it doesn't."

I look at the warriors watching me carefully. "If any of you ever come after anyone in this pack again, we will kill you, your mates, AND your pups. You're lucky my Alpha isn't like yours, otherwise your families would already be dead," I snarl. "For now, you're free to go."

I turn to my warriors. "Let them go. If they make any move to fight, kill them all," I say. I know it's against what Warren and I believe, but I won't risk our pack.

As each cell is opened, the warriors pull their loved ones to them, wrapping them in a protective embrace as best they can before quickly leading them out of the cells.

The entire time, I stay focused on Quinton, knowing my warriors will take care of the rest. If he attacks, I need to be ready to take him out. When all the cells are empty except the one with his son and mate, I walk forward.

"Step back," I say to him. He does as I say, and Luna Yasim stands, stepping forward.

"If you make any move against my warriors, I will kill your son," I tell him. He nods, and I gesture for my warrior to open the cell.

The moment the door is open, Quirin rushes to his father's arms. Quinton wraps his arms around him, hugging him tightly. "Go with your mother. Always remember that I love you."

"Dad! DAD!" he yells as Yasmin wraps an arm around her son and begins pulling him away.

"Son. You're an Alpha. Remember that Alphas always act like Alphas. Stand on your own two feet and walk out of here with your head held high," Quinton says.

Yasmin puts her son down, and he stands, glaring at me as he passes. When Yasmin goes to pass me, I put a hand on her arm, feeling her jerk. I'm sure she's wondering if I'm going to kill her or worse. I'm sure the other Alphas would have let their warriors take turns on a captured Luna. But that's not how we operate in this pack.

"Into the cell, Quinton," I say.

He looks at his mate, then his son, and does as I ask. I nod for my warrior to lock him in, and then I turn my attention to Yasmin.

"You should reject your mate. I don't know what my Alpha will do with him once he returns. That's up to him. But I expect that he will kill him for his role in what's happened to our Luna. If he does, it could kill you, too."

I hear Quirin begin to sob as quietly as a young pup can who knows that he is going to lose his father.

Yasmin nods, turning back to Quinton. "I, Luna Yasmin Harris, reject you, Alpha Quinton Harris, as my mate and Alpha," she says, watching him.

He looks at his son, then his mate. "Protect him. Guard him with your life," he says.

"You know I will," she says.

He nods, too. "I accept your rejection."

I watch as both of them hunch over, clutching their hearts.

"DAD!" Quirin yells.

"Get him out of here!" he yells at his mate.

She wraps an arm around her son and begins moving out of the cells.

I watch her go, then turn back to Quinton. "Get comfortable, Alpha. You have some time before my Alpha returns."

'Beta, we need you upstairs,' one of my warriors says. I turn and head upstairs. When I get there, I see the warriors and their families standing by.

"I said you're free to go," I tell them.

They all look at each other, then at Alpha Quirin, who is technically their Alpha now. His arm is around his mother, who is still hunched over, dealing with the pain of the rejected mate bond.

"Beta, we have nowhere to go, no pack to return to, and no offense, young Alpha, but most of us aren't comfortable swearing our allegiance to an Alpha as young as you," one of the warriors says before turning to me. "We want to stay. We want to join your pack."

I'm shocked, and I have to think quickly.

"That's not for me to decide. You'll have to wait for my Alpha to return and make that decision. However, as long as you agree to abide by the rules of this pack, we'll find rooms for you to stay in. Just know that if you make any sort of aggressive moves against anyone in our pack, we will kill you."

"Yes, Beta," they all say.

"Come on, Quirin. Let's go," Luna Yasmin says, guiding her son away. I watch him, staring at his father's pack members as if he can't believe they've just rejected him as their Alpha. Personally, I would do the same. In a time of war like what we're in, you need a strong Alpha, and he might have gotten there one day, but he's not there yet.

"Let Luna Yasmin and Alpha Quirin leave the pack. They are not allowed to return without speaking to me or Alpha Warren. Everyone else, follow me. Let's find you some rooms."

Chapter 63: *Unexpected Ally*
Yara

I come awake slowly. My body is stiff, and my arms are aching, like I've somehow managed to get tangled up in them while I was sleeping, and they're stuck behind my back. I try to move them out from under me, but I can't. My head feels fuzzy, and it hurts. What's going on?

'Wake up, Yara,' Annika says urgently.

'I'm trying, Annika. What's going ...'

"There she is. Finally," an angry voice says nearby. My eyes flash open. I recognize that voice. I don't, however, recognize my surroundings.

'Annika, where are we?'

'I don't know. He knocked me out, too.'

A hand grabs my hair, pulling me into a sitting position roughly. My arms are tied behind my back, and my legs are wrapped up tightly. My body is stiff and sore. I must have been like this for a while.

"You just had to go and fuck him, didn't you?" Simon snarls in my face.

He looks crazed. His hair is shooting out in all directions like he's been tugging on it so long that it doesn't bother trying to go back into place again. His eyes are furious, and he's glaring at me. Thank the goddess Warren already marked me.

I start to reach out in the mind link, wanting to try and reach my mate, when Simon backhands me hard. Pain shoots out across my cheek, into my ear, and across my nose. I fall back to the floor, unable to stop my face from slapping against the rocky floor of this cave.

"Don't you dare try to fucking call your mate!" He yanks me back up by the hair, and I cry out from the unexpected pain. "If you do, I'll kill him," he says, showing me the gun.

"Bradley ..." I say, the memory flooding back into my mind. "You killed Bradley!"

"He was in my way. If you had just come with me the last time, Yara, no one would have died, but now ... their deaths are on you."

"Warren will kill you when he finds you," I growl.

"Warren ..." he snarls, grabbing me by the throat before taking a deep breath. "Warren needs to die so that I can put my mark on you."

"Then why don't you let me call him, tell him where I am," I say, my tone condescendingly sweet. I have no doubt that Warren will kill Simon. I don't care how many silver bullets Simon shoots into him.

"Oh, I will. When the time is right."

I begin laughing. It makes everything in my body hurt, but I don't stop. "There will never be a right time to kill my mate. You are a coward and a bully. You always have been. I know it, and your father knew it. That's why he helped me get away from you."

He snarls, his claws coming out as he slams them into the floor on either side of me. "And he died for betraying me."

"I knew it was you who killed him. Your father was a good man. You must take after your mother," I say, earning me another backhand, this time on the other side of my face. Now, each side is throbbing in time with the other, like the ticking of a clock. Throb-throb. Throb-throb.

"Don't ever speak about my mother again," he snarls.

I spit blood onto the floor beside me. "You better hope these bruises are gone before Warren finds me. If he sees that you've hurt me, he'll make your death much slower."

"He will never find us here."

I laugh again. This time, both sides of my face and the rest of my body hurt.

"My mate, the most incredible Alpha and man I've ever met in my life, will find me. He will not stop until he has me back in his arms. Of that, I have no doubt. Your days are numbered, Simon. All you had to do was walk away, but it's too late now."

"You think much too highly of a man who let me get close enough to capturing you not once but twice," he says, smirking.

"Being attacked by three packs at once would be difficult for anyone. I'm still betting that MY mate finished off those Alphas and is out hunting for me. Tell me, did you leave your pack to die? Did you send them home, being chased by my mate? He would have killed them, all of them," I say, watching as the smug look falls away, replaced by fury.

"How did you make him so fucking strong?"

"I didn't have to. I told you; MY mate is the most amazing man I've ever met. He is strong in ways that you'll never understand. He's compassionate and loving, and when he was inside me ..."

This time, when he backhands me, darkness surrounds me.

'Yara, wake up!' Annika says. This time, I know where I am. My swollen, bruised face is an immediate reminder.

I feel hands on me, touching me, and I jolt awake, kicking and ready to scream. A hand clamps down on my mouth, and when I open my eyes, it's not Simon.

The woman looks at me, putting a finger to her lips, before quickly looking behind me. I turn my head, seeing Simon asleep inside the cave where he's brought me.

"Hurry," she mouths to me. The woman is small but wiry in a way that lets me know she's stronger than most people probably give her credit for. When she moves into the light, I recognize her. Farrah.

She slices through the bindings around my arms, looking over my shoulder at Simon again. I try to move my arms while she moves to my legs. They're stiff, and one is completely asleep. I can't move it. The other feels like I have an entire surgical ward of needles stabbing into me at one time.

The moment she undoes the bindings on my legs, I feel blood begin rushing through them, waking them up in the same painful way that my arm is waking up.

"Can you stand?" she mouths to me.

I try to move my legs, but I can barely bend my knees.

I shake my head no.

She nods as if expecting this. She puts her finger to her lips again. When I nod, she slides her arm under my knees, wrapping the other one around my back. The movement sends shockwaves of pain through my body as my blood continues to try and wake up my limbs.

I bite down on the cry of pain as Farrah lifts me, quickly carrying me out of the cave. It's up on a mountain, and I already know she's going to struggle to carry me down.

"I'm going to throw you over my shoulder. Just stay quiet," she says softly, her voice barely audible on the night breeze.

I'm thankful she gave me the warning because the pain of the movement sends another round of shockwaves through my body. My second arm is now waking up, and it feels like I'm being stabbed all over my body.

She begins carefully climbing down the mountain. I try to reach out to Warren or anyone from our pack, but we must be too far away. When I can, I wrap an arm around Farrah's waist to help steady myself on her shoulder. It must work because she begins moving faster after that.

When we get to the bottom of the mountain, she carefully sets me on my feet.

"Can you shift?" she asks.

"Yes. Do you know where we are?"

"We're between Alpha Harold and Alpha Quinton's packs. You need to get to Alpha Harold. He will help you."

"I don't know the way."

"I'll take you. Hurry, we need to be long gone before Simon wakes up."

"Wait. How did you know I was here?"

"I saw him dragging you over here, and I followed you."

"Why did you help me? You ran to get away from our pack," I say. I'm pretty sure I can trust her, but she did leave, and she could still be angry at me for saving her life when she wanted to die.

"A life for a life. You saved mine, and I don't like having an unpaid debt."

"Thank you," I say. She nods, and then we both shift and begin running to Harold's pack. I need to get a hold of my mate. I know he will be sick with worry, tearing this world apart trying to find me.

Chapter 64: The Gift
Harold

When Franklin returned after attacking Brady's pack, he let me know that Brady survived, but his pack had been nearly decimated. I sent scouts to watch his pack and make sure that he didn't leave. I doubt he will, but now that our pack is getting stronger, I can afford to send a couple of warriors to keep watch.

Savannah was beside herself, wanting to go back to her old pack to help, especially after hearing that Simon had kidnapped Yara. I told her what Beta Charlie said, and she'd become even more distraught.

"Bradley was shot? Even I wouldn't know how to save him. Poor Noelle," she said. Franklin had taken her to their room and tried to console her. I'd waited a few hours and called Beta Charlie.

"Alpha Harold?" he answered, sounding exhausted.

"I'm sorry, Beta. Did I wake you?"

"It's okay. Alpha Warren isn't back yet, so I'm still running the pack."

"I wanted to update you on Brady and find out what happened with Alpha Quinton."

"Quinton turned himself in, basically gave his life for his son's. He's in our cells. Luna Yasmin and Alpha Quirin are gone," he says. I hear him move around, and then I hear a soft voice murmuring beside him.

"No, it's Alpha Harold," he says, I'm guessing to his mate.

"So, your Luna is still missing?" I ask.

"Yeah. I doubt Warren will come home until he's found her," he says. "We haven't felt the tether to her snap, so we know she's still alive, but none of us can hear her, so she's either unconscious or too far away to connect. Tell me about Brady."

"Franklin and my warriors were able to take out several of his warriors while they ran to their pack. Brady's alive, but the pack is severely impacted. I've got warriors watching him to make sure he doesn't go anywhere."

"We need to figure out a way to get past his barricades," he says.

"Agreed. Once your Luna is safe, we can talk about that. And ... Savannah was concerned about Bradley. Did he survive?"

This time, Charlie's tone is full of pride. "Yeah, he did. My mate was able to get the bullet out. She's not sure if she stitched his lung up properly, but hopefully, his wolf will get strong and be able to help him heal. If not, maybe when Luna Yara returns, she can check and make sure he's stitched properly. For now, we're keeping him sedated. But the important thing is that he's alive."

"That's good to hear. Thank you, I'll let Savannah know. And if you need anything at all, please let me know."

"Thank you very much, Alpha Harold. Just dealing with Brady is a huge help."

We hang up, and I mind link Franklin to let him know about Bradley.

"What can I do, Dad?" Henry asks, walking into my office.

I smile at my son ... so very proud of the young man that he is. I order dinner for us, and we talk through all of the things that are happening, how they could impact our pack, and what our next steps should be. My son is very intuitive and inquisitive, asking intelligent questions and making thoughtful suggestions.

I decide to try some of his suggestions, even though I think they'll fail. If they do, it's a good learning experience for him, and if they don't, it's a good learning experience for me.

Before I send him off to bed, I tell him to close his eyes. When he does, I do the same.

"Open your mind to the pack. Don't focus on any one person. Just open your mind to the entire pack."

I give him a few moments, helping to mentally guide him to opening his mind. When he does, I sit back, letting him stretch his mind link.

"What do you feel?" I ask him.

I wait, letting him sift through the feelings in the pack. It's hard at first, trying to focus on the overall feeling, not on individual feelings. Some are sweet and happy, some are frustrated or angry, and some are lustful and intimate, but the overall feeling of the pack has become much more settled and happier since we entered the alliance with Warren, and Yara came to help heal our pack members.

"It feels good," he says, finally. He opens his eyes and looks at me. "Right?"

I smile. "Yeah. It's been a long time since it felt this good in our pack. That's a very good thing. Now, you have to think about what has caused the shift, the happiness in the pack. What did we, as their Alphas, do for the pack to feel this way?"

"We entered into an alliance with Alpha Warren."

"Yes, but it's more than that. An alliance is merely a piece of paper to the pack. They don't have the relationship with him that we do."

I watch him frown, thinking through what changed. "But that alliance has brought healing to our pack."

"Correct."

"And healing has strengthened the pack, which makes them feel more confident in our leadership as Alphas."

"Absolutely correct. Making the pack strong makes us stronger, but that's partly because the pack becomes more confident in our leadership, accepting their Alpha more fully, which also makes us stronger in our role. So, today's lesson to you, my son and Alpha heir, is to make sure you're keeping tabs on the feel of your pack. If this feeling that you have right now begins to change or lessen, you need to ask yourself why. What are you, as their leader, not doing or are doing wrong? Figure out what it is and change it if you can because you can only lead if the pack will follow. Okay?"

He nods, smiling.

"Alright, off to bed with you," I tell him. He hops up, coming to hug me before heading to bed.

I do a little more work before I go to my own bedroom. As always, I look at my empty, cold bed. I'm not sure why I never took another mate, but when you find your fated mate, and she's everything to you, nothing less will do. I enjoyed the few years that the Moon Goddess gave us, and that has to be enough to get me through the rest of my life.

I get ready for bed and fall asleep easily now that the pack is content. I have no idea how long I've been asleep when there's a howl that there are intruders at the border. I leap out of bed and shift. I'm running before I open the mind link to the patrols.

'Who is it? Who's attacking?' I ask, used to being woken in the middle of the night and rushing into battle.

'Not an attack, Alpha. It's Farrah ... and she has Luna Yara with her.'

'Are you sure?' I ask the patrols, and Conrad pushes harder to get to the border. It feels good to have my wolf back and getting stronger again.

'It feels good to be back,' Conrad says.

'Yes, Alpha,' the patrols respond.

'Franklin,' I call in the mind link.

'Are we under attack?' he asks.

'No. It's Luna Yara. I'm going to confirm, but once I do, I need you to call Alpha Warren. I don't want to call until I know for sure that it's her.'

'How did she get here?' he asks.

'No idea,' I say, just as the sweetest scent I've ever smelled enters my nose, earthy and daintily floral. I cut the link with Franklin.

'Conrad?' I ask.

I've only ever smelled something this delicious once before. When I found my mate. When I get close, I can see the two of them standing there, Luna Yara and ...

'Mate,' Conrad says.

I watch Farrah's eyes go wide and I know her wolf must have just announced us as her mate as well.

I shift, staring at Farrah before dragging my eyes to Luna Yara. When I do, I see that her face is horribly swollen and bruised.

"Luna, let's get you to the pack hospital."

"I need to call my mate," she says.

'Franklin, it's her. Call Alpha Warren and get him here now.'

'Yes, Alpha. Savannah is on her way,' he says just as I hear paws pounding behind me.

Savannah shifts and rushes up to her previous Luna, wrapping her arms around her in a tight hug.

"Oh, my goddess, Luna. We've been so worried about you. Oh, that fucker hit you? Alpha Warren will flay him. Come on," she says, taking charge and leading her toward the pack hospital.

"I need to call Warren," she says again.

"Franklin's calling him right now. He'll meet us at the pack hospital," she says as they walk away.

I watch them for a moment before turning to my mate.

"Farrah," I say, extending my hand for her to join me. She hasn't crossed back into the pack yet. The last time she was here, her mate and son were murdered, and she was captured and taken away, forced into another mate bond, and from what I understand, was raped until she became pregnant. Then, she nearly killed herself trying to end her pregnancy.

She looks resigned but steps into my pack lands. She reaches out, and when her hand touches mine, the tingles that I haven't felt in years light up in my body. I see tears well in Farrah's eyes, and I know she feels the same way.

I lead her to a place where we can have some privacy, and then I turn to her.

"You and I need to talk. Now is not the time; I need to be available when Alpha Warren gets here, and I need to guard his mate until he arrives. But ... rejection is not open for discussion, Farrah. I know you've been through a lot. I know you wanted to die, and I know you may not want this. But you are a gift given to me by the Moon Goddess, one I never expected to receive. So few people get one fated mate in their lives, and now you and I have both been blessed with two. Before you think about throwing that away, I want to talk. I want to see if we can find a way to come together. There's a reason the Moon Goddess put us together, Farrah. Don't throw this away without giving it a chance."

I watch as she looks at me and then looks around. I can feel her sadness, her sorrow at the memories that she has here.

"Okay, Alpha," she says, finally looking back at me.

"Call me Harold, Farrah."

"Okay, Harold."

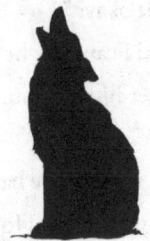

Chapter 65: The Call

Charlie

I haven't gotten more than two hours of sleep since Luna Yara was taken and Alpha Warren left the pack. I'm beyond exhausted, but more than that, I can feel the tension in the pack, the anxiety about not knowing what's going to happen to their Alpha and Luna. I have the same anxiety, but I'm the pack's current leader.

In the past, I would have also felt the pack's desire to test me, to test the strength of the leader of this pack. It's nice to know that Luna Yara's influence has extended past her and Alpha Warren. She's somehow made the pack feel whole like it should. So now, anyone who would try to go against me would break that bubble of security, and I think the entire pack would turn on them now.

My phone rings, and it's a number I don't recognize.

"Beta Charlie," I answer.

"Beta, this is Beta Franklin, Alpha Harold's Beta."

"Yes, I know who you are. Is everything okay?"

"Beta, we have your Luna. She's safe."

"What? Where is she? How? Does Alpha Warren know?"

I hear my Luna's sweet voice in the background, and then the phone is being transferred.

"Charlie?" My Luna's voice has never sounded so close to tears.

327

"Luna! Oh, goddess, Luna. We were so worried about you."

"They can't get a hold of Warren, Charlie. Do you know where he is?"

"He's out looking for you. Are you okay?"

"I need him, Charlie," she says, and I can hear her fighting hard to hold back her tears.

"I'll find him for you, Luna. I'll get him to you. You stay there. Is Savannah looking after you?"

"You know I am, Beta," I hear her voice in the background, making me sigh in relief.

"We'll be there as soon as we find him, Luna. Hold on."

"Okay," she says, and she passes the phone back to Franklin.

"Let your patrols know, my Alpha will be coming in hot."

"Will do, we'll be ready."

I hang up and turn to address the pack, seeing all of them have stopped what they are doing to watch me.

"You all heard?"

"Yes, Beta!"

"Good, your Luna is safe, but she needs our Alpha. Haynes, the pack is yours. You three, with me. We need to find Alpha Warren and get him to Luna Yara. Keep the phone lines open. I'll call as soon as I have news."

Noelle runs up with a small bag with a large strap, taking my phone while I quickly shift. She straps my phone to Gregor's body before wrapping her arms around us. "Take care of my mate and go get our Luna!" she says against my ear.

Gregor turns his head and licks her quickly before taking off, the other three wolves rushing to catch up. I cross the borders, searching for Simon's scent and following it out to a river. I keep the mind link open, hoping that I'll get close enough to Warren to let him know where Yara is.

When we get to the river, I lose the scent of Simon, Yara, and our warriors, so I know they crossed.

I look across the river, wondering if Warren crossed. Is he still over there, or did Simon double back? This isn't the way to his pack.

I lift my head to the sky, howling for my Alpha. It takes a moment, but then I hear him coming from the other direction.

I turn, and we run in the direction that I heard his howl. The moment the mind link clicks back into place, he's in my head.

"What are you doing out here? Is everything okay?"

"They found her. Luna is in Alpha Harold's pack. She's safe."

I feel a flood of relief, which quickly becomes an intense need to get to his mate.

"I talked to her. She said she needs you, Alpha! Go! They're expecting you."

I feel him and our warriors shift as he howls to his mate that he's on his way to her.

~ ~ ~

Simon POV

I wake up stiff and sore. After I'd knocked Yara and her smart mouth out, I'd had to get my anger out somehow. Rather than killing the bitch who is now responsible for the death of most of my pack, I'd punched the walls of the cave until my knuckles were raw and bloody.

Then, I'd sat and stared at her. She will pay for what she has put me through. She will pay for not staying with me, for not coming with me when she had the chance. I intended to make her my Luna, to be treated with the respect she deserved, but now, she deserves no respect, and I don't need a doctor if I don't have a pack to heal.

I underestimated just how strong Warren is. I thought if my warriors got home, they could fight, but I'd been wrong. I felt every one of their tethers break. The only thing that finally settled me was knowing that I could keep her as a breeder. She will give me as many pups as I can fucking put in her, and when she's used up her value to me, she can rot.

The thought finally calms me enough that I can get some sleep.

However, when I wake, the fucking bitch is gone! I quickly rush to the edge of the cave, looking out over the early dawn morning. She is nowhere to be seen. I shift and let Hegir sniff the area and smell another scent, a she-wolf.

I leave the cave, quickly following their scent. I can use the meddling she-wolf as an example: killing her slowly in front of Yara to let her see what happens when she defies me. I don't have to hurt her. I can hurt those who help her.

I'm about halfway to Harold's pack, following the scent, when I hear a wolf calling to another. I stop, listening and waiting. It didn't sound like Yara.

A few moments later, I hear the unmistakable answering howl of a wolf. Fuck! Warren is already back. I turn, changing directions. If Yara went to Harold's pack, then they will protect her until Warren gets to her. Right now, Warren is between my pack and me, and I can't risk him capturing me.

I turn and begin making my way to Quinton's pack to ask for sanctuary. It's my only option. I'll have to appeal to his Alpha arrogance, letting him know I've lost my pack, but I can pretend to grovel if needed. I did it all the time with my father.

Chapter 66: Safe

Warren

I felt something deep inside me ease when I got Charlie's mind link about Yara. I'm still about an hour away from Harold's pack, but Arric pushes us hard to get there, leaving our warriors behind. Yara said she needed us. I don't know what happened to her, what Simon may have done to her, and I don't care right now. We'll get through it. I'm just so thankful that she's safe.

When I get close to Harold's pack, I howl that I'm coming in. Hopefully, they know that I have no intention of waiting for the patrols to let me through. I need to see my mate, and nothing will keep me from getting to her.

As we catch her scent, Arric pushes even faster, following her scent, along with the scent of antiseptic, to the pack hospital. Arric rushes into the hospital, and I shift without stopping. Everyone in the waiting room, including Alpha Harold, just points, and I rush to her room, slamming the door open.

The first thing I see are her bruised, swollen cheeks. Simon will die slowly for touching what is mine. Then her lips begin to tremble, and she sniffs. She's in my arms before the first tears fall from her eyes.

"I'm here. You're safe," I say, feeling like I can breathe for the first time in days. I hold her while she cries, walking around the room as I kiss her head and nuzzle her hair.

"I'm here, baby. I'm right here. I'm not going anywhere," I murmur softly. I will, though. I will hunt Simon down like a dog and kill him. But not today. Today, I will take care of my mate.

I'm not sure how long I hold her, but she cries herself to sleep in my arms. When she does, I open the mind link, feeling my warriors and even Charlie are here now.

'Charlie, I need Savannah,' I mind link him.

A moment later, she knocks softly and then steps in.

"She's asleep?" she asks softly, and I nod. "Good. She wouldn't rest until you got here."

"What happened to her? What did he do to her?"

"Mostly what you see. He hit her three times, according to Farrah."

"Farrah? The one who left our pack after Yara saved her life?"

"That's the one. She found her and brought her here."

"I need to talk to her. What other injuries? Did he..." I can't ask. I'm trying to stay calm so Yara can get the sleep she desperately needs.

"He didn't. Luna swears he didn't. It aligns with what Farrah said. However, he tied her arms behind her back, and she apparently didn't realize that her arm was dislocated, so when she shifted, it tore. Annika is still weak from the chloroform that he used on them, but she's getting stronger now that they are safe. Yara wanted her to heal her face first so you wouldn't see it, but I insisted that Annika focus on the more serious injury."

"Is it okay that I'm holding her like this?" I ask, looking down at my mate.

"I'm sure being close to you is strengthening Annika even more, and Luna wouldn't have been able to fall asleep if she had been in pain."

I take a deep breath, smelling her cinnamon and nutmeg scent.

"Do you want me to get you a chair, Alpha?" she asks.

"No, thank you. I have too much energy to sit. Can you send Farrah and Charlie in for me?"

"Sure thing, Alpha."

Yara shifts in my arms, tucking her face against my neck. Arric begins purring to help keep her calm. The door opens, and Farrah, Charlie, and Alpha Harold all walk in. I frown, unsure why he's here.

"Farrah, you found my mate?" I ask her.

"Yes, Alpha."

"She was with Simon?"

"Yes. I saw him taking her toward a mountain out east, in between Alpha Quinton and Alpha Harold's packs. I followed them. I'm sorry. I couldn't get to her right away. But I waited. I watched. If he'd tried to ... I would have done something. But I knew he had to sleep at some point, and when he knocked her out ..."

She cuts off as I growl. Yara shifts in my arms again, and Arric begins purring again.

'Focus. Our mate is more important than our anger,' Arric scolds me.

I take another deep breath, feeling Yara's weight relax in my arms again as Arric's purr puts her back into a deep sleep. When she tucks her face against my neck again and sighs, I refocus my attention back on Farrah.

She watches our interactions, smiling a bit. "She knew you'd come for her. She knew that you would find her and that you would kill Alpha Simon. She even told him that he better hope her bruises were gone before you saw them, or you'd kill him slowly. I haven't seen love and trust like that between an Alpha and a Luna since ..." She stops, looking at Harold.

Arric begins purring again knowing that our mate knew we'd come for her and that she trusted that we would find her.

Farrah turns back to me.

"She kept calling you 'my mate', almost as if she was taunting him. She's stronger than she looks," Farrah says with admiration.

"Yes, she is. I am in your debt," I begin, but she shakes her head.

"Your mate asked me why I was helping her. I told her that she saved my life, and it was my turn to save hers. When I was in your pack, I didn't want to live, but she made a good point. If the Moon Goddess didn't let me die, then she must have plans for me. I guess your mate was right," she says, looking at Harold again. I'm beginning to understand why he's in here.

"My mate usually is," I say, smiling down at her. Then I look up at Charlie.

"You look like hell. I was going to send you after Simon ..."

"I'll go. You need time with our Luna."

"Send Haynes. I'm guessing that he's the one you left in charge of the pack?"

"Yes."

"Send him. Get home and get some sleep. You need it," I tell him.

When he doesn't argue, I know I'm right. Yara would have put him on reserve duty, so I will in her stead.

"Do you want me to send a car for you?" he asks.

"Yeah. I don't want her shifting until her arm is healed and I don't want to be out there with her alone if Simon, Brady, and Quinton are still out there. Is Quinton still out there?" I ask.

"The short answer is no, but there's a much longer conversation that we'll need to have once our Luna is settled. I hope you'll agree with the decisions I made."

"I usually do. That's why you're my Beta. Get home, get some rest. If you don't, I'm going to let Yara go at you when she's back to herself."

"Oh hell, no. I'm not going toe to toe with our Luna," he says, making me smile.

"Good, send the car, and I'll see you when you wake up," I tell him.

"I know you're feeling protective, Alpha, but the warriors would feel a whole lot better if they could see our Luna before we head home. And then they could spread the word that she's safe," he says.

I nod, then look at Harold. "Harold, I'm assuming it's okay to remain here while we wait for the car?"

"You can wait here as long as you like, Warren. My pack feels almost as strongly about your Luna as yours does. We've become much stronger because of her, and we're remaining strong because of our new Beta female."

"Savannah's wonderful," I say, suddenly remembering. I turn back to Charlie. "Bradley?"

"He's alive, but Noelle is happy to know that Luna Yara can now look at him and make sure she stitched him up properly. The bullet punctured his lung, and it was all new to her, but she did a great job of saving his life."

"Tell her I'm proud of her," I say.

"Tell her yourself when you get home," he says, smiling at me.

"Get out of here," I say, following him and the others out of the room.

When I walk out of the hospital room and into the waiting room, it's filled with my warriors.

"How is she, Alpha?" someone asks.

"Exhausted. Charlie is sending a car, so we'll be home soon. He thought you'd want to see her. She's sleeping now."

"He hit her," someone growls, and others do as well, but very softly so they don't wake Yara. It says a lot about my warriors and their love for their Luna, that they are managing their anger to let her sleep.

"We're getting a hunting party ready to go after Simon and hunt him down. Anyone who isn't exhausted can go. If you are, and you decide to go anyway, you'll answer to your Luna when you return in the less than exceptional shape she expects you to be in," I tell him.

They all chuckle, but I see a couple look resolved to not going. These last few days have been trying for the entire pack.

"Bye, Luna."

"We're glad you're safe, Luna."

"We love you, Luna," the warriors say softly as they file out of the hospital.

I turn, seeing Farrah watching me. She looks at Yara and then back up at me. "I can see why the two of you are mated together. You're both very strong but in very different ways. You complement each other."

"We do. People underestimate my mate, but they shouldn't. She's a powerhouse of strength, just not in the way that most of us are used to seeing it," I say.

"Mates should complement each other," Harold says, and I'm guessing after all she's been through, Farrah needs a bit of convincing to accept their mate bond. I have faith that Harold will succeed.

"I'm going to go find a place to sit in the quiet while we wait for the car," I tell them.

"I'll let you know when it's here. If you need anything else, let me know."

"Everything that I need is right here," I say, kissing Yara's head.

I go back to the hospital room and sit, getting comfortable and carefully readjusting Yara to make sure she's comfortable, too. Arric begins purring again, and before I know it, I've dozed off, too.

Chapter 67: Home

Yara

I wake with the smell of teakwood in my nose and the feeling of warm water surrounding my body. I jolt awake, unsure of what's happening.

"Shhh, we're both filthy, and you smell like Simon. I didn't want to go to sleep like this, so we're getting a bath. You can relax, I'll take care of you," Warren says. Just the sound of his voice soothes me.

I snuggle closer to him, needing his touch and smell after having been with Simon.

"Are you okay?" I ask him. I can feel the warring emotions inside of him.

He squeezes water over my shoulder, letting it rinse off the smell of the cave that I have on me. That and the scent of Simon. I don't even want to know why my body smells like him.

"I should be asking you that. But I'm better now that you're here and safe in my arms," he says.

I look up at him, and when he looks at me, his teeth snap together, and he looks away.

"I'm sorry you have to see me like this," I say softly, knowing my bruised face is a reminder to him of what he considers an inability to protect me.

"Don't you dare apologize for what that piece of shit did to you," he growls. I can tell he's barely able to hold on to his anger at Simon. But more than that is his anger at himself for not keeping me safe.

I reach up and stroke his cheek. "I knew you'd come for me," I say.

His eyes return to mine, a bit softer this time. "I would never have stopped until I found you."

"I know. I basically told Simon that," I say, smiling. He smiles a bit, too, gently taking the washcloth and running it over my face.

"I heard. Farrah heard part of your conversation with him. Were you trying to piss him off?" he asks, his smile not reaching his eyes.

"I only told him the truth, that you're the strongest man I've ever met, and yet, you're still somehow compassionate and loving ... and I might have taunted him by starting to tell him about how good you felt inside me," I say, cupping water in my hand and pouring it on his chest.

The hand that is washing me stops.

"You said what?"

I shrug. "He could never be the man you are, and he needed to know that."

He gently tilts my head up to look at him. This time, there's a bit of a smile in his eyes. "I would say next time, let's not taunt your kidnapper so that they hit you hard enough to knock you out, but there will never be a next time that someone gets to you, so it doesn't matter."

"I was only telling the truth. You did feel amazing inside of me," I say, looking up at him through my lashes.

I shift so that I'm straddling him as I continue to run the washcloth over his body. He watches me as his hands begin to stroke my breasts in a way that's more than just bathing. I let my head fall back, enjoying the feel of Warren's hands on me.

We continue bathing each other, and the more I touch him, the more my need for him grows. I can feel his need for me growing underneath me as well until, finally, I can't take it anymore. I lift up and slide myself onto his length, hissing at the sting. We've only been together that one night, and my body isn't exactly used to this. But I need him, and the feeling of him filling me is more than worth the moment of pain.

Warren pushes up out of the tub and stands, grabbing a towel as he walks us to the bedroom. "Did you need something, my beautiful, sassy-mouthed mate?" he asks, kissing me gently.

"I need you, Warren. I need you right now," I say to him, beginning to feel desperate in my need for him.

He lays me on the bed, somehow managing to stay inside me, then settles himself over top of me, his arms on either side of my head, as his fingers gently caress my cheeks.

"I've never felt fear like that before, Yara," he says as he begins to move slowly inside of me. "I don't ever want to feel fear like that again. You are so precious to me. I waited so long for you, and all I could think about was that I hadn't protected the greatest treasure I've ever been given."

I pull my legs up, wrapping them around him, needing to feel closer to him, needing to feel him deeper inside me.

"Of course, you did, Warren. I'm here, aren't I?"

"I should have ..." he begins, but I put my fingers on his mouth, stopping him.

"Don't second guess yourself. I know you would never intentionally put me in harm's way. What you did, you did because it felt like the right decision at the time, a time when you were in the middle of fighting two, maybe three Alphas and their packs at once. If I don't get to apologize for what Simon did, you don't get to apologize for making the best decisions you could in the heat of the moment."

"Goddess, I love you, Yara," he says, leaning in to kiss me. This time, he isn't so gentle, and I meet his passion with my own. My hands are everywhere, not able to get enough of him, not able to get close enough to him. I can tell he feels the same, and as he pushes us through one orgasm, he doesn't stop, needing more, desperate for more, just like I am.

I have no idea how many hours go by, how many times we mark each other, or how many orgasms we have when he finally pulls out and collapses beside me, pulling me against him and wrapping his arms around me.

I sigh, feeling peace settle between us. I know that will change soon. Simon is still out there, and he will die for what he did. But right now, tonight, my mate and I are together and happy.

I've just about fallen asleep when I feel the bed shake and hear what sounds like a roar. I jolt, looking up at Warren.

"What was that?" I ask him.

He smiles, kissing my nose. "I do believe our Beta couple is now officially marked and mated."

Chapter 68: Marked

Noelle

When Charlie left, going to find Alpha Warren, I realized something very important. If he didn't return, I'd be devastated.

I've watched him tirelessly run this pack while Alpha Warren has been gone. He's strong but fair, allowing Quinton's pack members to remain here until Warren can decide if he'll accept them into the pack. He's a better Alpha than Thomas ever was, and he's not even an Alpha.

I haven't had time to join the pack with everything going on, so I don't have a mind link to make sure that my mate is safe. And he is my mate. He is everything I have ever wanted in a mate and so much more. And now that I've made my decision to accept him, I want to make it official right now.

Of course, that's not an option. The pack is in chaos; our Alpha and Luna are gone, and now our Beta is gone. I may be the unofficial Beta female, but without a pack link, I'm useless to assist.

The same is true for my sister. With Haynes acting as Alpha, she could help him if they were marked and mated, but they aren't yet either, and like me, there's been no time for her to join this pack. We haven't even had a minute to talk about whether or not she will, although I've seen her staying close to Haynes, so I'm hoping that's a good sign.

"You okay?" Laney asks me. I've just returned from the hospital, looking over Bradley and the other warriors who were injured by Simon. Most of them have healed and are back to normal, but a handful and definitely Bradley will take longer. I'm hoping we find Luna Yara sooner rather than later so we can make sure he'll heal properly.

"Yeah, I just ..." I look at my sister. She's always been my protector. She's a great sister, and I love her dearly, but I'm not sure how she'll feel about me taking Charlie as a mate. He'll become my protector, then. Her whole life, she's protected me, and now, I won't need her to do it. Maybe then she can focus on her own mate.

"I'm ready for Charlie to mark me," I tell her.

She raises an eyebrow and smiles at me. "Is that so, Beta?" she asks me.

I laugh. "Yes, that's so. What do you think?" Her opinion has always been important to me.

"I'm not sure you could have been mated to anyone more perfect for you. Beta Charlie is a good guy and a great leader. This pack isn't like our old pack. What they have here in this pack starts at the top. You, my dearest sister, will only add to that."

Her praise made me feel better. When Charlie returned, he let us know that he'd found Alpha Warren, and Luna Yara was safe. He sent Haynes and a hunting party that included Laney, out to find Simon. But my mate was exhausted. I'd gone upstairs to the bedroom we share and talked to him while he showered. When he'd gotten out of the shower, I'd felt my body responding to his naked one. It's a feeling I've never had with another person, this intense desire to be with someone.

'That's the mate bond,' Beatrix, my wolf, says. 'That and our mate is one sexy man,' she purrs.

Charlie looks up at me and smiles. "Like what you see?"

"I definitely do, but you need sleep."

"Mmm, I'm not feeling so tired now. Come lay down with me."

I did, and my mate was asleep almost before his head hit the pillow. So I snuggled against him and fell asleep, too. However, I woke up feeling a deep ache in my body. I need to complete the mate bond. I know Charlie is tired, but ...

I begin running my fingers over his chest and stomach. I smile when his body begins to respond, even in his sleep. I kiss his chest, letting my hand move lower until I graze his now hard length.

He moans softly in his sleep, making me smile. Charlie's been careful about us not going too far. He said Gregor would want to mark me if we had sex, so he preferred to wait until I was ready to be marked. Well, I'm ready, and my body and my wolf are demanding it.

I take his length in my hand, feeling how hard he is underneath the soft skin. I stroke up and down, watching my hand and feeling pretty proud of myself when I see the bit of precum coming out of the tip. Charlie smells like glazed donuts, my favorite food in the world. I have a sudden, irresistible desire to see if he tastes as good as he smells.

I lean down, licking the precum off the tip of his hard length, and my eyes roll back into my head. He tastes better than any donut I've ever had. I'm about to try and get more when I hear his deep, husky voice.

"Noelle, what are you doing?"

I look up at him, biting my lip. "I know you're tired, but I want you to mark me."

In an instant, he has our positions flipped, and I'm on my back with him lying over top of me, no longer looking sleepy.

"Are you sure?" His eyes search mine, making sure I mean what I say.

I nod. "I've never been more sure of anything in my life."

He kisses me much more passionately and possessively than he has in the past. When he starts to move down my body, I grab him.

"No, I need you inside me," I say, practically desperate for him.

"Noelle, you need to be ready, as ready as possible. I'll give you what you want. Just let me make sure your body is ready to take mine."

"It's ready. I'm ready," I insist.

He slides his hands between us and groans. "Fuck, you're soaked."

"I need you, Charlie. Please."

He slides a finger inside me. "Is this what you need, baby?" he murmurs, sliding his finger in and out of me as he rubs the heel of his hand against my clit.

"Yes. Yes," I moan. It's not enough, but I know Charlie will give me what I need.

My first orgasm comes quickly, and Charlie captures my cry with his kiss, keeping my orgasm going as he slides a second finger inside me. I begin to whimper and moan as his kiss becomes even more possessive, and he begins growling.

When I come the second time, he pulls away from the kiss, his canines sliding out.

"Are you ready for me to make you mine," he asks before sucking his fingers into his mouth. His eyes are nearly black when he looks at me.

"Yes," I growl, feeling Beatrix pushing forward and wanting her mate.

He moves in between my thighs, settling himself so the tip of his cock is pressed against my opening. I hold his gaze as he slides inside me, stretching me and filling me. The intense pleasure isn't lessened by the sting of pain, and when he reaches resistance, he stops, looking at me possessively.

"You're mine now," he growls, pushing through the resistance and bottoming out inside me. I feel Beatrix healing me quickly, wanting to get past the pain so we can feel the pleasure.

Charlie kisses me softly, careful of his canines until I start moving my hips.

Then he begins moving in and out of me while sucking on my marking spot. I begin to do the same, feeling my mouth water as my canines slide out.

He pulls my leg up, hooking it over his arm, allowing himself to go even deeper. The new position hits me in just the right spot, and I arch my back as pleasure explodes through my body.

I cry out as the orgasm rips through my body, and I open my eyes, Beatrix focusing on Charlie's marking spot. With a possessive snarl, she sinks her canines into his marking spot, pushing her venom into our mate, making him ours forever.

Charlie's body jerks with his own orgasm, and he roars his release a moment before his canines sink into my marking spot, sending another wave of exquisite pleasure exploding through my body.

'MINE!' I hear him say in our new mind link.

'Yes, I am. And you are mine,' I purr.

He continues to stroke inside me, our orgasms continuing to come one after another while our wolves push their venom into our bodies.

When our wolves finally release each other, our canines snicking back into our gums, Charlie collapses beside me, pulling me against him.

"Mine," he says as he tucks me against his side, my head on his chest.

"Mine," I say, wrapping an arm and leg over him, practically laying on top of him.

He chuckles and kisses the top of my head. "I love you, Noelle."

"I love you too, Charlie."

This time, we both fall into a deep, very satisfied sleep.

Chapter 69: Unprotected

Yasmin

There was only one place for Quirin and I to go – back to our pack. There's no one there now. My son is the Alpha of nothing, thanks to his greedy father, but that's okay. We'll find a way. I'll find a way to bring my son back to the position he was born for. The only reason I accepted Quinton as my chosen mate was so that my son could be an Alpha. Quinton was fine as a mate, he never forced himself on me, but there was never any love there. It was always an understanding. I give him what he wants, and he will take care of me for the rest of my life.

I held up my end of the bargain, but he's completely fallen short on his. He can't take care of me if he's dead. And now, I'm weak, and I have to protect my young son.

It takes us nearly a day to get back to the pack at the slow pace we have to go because my wolf is silent. I can only walk so far before I need to stop and rest. Quirin is quiet, and since there's nothing that I can say to make losing his father better, I stay quiet, too.

I breathe a sigh of relief when we get to the pack lands. They aren't protected any longer. There's no one here to watch the borders, but it still feels safer than being out in the woods with me weakened and my son too young and immature to fight off any warriors that may come along.

We walk through the pack lands, and the smell of death and bodies that are beginning to rot is everywhere. When we walk into the packhouse, it's eerily quiet. Usually, the packhouse is bustling with energy and activity, but there's no one here. At least there are no dead bodies in here.

"Let's get something to eat, Quirin," I say.

"I'm not hungry."

"You need to eat."

"I'm not hungry!" he growls. He'd been helping me to walk, but he releases me and rushes upstairs. The sound of his door slamming echoes in the empty packhouse.

I hobble into the kitchen. I never learned how to cook, having been born into a Beta family, so I look around and see what there is that's easy to make. I find some hard-boiled eggs and some bread. I look around, and not seeing a toaster, I just pull off chunks of the bread, making a plate for Quirin while I eat. I'll need to figure out how to make food, or we'll have to find another pack to join.

The thought makes me ill. We can't join Alpha Warren's pack. Quirin will never accept it, and he and Quinton were enemies anyway. Alpha Thomas is dead, and I heard that Alpha Brady had attacked Alpha Warren but had retreated. Maybe his pack is an option. I don't think he's found a mate. Maybe he would take me as his mate. I'm still young enough that I could bear him a son. He needs an heir for his pack. It would keep Quirin and me safe until he was old enough, and then he could potentially fight Brady and take over his pack.

I need to come up with a plan. We need to burn the bodies before scavengers begin hunting for them, but before I do that, I need to rest. I need to get my strength back so I can figure out what to do and I can protect my son. The one good thing about Quinton is that he loved our son with everything in him. I wasn't surprised that he was willing to give his life for Quirin. I knew he loved him that much.

I knock on Quirin's door, but when there isn't an answer, I leave the plate by his door.

"There's food here when you're ready," I tell him.

Then I go back to my room. It smells like Quinton. I stand inside my room, breathing in his scent. It now smells like false security to me. He will die, and I have nothing and no one to help me protect my son. I wonder if we could live here, off the radar. Eventually, the electricity and water will be shut off unless I can find a stash of money or bank books. But if they aren't in mine or Quirin's name, we're screwed. Hopefully, Quinton was smart enough to leave everything to his son.

I lay down, thinking that this will be the first thing I do when I wake up. Well, that and check on Quirin. Then, based on what I find, I'll come up with a plan. Maybe there's enough money that we can put up security fences or something.

It's the last thought I have before I fall asleep.

When I wake, the room is dark. I look at the clock and see that it's the middle of the night. I've been asleep for hours. I reach out to Sasha, my wolf, but she's still too weak to respond.

I get up, wanting to check on Quirin. When I step into the hallway, it's dark. The hairs on my arms go up with the complete silence surrounding me. I never thought of this packhouse as feeling creepy, but it does. I almost feel like an intruder in my own home.

The plate in front of Quirin's room is gone. That's a good sign. I quietly open his door and look inside. His bed is unmade. I step in, looking around.

"Quirin?"

I flip on the lights and see a note on the bed. I feel like my heart stops beating as I rush to the bed and pick it up.

'Mother,
I have to go after him. I at least have to try to save him. I'll be back soon.
Quirin'

Oh no! Fear and dread rush through me. Quirin has his wolf. He'd have been able to run much more quickly than I'd be able to get to Alpha Warren's pack. If they catch him ...

I turn, racing down the stairs, and then stop, hearing a clanging in the kitchen. I race in, hoping to catch him before he leaves, only to see a stranger in my kitchen.

"Who the hell are you?" I ask him.

He turns and smiles at me, a sickening smile.

"Who are you?" he asks me instead.

"I'm Luna Yasmin. This is my pack. You are an intruder here!" I say, standing my ground.

The man arrogantly looks around. He's definitely an Alpha. He's built like one, and he acts like one. What the hell is a strange Alpha doing here?

"Luna of nothing, it appears. You have dead warriors outside, no omegas inside, empty safe rooms ... Where's your mate? Where's Alpha Quinton?" he asks.

I lift my chin. "He's out fighting a war. How is it that you're here, Alpha, with no warriors of your own."

"Ahhh, an interesting question," he says, looking around. "Much like you, I don't have a pack left either. I'm guessing this is Alpha Warren's work?"

When I don't say anything, he returns his focus to me. "So, I'm an Alpha without a pack or a mate, and you're a Luna without a pack or a mate. How convenient."

I growl, but without Sasha, it's weak, and this arrogant Alpha grins at me.

"Where is your son?" he asks.

"What son?" I ask him. I have no idea what he may or may not know about Quirin.

"Quinton's son. If you're his Luna, I'm guessing it's your son too. Although Quinton may have taken a mistress if you couldn't bear him a child."

"You haven't told me your name, Alpha," I growl again, ignoring his question. He ignores mine just as easily.

"If your son is here, I'd like to speak with him. If your pack is gone, that means that Quinton is either captured or dead. Since you don't seem to have a wolf, I'm going to go with dead, although you don't seem as impacted as I've been led to believe mates are when one dies."

He stands there studying me. Then he looks around again. "Or perhaps your son was captured, and Quinton gave himself up for his son," he says, his gaze returning to me. "Yes, that sounds right. That's why all the omegas are gone, too."

His eyes narrow on me. "So, you rejected him before Warren killed him, is that it? That would weaken your wolf, but it wouldn't kill you. Yes, I think that's it. I think Alpha Quinton gave his life for his son, and then you rejected him so that you could care for the boy. So where is he?"

"He's not here," I say.

"Tsk, tsk, Luna. Don't lie to me."

"I'm not lying. He's not here." Now I'm grateful that he isn't, but I still need to get to Warren's pack before he gets caught.

"So, the boy's like his father? Going to try and rescue the only person he loves, leaving you here, alone? Unprotected and wolfless," he says, taking a step toward me.

I turn, rushing to get away. I don't get far before he grabs my hair and yanks me back to him.

"Get off of me! Get off of me!" I scream at him.

"Settle down, Luna, or I'll fucking mark you," he snarls in my ear.

I'm no match for his strength without my wolf, so I calm down, trying to think of a way out of this. He begins stroking my hair, still holding me against his body with his free arm.

"Now, as it turns out, I just lost the woman I intended to make MY Luna. The woman who was going to give me my heir. But since I've got you now, I think we both know that you're more than capable of carrying an Alpha heir, aren't you?"

"Fuck you!" I growl at him.

"Oh, you're going to, don't worry, and you're going to do it willingly, or when your son gets back, I'll kill him. I'm going to let you go, and you're going to be a good little Luna and take your clothes off, bend over that couch, and I'm going to fuck you until I put a pup in you. Then we're going to figure out how to keep the electricity and water on here until I have my male heir, and he's old enough for me to take away from here. Then, and only then, will you be free to go. Do you understand?" he asks.

When I don't answer, he yanks my head back by the hair. "Do you understand," he growls in my ear.

"Yes. Yes, I understand."

"Remember, your son's life is at stake," he says, tapping my cheek hard before releasing me. "Now, turn around and strip for me."

I take a step away from him, willing myself not to cry. I can't help the fear that I know he must smell and is obviously getting aroused by if the bulge in his pants is any indication.

I turn around, and from the corner of my eye, I see movement. I've been a Luna long enough to have learned how to keep my features schooled. I don't look, even though I'm desperate to know if it's Quirin. However, I don't smell my son.

"Do I at least get the name of the man whose pup I'm going to bear?"

"Simon, but you can call me Alpha."

Suddenly, there's a flurry of activity, and I'm slammed against a wall. The group of warriors takes Simon down to the ground, and a large man comes sauntering over.

"Luna Yasmin, are you hurt?" he asks, looking over at me.

"No," I say, recognizing some of these warriors as Alpha Warren's.

"Is your son alright?" the female warrior in front of me asks.

"Yes," I say. I have no intention of telling them that he's gone after his father.

"Alpha Simon," the big man says, looking at my would-be rapist. "Alpha Warren wants to have a word with you. He isn't happy with the bruises you put on our Luna," he snarls, and almost as one, the warriors begin kicking the Alpha until he's a bloody mess.

"Let's drag his ass out of here," the big guy says, and the woman in front of me tosses him some rope. They tie Simon's hands behind his back, then tie his legs together, leaving two long pieces of rope. I have no idea what they're doing until two of the warriors shift, and the ends of the ropes are tied around their necks.

"Let's get him home," the big guy says, and the wolves take off, literally dragging Alpha Simon behind them.

When the big guy turns and looks at me, I try to press myself tighter against the wall.

"Luna Yasmin, we're not here for you. As long as you and your son stay away, we won't bother you. And rest assured, Alpha Simon won't be bothering you again either."

I nod.

The man looks at the woman in front of me. "Let's go, Laney."

She nods at me, and then the two of them shift and take off.

I give them a twenty-minute head start before I begin following them. I need to get to my son before he does something stupid!

Chapter 70: Simon's Return

Warren

Waking up with Yara back in my arms and safe is incredible. Waking up with my mate straddling me and sliding herself down my hard length is fucking fantastic.

I'd spent hours reconnecting with Yara, mentally and physically, last night, needing to feel the connection to her, needing to feel her. And now, apparently, my mate needs more. You won't hear me arguing, especially when I get to watch her beautiful body bouncing on me, feel her body clenching around me as she comes, hear her sweet sounds as she finds her pleasure, and then see those intense eyes when they focus on me. I knew this woman would be all passion when she finally let go, and here she is.

"More!" she growls, still hungry for me. Just me. The possessiveness in me is unlike anything I've ever felt. Yara has become the air that I breathe. She is everything that I need in this world, and this world would be nothing without her.

I flip our positions, putting her on her back and pulling both legs over my shoulders, grinding my hips into her until I feel myself touch her cervix.

"Yes!" she screams.

"Is this what my mate needs?" I growl.

"Yes!"

I thrust hard into her, giving her what she needs, what she's demanding, and when she comes again, I flip her onto her hands and knees, taking her hips and continuing my punishing pace as she mewls and whimpers before both of us find our release together. I'm pretty sure my possessive roar rivals Charlie's from last night.

When I collapse beside her, I pull her to me. "Feel better?"

"For now," she says, smiling with the promise of what's to come later. I growl softly at her as she lifts up onto her elbow, resting her head on her hand and beginning to trace the scars on my chest.

"What do you see?" I ask quietly. I know I've earned every one of these scars and fought hard in order to have them and survive them, but I wonder what my mate sees when she looks at my mutilated body.

She looks up at me, then back down to watch her fingers trace the crisscrossing pattern of scars that cover my body.

"I see strength," she says, not looking up at me. "It's how I knew you'd come for me, no matter how long it took you. It's how I knew that I'd be safe eventually. I knew that nothing and no one would ever keep you from finding me. These battle wounds are a testament to your tenacity. Some might call it stubbornness," she says, smiling up at me.

"What do you call it?"

"Determination. When I look at you, I see a man who will do anything to protect his pack, his family, his mate, and one day soon, I hope, his pups."

Excitement shivers through me. "You want my pups?"

"I already said so, didn't I? I didn't mean to say it out loud then, but I'm saying it out loud now. You will be an incredible father, and I cannot wait to see you raise our pups."

"How many?" I ask, hoping she wants a lot.

"As many as you want," she purrs, and I can feel Annika pushing forward.

"With you, I want a LOT of pups," I growl, feeling that same powerful possessiveness fill me again.

"You'd better get working on that, Alpha. I've only got maybe ten more years to give you pups," she says.

I flip her over, sliding inside her again. "Just in case it didn't work the last few times I came inside you, we should definitely do it again," I say, making my mate laugh.

"We definitely should."

After making my mate come several more times, we shower together, and I make her come again.

"Is this what our life is going to be like now?" she asks me.

"I'm just being thorough, my love," I say, making her laugh again.

She steps up to me, looking at me in a way that takes my breath away. "I love you so much, Warren."

"I love you more than anything, Yara."

I've just leaned in to kiss her when I get the mind link from Haynes.

'Alpha, we got Simon.'

I kiss Yara quickly and gently stroke her cheeks, which are now showing just the faintest hint of yellow from her bruises.

"Simon's back. Did you want to come show him that you're alive and well?"

"Yes, I do."

We finish getting dressed, and I take her hand as we head downstairs and outside.

"Do I smell like you? I mean, really smell like you, like we just had sex?" Yara asks me.

"Yes ..." I say, surprised she's asking.

"Good. I want Simon to know without a doubt that I'm yours."

I'm laughing as we step outside. It's a bit more than is necessary, but Yara's right. Simon needs to see that he lost and we've won at everything.

When I see him, I'm surprised, even though I shouldn't be. Our warriors love their Luna. Anyone who treats her poorly will pay the consequences.

"What did they do to him?" Yara asks, and I'm thankful that she doesn't seem upset about his poor state.

"It looks like they dragged him from wherever they found him," I say. His clothing is shredded, and his skin is torn in large slabs all over his body. Even his face has places where the skin tore away, chunks of it hanging off his face.

I step away from Yara, walking over to him. "Where did you find him?"

"Alpha Quinton's pack about to rape Luna Yasmin," Haynes says.

"Well, aren't you just special?" I say, squatting down. "That looks like it hurts," I say, poking a particularly raw-looking part of his body.

He snarls but doesn't reply.

"Alpha Simon, I did tell you that my mate would kill you if he saw my face before it healed. I guess I forgot to mention that my pack would, too," Yara says, coming to stand behind me. I feel her hand on my shoulder, and I watch Simon's nose twitching, his lips curl as anger flares in his eyes. Yara was right about having my scent on her. He's furious.

353

"Yara and I had one hell of a homecoming last night and again this morning," I say, taunting him. She runs her fingers through my hair, and I stand, turning to her. "Didn't we, baby?"

"We did. I tried to explain to Simon how fantastic you feel when you're inside me ..." she begins, but Simon begins snarling. It cuts off quickly as the warriors begin kicking him, but Yara never looks away from me.

I lean in, kissing her softly, and she presses her body against mine.

"You BITCH!" Simon screams. I hear the kicking begin again, but I wrap my arms around my mate. For all of her care and concern for the people in her hospital, the people she loves, when you cross her, she's just as vicious as I am. The punches she throws are aimed differently, but apparently, they hurt just as much as mine do.

I take my time kissing my mate. She seems to enjoy the kiss as much as I do. When I finally pull away, I smile at her.

"Get him up, take him to the cells," I say, not looking away from Yara. "Ready for breakfast, baby?"

"I am. I have to keep my strength up if I'm going to give you that pup you're working so hard to put in me," she says. I know it's mostly to taunt Simon, but I love that she just announced our intention to have a pup in front of the pack.

"I might have to try again after breakfast," I say, taking her hand.

"Let's hurry up and eat then," she says.

Simon makes the mistake of starting to scream obscenities again. I'm not sure if they're directed at me or Yara, but either way, they cut off as the warriors punch and kick him some more. At this rate, I won't have to torture him. The pack will do it for me.

Just as we start walking back to the packhouse, I see Trena come outside. I'd forgotten all about her when I'd found Yara.

"Trena?" Yara says, tilting her head.

"Hello, Luna," Trena says, but her eyes are focused on Simon.

I watch as she passes us, walking right up to him.

"Traitor," he snarls at her.

"Rapist!" she snarls back. Then, faster than a snake, her hand slams up between Simon's legs, and she rips his ball sack off.

I see my warriors flinch, and I'm pretty sure I did, too.

"Let's see you rape someone now, asshole!" she says as Simon screams in pain.

"Will he bleed out?" I ask Yara.

"Depends on how strong his wolf is. We could cauterize it if you're not ready for him to die yet," she says dispassionately. I've only seen Yara like this once before. When she squeezed that Beta's organs to make him let go of her. It's a side I don't see often, but when I do, she's a little scary.

"Cauterize the wound. Simon hasn't suffered enough for taking what's mine," I tell my warriors.

The smile they give me isn't pleasant at all. They will enjoy burning Simon.

"Trena, do you have everything you need here in the pack?" I ask her as she watches Simon being dragged away.

"Yes, thank you, Alpha," she says, looking over at us.

"Trena, come see me at the hospital today. We can catch up, and I'd like to look you over," Yara says, returning to her normal, compassionate self.

"Yes, Luna," she says before heading inside.

Yara watches her, then turns to me. "I do need to eat, but then I need to go check on Bradley."

"Then let's get you fed so you can get our pack back in shape, my Luna."

"With pleasure, my Alpha."

Chapter 71: Catching Up

Yara

I probably should care more that Simon will die a painful death because of what he did to me, but I don't. He didn't just hurt me. He hurt Piper, he hurt my pack's warriors, he hurt Bradley, and most importantly, he hurt Warren. My mate is a strong, powerful man, and I'd felt the lack of confidence in him, the feeling that he'd failed me. No one gets to make my mate feel like that. No one. So, for all of that, he can suffer.

I know Warren and the pack will make him suffer in their way, but I know how to hit Simon where it hurts. He's wanted me for a very long time. He even killed his father for protecting me and keeping me hidden. So, yeah, I knew that flaunting my relationship with Warren in front of him would make him crazed, and I'd been right.

Of course, I had the added benefit of claiming my mate in front of the pack. As angry as they are with Simon, and there's a lot of rage there, I felt their excitement when I announced that Warren and I were trying for a pup.

When we walk into the packhouse, Charlie and Noelle are there.

"Luna!" Noelle cries.

"Let's see it," I say, smiling at her.

She blushes prettily, looking at Charlie, who is smiling possessively at her. She pulls her shirt away from her neck, and I make a point of looking it over.

"Nice job, Beta," I say to Charlie.

"Thank you, Luna."

"I was talking to Noelle, Charlie," I say, making Warren chuckle.

"We definitely have a lot that we need to do. Not the least of which is to have an entire pack ceremony. We have our Luna, our new Beta female, and we need to make a decision about our Gamma," Warren says.

"I thought we'd already made that decision," Charlie says, raising an eyebrow at Warren.

"We're in agreement?"

"Absolutely."

"Let's make it official today, then. Do you know if we'll have our Gamma female as well?" Warren asks.

"Not yet," Charlie says as the four of us get some food and sit. This feels nice, like what a morning in a packhouse should feel like. Like we're talking over our plans for the day before we go off to our respective jobs. No one is talking about war, which is a nice change.

"Who are we talking about?" I ask Warren.

'Haynes,' he says in the mind link.

"Oh. Good choice."

"Yara approves. We're good to go."

"Is it possible for me to accept you as my Alpha so I can get into the pack link? It would be really helpful for me to be able to hear everyone and not just Charlie now. Oh, and Laney will need to as well."

"Laney already did, but we can do that quickly before you go with Yara this morning. I'd prefer it if you could contact me or the warriors if something happens."

"When did my sister accept you as her Alpha?" Noelle asks.

"Before you got here. That's how I knew I could trust her."

"Oh, so it was just me then. Well, we definitely need to fix that!" she says.

"Once we get our Gammas agreement to the position, I'll announce to the pack that anyone can challenge him for the position, then we can schedule the pack ceremony," Warren says, smiling at Charlie. "It feels good that it's more than just you and I now."

Charlie smiles at Noelle and then at me. "It really does."

As we finish eating, I have Noelle tell me what she did with Bradley. She's so nervous that she did something wrong.

"Noelle, you saved his life. He's alive, and we can fix anything else if his wolf hasn't already," I tell her, reaching out to squeeze her hand.

"See, I told you. You did the hard part, Little Beta. You got that bullet out."

When we're done, Noelle quickly accepts Warren as her Alpha. Then she and I kiss our mates and start to leave the dining hall. It's full of our pack members who are having breakfast, talking to family and friends, saying hello, and welcoming me back as we pass. The feeling here is so much different than it used to be, so much better. Because it is, I turn back.

"Alpha Warren, don't forget you have work to do later," I say, raising my voice so he can hear me across the room. The room goes quiet as everyone looks at Warren. He frowns and I can see him trying to figure out what he forgot.

"Until you put a pup in me, I won't give you a moment's rest," I see, hearing our pack members chuckle as Warren smiles wide.

"Oh, my little Luna, there is nothing about putting a pup in you that is work. But you're welcome to put me to 'work' as long and as often as you'd like," he says, the smile on his face twinkling in his eyes. Damn, my man is hot.

I smile at Warren as the pack howls and cheers. Happy with our interaction and the feeling in the pack, I turn and head to the hospital with Noelle.

When I arrive, I see Piper, who looks exhausted, with Travis standing beside her.

"I need to check on both of you, but I need to check on Bradley first. Piper, you're overdoing it. You're off duty starting right now. Who else is here?"

"I am, Luna," Erica says, walking out. "It's good to have you back."

"It's good to be back. Piper, have a seat. Travis, you, too."

"Yes, Luna," they both say.

"Noelle, with me."

We walk into Bradley's hospital room, and I look over his medical file before checking the incision.

"Let's open him up and see what his lungs look like," I say, pulling on gloves as Noelle gets what I need.

"The tissue of the lungs was weird. I wasn't sure how much pressure I could put on the stitches, so they might be too tight or not tight enough," she says as I slice through her stitches. When I have to cut flesh to get to his lungs, I know his wolf is trying to heal him. That's a good sign.

I retract the skin and muscle and see that Noelle worked around his rib cage instead of cracking him open.

"That must have made things much more difficult for you," I say, looking over the stitches.

"I used a camera, so I had a better view, and because the bullet was low, I was able to work from under this rib cage. Do you want the camera?" she says, holding it out for me.

"Let's have a look."

When the camera is in, I realize that Noelle did a really good job, especially since this was her first time, and she had very little space to work, having to go under and between his ribs to access his lungs.

"Nice job. In the future, I'd make sure you get all of the singed lung out," I say, taking a scalpel and slicing off a piece of lung that is dead. "Otherwise, it could decay inside the body and cause other problems. But well done, Noelle. If this is what you want to do, and I hope it is, you need to start taking classes. Warren and I talked about me doing online classes, and I know there are werewolf universities where we can go, too. They'll be more agreeable to us working in the packs and using our work here as our practical knowledge," I say as I stitch Bradley back up.

"I would love that. And I think Piper and Anna would like to take classes as well," she says.

"We might have a fully functional hospital here one day. Who knows, Noelle, maybe once things settle with the packs, we could bring others in here and help train them to care for their pack members."

I turn off the sedation that was keeping Bradley under. "Let's let him wake up. He won't be going anywhere for a couple of days, but once his wolf isn't drugged, he can start healing him faster."

When we walk out, I stop. Piper and Travis are in the hallway, and he has her against the wall, kissing her in a way that mates kiss each other.

"Am I interrupting?" I ask, teasing.

"Oh my goddess, Luna, I'm so sorry," Piper says, her voice raspy.

"You're sorry for kissing your mate? Or you're sorry for speaking before I checked your throat?"

"How did you ..." she begins before Travis gently puts his hand over her mouth.

"She just warned you about speaking, Pipes. From everything I've heard, you don't want to cross your Luna," he says, smiling at me. "Hi, Luna. Yes, we're mates. Since I don't have a mind link, I've been waiting for Piper to be able to talk. But I don't want her to injure herself to do it."

"Looks like you've found a way to communicate," I say, walking over to her. Noelle hands me a mini flashlight, and I look at her throat.

"This is healing nicely. Is your wolf back?" I ask her.

She nods.

"How are your vocal chords?" I ask.

"Still healing, Luna," the deeper voice of her wolf says.

"What about swallowing? Are you able to get regular food down?" I ask, and she nods.

"Minimal conversations only. Do as much as you can in the mind link. Come back and see me tomorrow," I tell her before turning to Travis.

"How about your wolf?" I ask.

I watch his wolf push forward. "I'm here, Luna."

"Full strength?"

"Not quite."

"No fighting until I clear it. If another battle breaks out, get here. You can help guard the hospital or triage like you did before."

"Yes, Luna."

They turn and head out.

"Is this what our lives would be like if there was no war?" Noelle asks.

"Probably," I say, just as Trena walks in the door.

"Hey, Trena, how are you ..." I stop, seeing tears filling her eyes.

"I can't! I can't!" she says, turning and rushing out of the hospital.

"What's that about?" Noelle asks.

I turn, looking down the hall behind me. There's only one person in the hospital, and he's unconscious.

"I'm pretty sure I know."

Chapter 72: Gamma
Warren

I love that Yara keeps claiming me in front of the pack. I can feel the difference in them, the settled feeling that they get knowing that their leaders are happy together. But more than that, it settles me and makes me feel like a fucking king.

The woman I care about most in this world, admire more than anyone, and love more than anything keeps telling anyone who will listen that she loves me and wants my pup. The first time might not have been intentional, but this time it was very intentional.

When I hear my pack members murmuring, 'Well done, Alpha,' I can't help but smile smugly. That's right. That incredible woman loves ME.

"You know what this packhouse needs?" I ask. Not waiting for a response, I look at Charlie. "More flowers," I say and turn to walk out of the dining room as the room erupts into laughter and cheers.

"Lots and lots of flowers," I say.

"Do you want us to order them for you, Alpha?" a couple of omegas ask me.

I stop and look around the place, thinking that every pack member should have flowers in their rooms, too, and if I do what I'm thinking, they'll have a variety to choose from, and so will my mate.

I tell them what I want, and their eyes go wide.

"Are you sure, Alpha?" they ask. "That's a lot of money."

"Our Luna is back safe and sound. We've eliminated one threat to our pack and have two more in our cells. I think that's cause for some serious celebration, don't you?" I ask.

The room cheers again. "OH! And no one tells our Luna. It's a secret," I say, my smile widening when I think of her response. "And get them here before she gets back from the hospital today if possible."

"Yes, Alpha," the omegas say, and I see several more join them as they rush off to get this done.

"Damn," Charlie chuckles as we walk out of the dining hall. "How the hell am I supposed to compete with that?"

"That's your problem," I say, smiling at my Beta. I feel light as fucking air. I know we have a lot going on, a lot yet to do, but damn, does it feel good to have my life falling into place.

Charlie and I walk to my office and sit. "Okay, Haynes or Quinton first?" I ask him.

"Let's start with Haynes. Maybe give him time to talk to Laney before we have our pack ceremony. And if he agrees, then we'll need to schedule his challenge. But if all goes well, we'll have our ranked members, Quinton will be dead, and Simon can watch as you make Yara your Luna, and our pack members swear their loyalty and allegiance to a unified leadership before he dies."

"I want to keep him alive until we know Yara is pregnant. I want him to know that he lost all the way around ... that it's my pups that will be growing in her belly, my pups that she'll be giving birth to, my pups that she'll be nursing and raising," I say, beginning to growl possessively at the idea.

I look at Charlie. "Are you and Noelle going to have pups right away?"

"I don't know yet. We didn't get that far in the conversation. She said she was ready for me to mark her, and so I did," he says, smiling smugly.

I smile at him. "Okay, let's get Haynes in here. I want Quinton dead before Yara gets back. When she's back, I want to celebrate."

"I'll let the omegas know that we want to have a party tonight," he says, and we both stop, staring at each other.

"Did you ever think I would say those words?" he asks softly.

"No. And I never thought we'd be safe enough or healthy enough to even consider having one. We definitely need a party. A BIG one! Tell them to keep it a secret as best they can. Let's make that a surprise for the pack. They deserve this as much as we do," I tell him.

While Charlie mind links the omegas, I mind link Haynes.

'Can you come to my office?'

'Yes, Alpha,' he says. There's a knock on the door just as Charlie refocuses.

"They're thrilled. I don't know what they're going to do or how much it's going to cost us, but I told them money was not a problem."

"Let's hope it's not," I say before turning to the door. "Come in."

"Alpha, Beta, you wanted to speak to me?"

"Haynes, come in," I say, gesturing for him to sit beside Charlie.

He does, looking from Charlie to me, hopeful energy emanating from him.

"So, you've had to lead the pack a couple of times while Charlie and I were out. How did that go?" I begin.

"I think it went well. I know I still have a lot to learn, but I felt more comfortable the second time you left me in charge."

"How about leading the group to find Simon?" Charlie asks him.

"That felt really good. The warriors seemed to respond well to me. We were methodical and careful, and obviously, we found him."

"What's going on with you and Laney?" I ask.

"She wanted to take things slow, although now that her sister is marked and mated, I think she's feeling a bit out of her element. She's been watching over Beta Noelle for so long that she doesn't really know what to do with herself now that she's safe and has someone else watching over her."

"What do you think of Laney being a Gamma?" Charlie asks him.

His gaze focuses on Charlie. "I think she'd be fantastic. From what I've seen, she's an excellent fighter, strong and smart. She's taken down several of our warriors during sparring sessions, and she's gained their respect."

"When do you think the two of you will complete your mate bond?" I ask him.

"I'm not sure. I won't rush her. She needs to be ready to give herself to me," he says firmly, making me smile.

"Good for you, Haynes," I say, looking at Charlie, who shrugs, intentionally spreading out Haynes' torment.

Haynes' eyes begin tracking back and forth between us, waiting and practically bouncing in his seat with anticipation.

Finally, I smile. "How about you, Haynes? How do you feel about being a Gamma?"

"Are you offering me the position?" he asks, his excitement spiking quickly.

"Yeah, we are," Charlie says, smiling at him.

"Hell fucking yeah! Yeah, I want it!" he says, jumping out of his seat. "I mean, it would be an honor," he says, sitting back down and forcing himself to be calm.

Charlie and I both laugh. "Good. We have to announce your nomination, and you'll be open to a challenge, but I'd like this done in a couple of days so we can have a pack ceremony and bring all of our new leaders and pack members into the pack."

"Thank you! Thank you for this opportunity," he says, jumping up again.

"You've earned it, and you'll earn it every day in this pack, you know that," I say.

"I look forward to it!" he says.

Charlie chuckles. "Go. Tell your mate. I know you're dying to."

He rushes to the door. "Thank you again," he says before rushing off to find Laney.

~ ~ ~

Laney POV

I've been practicing some new moves that Haynes taught me. I need the repetition to make it more seamless in sparring. Punch, kick, duck, come up swinging another punch. He's good at combos, and he's also good at mixing up his combos, so his opponent never knows what to expect from him. He's taken me down more times than I've taken him down when we've sparred together. And since I know he goes easy on me, it's a testament to how much better he is at fighting than I am.

As I go through the motions, my body goes into autopilot while my mind kicks in. What am I going to do about Haynes? I've put him off, worrying about Noelle and trying to let go of the fear of becoming someone's mate. I've seen the good and the bad of mate bonds in Thomas' pack, mostly the bad. However, this pack is different in so many ways. There aren't bad mate bonds here. Mates aren't flirting and cheating on their mates like they did in Thomas' pack. Not only is it arrogant and demeaning, but it's stupid. That kind of behavior weakens your warriors and, therefore, your pack. The fact that Thomas and most of his pack members are dead now just proves my point.

But Haynes isn't that way. I haven't been here very long, but I already know that he's not like the warriors from Thomas' pack. He wants me as his mate. He doesn't flirt with other she-wolves and doesn't even show more than a typical pack member's interest in them and their lives.

"LANEY!" Haynes says, rushing up to me. He has a huge smile on his face. "Come with me!" he says, taking my hand and practically dragging me away from the packhouse toward the forest nearby.

"Haynes! What are you doing?" I ask, laughing. Okay, sometimes he pulls me away, and we make out. I mean, the man's mouth is soft and warm, and when his arms are around me...

He stops, pulling me into his arms. I expect him to kiss me, but instead, he smiles down at me.

"Alpha and Beta offered me the Gamma position."

"Oh, Haynes! That's amazing! You're a great leader! You deserve this!" I say, meaning it. I'd watched him while he led the pack. The second time, he'd been more confident than the first, and it had shown. Then, leading the group to get Simon, he'd been amazing, a true leader, someone that others were willing to follow. Someone that I am willing to follow.

He brushes my hair away from my face. "They asked me what I thought about you being a Gamma," he says softly, making my heart flutter.

"What did you say?"

"That you'd be incredible, that you've already gained the respect of our warriors, that you're strong and smart. I didn't mention that you're beautiful and passionate, but you're those things as well," he says softly.

I love the way this man looks at me. He doesn't hide how much he wants me, how much he loves me. I'm pretty sure the only reason he doesn't kiss me in front of the other pack members is because he thinks I don't want it. And at first, I didn't. But that's been changing. Now, the thought of this man letting everyone know that I'm his ...

"Do I get to challenge you for the position?" I ask him, smirking up at him.

"I refuse to fight with you," he says, his voice still soft but more intense.

I slide my arms around his neck. "What about marking me? Are you going to refuse to do that, too?" I ask, just as softly.

He shakes his head at me. "Anytime you're ready, I'm ready."

I rub my nose against his, putting my lips a hair's breadth away from his as I hold his gaze.

"I'm ready," I murmur, knowing that I am. Not because he's going to be a Gamma, but because it's time for me to accept that this man is the real deal. He's mine, and I won't let anyone else have him – ever.

His mouth is on mine in an instant, and I wrap my legs around him.

"Our room or out here?" he asks, barely taking his mouth off of mine.

"Make me yours under the sunlight in the forest," I say, and he begins carrying me deeper into the forest.

I smile as he lays me down in a spot where the sun is filtering through the canopy of trees around us.

I'm going to be a Gamma, my sister's Gamma. But more important than that, I'm going to be mated to the most wonderful man I've ever met.

Chapter 73: Mothers and Friends

Yara

I'm about to go searching for Trena, when Katie comes in with her new baby girl.

"Hi, Luna. I know you just got back, but I was hoping you could look over my daughter for me."

"Is everything alright?" I ask her.

"I think so, but I'm not sure I'd know if something was wrong. She smells fine, and she's sleeping well, but ... she's not nursing well."

"Okay, let's have a look," I say, getting Noelle to put them in a room while I quickly check that Anna and Erica are okay.

When I get into the room, Katie is pacing while Noelle weighs her daughter.

"What did you name her?" I ask.

"Emery," she says, smiling at her daughter.

"How are you and your mate adjusting to having a newborn?" I ask her.

She blows out a breath. "It's great, you know, but ... well, we both worry every time she makes a sound. I've never had so little sleep."

"What does your wolf say?" I ask her.

She chuckles. "That I'm being overprotective, but that she's worried about her not latching on and eating enough."

I walk over to where Noelle is taking her measurements. She's a little underweight, and she's opening her mouth like she's hungry, being fussy.

I take a moment to look in her mouth, not seeing anything that would keep her from being able to latch on.

"Okay, let's see how you do this," I say to her.

"You mean right now?" she asks, and I can feel her nervous energy increasing. I pick Emery up and smile down at her as she searches for a breast to nurse on.

I look up at Katie and see the panic on her face.

"Have a seat, Katie. Take a deep breath. I can feel your nervousness from here. If I can feel it, your daughter will, too. Sit down, relax, breathe, and calm yourself. You want your daughter to feel good when she's in your arms and nursing. If you're nervous and anxious, it will make her nervous and anxious," I tell her.

I know this isn't always the answer. Some babies, for whatever reason, don't nurse from their mothers. But sometimes, it is about the energy that the mother is giving off, and in this instance, I have a feeling that Katie's 'overprotectiveness' is making her daughter anxious.

She pulls her breast out, but her energy is still high.

"Sit back, get comfortable, close your eyes, and breathe," I tell her.

She looks at me for a moment, looking terrified, but then she does what I ask. It takes several breaths before she finally takes a full, deep breath.

"Good, a couple more like that," I say, forcing her to relax even though Emery is getting fussier.

When she opens her eyes, I smile encouragingly at her. "Ready?"

"Ready," she says.

I lay Emery in her arms, and she immediately searches for Katie's breast.

I feel Katie getting tense, so I put my hand on her shoulder. "Deep breaths. Help her find your nipple. There you go," I say when Emery latches on.

"What if she doesn't stay on?" Katie asks, looking up at me.

"Take a deep breath. Make sure that you're giving her a calm environment to nurse in. If that doesn't work, we'll try something else," I say.

"Will you stay with me?" she asks.

"Of course," I say, sitting down and watching. When it looks like Katie is starting to get nervous again, I distract her.

"What's the best part of being a new mom?" I ask her.

"Everything!" she says, smiling. She begins telling me about watching her daughter when she's looking at her and hearing her sweet sounds when she's sleeping.

"Poop is gross, and, uh, it gets everywhere," she says, laughing, then tells me about how her mate wasn't careful, and Emery basically pooped all over him and then proceeded to pee on him.

She begins laughing while she's talking, and I see Emery look up at her. "See, your daughter knows when you're happy."

"Hey, beautiful girl," Katie says, stroking her cheek. Emery goes back to nursing, and momma and daughter continue to look at each other, Katie cooing at her.

"I think you've got this," I say softly, nodding to Noelle that we should leave and let them bond.

"How did you know what to do?" Noelle asks when we step out of the room.

"I didn't. But part of being a doctor or even a nurse is assessing the situation. Katie came in uptight and even said her wolf called her overprotective, which said to me that she was anxious. Once you get anxious about something and it doesn't work, you start expecting it not to work, and then the anxiety gets worse, and it can become a terrible cycle. I just tried to break the cycle. If it hadn't worked, we'd have had to try moving her to a bottle, but this seems to be helping. So, hopefully, momma and baby can begin bonding during feeding times, and Katie will learn to relax."

"You're going to be a great mom," Noelle says to me.

"Something tells me that you will be, too."

I check on Bradley while I wait for Katie to come out of the room. When she does, she has a sleeping Emery in her arms. "All good?"

"Yes, thanks, Luna."

"If you find yourself getting anxious, talk to your mate. Find something happy to talk about or something that she did that made you smile so that you can keep yourself calm while you nurse."

"I will, thank you."

When she leaves, I turn to Noelle.

"I'm going to go find Trena. Mind link me if you need anything."

Noelle smiles. "I almost forgot I could do that!"

"How could you? The pack is all kinds of excited. I wonder what they're doing over there."

"I guess we'll find out later," she says.

I catch Trena's scent and follow it into the woods. It's only been an hour, but she's still out here crying.

"Trena," I say softly as I approach her.

"Oh, Luna. Hi. Did you need something?" she asks, wiping her tears off her eyes and cheeks.

"I needed to see how you're doing."

She looks at me, and her lips begin to quiver. I go to her, wrapping my arms around her and letting her cry. I knew Trena from Alpha Solomon's pack, but we'd never been really close. Alpha Solomon was busy keeping me away from Simon, which meant that I was kept away from most of the pack members my age. I focused on my studies, and as I got older, I avoided pack gatherings altogether unless Alpha Solomon was going to be there to help keep Simon in check.

"I'm so sorry, Luna. I don't know what got into me," she says, finally pulling back.

"Don't you?" I ask her.

She looks at me, and I know I'm right.

"I can't have a mate, not after what Simon did to me. No one would want me, anyway. He wasn't exactly private when he'd take me," she says. "His warriors ..."

"Are all dead now. And anyone who would say anything about that time of your life would answer to me, or better yet, Warren."

"It doesn't matter. I don't know that I could ever have someone touch me ..." she slaps her hand over her mouth as if she's going to be sick.

"I understand. But I will say this. Bradley is a good man. He took a silver bullet from Simon to protect me. He's basically my guard when I'm at the hospital. He's strong, but he's also compassionate, attentive, and trustworthy, and I'm pretty sure he'll be excited to have found his mate when he wakes up. I can't say what the best option is for you or if the two of you could ever find your way together. But I would ask that, even if you aren't willing to give your mate bond a chance, that you wait to reject him until he's healthy."

"Simon shot him?"

"He did ... in the lung, with a silver bullet. It will be a while before he can heal from that. I don't know how long it will take for his wolf to return. But I do know that he's lucky to be alive. So, both of you have suffered at Simon's hand. Maybe that's enough to start building trust, maybe not. That's for you to decide."

She nods.

"Now, I do want you to come in so I can examine you. Did Simon hurt you?"

"Yes, but nothing my wolf couldn't heal from. It was mostly bruises and some tearing."

"What about a pregnancy?" I ask.

"After the first time, I got the pack doctor to put me on birth control. So, I'm good there."

"How is your wolf?"

"Sad that I'm afraid of our mate. She wants him, of course."

"I understand that. Annika was the same way when I met Warren. I was terrified, having only really known Alphas like Alpha Solomon and Simon."

"Alpha Solomon protected you, didn't he? That's why you never spent time with the pack when Simon was around, and it's why you disappeared?"

"Yep, and it's also why Simon killed his father. Because he protected me. Simon hurt a lot of us. You most of all. But in this pack, we heal. I insist on it. Ask anyone," I say, smiling.

"Oh, I've already heard," she says, chuckling for a moment. "I wish I'd known you better in Alpha Solomon's pack. Maybe we could have been friends."

"There's no reason we can't be friends now. Just because I'm your Luna, or I will be when Warren has the pack ceremony, it doesn't mean that we can't be friends."

"I'd like that."

"Do you think there are others in Simon's pack that would want to come here? Be a part of this pack?"

"I honestly don't know, Luna. I separated myself from them, and I think they separated themselves from me, worried that if Simon saw them with me, he might start calling them to his office."

We're quiet for a moment.

"What's going to happen to Simon?" she asks.

"Eventually, he'll die. But Warren and this pack will make him suffer as much as possible before then."

"Good. He deserves it," she growls.

"Yes, he does. Come on, want to walk back to the packhouse with me? Something is going on, and it's making me crazy. I need to know what they're doing over there. I can feel all the energy but can't get a read on what anyone is thinking."

"Sure," she says. We stand, and I hug her again.

"You're not alone, Trena. If you need to talk, need company, or just need a friend, come see me."

"Thanks, Luna."

We walk back to the pack, and I'm surprised that there are so few people on the road. The ones that are there all say hello, but they've got stupid smiles on their faces like they know a secret.

I frown. What is going on?

"I have no idea," Trena says, and I realize I spoke out loud.

I turn as we walk up the steps to the packhouse and see that the people wandering around outside have all started following me back.

Trena walks inside ahead of me as I look over the group, frowning.

"What the ..." Trena says.

When I turn and step inside, I suddenly understand.

"WARREN! WHAT DID YOU DO?"

Chapter 74: Quinton

Warren

As soon as Haynes walked out of my office to find Laney, I turned to Charlie. "Let's deal with Quinton. I want this done before Yara returns, and I want the pack to be able to settle in and enjoy the party tonight."

"You know I'm with you, Alpha," he says as we stand.

I stop, turning to him. He has always been with me. Always.

"You are now and have always been my greatest ally and friend. You, more than anyone, stood beside me when we were in our darkest times. You never betrayed me. You never took advantage of times when I was weakened. If anything, you fought harder to make sure I got stronger so I could continue as this pack's Alpha. Now, as the sun begins to rise on our lives and the darkness is washed away, I want you to know that I will never forget that. You have my trust and my loyalty, always."

"Thank you, Alpha. You've always been the kind of Alpha that I wanted to follow," he says, his voice thick. I wait while he gets hold of his emotions. "Besides, your job sucks. Mine's much better," he says, and both of us laugh as we leave my office.

When we get down to the cells, Simon is moaning in his, rolling back and forth on the floor. I ignore him and turn to Quinton. He's watching Simon dispassionately.

"You planning to do that to me?" he asks.

"If you had ever gotten your hands on my mate, had left bruises on her, had intended to rape her, yes. Lucky for you, you never got the chance. Your death will be quick. Does it matter to you that my warriors found him trying to rape your mate?" I ask him.

He's on his feet in a flash, his teeth bared. "Did he touch my son?"

"Not to our knowledge. Yasmin told my warrior that he was fine. They didn't see him."

"What the fuck kind of asshole goes around trying to rape Lunas," he growls.

"Want to take a turn at him before I kill you?" I ask him.

His head snaps to mine. "You'd let me?"

"Don't kill him. I'm not done with him yet, but he went after your mate, too. You may not love yours the way I love mine, but as an Alpha, I know I'd want to make him hurt."

"Yeah, I'd love to kick that arrogant asshole right in the face," he growls.

"No!" Simon groans.

I stand back as Charlie opens the door to Quinton's cell. He stays behind him as another warrior opens the cell door to Simon's cell.

Quinton stalks into the cell. "You were so fucking arrogant the last time we talked. Now look at you. At least I'll die with dignity," he says, stomping his foot onto Simon's hand and smashing the bones. Simon screams in pain.

He kicks him hard between the legs. I know he must be sore from being cauterized, but having your dick smashed is going to hurt almost as bad. It must be because Simon turns to the side and vomits. "That's for touching my mate. I promised to keep her safe, and you made me break that promise."

Then he stomps on his knee, snapping it out of joint, probably breaking it. "That's for thinking you could walk into my house like you fucking own it. You don't."

He turns, stepping back out of the cell. "Thank you for that."

I look at him for a long moment. "If you were a different kind of person, I think we could have been friends. But you let greed take over your life."

"Don't get melancholy on me now, Alpha. Let's get this done," Quinton says.

"Very well," I say, turning to head outside. I know my warriors are flanking him, and Charlie is behind him, so I know he can't attack me.

We walk upstairs, and I can see that the first delivery has arrived. I smile as I walk farther away from the packhouse. I don't want any blight on my pack's celebration.

"Having a party?" he asks, his tone angry.

"We are actually. I have my Luna home with me, where she belongs. Charlie has found his mate, and we've made our choice for Gamma. We have a lot to celebrate in this pack. My warriors deserve it. We've been at war for far too long."

"Seems like that war is coming to an end," he says as I stop and turn to him.

"It is. On your knees, Alpha."

Several warriors have come to watch me execute the man who caused our pack so much pain and anguish over the years.

"Alpha Quinton, you have waged war against my pack because of your greed and desire to take my mate from me. My pack members have died because of you. For your sins, I sentence you to death, effectively immediately. Do you have any last words?" I ask him.

"Please don't hurt my son."

"If your son leaves me alone, I'll leave him alone. If he comes after me, I will kill him."

He nods, holding his head high as I extend my claws.

"Goodbye, Alpha Quinton," I say and remove his head with one swipe of my claws.

My warriors lift their heads to the sky and howl happily that one of our tormentors is gone. I have no such positive feelings. I take no pleasure in killing, especially an Alpha who had as much promise as Quinton.

"Burn the body," I say, heading back inside. My gloomy mood follows me inside until I see more flowers being delivered.

"Is this all of them?" I ask one of the omegas.

"Oh no, Alpha, we've only gotten two deliveries so far," she says.

As bad as my mood is, the thought of Yara's response when she walks in helps to lighten it. I walk back to my office, Charlie following me, looking behind him and shaking his head.

"So, is this what our lives are going to be like now? Parties and antagonizing our Luna?" he asks me.

"Goddess, I hope so. But after tonight, and after we finalize our ranked members, I want to meet with Harold. Quinton made a good point."

"What was that?" he asks.

"This war needs to end. There's only one Alpha left, and we need to take him out."

"He's the worst one, the hardest one to get to."

"I have an idea about that, but let's wait until we meet with Harold. I think I'll invite him and Henry to our pack ceremony. What do you think?" I ask Charlie.

"Why not? That's what allies do, right?"

"I honestly have no idea. We've never had allies before. If he comes, then maybe we can talk then."

We talk a bit longer before Charlie goes to work. He and I have had to restructure our days now that we're not fighting all the time. Before, we would take care of what was most pressing before the next attack. Now, I finally feel like I'm able to start managing our pack like I always should have been.

I've lost track of time when I hear her.

"WARREN! WHAT DID YOU DO?"

The moment I hear her voice, my heart lightens and a smile spreads across my face, which is so wide it hurts. I stride from the office, walking out into an explosion of flowers. Holy shit! I had no idea it would look like this. It's like a fucking jungle in here. It's perfect!

"Hi, baby! How was your day?" I ask her as if there's nothing out of the ordinary about having a packhouse full of flowers.

"How was my day? HOW WAS MY DAY? What the hell is this?"

"Well, the pack and I," I say, looking around and including all of them in the fun. "We were so glad to have you home that we wanted to celebrate by giving you flowers."

Her mouth falls open, and she looks at me as if I've lost my mind. It takes every bit of Alpha training for the last thirty years for me not to laugh out loud. Goddess, I love this woman.

"How many flowers did you buy?" she asks, looking around.

"Umm, Carrie, how many did it end up being?" I ask, not looking away from Yara.

"I believe we decided to buy out five florists, Alpha. The largest we could find," she says.

"Five..."

"Welcome home, my love," I say, walking up to her and pulling her to me.

"Tonight, we're having a celebration! Our Luna is home! Our Beta has found his mate! And our Gamma position has been offered and accepted. Let's party!" I yell, watching my mate's smile spread across her face.

As the pack cheers around us, I take my mate's mouth in a fiery, possessive kiss. Her arms wrap around me, and I kiss her until there's nothing around us, no cheering, no scent of flowers, only her, her smell, her taste, and her body pressed against mine.

~ ~ ~

Quirin POV

I watch as my father is brought outside.

"Quirin, no! We need to go!" My mother found me about an hour ago, and she's been trying to get me to leave, but I refuse. If I can't rescue him, I can at least be here to watch him die.

They say words back and forth, Alpha Warren and my father. And then my father raises his head, proud until the end. When Alpha Warren removes his head, my mother looks away, but I don't. I watch as the warriors all howl their dominance over my father.

I watch Alpha Warren walk back to his packhouse. I'd seen the flowers coming in all morning. They're going to have a party. They're going to celebrate that my father is dead.

The pain in my heart turns to hatred as I watch him walk inside.

One day. One day, I will have my revenge.

Chapter 75: Party

Yara

I can't believe my mate. Well, maybe I can. He seems to like finding ways to surprise me. I think he enjoys watching the flood of emotions I feel when he does something frivolous and crazy, like literally filling our packhouse with flowers.

After he announced the party, we went upstairs to shower and change, and of course, my mate is still working to give me that pup, so we took some time to have our own celebration with a promise of more to come later.

I'm honestly not sure who is more excited, him or me. The feeling coming off of my hardcore fighter of a mate is almost giddy. He's so full of excited energy that he's practically bouncing on the balls of his feet as we get ready.

"Did I not wear you out enough?" I ask him.

"Yara!" he says, swinging me around in his arms and making me laugh. "Do you feel the pack's energy? Do you feel how happy they are?"

"Yes, I do."

He sets me down, smiling at me with so much love in his eyes that it makes my heart feel like it's going to explode.

"They've never felt like this, Yara. In the two decades that I've had Arric, the pack has never felt like this. And it's all because of you," he says, stroking my cheek.

"You are giving me WAY too much credit, my love."

"I don't think so. My entire life has changed since you entered it. This pack has never been stronger than it is now that you're here, taking care of them and giving them hope and life."

"They wouldn't be here if it weren't for you, Warren. You kept them alive. You fought for them and for me. Maybe I've healed them, but they wouldn't have been here to heal if it weren't for you and your strength."

"Hmmm, I guess that's why we're perfect for each other," he says, leaning in to kiss me.

"And why we're perfect for this pack," I say, taking my time as I press myself against my mate, letting our love and happiness combine and swell around us as we kiss.

When we finally pull apart, he smiles at me for a moment, and then the excitement is back.

"Come on, let's go!" he says, grabbing my hand and practically dragging me downstairs as I laugh. It is a good feeling, a really good feeling, not only from the pack and my mate, but inside me. I realize that I never expected to have this kind of happiness in my life. But with Warren, apparently, all things are possible.

I shake my head as we walk through the forest that is the packhouse.

"What are we going to do with all of this?" I ask him as we navigate through the plants.

"I thought we'd let the pack members pick what they wanted to decorate their rooms. What do you think?" he says, turning to smile at me. Goddess, this man is gorgeous when he smiles. The smile widens as he hears my thoughts.

"It's a great idea," I say.

I can smell the food before we get outside, and my mouth begins to water. Someone has put music on, and people are eating and drinking, some dancing with their pups, their mates, or both when we walk outside. There are tables set up everywhere, and everywhere I look, people are talking and laughing.

"There they are! We thought you'd never arrive," Charlie says loudly, getting the pack's attention. They cheer as we walk out.

"Hey, my mate wants a pup, and I'm working hard to give her one. That takes time, Charlie. You don't rush those things," Warren says, making me blush but making the pack laugh and cheer.

"I just have a few announcements," Warren says. He pulls me to his side as someone turns the music off.

"First and foremost, our Luna is home. She is safe and back under our protection," he says, kissing the top of my head while the pack cheers. "Second, let's give a round of applause to our omegas! They worked hard to put this feast together AND keep it a secret from all of you."

The pack cheers again, and I can see and feel the omegas' pride and happiness that Warren acknowledged them and their efforts.

"Third, it's time for us to have a pack ceremony. We have our beautiful Luna," he says, and everyone cheers again. He smiles at me, waiting for the cheers to die down. Then he looks back up and around.

"Where's Charlie?"

I hear Noelle yelp as Charlie lifts her up by her waist and puts her on his shoulder. "We have our beautiful Beta female," Charlie announces to everyone's cheers.

"And, we have our nomination for Gamma, Haynes. Haynes, where are you?" Warren asks, and we both look around. Warren sees it at the same time that I do. "Uh, apparently, we have our nomination for Gamma COUPLE! Congratulations, Haynes and Laney, on your mating."

"WHAT?" Noelle exclaims.

As she rushes over to her sister, the pack cheers, and Warren raises his hand for silence. "I want to have the pack ceremony this weekend. I intend to invite our allies, Alpha Harold and his son, Alpha Henry, to come watch and stay for a while. Before that occurs, you will have the chance to challenge Haynes for the Gamma position. Those challenges will take place in two days, so tomorrow, if you want to challenge him for the Gamma position, put in your request before the end of the day."

As I look around, I don't see anyone who looks unhappy with Haynes' nomination, but some will probably challenge him just to see how strong he is. It's not uncommon since he will be a ranked member and their leader.

"We have a lot to celebrate tonight. Two of our enemies are dead, and one is in our cells. Feel free to go flaunt our happiness in Simon's face," Warren says, making everyone laugh. Not all the laughs are nice. Simon won't have an easy night, but I don't care. He brought this on himself.

"Whatever you do, don't kill him. He stays alive until we have proof that our Luna is carrying my pup. I want him to see that everything that he wanted in this life belongs to me. Yara is MY mate, OUR Luna, and the mother of MY pups. And I want him to know that before he dies."

There's more cheering from the pack. Oh yeah, Simon will have a rough night with a lot of taunting.

"We have one enemy left. I will be speaking to Alpha Harold and discussing ways to eliminate our last and final threat. My goal, our goal, is to end this war. We've had enough fighting to last multiple lifetimes. I think it's time we all got to relax and enjoy our lives for once. I know I intend to," he says, pulling me even closer to him.

"And last but not least, your Luna, in all of her generosity, has agreed to share her flowers with all of you. Please take some flowers or plants to your rooms tonight. There are plenty to choose from and enough to go around," Warren says.

"PLEASE take some," I reiterate, making everyone laugh. "And thank you for showing me so much love. I love all of you and this pack. I couldn't be happier being mated to our Alpha, and I can't wait to become an official member of this pack and your Luna."

Warren leans in to kiss me as cheers go up again.

Finally, he pulls back and looks around. "LET'S PARTY!"

Our celebration goes late into the night, and when Warren and I finally get to our room, the celebration continues well into the morning.

Chapter 76: Bradley

Trena

I know this pack is different than Simon's. It's obvious in everything that goes on here, every interaction that occurs with Alpha Warren, Beta Charlie, and this pack. Even Yara is different than I remember her from before. Somehow, she seems stronger, as if finding her mate and becoming a Luna has brought out something inside her that was waiting to blossom.

But I'm in no mood to celebrate. I begin walking around the pack, hearing the periodic sounds of cheering, music, and laughter. It's the exact opposite of my own emotions, making it feel almost otherworldly.

Eventually, I find myself standing outside the pack hospital. Just like with the patrols, the nurses here are taking shifts so everyone can go to the party. However, I know there is only one person in the hospital right now. My mate. Bradley.

I walk inside and wave to Katie who is currently on shift.

"How's the party?" she asks excitely.

"In full swing," I tell her.

"I can't wait to go. This pack has never had a party before."

"I don't know of any packs that have had parties. We've had so much war for so long."

Katie looks off to where we can hear cheering again. "It makes me even more proud to be a part of this pack." She looks back at me. "Are you going to stay and join our pack?"

"I'd like to, but ... we'll see how things go. Is it okay if I go see Bradley?"

"Sure. He's still unconscious."

"That's okay," I say.

She nods, giving me a knowing look. Why else would I want to see Bradley unless he was my mate?

I walk into the room and over to the bed, taking my first look at the man who smells better than anything I've ever smelled, like cigars and whiskey, warm and inviting. He's very attractive, with dark brown hair, and a longer mustache and beard. He looks rugged, but that's probably because he's covered in scars like most warriors these days. He's a big man, and I can see why Alpha Warren chose him as Luna Yara's guard. He'd be a hard man to get past.

I reach down and take his hand. I wonder what it would have been like meeting Bradley if Simon hadn't done what he did to me over the past year. I wonder what it would be like to find my mate before I'd lost hope and didn't have the negative feelings to go along with it.

"Luna Yara told me you were a good man. But trust me, you don't want me," I whisper.

"How do you know?"

My eyes flash up to the man who was supposed to be unconscious. I try to yank my hand out of his, but he's surprisingly strong for someone who nearly died.

"Please don't rush off. My wolf is silent, but that doesn't mean he doesn't feel your presence," he says.

I nod and lean back against the bed, letting him hold my hand. He begins to rub his thumb over the back in slow circles. It sends tingles up my arm and through my body. It feels so nice, but I know I can never have this in my life. Tears spring to my eyes, and I'm angry at Simon all over again for what he did to me.

"You want to tell me why you think I won't want you?" he asks me gently.

I shake my head no. Then I look at him. "I don't want to tell you, but you need to know so you don't have any misconceptions about us becoming mated."

His eyes narrow. "Okay. Why don't I want you?"

My stomach roils, and my throat tightens. I look away from him, unable to look my mate in the eyes when I tell him.

"I was Simon's whore. Whenever he wanted ... sexual release, he called me."

"Was it consensual?" he asks.

I shake my head no. "But he was my Alpha ..."

"Simon's a fuckhead who doesn't deserve the title," he growls. "Is he dead yet?"

"No, he's in Alpha Warren's cells. They're torturing him before they kill him."

"Good, I'd like to have a go at him. I'm a little surprised that you didn't have a go at him. You seem pretty angry," he says, watching me.

I can't hide the smile that comes to my face. This time I do look at my mate. "I ripped his balls off."

He blinks twice before he bursts out laughing. "Aww, shit, that hurts," he says, wrapping his arm across his chest as he begins coughing. I rush to get him some water and help him drink it.

When I set the water back down and turn back, he's looking at me thoughtfully. "You know he's the reason I'm in this bed, right?"

I nod. "Luna Yara told me."

"Don't reject me just yet. Get to know me first. I want to get to know you."

"I told Luna Yara that I wouldn't reject you until after you're healed, so you don't have to worry about that."

When he doesn't respond, I look back up at his face.

"That's not what I'm worried about," he says softly. "If things hadn't changed, I may never have found you. I never expected to find my mate when I realized she wasn't in this pack. And look, I'm no saint. I didn't save myself for you. So, I don't care that you've been with others. I DO care that the shithead raped you, and for that, I'll finish what you started and rip his dick off. But, if you look at this a bit differently, you and I got lucky. Neither of us died in these wars, neither of us took chosen mates, and we've found each other in spite of everything. So maybe give us a chance. Don't assume I don't want you. I do want you. And I'm a patient man. I can be as patient as you need me to be. Just give us a chance, okay? Will you do that for me, for us?"

I search his face but find only truth in his words. "Okay."

He smiles, a big, beautiful smile, and holds out his hand. "I'm Bradley."

"Bradley, I'm Trena," I say, shaking his hand.

"It is very nice to meet you, Trena."

Chapter 77: Possessive
Warren

I wasn't surprised when we had several of our warriors submit requests to battle Haynes. I would have been more surprised if they hadn't. The pack hierarchy is built on strength and leadership. Haynes has shown his ability to lead and to learn what he doesn't know, but now he'll have to prove his strength. I'm not worried. If I didn't think he had the strength to defeat the other warriors, I wouldn't have chosen him as my Gamma, and neither would Charlie.

After waking with my mate lying on top of me and giving her my best effort to ensure she's carrying my pup, I head downstairs to call Harold.

"Good morning, Alpha Warren," he answers.

"It is a good morning, indeed, Alpha Harold."

"It sounds like it. May I ask what has you so happy?"

I tell him about our pack's party last night, celebrating our strength and togeth- erness.

"That sounds ... incredible. Perhaps I should consider doing something like that here," he says.

"I honestly didn't realize how much our pack needed it, Harold. If you have the chance, I would suggest doing something like that. The feeling in my pack this morning is just amazing. It's unlike anything I've ever felt before."

"I'm very happy for you. I'll definitely have to think about that and what we could do here. But I'm guessing you didn't call just to tell me that," he says.

"No, I called for two reasons. First, to tell you that I executed Quinton yesterday."

"How are you doing after that? Executing another Alpha is never easy."

"No, it wasn't easy. Maybe because I don't consider Simon an Alpha, torturing him is easy. Killing Quinton ... honestly, it sucked. He and I, in a different life, could have been friends."

"The two of you had a lot in common. You were both passionate about your packs. You were strong leaders and great fighters. I think you're right. It just goes to show you how two people who are so similar can go down very different paths. Where is his son?"

"As far as I know, Luna Yasmin moved the two of them back to their pack."

"Perhaps Henry and I will go see him, see if he and his mother want to join our pack. Perhaps we can change the direction of the son, so he doesn't end up like his father."

"I think a conversation like that would be better coming from you since I'm the one who executed his father," I say.

"I agree. I'll make plans to take a trip over to their pack and talk to them."

"Which brings me to the second reason I'm calling. I wanted to invite you and Henry to my pack to bear witness to our pack ceremony as we bring in all of our newly ranked members. I'll be honest, I've never had an ally before, but it feels like the kind of thing you invite your allies to attend. It would also give us a chance to talk in person about the ideas I have for taking Brady out, and of course, you'd be closer to Quinton's pack if you were here," I say.

"I would love that. And I think Henry would, too. Would it be okay if I brought Farrah? We're still building a relationship, but I think it might be good for her to see what a strong, healthy pack can look like."

"We'd be happy to have your mate. She didn't really spend any time here when she first came in. I think it would be good for her to see what we're building here. Maybe it will help her to see what's possible in your pack now that our war is finally ending."

It's quiet for a moment. "I never thought I'd see the end of the war, but you're right. Thomas and Quinton are gone, Simon is out, and that only leaves Brady. Once he's gone..."

"Peace. And that's what I'm striving for."

"That's what WE'RE striving for. We're allies, remember," he says.

"Yeah, we are. And that feels good, too. I'll have three rooms made up for you, just in case. If you'd like to come Friday, we'll have the ceremony on Saturday, and you can head over to Quinton's old pack on Sunday if that works for you."

"That'd be great. I'll see you then."

"See you then," I hang up and mentally reach out to Yara. She's humming with happiness. Goddess, the feeling in the pack is making me feel high.

When I step out into the packhouse, I see smiles on the faces of my pack members. People look hopeful, and the camaraderie from last night continues. Some omegas and warriors are talking about where to put the plants that remain in the packhouse.

"Why don't you take some over to the hospital? Your Luna spends a lot of her time there," I suggest.

"Great idea!"

I have work to do, but the feeling coming from the pack feels so good that I spend my day going around and helping others, spending time with my pack members, and getting reacquainted with them.

I get involved in helping some warriors who are rebuilding some of the areas around the pack that have been destroyed in our wars. I'm having such a good time that I completely lose track of time. It's a warm day with the sun shining down, so most of us have stripped down to shorts as we work.

"That sexy as fuck man is all mine. With a body like that, he'll be giving me lots of pups," I hear Yara murmur behind me.

I stand up, looking at my warriors, who all try and fail to hide their smiles and snickers. I don't bother trying to hide mine.

I look behind me. "Did you say something, my love?"

"No," she says. Her arms are crossed over her body, and she's leaning against a wall ... watching me. Even from here, I can see that her eyes are dark with desire.

"Something on your mind, baby?"

"Did you have them send plants over to the hospital?"

"I did. I thought you'd like to have them over there, too," I say, tilting my head as I watch her still looking over my body. The feeling I'm getting from her is very, very possessive. It's not something I'm used to feeling from Yara, but I like it.

Her eyes track back up to mine. "How much longer do you have out here?"

"Not much longer."

"I'll be upstairs," she says, turning and walking back inside.

I turn and look at my warriors.

"We're done here, Alpha."

"Thank the goddess," I say, rushing inside and scooping up my mate. She doesn't seem to care that I'm drenched in sweat. She wraps her arms around my neck, and for the first time since I met her, her kiss is more demanding than mine.

I don't release her mouth as I walk us into our room and straight to the showers. I turn on the shower and then set her on the sink, moving between her legs as she wraps herself around me.

When I finally pull back, I look at the smug look on her face.

"What's going on in that pretty head of yours?"

She bites her lip and smiles. "I'll tell you after we shower."

I pull her shirt over her head, unhooking her bra and tossing it aside as I kiss her again. I could probably dig around in her head and figure out what's going on, but she seems very proud of herself, so I want to let her tell me.

I set her back on the floor, and we remove the rest of our clothes before getting into the shower. She makes a point of getting the soap and rubbing it over my body, watching her hands as she does. The possessive feeling I was getting before increases the longer she touches me.

When she looks back up at me, I can see that Annika is forward. "Mine!" she growls.

Arric pushes forward, too. "Yes, I am. All yours."

I press her against the shower wall, lifting her leg and sliding inside her.

"Is this what you need?" I ask her, beginning to move inside her.

"I need you," she breathes, kissing my chest and my neck.

She wraps her arms around my neck and then lifts up to wrap both legs around me. I grab her hair, pulling back to look at her while I thrust inside her. She's never felt this needy before.

I'm about to ask her if she's okay when her canines slide out. I tilt my head, giving her access, and Annika presses her teeth into my neck, causing me to come immediately. I growl as I thrust harder inside her, Arric letting our canines slide out before sinking them into Yara.

Her body jerks with her release, contracting around me and making me shoot off again. Annika doesn't release me, purring loudly as she pushes her venom into my body.

When she finally lets go, I pull back and look at her.

"What's all this about? Where's all this possessiveness coming from?" I ask her.

Yara smiles, then steps out of the shower. I quickly finish washing as she wraps a towel around herself, then lifts her pants off the floor, pulling something out of the pocket.

When she turns, she has a plastic stick in her hand.

"What's that, baby?" I ask her, stepping out and grabbing a towel. It must be some medical thing. It has two pink lines in the middle of it. "What am I looking at?"

When I look at her, she's smiling, and there are tears in her eyes. "It's a pregnancy test."

I stop drying myself, holding my towel as I go still.

"And what do two lines mean?"

"Positive."

"Positive? You're pregnant?"

She nods.

I whoop with excitement, grabbing my mate and swinging her around in my arms before taking her mouth in a kiss just as possessive as hers was earlier. I carry her to the bed and lay her down.

"Can we wait to tell the pack during the pack ceremony this weekend?" I ask her.

"That's when I was hoping to tell them. We have so much to celebrate, Warren."

"Yes, we do. We should start right now," I say, sliding back inside her and having our own personal celebration for several more hours.

Chapter 78: Secret

Yara

I knew Warren would be excited. What I didn't expect were the feelings that stirred inside me and Annika when we found out that I was pregnant. I began feeling very possessive of him. I am the one that will give him his pups. Only me. He is mine. Only mine.

Thankfully, he didn't seem to mind my possessive neediness or Annika's. I guess that's why they're mated to us. If anything, he almost seemed pleased that Annika felt the need to mark him several more times last night and again this morning. She finally relaxed a bit when our scent on him was almost equal to his, and his on us was the same. No one can say they don't know that he is mated to me. Or at least, that's Annika's thinking.

I walk into the bathroom, watching as he showers off our sex before going to warrior training. Annika begins purring loudly as I look him over. He really is one hell of a gorgeous man: sexy, strong, and powerful, yet kind and loving, patient and thoughtful.

He leans his head away from the shower head, wiping the water from his eyes. "Again?" he asks, raising an eyebrow.

"I'm allowed to purr at my sexy mate."

"How about my sexy mate gets naked, and then she and my pup can join me."

I pull the shirt over my head, letting it drop to the floor. Now it's his turn to purr at me.

When I step in, he begins stroking my nipples, making my body hum. "How long before we know if we're having a boy or a girl?" he asks.

"That depends on how fast and powerful your Alpha sperm were. If they caught my egg on the first try, we may know by the weekend, but that's a big if. I think the pack will just be happy to know that we're having a baby."

"You know the warriors are going to become even more protective of you, right?" he asks, turning me to face the wall as he slides inside me again.

"Do you think I'm going to be like this my entire pregnancy?" I ask.

"Like what?" he asks, sliding in and out of me as I arch to take him deeper.

"Desperate for you?"

He nips my shoulder. "Goddess, I hope so."

When I've finally had enough, for now, we get dressed, and I head over to the pack hospital. I know that Warren is leading Haynes' challenges for Gamma this morning, and some of the warriors may end up injured.

When I walk in, Anna is smiling at me. "Good morning, Luna. Last night was amazing. We all had such a great time."

"It was great, wasn't it? Things are really changing, aren't they? Warren is such a great Alpha."

"Every great man needs a great woman, and you are that great woman, Luna. The entire pack recognizes that everything changed once you got here. Maybe it's the two of you together, but it's only because of you that our lives have improved so much."

"Anna, that is so sweet to say. I'm not sure I can take all the credit, though."

"Whether you accept the credit or not, we're giving it to you. And it's not just us, Luna. All those other Alphas that wanted you? They recognized it, too. They could see that you have made this pack stronger. That's why they wanted you. Well, maybe not Simon. He's just a creep."

Something about the way she says it makes me look at her.

"Did you go taunt him last night?"

"Am I in trouble if I did?" she asks.

"No. I expected the pack would taunt him. He's hurt enough of us that he deserves whatever he gets."

She looks at me guiltily.

"What did you do?"

"He hurt Piper. He almost killed her! Some of the warriors held him so I could punch him in the throat. I'm sure it didn't hurt him as much as I would have liked for it to, but some other women kicked him in the crotch for threatening to rape you and Luna Yasmin and for what he did to Trena. Now that we know she's mated to one of ours ..."

"Wait, how did everyone find out about that?" I ask.

"Katie figured it out, and it's been pretty obvious to those of us here that they're mated. I mean, Trena's been here all night. They've been talking and sleeping off and on."

"That sounds like a good sign."

"I think so. Bradley's a good guy. And I'm pretty sure she told him what happened. I mean, the rest of us can guess because of what she did and said to Simon, but I'm sure it's different when you tell your mate. That would have been hard."

"Trena's tough, maybe tougher than she realizes. If she gives Bradley a chance, I think they'll find their way together."

"I think so too, Luna. Should we check him over before Haynes starts sending warriors to us?" she asks.

"Yep, let's do it."

We walk in, and I'm a bit surprised to see Trena curled up on the bed beside Bradley. His arm is around her and she is sound asleep. He, however, smiles when I walk in.

"Luna, it's good to see you alive and well and home."

"Bradley, it's good to see you awake. I'm missed having my guard around."

"Hopefully, I'm ready for active duty again."

I raise an eyebrow at him. "Do you think so?"

He looks at me for a long moment. "No, not yet. But if my mate keeps sleeping beside me, I'll heal a lot faster."

"Is that how you got her to lay next to you?"

"That and she was exhausted. Nightmares," he says, pressing his lips together tightly. "Can I let you know, or should I link Alpha Warren that I want a go at Simon."

"You have a couple of days before he dies. But I'll let Warren know. You may want to wait anyway. I hear the pack had a really good time with him last night."

He gives me a scary smile, menacing in a way that I don't usually see on Bradley's face. I think I understand why Warren chose him as my guard.

Trena shifts and when her eyes open, she jolts up. "OH!"

"Good morning, Trena. Did you sleep well?" I ask as if finding someone in a hospital bed with their mate is an everyday occurrence.

"Uh, yes?"

"Good. I need some space here if you don't mind, so I can look Bradley over."

She scrambles off the bed, but he captures her hand before she can get too far. "Don't go," he says softly to her.

"I'm going to use the bathroom, and I'll come back." When he doesn't let go of her hand, she watches him. "Promise."

He pulls her hand to his lips and kisses it before releasing her. "Hurry back."

I smile as I start looking over Bradley's paperwork, then turn to look at him.

"How are you feeling?"

"Better, but not 100%. I'd try to lie, but you'd just catch me in it," he says, smiling.

I smile back, looking at the incision. "Your wolf?"

"I can feel him moving around, starting to wake up, but he's not back yet."

"I'm going to have you get up and walk around the room, see how you're breathing," I say.

He does, but he struggles to get around the room, and he still can't take deep breaths.

"Okay, back into bed. Here are your options - you can stay here and rest or I can release you to the packhouse where you will rest. If you don't rest there, I'll send you back here. No work yet. But, as your wolf gets stronger, you can walk further distances. I'd prefer it if you went with someone, especially in the beginning, while your lung is still healing. I don't want you overdoing it and passing out on me."

"Yes, Luna. Perhaps my mate will walk with me," he says, looking at the door as he gets back in bed.

"What happened?" she asks, rushing to the bed.

"I was assessing his ability to breathe. Obviously, he's not able to do much before becoming winded. If I release you, you'll have to be wheeled over to the packhouse. You won't make it otherwise, but I know you'll heal better in your own bed. I'll still want to see you every day until I clear you to go back to work."

"Yes, Luna. Hopefully, Trena will agree to be my walking buddy," he says, panting as he lays back.

"Well, you definitely need someone to help you," she says, pulling the blanket over his legs.

"I'll get your discharge orders, Bradley. I can't stress to you enough that if you don't follow them, I am readmitting you," I say sternly.

"Yes, ma'am."

I turn, making my notes in his chart. Now, I just need to find that ultrasound machine and see if I'm having a boy or a girl.

"Who's she talking to?" Trena asks.

I turn back and see Trena looking confused while Anna and Bradley smile at me.

"She forgets she's talking out loud," Bradley says.

My eyes go wide. "Did I..."

Anna nods her head excitedly. "Congratulations, Luna!"

"Oh no! It's supposed to be a secret. Warren wants to announce it to the pack this weekend. Please don't tell anyone," I say, worried that I've let the secret slip without meaning to.

"Your secret is safe with us, Luna, but that just means I need to get healthy fast. Alpha's going to want a guard on you all the time now."

I smile, thinking of my mate. "Yeah, he will."

"Do you want me to help with your ultrasound, Luna?" Anna asks me.

"That would be great, Anna. We'll get a wheelchair for you, Bradley, and then you can leave whenever you're ready. No rush."

When Anna does the ultrasound, it's still too early to tell, but we can see my baby's heartbeat. "Do you want me to take a video of it, Luna?"

"Yeah. Warren will love hearing that sound," I say.

"We should try again on the morning of the party. Maybe we'll get lucky."

"Sounds like a plan. Thanks again, Anna. I really appreciate it."

"Anytime, Luna."

Chapter 79: Heartbeat

Warren

I'm running the challenge with Haynes. There are five individuals challenging him. Depending on how long each competition takes, this could be quick or go on for hours. Most of the challengers are strong warriors, so I'm assuming this will take all morning and part of the afternoon.

Since I don't want my warriors injured too much, I'm calling the fights. Injuries during challenges are common, and I know Yara is available to treat my warriors if they get injured, but now that we're a healthy pack, I want to keep us that way.

Haynes takes the first guy down, and I call it after he dislocates his shoulder. The first match took an hour, and I expect the others will be about the same.

"Go see your Luna," I tell my warrior, then call a brief recess for Haynes to catch his breath.

The second battle lasts a bit longer, and this time, Haynes dislocates my warrior's knee. I call it and send him to the pack hospital before giving Haynes another break.

We're just about to start round three when I feel her. I look up and see my mate smiling at me.

"Take a break," I say.

"Alpha, I'm good to go," Haynes says.

"Yeah, but I need a break," I say, jogging over to Yara, pulling her into my arms, and kissing her with everything in me.

I'm so excited that she's carrying my pup that I can hardly stand it. I've heard the word elation before, but I never really understood what it meant until now. I never understood the emotion that went behind it. Now, though, I'm elated, overjoyed, thrilled, euphoric. You name it, I'm feeling it.

I pour every bit of emotion that I have for my mate into her as I kiss her. She holds on to me, whimpering softly as she melts in my arms, just as happy as I am as our emotions mix together.

When I pull back, I nuzzle her nose with mine. "What brings my beautiful mate out here?"

"I wanted to let you know that I've released Bradley, but he's still not allowed to work. He's got his therapy, and if he doesn't follow through, I'll readmit him," she says, her eyes closed as she enjoys our closeness.

"You could have told me that later," I say, wondering if she needed my touch as much as I needed hers.

"I also have a surprise for you. I was hoping you were almost done, but it looks like you still have a ways to go."

"What kind of surprise?"

"The private kind," she says, opening her eyes to look at me.

'The baby kind?' I ask in the mind link, and she nods.

"I can take a longer break," I say out loud.

She looks at my face, her fingers running through my hair. "No, let's wait. I'd rather take our time and not be rushed."

"Wise words from my Luna. And just so you know, Alpha Harold, Alpha Henry, and Farrah will be coming for our pack ceremony this weekend."

She smiles her big, sweet smile, making me hungry for her again. "I'm so glad. I think the pack should know what Farrah did for me."

"For us," I say. "She brought you back to me. For that, I will be forever indebted to her."

She runs her nose against mine. "I really enjoyed our celebration last night. Maybe we can celebrate again tonight."

"My sweet little mate, I intend to celebrate like that with you every single night for the rest of our lives," I purr at her.

"My life just keeps getting better and better. Now," she says, slapping her hand on my ass cheek, then grabbing hold. "Go finish so we can play," she says, giving me a very naughty look.

I shake my head as she pulls away, smirking at my semi-hard state as she turns.

"Haynes, how many more can I expect in my hospital today?"

"Just three more, Luna," he calls out.

"I expect to be able to congratulate you later. Don't disappoint me," she says to him, and I know, without a doubt, that no one is defeating Haynes now. He, like every other warrior here, would never want to disappoint his Luna.

"Yes, Luna!"

"Alright, let's get back to it!" I say, clapping my hands together as I jog back.

"Why bother, Alpha? No way Haynes is losing now," one of my remaining warriors says.

"Test your Gamma. Those of you who wanted this challenge are some of my strongest warriors. You need to know without a doubt that he's stronger than you are. So, let's do this so there's no chance that you ever question yourself or him," I say.

When the next warrior is back in position, I call the start.

A broken ankle, a dislocated elbow, and a broken wrist later, I announce that Haynes has officially won his spot as the pack's Gamma.

It's mid-afternoon, and while the warriors and Charlie congratulate Haynes, I go tell the omegas to prepare another celebratory dinner for tonight.

"We were already working on one, Alpha," my Lead Omega says.

"Perfect," I say, turning to leave. I stop and turn back, realizing that now that I have time, I can ask some of the questions that I never had a chance to ask my pack members before.

"Is there anything that you need that will make your lives or your jobs easier?"

After a startled moment, they look at each other, and then I get a list of things that would make their lives and working in the kitchens easier.

Feeling better and better about my life and this pack, I head upstairs to shower and get ready for Yara. I expect she'll be here after she sets the bones in my warrior's wrist. As I strip off my clothes, I look out the window and see Bradley walking very slowly. His arm is wrapped around Trena's shoulders, and her arm is wrapped around his waist, helping him walk. As I watch, I see that he has to stop every couple of steps. He may actually have to stop, but part of me wonders if he's laying it on thick so that his mate will continue to touch him, and they can spend more time together.

As I watch, I see Trena look up at him, and even from here, I can see her cheeks flush before she looks down. But not before I see the smile on her face.

Well done, Bradley. Well done.

I hop in the shower, thinking of my mate and her possessiveness last night. I do wonder if her need for me will continue to be so strong throughout her pregnancy. I won't be unhappy about my mate needing and wanting me all the time. I don't even mind her possessiveness. After our slow start, I actually like it a lot. I love how much she wants everyone to know that I'm hers.

I smell her before I hear her. Her gentle arms wrap around me from behind, and her lips press against my back.

"Hello, my mate," she purrs.

"Hello, my sweet, sexy woman. Did you get the warriors all patched up?"

"I did. I'm not keeping any of them overnight, but they're all off-duty for the night. I'll check them tomorrow, but the dislocations should be completely healed by then, and the breaks a day after that."

Yara begins stroking me, making my semi-hard length rock hard in her hands. I take her in the shower, taking my time since Annika doesn't seem overly possessive at the moment. She still sinks her canines into my neck, and Arric does the same to her, but that only makes our orgasms that much stronger.

When we step out, she wraps her hair in a towel before wrapping another towel around her body and rushing out of the bathroom.

"Yara, what are you doing?" I ask.

When she comes back in, she has her phone. She pushes some buttons, and then I hear what sounds like a heartbeat. It's soft and fluttery, but I'm pretty sure that's what it is.

Because she's looking at me the way she is and because she told me she had a baby surprise for me, it suddenly clicks that this is my pup's heartbeat.

"Is that...?"

"Mmhmm," she says.

404

I pull her against me, closing my eyes as Arric pushes forward so we can both hear our pup's heartbeat. I can feel Arric's desire to start purring, but he holds off, not wanting to mute the sound of our pup's heartbeat.

When it's over, I look at her. "Play it again."

She chuckles and hits replay. I press my lips to the top of her head, closing my eyes again. Next to the sounds that Yara makes when I'm making love to her, this has become my favorite sound in the world.

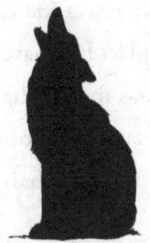

Chapter 80: Gammas and Betas

Laney

I watched my mate, my official mate of three days, while he fought for his position as Gamma. I had no doubt that he would win. He's a great fighter but an even better instructor, which is what the Gamma position would do - train the warriors in our pack.

Our pack. I'm still getting used to the idea of being a part of this pack. I watch as Alpha Warren jogs over and kisses his mate in front of the pack, the goddess, and anyone else to see. The love that is shared in this pack is unlike anything that I've ever seen and definitely unlike anything in Thomas' pack, even when his father was Alpha.

This pack feels good. The camaraderie, the cohesiveness, is unlike anything I've ever seen or felt. This pack acts like a pack should. They act like a family, protecting each other and working together. Even this competition against Haynes feels different.

I'd been terrified that these five warriors would work together to take Haynes out. It's what would have happened in my previous pack. They would have worked together to find his weakness, and one by one, they would have played on his weakness until one of them took him out, most likely forever. Death in these types of competitions wasn't uncommon in Thomas' pack. But it's just another difference here.

When Luna Yara tells Haynes that she expects to congratulate him later on his win, I'm surprised again. First, she clearly identified who her preference is. Second, rather than making it more of a competition, the others realized that Haynes wouldn't let his Luna down. They were ready to give up and let him have the position.

Then, the biggest surprise of all was that Alpha Warren told them to continue. He's right. Not knowing for sure could cause animosity in the future. It could mean that warriors test Haynes and, therefore, me more than they should because they never truly found out if he could defeat them.

In between each battle, Alpha Warren gives Haynes a break to breathe and get some water. He always jogs over and kisses me, each kiss becoming more and more sweaty. But I don't care. At first, I thought it would feel strange for him to kiss me in front of others. In this pack, though, it feels right. I'd almost be upset if he didn't kiss me in front of everyone.

When he defeats his final opponent, he first checks to make sure he's okay, congratulating him on a good fight, and then he turns to me. I race into his arms, slamming my body against his as I wrap my arms around him.

"You did it!" I say excitedly before kissing him.

I can feel his growl of happiness vibrating against my body as I kiss him.

"Congratulations, Gamma," several warriors say. I can feel them slapping him on the shoulder as they pass, but he doesn't stop kissing me.

When he finally pulls back, he smiles at me. "I think they were talking to you."

I bark out a laugh just as Beta Charlie and my sister come out to congratulate Haynes.

"Gamma Haynes," Charlie says, walking up.

"Gamma Laney," Noelle says, smiling at me.

"Beta Noelle," I say before pulling her into a hug. A year ago, I was terrified that I wouldn't be able to protect my sister and keep her away from Thomas or the others who wanted her. But now, here we are in this amazing pack, and we're both ranked members.

"Why don't you go get cleaned up? I believe our Alpha is planning another celebration for you tonight," Noelle says.

"Another one?" I ask.

"We have a lot to celebrate. Good things are happening in this pack. We should always celebrate good things, and now we can," Charlie says.

I look at my mate. "We should definitely celebrate," I say proudly.

"What kind of celebration are we having?" he asks, his eyes darkening.

I laugh. "Every kind possible."

"Perfect, let's start now," he says, scooping me up and carrying me into the packhouse.

"Get something to eat," Charlie calls from behind us.

"Oh, I'm definitely going to be eating," Haynes says, making me blush. I've never blushed as much as I have since I met this man. I don't think I'd ever blushed before, ever. But now, I know exactly what he's saying, what he means, and what it will feel like when he has his face between my thighs.

I can't wait.

Noelle POV

I lean into my mate as we watch Haynes, Gamma Haynes now, carry my sister up to their room, where I'm sure they will begin celebrating right away.

Charlie kisses the top of my head. "Come walk with me," he says, taking my hand and leading me away from the packhouse.

I know my mate. I know he's focusing on the patrols, making sure they're running as they should be, making sure that the feeling in the pack is positive, and nothing seems out of place. He, as much as Alpha Warren, manages this pack and everything in it. For the longest time, it's just been the two of them, and they have done a fantastic job of taking care of everything. Now, though, they have Luna Yara and me. And now, we also have a Gamma couple to help run the pack. I know it will take my mate a while to finally let go of what he's been doing his entire adult life.

I wait until he's finished with his mental overview of the pack, watching this strong, sexy man as we walk.

"You're staring at me," he says, turning to smile at me.

"I'm not staring at you. I'm looking at you."

"Is there a difference?"

"Yes, one is creepy, and the other isn't," I say, smiling up at him. He chuckles. It's a warm, deep sound that I love hearing.

"Why are you looking at me then?"

"Well, besides the fact that you're bringing me out here for a reason, and I'm waiting to hear it, I was watching you assess the pack. You're very good at it. You could have been an Alpha, you know?" I say.

He shrugs. "Like I've told Warren, his job sucks. Being a Beta is MUCH better," he says.

"Is it, because truthfully, the two of you do almost the same things for this pack. I've been watching you run this pack, and the two of you move in a seamless synchronization. When he takes care of one thing, you shift to cover what he's not watching, and the same is true for him when you move to focus on something. It's impressive. And the two of you have obviously been doing it so long that I don't even think you realize you're doing it anymore. Like now, you know Alpha Warren is upstairs, waiting to talk to Luna Yara about whatever she came by to tell him earlier, so you've just automatically taken over monitoring the entire pack. When he comes back down for the party later, he'll re-engage, and you'll shift to covering only certain things."

I stop and pull him to a stop with me. "It's a testament to what great leaders both of you are. Betas are frequently overlooked for the hard work that they do in the pack, or at least, that's been my experience. So, I wanted you to know that I see you. I see what you do, and I recognize the value that you bring to this pack. Alpha Warren may be the Alpha, and he's a great Alpha. But without you, I don't think he'd still be an Alpha. I'm not even sure he'd still be alive."

I watch my mate's jaw tick as I feel the strong emotions welling inside him. I'm not sure anyone has ever told him how impressive he is. Alpha Warren, possibly, but what I said is true. Betas are often overworked and underappreciated.

He pulls me against him. "You're proud of who I am?"

"I'm proud of the Beta that you are, I'm proud of the man and wolf that you are, I'm proud to be your mate, and I'm proud that one day, I will be the mother of your pups," I say, reaching up to stroke his cheek, rubbing my thumb over his jaw until he relaxes.

He leans down, kissing me deeply, opening his mind, and letting his emotions and pride in my words flow through me. I open myself to him, letting him feel just how much I meant every word I said, how much I love him, and how grateful I am to have him as my mate.

He pulls back and leans his forehead against mine. "You want to have my pups?"

"I do," I say.

"That's what I wanted to talk about. Now that our Alpha and Luna are trying for a pup, I thought that maybe we could start trying. I mean, if you're ready."

I kiss my mate again, then kiss his jaw, making my way to his ear when I nibble on his earlobe before whispering in his ear.

"I already am."

He jerks back, looking at my face.

"You already are ..."

I smile. "Pregnant. I just found out this morning."

He lifts me up, swinging me around as he lifts his head and howls happily. Then he sets me down and kisses me as passionately as he does when we're making love.

"You've just made me the happiest man in the world."

"Congratulations, Daddy. You're going to be a father!"

He howls again as I laugh, and then he pulls me deeper into the forest and shows me just how happy he is.

Chapter 81: Career Paths
Yara

Haynes' congratulations party was wonderful. The happiness in the pack was contagious, and everyone laughed and enjoyed themselves. It feels like the bonds that weave a pack together are strengthening, and the pack itself is becoming stronger because of it.

I was even more excited when Charlie and Noelle pulled Warren and me aside to tell us that they were expecting and that they wanted to announce it at the party.

"Do you mind waiting until the pack ceremony?" Warren asks.

"Sure, we can wait. I think," Charlie says, smiling at Noelle. He looks like I feel ... ready to burst with the news. And apparently, I already did. "But is there a reason you don't want us to add to the celebratory feeling tonight?"

Warren smiles down at me.

"What?" Noelle gasps, reaching out to take my arm. "You're ...?"

I nod excitedly, and we hug, doing a strange jumping, rocking motion while our mates just smile at us.

"You're good with both of us announcing together?" Warren asks Charlie.

"I hope you're planning a HUGE celebration. This pack is going to go nuts!"

Warren's happiness and excitement ripples through the bond. I love feeling my mate so happy.

"How about Noelle and I take care of the party arrangements, and you two do ... whatever you do," I tell them.

Warren smiles at me, then looks at Charlie. "I guess we'll get Haynes and do 'whatever we do'."

"Yeah, whatever that is," Charlie smirks, winking at his mate.

I look at Noelle, who raises an eyebrow. "Running the pack?" she asks.

"Managing the finances?" I add.

"Keeping us safe?"

"Keeping our warriors strong?"

"Keeping us fed," she and I begin counting off all the things our mates do for us and the pack.

Warren pulls me to him. "I'm pretty sure it's OUR mates who keep our pack strong, but the rest ... yeah. And let's not forget our most important job."

"What's more important than the pack's safety?" Noelle asks.

"Loving our mates," Charlie says.

"Making sure we give them pups," Warren says.

"Making sure they're always happy."

"Making sure they always have flowers."

"Making sure they know they are more important to us than anyone."

Noelle and I begin laughing. "Okay, okay. Damn, you two. You should have been brothers."

"We're brothers from different mothers," Charlie says, smiling.

"Let's go, bro. Let's go find our little bro and harass him," Warren says.

"YES! That's what big brothers do," Charlie says excitedly.

Noelle and I watch them walk off to find Haynes.

"Is it me, or is their happiness intoxicating?" I ask.

"I feel like I'm getting high on it," she murmurs.

The next couple of days go by in a blur. Since there's no one in the hospital, I do inventory, showing everyone how to check the supplies, and we make a list of what we need. I have Anna call Savannah to find out who we order from and then have her put in the order for more medical supplies.

Right now, things are good. But we have one more Alpha to destroy, and I know Warren is going to talk to Harold this weekend about taking Brady out. There's no way our pack will walk away unscathed, so I want to be prepared and ready for anything.

While we're there, pack members come and go, finally able to bring in pups who have scraped knees or have splinters in their hands or feet. We see pregnant she-wolves who want to get their unborn pups checked and other minor, everyday reasons that a pack needs a medical facility.

I keep Noelle by my side, and I realize that if this becomes our norm, I will be able to go back to school. Maybe, since Noelle is just starting her classes, we can work it so that one of us is always available in case someone needs us. With that in mind, she and I sit down and research online medical courses, focusing on werewolf facilities that are more likely to let us do our practical work in our packs rather than at the university.

Piper has also shown an interest but in nursing, as has Anna. So, the four of us look at classes and I have the three of them sign up. I'm waiting until after the war to make sure that I'll have time to continue my education.

When Katie and Erica hear about the classes, they also want to join, although Katie decides to wait another semester so that her pup is a bit older before she starts.

"Luna, you realize we're going to have the largest, most well-trained medical team possibly in the country?" Noelle says.

I stop and look at her. "You're right."

"You know, many packs need medical professionals. I don't know what it's like everywhere else, Luna, but here, we could provide them with hands-on training, especially for doctors. We could charge them for the service, maybe have them come a week at a time, monthly or quarterly, so they could learn with us, like what you're doing with me. It would be a great way to increase the income of the pack and make a name for ourselves. We both know that the universities can't give doctors the same experience that we're getting here."

"And sparring accidents happen all the time. There's always someone who dislocates or breaks something, so no matter when they came in, we'd have medical needs. We could even rotate and have students coming in every week. We'd have to figure out the limit. We wouldn't want too many at once because then they wouldn't get the hands-on training they need, but ... that's a fantastic idea."

We look at the hospital layout and realize that the side of the building where both Piper and I were attacked is unused, even during wartime.

"This could be our classroom and teaching area," Noelle says.

I nod, picturing it in my head.

'You don't have to talk to me about it. If you want to do it, just do it,' Warren's voice filters into my mind. He's always listening to my thoughts. I wonder if he knows I accidentally told Bradley and Anna about our pup.

'Of course, I know, baby. You mumble all the time, it was inevitable. But you haven't done it so much that the secret is out, and we'll be telling the pack this weekend, so we're good,' he says, and I can feel him chuckling.

'I'm glad you're not angry.'

'I know my mate, and I love you and your mumblings,' he says before closing the link.

"Warren says to do it. Once Brady is gone, let's figure it out and talk to the university about partnering with them."

"EEEK! I'm so excited!" Noelle says, and honestly, I am, too. This isn't exactly what I thought my career path would be, but I like it. It feels good to know that I can help others gain the skills they need to keep their packs strong.

On Friday, Alpha Harold, Alpha Henry, and Farrah arrive. From the moment they step out of the car, I can tell they can feel the happiness in our pack. As I said, it's contagious, but it's also something that these packs, our packs, haven't had in our lifetime.

"Welcome to our pack. We're very glad to have you," Warren says.

I say hello to Alpha Harold and Alpha Henry, but my focus is on Farrah, the woman who saved my life so I could have this life.

I walk up and take her hands in mine. "It's good to see you again, Farrah."

She looks almost embarrassed with my attention. "Thank you, Luna. It's nice to be back, especially under different circumstances."

I notice that she isn't wearing a new mark, but she's here, and I take that as a good sign. I loop my arm through hers and lead her inside. When we step inside, I see everyone milling around, working to prepare for our pack ceremony and celebration tomorrow.

"Attention everyone!" I say, getting the pack's attention and waiting until the room is quiet. I hear Warren, Harold, and Henry walk in behind us.

"For those of you who don't know, this is Farrah," I say, turning to look at her. She gives me a look like she's worried about what I'm going to say. From the corner of my eye,

I see Harold take a step forward as if he's coming to protect his mate, but Warren puts a hand on his arm, holding him back.

"I wanted all of you to know that this is the woman that helped me escape from Simon. She put herself at risk to free me, and then she guided me to Alpha Harold's pack so that Warren could get to me. I'm sure you all would have found me eventually. Of that, I'm positive. But Farrah got to me before Simon could do anything more than leave a few bruises on me. I wanted all of you to know that this is the woman who is responsible for bringing me back to you."

As I knew they would, the pack presses forward, thanking Farrah for what she did, letting her know how much they appreciate her, and if there is ever anything that they, or we as a pack, can do to repay her, we will.

I step back, letting the love of my pack embrace Farrah.

"I didn't do anything," she says softly, tears starting to fall.

As Harold walks up to stand behind her, lending her his strength, Warren wraps his arms around me, and our pack assures her that she gave them back one of their greatest gifts and that we will always remember and be thankful for what she did for us.

Chapter 82: Planning for War

Warren

We spent Friday night with Harold, Henry, and Farrah, showing them around the pack and letting them get to know our pack members. I could tell that Harold was impressed. It's one thing to hear that your pack is happy, but it's quite another to feel it. And because of my amazing mate, Farrah got the full force of our pack's love and admiration.

The next morning, after breakfast, Harold, Henry, Charlie, and I all head to my office.

When we sit, Harold turns to look at me. "It is really impressive what you've done here, Warren."

"Thank you, Harold. Most of that is because of my mate. The pack fell in love with her before she agreed to be my mate. Thankfully, she found something in me that was worthy of her love and trust."

"Thankfully? It sounds to me, based on what I've been hearing from your pack members, that you ARE worthy of everyone's love and trust."

"He is," Charlie says before I can answer.

"You and I both know, Harold, that the love and trust of your mate are the most important things they can give you. So yes, Yara accepting me for the man I am is more important than the pack's love and trust."

"But how did you get the pack to feel like this? I know I'm young, but I know our pack doesn't feel like this, and we should try to get this feeling in our pack, too, right, Dad?" Henry asks.

"We definitely want something like this in our pack. Your pack is obviously stronger because of it."

"They are, and I wish I could tell you that it was this or that, but in reality, I think it was a lot of little things combined. First, Charlie and I have a strong bond. We've run this pack on our own since we lost our Gamma in the war. No matter how injured I was, I always knew that I could count on Charlie to support me and manage the pack in my absence. That was key. But then Yara arrived," I say, unable to stop the smile that spreads across my face when I think back to our first meeting.

"She came in like a breath of fresh air. You've heard her mumbling. She does it all the time. The pack adores it, adores her. It didn't hurt that she's one hell of a doctor. Believe me when I tell you that when you're in her hospital, she's in charge. She may not be a warrior, but she'll go toe-to-toe with anyone that she thinks isn't strong enough to fight."

"And believe me, our Luna doesn't hold back when she tells you all about yourself. Alpha's biggest threat to our warriors is that they will have to face our Luna's wrath," Charlie says, smiling. I know he also has fond memories of Yara's arrival here. I'm just glad he found Noelle, so that's all they are – fond memories of his Luna.

"Once Yara arrived, it was like everything began to fall into place. Even with the constant fighting, my pack was getting stronger. Yeah, we had fewer warriors fighting, but they were stronger because of her. Then Charlie found his mate, and we finally had time to choose a new Gamma. Now, our pack feels complete and whole. The pack feels it and is excited about life again."

I can see Harold thinking through what I've said. He knows as well as I do that it starts with his Luna. I don't want to ask in front of the others, but his relationship with Farrah is key.

"So, you wanted to talk about Brady. I hope it's okay that I brought Henry in to listen. He's getting older now, and I think it's important that he hears strategy and what goes into a war, as well as keeping the pack safe," Harold says.

"I couldn't agree more, and as I said before, I know that our alliance will begin once you step down, so I think it's important that Henry sees how I operate now so there are no surprises when he takes over as Alpha."

"Thank you, Alpha," Henry says.

"So, this is my plan. I think we need to spring all of Brady's traps and then attack."

"Spring them how?" Harold asks.

"We need weights. Something heavy enough, something that weighs as much as a wolf or man, so that the traps spring. Now, I'm well aware that they aren't all just around his pack lands. I found that out the hard way. And I know we probably won't be able to get all of them. But we have Yara now. And if we use our hospital as ground zero for our injured, bring Savannah over here to help out, then I don't think we'll have casualties. We'll definitely have injuries, but I think Yara can help our warriors heal from just about any injury."

Harold sits back, thinking about what I said. I have to fight to hide a smile when I watch his son mimic his position and get a very similar thoughtful look on his face. I don't care if Yara has a boy or a girl this time. I already know she's willing to give me more pups. One day, I hope it's my son mimicking me just like Henry is doing with Harold. I get a sudden flash of a little girl, looking just like her mother, walking around the pack and mumbling to herself, just like Yara. Damn, I can't wait to have a family with my mate.

"Carrying that much weight would exert a lot of effort. How do you propose that we get whatever that weight is to Alpha Brady's pack?" Harold finally says.

"I was thinking the same thing, Dad," Henry says, nodding. Yeah, I can't fucking wait to have a son.

"So, I have a couple of thoughts on that. First, we load up trucks and drive in like we own the place, encircling the pack lands and dropping the weight. I'm currently leaning towards using sections of tree trunks that we could dump onto his land until they blow. That way, our men aren't tired because they've been carrying large loads of wood with them. Another option is to find downed trees or cut some trees when we're close and then carry them the rest of the way. A final option, if we want stealth, is to carry the weighted objects to a place near his pack, rest overnight, and attack at first light."

This time, Henry turns to watch his father. I glance at Charlie and see the same desire to have a son on his face that I'm sure is on mine.

"While I like the idea of a stealthy approach, I don't think it's needed with Alpha Brady. He's arrogant because of his traps. He thinks he's safe behind them. Showing up with several trucks and beginning to blow his traps will send him into a fit. I've gotten the impression from him that he's impulsive and not intelligent in his fighting."

"I agree," I say.

"I think his knowledge of explosives and spring traps has kept him and his pack safe, for the most part. I think Quinton was the strategist and mastermind of the alliance. Goddess knows Thomas wasn't smart," Harold says, thinking out loud. I'm not sure if it's for my benefit or his son's, but either way, we're all following along.

He nods, thinking until he finally looks up at me. "I like the direct approach."

I smile. "I do, too. I think it sends a message that we're not afraid of him."

"Agreed. So, what do you plan to do with his pack members?"

"If they fight, they die. If they don't, they have the choice of joining one of our packs or going rogue. Do you agree?" I ask.

"I agree," he says, looking at his son. "What about you, Henry? Does this approach make sense to you?"

Henry thinks for a moment, then nods. "Yes, sir. I think this makes sense."

Harold looks back at me. "When do you want to schedule our attack?"

"Within the week."

"I'll call Franklin and let him know that we need to start preparing for battle since I need a couple more days to go see Luna Yasmin and Alpha Quirin," Harold says. "I also happen to have some downed trees on my pack lands that need to be cleaned out."

I smile at him. "I might have noticed that when I was there getting Yara. It's where my idea came from."

He shakes his head at me. "I didn't know that you noticed anything other than your mate when you came to get her."

"Not much, but as we left your pack and I had her in my arms, I had a few moments to look around." I shrug. "I guess it's the Alpha in me."

"I guess it is. Now, let's go find our mates, and you, Alpha, and you, Beta, have a celebration to prepare for."

"Yes, we do," I say, standing and smiling. Today is finally the day.

"Just one more thing, Harold. I'll be executing Simon tomorrow for what he did to Yara and my other pack members. You're welcome to stay and bear witness, but it's not necessary. I wasn't sure if this was a lesson you wanted your son to have or not. I will be honest; the pack has not been kind to Simon. His death will not be the honorable death that Quinton had. He hurt too many of our pack members and made it too personal for all of us."

Harold looks at Henry before nodding. "We'll stay. It's not an easy lesson, but it's an important one."

"Okay. For now, let's go find our mates."

Chapter 83: Getting Ready

Yara

Tonight, I'll take my place as Luna of this pack. It's an important moment for me and for this pack. I've accepted Warren, this pack, and my role in it. This is my future, a future I never truly expected to have, but I can't wait for each day to begin so I can live it.

Archie got my things from the university when Warren sent him to erase my presence there. Thankfully, he'd put all my school records back, but now I have my clothes from when I was in Alpha Solomon's pack. I don't have a lot of dressy clothes, but Alpha Solomon insisted that I have a couple of nice dresses for important dinners, pack events, and graduations.

As I stand in my closet, I remember the man who raised me, who looked after me, and who ultimately died because he protected me from his son. There was one dress, in particular, that I've only worn once. Alpha Solomon had chosen it for me. He said it made me look mature, yet elegant, but still feminine. It's a color that is close enough to the color of my eyes that it makes my eyes pop.

It has a crochet lace overlay on the bodice with a halter neckline, which means no bra. I smile, thinking of Warren's reaction to that. The long skirt has a chiffon overlay that falls from a fitted, banded waist. The dress also has a sexy slit that made me self-conscious before, but now, I can't wait to see Warren's reaction to it. It makes me wonder if Alpha

Solomon thought I'd one day need a dress like this for a Luna ceremony. Even if it didn't feel like the perfect dress for today, which it does, I'd wear it for him. I wish he was here to see me take my place as a Luna. I know he'd have been proud of me.

There's a knock at the door, and I call for the person to enter. Anna and Piper come in and gasp when they see me.

"Oh, Luna. Alpha is going to swallow his tongue when he sees you," Piper says.

"I bet he's stunned into silence, and how often does that happen?" Anna agrees.

"Never," the three of us laugh.

"You think he'll like it?" I ask.

"He'll love it. You look so beautiful, Luna, it almost makes me want to cry," Piper says. Her voice is still soft as she continues to heal, and she'll always have silvery scars on her throat where Simon tried to rip her throat out, but those scars only reinforce how strong she is. Of course, she also has a silvery mate mark that shines brighter than the scars on her neck.

"What's this I see?" I ask her, walking over.

"Geez, you even glide in that dress," Anna says, her eyes going wide.

I smile at her but focus on Piper. "Travis and I made it official last night," she smiles.

"Oh, Piper. I'm so happy for you," I say, hugging her carefully so I don't crush my dress.

"Thank you, Luna. It feels really good to have someone like him as my mate. I feel so lucky to have found him."

"So, what can I do for the two of you?" I ask.

"Well, first, we're here to help you," Piper says.

"Help me what?"

"Get ready, of course. We're multi-talented, Luna. We wanted to help you with your hair," Piper says.

"Yes, but also, Gamma Laney doesn't have a dress, and we were hoping you might have an extra one for her?" Anna asks.

"Do you think she and I are the same size?" I ask, turning back to my closet.

"Erica is helping her, and she'll find a way to make it work. Gamma Laney didn't say it, but I think she was feeling bad about not having anything to wear other than warrior clothes."

"What about Beta Noelle?" I ask. She's small like me, so I know my dresses would fit her.

"Gamma Laney made sure her sister had a dress for important events, so she has one. But our Gamma does not spend money on those sorts of things for herself," Anna says.

"Of course, she didn't. I'm sure Noelle always came first for her," I say, pulling out another dress, this one close to knee-length on me, but it would probably come mid-thigh on Laney. "The blue won't match her eyes, but it will go well with her blond hair," I say.

"It's perfect. Our Gamma is a warrior, and I'm sure her legs are fantastic. Gamma Haynes will drool over her in that dress," Anna says excitedly.

"Okay, take that to her. Is someone helping Noelle get ready?" I ask.

"Yes, Luna. Katie is helping Beta Noelle. We drew straws to see who got to come help you," Piper says, pulling a bag from her back that I hadn't noticed before. "Have a seat, Luna."

"Okay," I say, excited to dress up for Warren and the pack.

Anna returns before Piper is finished. "Alpha Warren sent these up for you, Luna," she says, handing me a bouquet of wildflowers. I can tell that he hand-picked them for me. It makes my heart flutter with love for this strong, powerful Alpha who picks wildflowers for me.

"Here, Anna, tie them with this ribbon. It will match the ones I'm putting in her hair," Piper says.

"Oh, perfect!"

When Piper's done, I turn to look in the full-length mirror at myself. I've never been one to dress up; always focused on my studies and wearing comfortable clothes and lab coats at school. I almost don't recognize the woman in the mirror. She looks exactly like what a Luna should look like: poised, elegant, and beautiful.

"Oh, Piper. I look amazing," I whisper.

"Luna, you looked amazing before. All I did was make your hair match your dress and you. It's the woman that makes the Luna, not the clothes," Piper says softly, our eyes meeting in the mirror.

"You really are our perfect Luna," Anna says, looking at me in the mirror.

"I'm going to cry," I say, my eyes filling with tears.

"Well, then, it's a good thing Anna hasn't done your make-up yet," Piper says.

"Make-up?"

"Not much, Luna. You're already beautiful. It will just enhance your natural beauty. Have a seat."

It isn't long before she's done, and when I look again, I can see that she really didn't add too much, just enough to enhance my looks, as she said.

"It's perfect, Anna."

"No crying now, Luna, or I'll have to start all over."

Anna looks at the time. "Piper, we have to go get ready. The ceremony starts in less than an hour."

"We'll see you down there, Luna," Piper says, gently hugging me again. I give Anna a hug, and after they leave, I look at myself again, taking a deep breath.

When Warren's voice drifts into my head, asking if I'm ready, I get my bouquet and begin to head downstairs. On the way, I catch Noelle heading down, and we both find Laney.

"Well, if our mates aren't struck speechless, I don't know what will make them so," I say, looking at Noelle and Laney. The dress works well with her like I thought it would, and it shows off her muscular legs. I can tell she's a bit uncomfortable showing so much skin while being so dressed up, but it suits her. I also notice that both women have small bouquets of flowers as well.

"Are we ready?" I ask.

"Ready, Luna," Noelle says.

"Ready," Laney says.

I hold my bouquet in both hands and open my arms for my ranked females. I want us to all walk outside together. When they loop their arms through mine, holding their own bouquets, I take one more deep breath, and we step out back.

As one, the pack turns to look at us. I can hear their murmurings, but my eyes are on the stage where our mates all turn their focus to us. I, however, only have eyes for Warren.

'Damn,' I see him mouth as his eyes darken possessively as we begin making our way to the stage.

Chapter 84: Luna

Warren

I've seen my mate looking sweet and shy when she's in front of the pack, I've seen her looking confident and powerful when she's in the hospital, I've seen her looking passionate and fiery when we marked and mated, but tonight, when she walks out, arm-in-arm with her other ranked members, I see her looking like the Luna that she is. She's breathtaking. And while I love that they are literally creating a unified front by walking out the way they did, I can't take my eyes off of her.

"Damn," I say, hearing my Beta and Gamma saying the same.

The entire pack goes quiet as they watch their ranked females making their way to the stage. Yara is holding the bouquet of wildflowers that I picked for her. I thought she'd appreciate the sentiment, and it seems like she did. They have a ribbon holding them together that matches the ribbons in her hair, which also matches her dress. Her head is held high, and I can see and feel that she's fully accepted her position in this pack.

When I watched my parents and the love that they shared, I knew I wanted it, knew that I had to have it. But I had no idea that it would be like this. This love, this admiration, this bond between us is everything. She isn't just the other half of my soul. She is my everything.

She is my life, my love, the mother of my pups, the Luna of my pack, the air that I breathe, the reason that I love getting up in the mornings, the reason that I can't wait to go to bed at night. This world isn't just a better place with her in it. She makes this life worth living. Even if we were still fighting all day, every day, knowing that I had her to come home to would make it all worthwhile.

As she makes her way to me, I feel her open the link in our bond, her love for me flowing through freely. I watch her as I open the link from my side, pushing every emotion that I'm feeling for her through the bond. I watch as she gasps with the power of my love for her, her eyes welling with tears.

As one, the three of us walk to the edge of the stage. I reach my hand out for Yara, helping her up the steps and leading her to the table that is set up for tonight's ceremony. Charlie escorts Noelle to our right, and Haynes escorts Laney to our left.

"My pack," I say, raising my voice and finally dragging my eyes away from my mate to look out over our pack members. "Tonight, for the first time since I've been your Alpha, the leadership of this pack is complete."

The pack roars with cheers and howls, the stage underneath us vibrating with the power of their excitement.

"Tonight, your ranked members will officially take their place in this pack, and you, our pack, will declare yourselves to us and this pack."

When the cheers die down again, I hand the ceremonial chalice to Yara, turning to face her.

"Do you, Yara Ellis, accept me as your mate and Alpha?"

"I do."

"Do you accept your role as the Luna of this pack, vowing to love and protect our pack members with your life?"

"I do."

"Do you swear to honor and love me and this pack until the day that you die?"

Yara turns to look out over our pack members. "I couldn't love any of you more than I do. I swear that I will honor and love all of you until the day that I die," she says, turning back to me. "And you as well, my mate, my Alpha, the love of my life."

She holds out the chalice, and I slice my hand, letting my blood drip into the cup, my eyes never leaving hers.

"If you accept your role and place in this pack, drink my blood and let it be so."

She pulls the cup to her lips, still holding my gaze as she drinks. It's as if the final tie that binds us wraps around us, sealing us together in this unified bond forever. When her eyes widen, I can see that she feels it, too.

I know we have more, much more, of the ceremony to go, but I just need to kiss her. The feelings inside me are almost overwhelming, and I need my mate to ground me. I pull her into my arms and kiss her, barely hearing the sounds of the pack as they cheer and howl again.

When I finally pull back, both of us are panting.

"Goddess, I love you, Yara Ellis."

"And I love you, Warren. But that's not my name anymore." She turns to look at the pack, raising her voice. "I'm Yara Hill now."

While the pack cheers, I pull her to my side, nodding at Charlie and Noelle to take their place at the front.

We go through the ceremony of officially making them our Betas. I finally have a moment to look at Noelle and see that she's dressed as beautifully as Yara. Although my mate outshines her, she looks every bit like the Beta female she is.

When they've sworn themselves to me and Yara, they step aside, letting Haynes and Laney stand in front and in between us. We go through it again, each time slicing our palms and adding our blood to the chalice so that when it's time, there is enough for each pack member to come forward and swear themselves to their new ranked leaders.

The ceremony takes a couple of hours, each member swearing themselves to us. Even some of the older pups who don't yet have a wolf wanted to participate, which Yara found endearing, so I allowed it. They'll have to do it again once they have their wolves, but she's right. It's wonderful that our entire pack wants to be a part of what we've created. I was happy to see that all of Quinton's pack members joined our pack, as did Trena. It reminds me that I still need to deal with Simon's remaining pack members.

When the last person has sworn themselves to us, I pump my fist in the air, Charlie and Haynes joining me as we wrap our arms around our mates, and the pack howls and cheers.

"I have a couple of announcements before we begin our celebration," I say, waiting until the crowd quiets down.

I look at Yara, and I know my love for her is shining in my eyes. "Your Luna is pregnant ..."

431

That's as far as I get before the pack roars with happiness again. I take the time while they are cheering to kiss my mate again, sending all my love through the bond that somehow feels even more unbreakable now.

When I pull back and the cheers quiet, I look up at Charlie.

"And I have an announcement," he says. "Your Beta is also pregnant..." and once again, anything else he says is drowned out by the overwhelming happiness and loud cheering of the pack.

Charlie does what I did, kissing Noelle through the cheering. I pull Yara to me, kissing the top of her head as I let the love and happiness of the pack flow through me. It really is intoxicating.

When the cheering dies down, the pack, almost as one, turns to look at Laney.

"He just marked me a couple of days ago," she says, frowning as if we're all crazy.

Haynes shrugs, pulling her against him. "Next week then," he says, making everyone laugh.

"Let's celebrate!" I say, and the pack begins to move around, getting food while someone turns on music. As we leave the stage, I see pack members dancing with their pups while others get their food and find tables to sit at and eat.

I never thought I'd see the day where this was our pack's life, but I'm so glad and thankful that it is.

Chapter 85: Tormenting Simon
Warren

I lead Yara over to where Harold, Farrah, and Henry are standing.

"That was..." Harold begins. "I don't even have words. I'm not part of your pack, but I can feel their overwhelming joy and happiness."

"Their excitement is exhilarating. I don't know how you can stand it," Farrah says, looking around the pack in awe.

"Intoxicating was the word that came to my mind. And if I'm going to get drunk, I'll gladly get drunk on my pack's happiness," I say.

"Could you create something like this in our pack?" Farrah asks Harold, looking around at the merriment in my pack.

"Not by myself," he says to her. I watch as she realizes what he's saying. I can see her desire to have this kind of happiness in their pack. Maybe that will be enough for her to decide that she's willing to take him as a mate. Time will tell.

We walk around, talking to our pack members, laughing and joking with them, eating with them, and just enjoying our time with them.

As the party winds down, I pull Yara to me. "I want to kill Simon tomorrow, but tonight, I want to flaunt what we have in front of him. I want him to know that he's lost everything."

Almost as if my words conjured him, Bradley steps up to me.

"Excuse me, Alpha. I don't mean to interrupt, and I don't want to put a damper on your festivities tonight, but I'm assuming now that our Luna is pregnant that you'll be killing Simon?"

"That's correct. I'm planning his execution for tomorrow."

"I want my pound of flesh, Alpha," he growls.

I turn and look at him, seeing Trena standing just behind him.

"You have a lot of reasons to hate him, as do I. Do you want your pound of flesh, or do you want to give the killing blow tomorrow?" I ask him.

He looks shocked for a moment that I would offer that to him, but he and Trena have suffered nearly as much as Yara and I have.

"Thank you, Alpha. I think you should deliver the killing blow. He's hurt more than just Trena and me. He's hurt others in our pack. So, I think it should be you, Alpha."

"I just wanted to give you the option. I was just about to take your Luna down to the cells and let Simon know he's lost. Depending on what you have planned, make sure you have someone to cauterize his wounds. He doesn't get to die until tomorrow," I tell Bradley.

"Yes, Alpha," he says, smiling a vicious smile. Yeah, Simon's last night will be a miserable one.

I take Yara's hand and lead her to the cells. She's unusually quiet, so before we go down to the cells, I turn to her.

"We don't have to do this if you don't want to," I say, stroking her cheek.

"That's not why I'm being quiet."

"Why are you quiet then? You're not even mumbling."

"My ways of torturing are different than yours and the pack's, but they are just as effective, I think," she says.

"More so, in some instances," I say to her.

She nods. "I think I know how to hurt Simon more than anything that Bradley will do to him later."

I smile, shaking my head at my mate. "You are scary in your calm. Most people get revenge when they are angry, but not you. You plan, you're thoughtful about it, and that makes it so much more vicious."

She smiles at me. "Let's get this over with. I'm ready to celebrate privately with my mate."

I kiss her, then take her hand, walking her down the stairs to the cells. The smell is awful. There's urine, feces, blood, scorched flesh, and fear all rolled into one disgusting scent.

Simon barely looks up as we walk in, that is until he sees Yara. Then he growls.

"Simon, I wanted you to know that I've taken my place as Warren's Luna. I am his, and I will always be his," she says, turning to look at me. I let her lead, knowing that she was right about one thing. Anything she does to Simon will hurt him much more than anything that I can do to him.

She reaches up, stroking her fingers over my face and into my hair. It's a soft, gentle touch, completely out of the element of what's around us.

"Something that you never understood, Simon, is that when a man is worthy of the love of a woman, the love of his mate, she will give herself to him, willingly and happily," she says before lifting her chin and submitting to me.

My possessive growl is instant, and I pull her to me, leaning in to kiss her throat, nipping at her, accepting and loving her. I had no idea what she was planning, but this, more than anything, will hurt Simon, watching the woman he wanted willingly and openly submitting to me in front of him.

She continues talking, and I continue to lick, kiss, and suck on her throat.

"Warren is the kind of man that a woman, a woman like me, would gladly give herself to. He's the kind of man who will always respect me, always appreciate me, always protect me, and always love me, every part of me. He will never try to make me less than the woman I am. He will never be intimidated by my strength because he knows his own strength and power, and he knows that my strength adds to his. He's the kind of man who has scars all over his body, proving how strong and powerful he is. But he's also the kind of man who picks wildflowers for his mate because he knows I like them. That is the man who deserves my submission. That is the man with whom I choose to spend the rest of my life," she says, gently pulling away from me and turning in my arms to face him.

I stand behind her, wrapping my arms around her, letting her lead. I see that while I've been focused on Yara's throat and her words, Simon has moved to the bars of the cell. He's panting with his anger and frustration at not having my mate.

"And he is the kind of man who I will happily give a pup, one that is already growing in my belly. The first of many," she says, tilting her head so I can kiss her neck again as Simon snarls angrily.

"And tonight, I will celebrate with my mate, his body deep inside of mine, all night long. Because that's the kind of man Warren is. He's the kind of man who takes his time, making me scream in pleasure, finding new ways to make my body respond to him before finding his own release and then falling asleep with me wrapped up in his arms."

She turns to look at me over her shoulder. "Are you ready to begin our celebration, my love?"

"I can't wait," I growl, kissing her again before looking at Simon. "Sweet dreams," I say, taking Yara's hand and leading her away. We pass Bradley as we go.

"He's all yours," I say before taking my mate to bed and doing everything that she told Simon I would do to her.

Chapter 86: Trena

Bradley

I've been taking advantage of my rehabilitation to get to know Trena. Maybe some days, I make it seem like I'm weaker than I am, but I don't do that a lot. Trena was already repeatedly manipulated by Simon, lied to, mistreated ... you name it, so I don't want her to ever think I'm that kind of man. But, if I'm struggling to breathe, maybe I didn't need to sit down for quite so long. I just wanted to so I could spend more time with my mate.

At first, she only let me touch her when she was helping me to walk. She was great about making sure she didn't wrap her arms around my waist until we were away from the packhouse. I hate feeling weak, and she seems to understand that I don't want others to see me as weak, either. So she waits to assist me until we're away from the pack. That's also been a good excuse to separate us from others so I can have some private time with her.

It's a couple of days after I left the hospital when I am finally able to walk her to a place where we have a small pond on our pack lands. No one has really ever been able to enjoy this spot since we've all been at war most of our lives. But I knew it was here, and I wanted to show Trena. It's a quiet area where the sun comes through trees, and if she ever needs space or to get away, this is a safe place for her to go.

"It's really pretty," she says, looking out over the water.

"Yes, you are."

I've been looking at her, unable to take my eyes off of her. She is beautiful. I have no doubt that this is why Simon chose her. She's the most beautiful woman I've ever seen in my life, with long, thick brown hair that gets wavy at the ends and soft brown eyes that are still haunted by what Simon did to her.

She looks up and sees me looking at her. She blushes and steps away from me. I let her go, never wanting to force her into any physical contact. I chose honesty since I know that is the only path that will ever lead us to a relationship.

"I'm sorry. I'm practically desperate to kiss you. Your lips are pink and perfect, and I know you don't realize it, but when you're talking to me, you frequently lick them, which makes me REALLY want to kiss you."

She looks out over the water. I can see her mind turning a mile a minute, her eyes looking all around as she thinks through my words, and I can practically see the steam coming out of her ears at my comment. I have no idea if I've completely offended her, scared her, impressed her, or anything else until she finally turns to me and smiles shyly.

"I've never been kissed."

I frown at that. How is that possible? "You've never ... but ..." How do you ask someone who's been raped why they've never been kissed.

"Simon didn't kiss me. He did things to me, or he told me what to do to him, but he never kissed me."

My anger at Simon flares, but right behind that is a deep, powerful possessiveness. I want this woman's kisses, all of them, every last one, for the rest of my life.

"Can I kiss you?" I ask gently.

She nods, and I hold back the urge to pull her into my arms and kiss her the way I've been wanting to since I first saw her, passionately and desperately. Instead, I step up to her, stroking my fingers over her cheek. "At any time, if it becomes too much, pull back. You don't have to kiss me if you don't like it or if it scares you."

She nods, and I smell the slight scent of her fear, but she agrees. So, I slowly move in, watching her as I do until I gently press my lips against hers. I slowly and softly deepen the kiss until she starts to lean against me, her hands fisting in my shirt. I carefully slide my hand into her hair and hold her head as I tilt mine, deepening the kiss even more.

When I slide my tongue over her lips, she gasps and pulls back. I wait to see if she will pull away, and when she doesn't, I gently slide my tongue over her lips until she opens them. Her scent of fear changes to a scent of arousal, her spiced cider taste mixing with her scent and making me groan with the pleasure of it. When I finally pull away, I press my forehead against hers as we catch our breath.

"I hope you liked that because I would love to do that again."

"I did like it," she says shyly. She bites her lower lip as she says it. I know it's not meant to be sexy, but with her, she's sexy without even trying.

I reach up and use my thumb to gently pull her lip from her teeth. "I should be the only one allowed to bite that lip," I said, making her smile.

After that, I've been stealing kisses as often as she'll let me. I never do it in public. Based on what she's told me, Simon never cared who saw them, and, in some instances, it seemed that maybe he preferred it, getting off on her embarrassment and humiliation. So, I know that's a trigger for her. Since we walk in the forest multiple times a day to help strengthen my lungs, it works that I can sneak kisses then.

It's a couple of days later, while we are resting under a tree, that I notice her nodding off. She has dark circles under her eyes most of the time, and when I ask her about it, she shrugs and says she has nightmares, so she doesn't sleep well.

I pull her against me, being careful when she goes rigid in my arms to just massage her head and rub my fingers over her back. I make sure it is loving and not sexual in any way, and it doesn't take her long to fall asleep. She slept for hours while I held her.

I offered to have her sleep with me at night, and last night, for the first time, she finally agreed. It took her longer than normal to fall asleep. Being in a bed made her uncomfortable at first. But Declan, my wolf, started purring softly, and I massaged her head, letting my fingers slide through her soft hair. We'd waited until she'd fallen asleep, and then Declan and I had fallen into the deepest sleep I can ever remember having.

When I wake up, I have the most painful erection I've ever had in my life. I moan, shifting, and when Trena yelps, my eyes flash open. Somehow, overnight, she had moved, and she is now lying on top of me, her head nestled against my chest.

Her eyes are wide. "I'm so sorry, I don't know..." she says, scrambling off of me.

"It's okay, Trena. I'm sure your wolf felt comfortable and wanted to be closer to me. I know mine wants to be closer to you. And..." I gesture to my hard length, standing at attention under my shorts. "I can't exactly do anything about that. You're beautiful, you're my mate, and you were lying on top of me. But you don't have to be afraid of me. I won't do anything. I won't hurt you, ever."

"I should ... go," she says, quickly getting off the bed.

"Can we go for a walk after breakfast?" I ask, wanting to know that we're okay.

She's already at the door, practically running to get away from me. But she stops and turns to look at me and nods.

"I'll meet you downstairs."

"Good. I'll see you there," I say, sighing as she leaves like she can't get out of my room fast enough. Maybe this was a bad idea.

I get up and shower, dealing with my hard-on while I take a cold shower. The cold does nothing to help me when I remember the feeling of my mate lying on top of me, and I have to take care of things again before I finally finish my shower.

Chapter 87: Revenge

Bradley

Today is the pack ceremony, and Trena has agreed to join our pack. I'm thrilled that she's comfortable enough to join our pack, and I'm hoping that means that she's comfortable enough with me to remain here, knowing that we're mates. It gives me hope that we'll have a future together.

We go for two walks before the celebration begins. She's quiet, but she does let me steal a few kisses. When it is time for the ceremony, she and I stand side by side, and when it's time for me to go forward and recommit to my ranked members and the pack, she comes with me.

After Alpha Warren and Beta Charlie announce that our Luna and Beta female are pregnant, the pack howls, and I do as well. I am excited about the good things that are happening in our pack. Trena, however, remains quiet.

"What's on your mind, beautiful?" I ask her, leading her away from the party.

"This is all a bit overwhelming for me right now. I think I'm going to go to my room," she says.

"Do you want me to go with you?" I ask her.

She shakes her head. "You should stay and enjoy this," she says, and I can see the tears starting to form in her eyes. I'm not sure what it is about this party that has her upset, but if she needs space, I'll give it to her, even if it goes against everything inside me to do it.

COOPER

"If you need me or just don't want to be alone anymore, come find me. No matter what time it is, okay?"

She nods her head, then uses the shadows to get back into the packhouse without anyone seeing her.

The anger that I'm able to keep at bay when she's around leaves, and I'm furious all over again that my mate is suffering because of that shithead in our cells. I know that Alpha Warren will be planning his execution, so I approach him, telling him that I want my pound of flesh.

I'm surprised when he offers to let me kill him, but I meant what I said about it being him. Many in our pack have suffered because of Simon, not just me and not just Trena.

I'm even more surprised when I turn around and see her standing there.

"Trena, I thought you left. Are you okay?" I ask her, instantly concerned.

"I came to make sure that you knew I wasn't leaving because of you," she says.

"Oh," I say, smiling at her kindness. "I knew that. I don't know exactly what about all of this is upsetting you, but I understand that there will be times when you just need to get away."

She looks behind me at Alpha Warren. "What are you going to do to Simon?"

"Finish what you started, like I told you I would," I growl.

Her eyes move back to mine. "You don't have to," she says.

"Yes, I do. Mostly for you because you're my mate, and he hurt you. He's made our lives more difficult because of what he did to you. But I'm also doing it for Declan and me. It's hard for us to know that we didn't protect you. I know that I didn't know you then. But I do now, and I hate that you suffered, and I wasn't there to keep you safe."

She smiles at me, cupping my cheek and lifting up on her toes. It's the first time she's initiated a kiss between us, and I don't hesitate to accept what she's offering.

"Why don't you go inside, and I'll find you when I'm done."

She shakes her head, putting her hand in mine. "I want to go with you. I don't want him to see me, but I want to be there for you."

I stroke her cheek. "Okay, let's go. I believe our Alpha and Luna had some words for him, so I'll have to wait my turn.

When we get to the cells, I look at one of the guards. "I need something to cauterize a wound," I tell him. I need to make sure I don't kill Simon. I'm sure it will be a public event for the entire pack to witness.

The guard gives me a wicked smile. "We've kept an iron hot, just in case anyone gets overzealous," he says.

I guess Simon has been suffering at everyone's hands. Good.

I lead Trena down the stairs, listening to Luna Yara as she tells Simon what a great man our Alpha is and why he deserves her submission. When I turn the corner and see that she's actually submitting to our Alpha, I step back. Alpha Warren wouldn't want anyone to see that. Well, other than Simon. I realize that our Luna knows exactly how to hurt Simon and by the time they leave, he's practically frothing at the mouth with fury and jealousy.

I send Trena back upstairs to wait. The smell down here is atrocious, and I don't want Alpha Warren getting upset if he thinks that we saw our Luna submitting to him. When they're done, they pass me on their way upstairs.

"He's all yours."

I smile, walking in to see Simon staring after our Luna. When his eyes meet mine, he snarls.

"You! I thought you were dead."

"I'm not so easy to kill," I say, smiling hatefully at him.

"What do you want?"

"Now, that is a very interesting question," I say, standing in front of him. "What do I want? What I want is to make you suffer for hurting my mate."

"Let me guess, the girl whose throat I ripped out?" he asks, not at all concerned that he nearly killed one of my pack members and possibly my mate.

"No. And for the record, you didn't kill her either. She's alive and well, thanks to our Luna," I say as the guards open the doors.

"Who then?" he asks, taking a step back.

"Trena," I say, and I see a flash of fear in his eyes before he covers it with malice.

"She's got a great mouth for sucking cock, doesn't she?"

I'm not sure if he's hoping that I'll kill him, but even if Alpha Warren hadn't told me to leave him alive, I would want him to suffer for what he did.

"I heard she ripped your balls off," I say, making a point of looking at his limp dick hanging between his thighs. It looks a little bruised, so I'm guessing that some of the pack members have been kneeing him and kicking him in the crotch. "So, I'd say she's got great hands for turning an Alpha into a eunuch," I say, hearing the guards snicker.

He snarls again, stepping farther back into the cell as I step in.

"She got her revenge. So what the fuck are you doing here?"

"I told her I'd finish what she started," I say, and his eyes go wide. He tries to rush past me, but my hand slaps against his dick, grabbing hold as my claws extend.

"No! NO!" he screams.

"I wonder how many times she said that to you," I say, my voice deadly calm.

"She never did. She never denied me," he says, his heart rate spiking.

"Well, you were her Alpha, weren't you? You didn't need to do anything other than command her, did you?"

"Please," he begs.

I snarl, and with one hard yank, I rip his dick off. He screams in agony.

"What I should do, is shove this down your throat, like you did to her," I snarl, holding his dick up for him to see. "But ... my Alpha says it's not time for you to die yet."

Before too much blood is spilled, a guard comes in, pressing the hot iron to the hole in Simon's crotch. He screams again, and I'm a bit surprised that he doesn't pass out from the pain. Maybe it's the Alpha genes.

When the guard is done, Simon is left panting on the floor.

"I guess you won't be needing this anymore," I say, and extending my claws, I shred his dick before dropping the pieces of it on the floor beside him.

"As my Alpha said, sweet dreams," I say, turning and leaving a sobbing Simon on the floor of the cell.

When I get upstairs, Trena is pacing while she waits for me. She turns as the door opens, hearing Simon's screams and sobs. She sees my hand and body covered in Simon's blood. When her eyes return to mine, I see her body relax.

"I was wondering if I could lay with you again tonight," she says softly.

I smile at my sweet mate. "Let me wash this scent of vermin off of me, and then I'm all yours."

This time, when I lay with my mate, she asks me to curl up around her. I wrap my body around her, letting her know that she's safe and that from now on, I'll always be here to protect her.

Chapter 88: *Allies and Enemies*

Warren

The first thing I do when I wake up with Yara the next morning is to open my mind to the pack. The feeling of love, contentment, and family is stronger than I've ever felt in my life, even when my parents were alive.

Keeping my mind open to the pack, I slide my hand over my mate's still-flat stomach, knowing that my pup is growing inside. Yara says that it is still too soon to tell if our pup is a boy or a girl, but she's going to keep checking until she knows. Since Savannah will be here soon, maybe I'll get my answer then.

Today is another important day. First, Simon's life ends. That is primary. But before that I need to check on his pack. I close the link to the pack and slowly begin to wake my mate. We were up late last night, and I know she's carrying my pup, but it's time for us to get going. Harold, Henry, and Farrah are leaving to go see Quirin and Yasmin today, and I don't want to make them wait too long before they head out.

So I slowly tease my mate until she's awake, then slowly slide inside her from behind, holding her against my chest until she begins to arch and take me deeper.

I take my time, kissing her shoulder and her neck as I bring her up and over the first time. I suddenly realize that this is my new life, a life where I get to wake up inside my mate every morning. My mate then shifts, sliding me out of her and turning, pushing me on my back, and straddling me.

"Was I moving too slow for you?" I ask, chuckling. I watch my sexy mate slide herself onto my length and then begin to ride me.

"I just wanted to feel you in a different position now that I'm awake."

"You will never hear me complain about being able to watch you make yourself come on my cock."

She gives me a possessive, sultry look as she begins to move faster. I slide my hands over her body, teasing her nipples and loving the feel of her soft skin under my rough, calloused hands. When she gets close, she throws her head back, riding me hard as her breasts bounce beautifully in front of my face.

I growl at her beauty, her submission, and the knowledge that this woman is mine before we both find our release together. When she starts to come down, she falls onto my chest, both of us panting. I wrap my arms around her, kissing the top of her head.

"Now that's what I call waking up properly," she murmurs from my chest.

I laugh, her body bouncing on mine as I do. "I'm happy to wake you up properly every day, my love."

She lifts her head. "I said that out loud?"

I grin at her. "You sure did."

"Well, good. Because I'll get used to this very quickly and begin to expect it every day," she says sassily.

"My Luna's wish is my command," I say, stroking her cheek. "Thank you for what you said about me last night," I say, remembering. No one has ever made me feel better about the man and Alpha that I am.

"Which time," she asks, putting her hand on my chest and resting her chin on it so she can look at me.

"What you said to Simon," I say.

"Every bit of it was true."

"I liked hearing you say it."

She sits up, my length still deep inside her. "You, my mate, are fierce and powerful," she says, running her fingers over the scars on my chest and stomach. "But you are also gentle and kind, loving and caring," she says as she begins moving on me. I can feel myself getting hard inside her again.

"You're intelligent and witty, funny and passionate," she says, running her hands over my body as she begins to ride me again. "But do you know what I love most about you?" she asks, her eyes meeting mine.

I shake my head, unable to speak with the strong emotions that she is eliciting from me.

"You're mine, Alpha. And this baby right here is yours. Every baby that grows in my stomach will be yours. I love the way you love me. I love the way you adore me and show me that I'm special to you. I love everything about you, Warren," she says.

I can't take it any longer. I sit up, devouring her mouth in a passionate, scorching kiss. I flip our positions and spend much longer than I had planned showing her just how much I love and adore her as well.

By the time we come downstairs, I'm famished. I say hello to Harold, Henry, and Farrah, inviting the first two to join me for breakfast in my office. I'm behind schedule, and I want to catch up.

I send a mind link to Charlie, Haynes, and Laney to join us in my office, before getting some breakfast, kissing my mate, and heading in to start my day. When they arrive, I have everyone sit around the large conference table.

"Haynes and Laney, I have your first assignment as my Gammas. I intend to kill Simon today, in the next couple of hours. I need you to go to his pack, see who is left, and offer them asylum." I turn and look at Harold. "Do you agree?"

Harold looks thoughtful for a moment. I'm beginning to realize that this is the norm for him. He likes to think things through before making decisions.

"What if they have some warriors, perhaps some she-wolves with young pups or she-wolves who have lost their mate due to the wars? They may be angry and want revenge."

"My thought was to offer them sanctuary conditionally. I'm sure they're angry if they survived. They might be angry with me for killing their pack members and their Alpha, but that anger would be misguided. Simon did this to his pack. He started this war. I ended it. But that is why I wanted you here. They may want to become part of a pack, just not mine if they lost a mate. I'd rather give them your pack as an option, knowing what we're planning with Brady's pack. If they choose to go rogue, if they choose Brady's pack, that's their choice," I say.

"Should we warn them that we intend to attack Alpha Brady's pack if that's their decision?" Haynes asks.

"No, I don't want him to have any warning that we're coming, and right now, only a select few of us know that we're planning to attack. I want to keep it that way," I say, looking back at Harold.

He sighs, leaning back. As I watch Henry, intently watching his father, I once again feel the strong urge to have my heir. I can't wait to raise my son to be the best possible Alpha he can be.

Eventually, Harold nods. "It's the unfortunate part of being in a war. Innocents die. However, as an Alpha, it is our responsibility to protect OUR pack members first. If we were to tell others of our plans and then they told Brady, we put our pack members in danger when it's not needed. At the risk of sounding callous, if they don't choose to join one of our two packs, they aren't our allies anyway," he says, looking at the others in the room. "I agree to take in any that want sanctuary, but not in your pack. If they prove themselves worthy, I'll accept them into my pack. If they don't ..."

"If they don't, they leave or die," I say.

I look around the room. "Are we all in agreement?"

"Do we know how many we're talking about? Any idea how large Simon's pack was?" Charlie asks.

"Yara and Trena might know. But Simon lost most of his warriors and all of his ranked members. The pack will lose their Alpha today once Simon is executed. So, that mostly leaves omegas, and as Alpha Harold says, some warriors with pups."

"I'll talk to Noelle and have her work with Luna Yara and Trena. We'll need to make arrangements for this many pack members. We're already pretty full, having taken in Quinton's pack members," he says.

"Good thinking."

"How do we get them back? Let's say we're talking thirty to fifty omegas and some warriors with pups. We can't walk back. It will take days. Haynes and I can't protect all of them if someone like Brady attacks us," Laney says.

"We can send them in the vans," Charlie says. "We have some from Quinton's pack, and we have ours. That should be enough. They can pick a few extra warriors to take with them, maybe even Trena, who can speak to the truthfulness of what our Gammas are telling them."

"That's a great idea. Okay, we have our plan. Any questions?"

When no one does, Charlie heads off to meet with Noelle, and I help Haynes and Laney get their warriors ready to go, making sure that the vans are set to carry a large group of omegas and pups back to the pack.

Harold calls Franklin, letting him know they may have more pack members coming while Henry follows me, asking me questions about what and how I'm setting up the vans. I explain that it's because omegas are weaker. They'll be frightened and will be weak without their Alpha, so I want the vans to have something soft to sit on and blankets in case they're cold from fright or just the weather.

As I'm explaining, I feel a warmth spread through my body, Yara's love flooding into my system. I turn and see her leaning against a wall, watching my interactions with Henry.

"That's the future father of my pups," she murmurs. Damn, I love that woman.

When the vans are ready, I send them off, then turn back to Yara. "Ready to send Simon off to wherever shitheads like him go?"

"I'm ready for his stench to be out of our pack, yes," she says.

I turn, taking one more moment with Henry. "I want you to understand that what has happened to Simon is not normal for me. But he's injured multiple pack members, he kidnapped my mate, he threatened to rape her, and he left bruises on her that were still there when I got to your pack. He does not deserve and has not received an honorable death like Alpha Quinton received. I just wanted you to understand when you see him today that this is sending a message to anyone who comes after me and my pack, but mostly, anyone who touches my Luna. Come after what's mine, and you will suffer."

"I understand."

"Okay, let's go find your Dad and Farrah, and I'll call the pack together. I know your father is anxious to get on the road, and I hope that you and he can talk some sense into Alpha Quirin. He's at risk being out on his own."

"That's what Dad said. I can't imagine being on my own, even with my mother. It's not enough, although most of the warring packs have been defeated. You never know who may come into your territory and try to take it over," Henry says wisely.

"A very good point. One that I hope you'll make to Alpha Quirin when you see him."

As Henry goes off to find his father, I take Yara's hand.

"Do you know how sexy you are when you act like the best father in the world?" she asks me.

I smile at her. "You could show me just how sexy I am to you later," I purr.

"Oh, I fully intend to." She stops and turns to me. "I have no idea how I'll ever be able to keep my hands off of you if you act like that with our pups."

I pull her against me. "I guess then I'll know if I'm doing something wrong. Because I want your hands on me all the time, my little Luna."

"It's good that we're on the same page, Alpha," she whispers.

I growl, wanting her now but knowing I need to take care of business first.

"Let's deal with this, and then you can show me just how sexy you think I am."

She gives me a heated look, and I know that Simon's death will be fast. I want my mate. Simon is nothing. Yara is everything.

I call the pack together and ask Harold to stand with me in front of them. My warriors drag Simon out. He's filthy, bloody, and burned. I can see that Bradley did just what he said he was going to do, and now, Simon is unable to walk, his body hanging limply as the warriors drag him in front of me.

I glance at Henry and watch his eyes go wide before he settles. I notice that Farrah puts her arm around him, squeezing his shoulder. I'm glad to see that he allows it.

The warriors drop Simon at my feet. He's barely able to hold himself up, using his arms to prop his upper body up.

He looks up at me, his eyes already dead.

"Simon Tolliver, you have attempted to murder two of my pack members. Your pack has attacked and injured multiple members of my pack. You kidnapped and beat my mate with the intent to claim her and rape her. For your crimes, I sentence you to death."

He begins to sob as I lift my hand, Arric extending his claws. "Do you have any last words?"

"Kill me," he begs.

With one swipe of my hand, I remove Simon's head from his body for once, giving him what he asked for.

Chapter 89: Gammas
Haynes

As we drive to Simon's pack, I look over at my mate. She's staring out the window, and I can feel her nervousness through our bond.

"What's on your mind, beautiful?"

She turns and looks at me, smiling bashfully. She's used to worrying on her own without anyone noticing or caring. She's still struggling with me being in her mind, constantly focused on her thoughts and emotions. She loves it when we're in bed together, but at times like this, she forgets, and I think it embarrasses her to get caught.

"Have you ever done anything like this before?" she asks me.

"Nope, I've never been a Gamma before. Just a warrior, like you."

She turns, looking back out the window.

"You didn't answer my question," I say. I'm glad that it's just us. I wouldn't be so direct if there were others in the van with us. But since we had to bring so many vans, we doubled up, and I made sure that my mate came with me.

"How do you know we won't be attacked when we arrive?" she asks.

I shrug. "I don't. We might, but I doubt there are very many warriors left, and any that are left will be young, too inexperienced to have fought with Simon, or suffering from a broken mate bond. There could be other warriors left to patrol the pack; that's possible, but I doubt it. Simon was focused on getting our Luna. He doesn't strike me as the type of Alpha that cared about his pack."

"So you're not worried about walking into a possible fight?" she asks.

I shrug. "How is that any different than what our lives have been until now? Why? Are you nervous about it?"

I watch as she thinks through my question. I feel the turmoil in her. She likes knowing what she's walking into, and not knowing is making her nervous.

"What's the worst thing that could happen?" I ask.

She turns and looks at me, and now I understand the fear.

"I could lose you," she says, barely above a whisper.

I take her hand and pull it to my mouth, kissing it while watching the road.

"I'm not Noelle, Laney. I'm a strong warrior, and I know you've spent a large portion of your life trying to keep her safe, but you don't have to worry about me. I'm not going anywhere. My life has improved dramatically since I met you. I'm not giving that up. I'm not letting some asshole take me out now, just when I've found you and I finally get a taste of the life that I've always wanted. No way that's happening. I have WAY too much to live for now, and not only that, but I have a kick-ass mate who I know will always have my back. So, even if someone gets past me, there's no way they're getting past her," I say, smiling when I see her lips twitching.

"Yeah, she is pretty awesome," she says, chuckling.

"She's the most incredible woman I've ever met," I say seriously. "And that's impressive considering who our Luna is."

I feel her settle as we talk. The fear is still there, but it's not at risk of overwhelming her. My mate likes to be in control, and in the bedroom, I'm happy to oblige. But in the real world, that's not always possible. I need her focused on what's going on today, not worried about me and making mistakes because she's too busy trying to protect me rather than protecting herself.

When we pull up to the gates of Simon's pack, it's quiet. I roll down the windows, listening. There's no one here, and I don't hear any patrols either.

'Anyone hear anything?' I ask in the mind link.

'No, Gamma,' I get from each car.

'Stay alert,' I say as I pull into the pack lands. Laney rolls down her window, and we listen. I know the others behind us are doing the same.

Luna Yara convinced Trena to come with us. She hadn't wanted to, but when she said she would, Bradley insisted on coming along, too. He's not going to let anything happen to Trena, not going to let anyone say anything bad about her, but we need her to let the others know that we're not here to kill them.

"This is creepy," Laney says as we pull up to the packhouse. It's still eerily quiet here.

"Stay alert," I say to her as I get out, looking around. I can smell stale food and fear. Lots of fear.

"Do you know if Alpha Simon is dead yet?" Laney asks quietly, walking to stand beside me.

"I would guess that if he isn't, that he will be soon. It took us just over an hour to get here, and I'm pretty sure Alpha wasn't going to wait to kill him. Maybe that's why it's so quiet."

I look at Trena as she walks up. I can see that her eyes are haunted by being back here. I hate that she has to face this, but it's necessary, and she's a tough woman. She wouldn't be mated to Bradley if she wasn't.

"What do you think?" I ask her.

I watch as her focus changes, and the haunted look becomes more calculating. "I think the omegas are terrified, worried that we're here to kill them, but someone has taken charge and told them to hide. That's who you need to worry about," she says.

"Any ideas who that might be?" Bradley asks. He's still not one hundred percent, but I know he'll fight if it comes to that.

"His Gamma, maybe. I'm not sure if he's still alive or not. I doubt the Lead Warrior is alive. He'd have been with Simon."

"Hello!" I call out. Nothing.

"They don't do booby-traps here, right?" I ask Trena.

"Not to my knowledge," she says.

I turn and look at the warriors behind me. "You five, in the back, the rest of you, with me."

"Get behind me, Trena," Bradley says, gently pushing her behind his back.

"You're the injured one, Bradley," she growls softly. He ignores her.

I look at Laney. "Ready?"

"Let's do this," she says. We walk up to the front door, and I nod for Laney to kick it in. I'm not risking that someone is on the other side waiting to attack.

She does, and I stand in the doorway, ready for someone to leap out at me, but no one does. The pungent scent of fear increases now that the door is open.

"Hello?" I call again.

"YOU KILLED HIM!" a woman screams, leaping at me from the shadows. Before I can grab her, Bradley's big hand grabs her by the throat, holding her in the air.

"Calm down!" he growls.

"Lina, calm down. What are you doing?" Trena asks her.

"Trena? We thought you were dead."

"I'm not dead. Who's in charge here?"

Bradley sets her down but doesn't release her throat. Lina scoffs. "Well, that's the question, isn't it? No one's left. It's just us."

'We're clear in the back, Gamma,' one of my warriors says.

I nod at Laney to enter along with the men I have with me.

"Where's Gamma Darius?" Trena asks.

"Dead. They're all dead. We felt all of their tethers break, including Alpha Simon's, not long ago. So are you here to kill us then?" she snarls.

"No. We're here to bring you back to our pack or offer you the option of joining Alpha Harold's pack. You have the option of going rogue, but I wouldn't recommend that," I tell her.

'Mostly terrified omegas and pups inside, Haynes,' Laney's voice says in my mind.

"Trena, can you go inside and talk to the omegas? Let them know that we're willing to take them into our pack," I say. She heads inside, leaving Bradley and I to speak to this woman who must have taken charge of the pack.

"Are you going to let go of me now?" she growls at Bradley.

"Are you going to stop trying to attack my Gamma now?" Bradley retorts.

"How many warriors are left?" I ask her.

"Only those of us who were unable to fight," she says. "Most of them are near death because they lost their mates."

"Our Luna can help them," I say.

"Your Luna ..." she scoffs again.

"Yes, my Luna. Maybe you've heard of her. Her name is Yara. She came from this pack. She's the reason that your Alpha and all of your warriors are dead. He came after our Alpha's mate. He didn't care how many of his warriors got killed, and, in the end, he

454

died because he tried to take her," I snarl. I'm over her attitude. "So, you have a couple of choices, Lina. Get your shit together and decide which pack you want to be a part of or try and make it on your own. You have until we get these omegas packed into the vans to decide. You come after me or any of my warriors again, and I'll kill you. Are we clear?"

I watch something in her shift. This woman may be a warrior, but she's no leader. She, like the others in this pack, needs a leader to feel safe. I realize that she's not only suffering from the loss of her mate but also from not having anyone to lead her and this pack. She took it over, but it's not her strength.

She lifts her neck in submission to my authority, and Bradley releases her. "We're clear," she says, much more calmly.

It's at this moment that I realize the importance of my role in the pack. Our pack accepted me because they knew me and knew my strengths. But there will be times, like now, when my position is important for other reasons, and being able to show others that they are safe, protected, and cared for goes a long way to making the pack cohesive and calm. I've always respected Alpha Warren and Beta Charlie, but that respect just increased knowing that this is what they have had to do, even in our pack, since they took over.

When I walk inside, I see the omegas are starting to stand. Their eyes go wide when they see me. Maybe my acceptance of my position and role in the pack has changed my aura, or maybe they just recognize a ranked member from another pack. Either way, they're concerned.

"Trena, have you explained to them what we are offering?" I ask, looking around.

"Yes, Gamma. Everyone would like to return to our pack. They don't know Alpha Harold, but I told them if they aren't happy in our pack, we will find a way to help them see Alpha Harold's pack."

"Good thinking. Everyone needs to collect their things and get in the vans. Only take what you can carry or can't live without," I say, and they all begin moving to their rooms to get their things.

I look at Bradley. "Let's see what food we can take. They don't look like they've been eating much."

He takes Trena, and together, they go to collect whatever food is salvageable.

Laney takes my hand and pulls me into an empty hallway. "That was so fucking hot, the way you went all Gamma on that woman," she growls, pressing herself against me. "When we get home, you're mine, Gamma."

I slide my fingers into her hair, gripping it and tugging her head back so she's looking at me. "I'm always yours, Gamma," I say before taking her mouth in a hot, dirty kiss.

We get everyone loaded into the vans, making sure they have food and water. As we drive back to the pack, I look at Laney, and I know she feels it, too. We may have had the pack ceremony to make us the pack's Gammas, but this assignment, getting these people back to our pack, has made me feel more like a Gamma than the ceremony did.

I understand my role now and my position in the pack much better, and I reach out my hand to take my mate's. I know that she feels the change in us as well. We are our pack's Gammas. We are leaders in the strongest pack in our territory.

Chapter 90: Quirin

Harold

"What are you expecting to find when we get there?" Farrah asks me as we drive to Quinton's old pack. We're taking it very slowly, mostly for her but also partly because of Henry. I want him to accept Farrah, not as a replacement for his mother, but as a mother figure. It's something he hasn't had and has needed in his life.

I'd noticed that Henry had allowed her touch when we'd watched Warren execute Simon. I saw his shock at Simon's state when they brought him out. I was glad that Warren spoke to him ahead of time, letting him know that this isn't the norm for his pack. Farrah's instinct, the instinct of a Luna and a mother, had been to help support him while he watched. My heart soared with my pride in both of them. Now that Farrah has accepted me as her Alpha, she feels the emotion. I don't shut myself off from her, wanting her to feel everything that I'm feeling so she understands and learns to trust me. Her eyes seek mine, and I see the hint of a smile.

Slow means that I get to hold her hand while I drive. It makes both of us feel calmer. And while we were in Warren's pack, she agreed to sleep in the same room with me, which ended up being in the same bed. Nothing happened, but being able to sleep wrapped around my mate had felt amazing. Based on how well she slept and with no nightmares, I think it did wonders for her, too.

"I know the pack is gone. Beta Charlie attacked them while Quinton was attacking our pack. Since we also know that Simon was there, and Warren's warriors indicated that there were dead bodies littering the ground, I'm going to assume that they haven't had a chance to burn their dead yet. We should all be prepared for the stench of rotting bodies when we arrive. That's going to be first. Then, I'd expect that Quirin will fight leaving. I'm not sure about Luna Yasmin, but I'm guessing after Simon's assault, she must realize how exposed she and her son are out here by themselves. I'm counting on both of you to help me get through to them. Farrah, you can speak to Yasmin, woman to woman, and Henry, you can speak to Quirin, Alpha heir to Alpha heir."

"Is he still considered an Alpha heir, Dad?" my son asks.

"He is the son of an Alpha. His pack may no longer exist, but knowing Quinton, he owned those pack lands, which means that when Quirin comes of age, he can start his own pack again."

I look in the rearview mirror and watch my son as he thinks through what I've said. "What if he ends up trying to steal some of our pack members?"

"Well, what I would say to you is this. All Alphas are different. Sometimes, people choose one pack over another because they prefer the way a certain Alpha leads versus another. And that's okay. However, I would also say that if it's more than that, if it's more than a simple preference, you, as an Alpha, should consider what you aren't doing or giving to your pack members that has them wanting to leave your pack. As a leader, your pack comes first, or at least a close second to your family and your mate," I say, smiling at Farrah. I love that she blushes when I say things like that.

"If your pack members start to leave, you need to think about what you, as their leader, aren't giving them. Why are they leaving? What do they need that you aren't providing for them? You can only be a leader and an Alpha if you have a pack to lead. It's not always just about being strong and protecting the pack. Just like you need more than a strong father, your pack will, too. If I were the type of father who made sure you were safe, fed, and educated, but I never gave you any of my time, you wouldn't like it, would you?"

He thinks about that. "No, I wouldn't. I enjoy our time together."

"Exactly. The pack is exactly the same. Even if you protect them, it wouldn't be enough because you aren't fulfilling their emotional needs, and maybe not even all of their physical needs. Does that make sense, Henry?"

"Yes, it makes sense," he says, turning back to the window. I know my son enough to know that he'll think through what I've said, and if he has questions, he'll come back and ask me about them later.

When I refocus on the road, I feel Farrah looking at me.

"What?" I ask her.

She smiles, shaking her head. "You're a good Alpha."

"I try. I don't know that I always succeed, but I do try."

She smiles and looks out the window. While I keep my mind open to her, she doesn't always do the same for me. It's times like these that I'm practically desperate to know what she's thinking. But I don't push. I want her to come to me on her own terms.

I'm not sure if she felt what I was thinking or not, but she turns and looks at me, opening her mind to me. What I feel has my heart soaring. She's wondering how she can resist a man who is such a good Alpha, who she knows is a good mate because she knew me when my mate was alive, and she knows that I was always true and kind to her.

She glances back at Henry, who is still deep in thought. 'I don't know that I'm ready to be physical yet, Harold, but I think I'm willing to accept you as my mate,' she says in the mind link.

I pull her hand to my mouth, kissing it. 'I'll take as long as you need. I know you've been through a lot. I will never rush you.'

I see my son turn his head and watch our silent interaction. He smiles and turns back to look outside. He's already noticing little things that go on around him, just like a good Alpha should.

'Maybe ... maybe when we get back, I could move into your room,' she says, still speaking in the mind link.

'I would love that.'

My heart is full of love as we pull onto Quinton's pack lands. Even from here, the smell of rotting flesh is strong.

"UGH!" Henry says, covering his mouth. "How can they live here? It's awful."

"They may not feel like they have another choice, which is why we're here," I tell him.

As we drive, we begin to pass bodies in various stages of decomposition.

"I'd like to offer to help them burn their dead. Even if they don't want to come with us, this will attract predators and could put them into a dangerous situation."

As we approach the packhouse, I see Luna Yasmin with a shirt tied around her mouth and nose. She's attempting to drag some of the bodies into a pile. She stops when she sees us, moving back to the packhouse and calling out to someone. Quirin comes running out to stand beside his mother.

I step out of the car, as do Farrah and Henry.

"Alpha Quirin, Luna Yasmin. I am Alpha Harold. This is my mate, Farrah, and my son, Henry. We've come to talk to you and to offer our assistance in cleaning up your pack lands."

"What do you want to talk about?" Quirin asks defensively.

"You and your mother are not safe out here."

"We're fine," he says defiantly.

I look at Luna Yasmin and raise my eyebrow. "You didn't tell him?"

Quirin's head snaps to his mother. "Tell me what, Mother?"

"It's nothing," she says, raising her chin.

"If Alpha Warren's warriors hadn't arrived when they did, it would have been something. You and I both know that," Farrah says, stepping forward.

"Mother?" Quirin asks.

When she doesn't answer, I look at him. "So, you weren't here when Alpha Simon showed up and attempted to rape your mother?"

Yasmin clenches her teeth.

"Mother?"

"You weren't here. Nothing happened. I didn't want to worry you," she says.

"It sounds like a lot happened," he growls, then turns back to me. "How do you know about all of this?"

"I'm in an alliance with Alpha Warren. My family and I witnessed the execution of Alpha Simon this morning. He and I are concerned about you, but he didn't feel that you would listen if he offered you sanctuary because he killed your father."

"Murdered him, you mean," Quirin snarls.

"Your father had a lot of very good qualities, but sometimes greed can turn those good qualities into something that is not so good. I'm sure you know that he intended to take Alpha Warren's mate from him. Believe me, if he did, he wouldn't have had the simple execution that he had. You didn't see Alpha Simon. Your father was not tortured before his death. He was given an honorable death. Alpha Simon was not."

Quirin grits his teeth. "What do you want?"

"I'm here to offer you and your mother sanctuary in my pack. You are an Alpha heir, but without a pack, you are at risk. I'm assuming that your father owned these lands..."

"Yes, he did. We found the paperwork," Yasmin says.

"That's good. When you come of age, you'll have a pack to return to. Perhaps, by then, you'll be able to start rebuilding this pack, gaining some pack members, and creating a positive environment here. I'm offering to have you come live with me. You are still an Alpha heir, as is Henry. You are nearly the same age, and I would teach you, as I'm teaching Henry, how to run and manage a pack. Luna Yasmin, you are welcome to join as well; however, you will lose your title. But you would be safe and protected within my pack."

I can see Quirin thinking about it, not sure what the right answer might be.

"Why don't we help you clean up your dead, and we can give them a warrior's burial? While we do that, we can talk, and you can ask questions. I know that I usually need to think things through before I make a decision. And your warriors need to be laid to rest," Henry says, coming to stand beside me.

"You're willing to help us?" Quirin asks.

"Of course. That's what good Alphas do. We help each other," Henry says, stepping forward. "And maybe, if you decide to come live with us, we can become friends. Maybe once we become Alphas of our own packs, we can create an alliance."

"I'll never join an alliance with Alpha Warren or his heir," Quirin snarls.

"You don't have to have an alliance with him to have an alliance with me," Henry says, turning to look at me. "Right, Dad?"

"That's right," I say, hoping that I can change this young man's hatred for Warren. Nothing good will ever come of it.

It was hours later before we finally got all of the bodies into a group, laid out and ready to burn. During that time, I let Quirin and Henry work together while I helped Yasmin and Farrah. They stopped to make food at one point, and I continued on my own, allowing my son to talk to Quirin, heir to heir.

When it was all done, I stood beside Quirin, staring at the massive number of bodies. "Would you like to say something?" I ask.

"Thank you for giving your lives for the pack. You will never be forgotten," he says, his voice thick with emotion.

I put my arm around his shoulders, squeezing his shoulder so he knows he's not alone, as Henry lights a torch and sets the bodies on fire. We stand in silence, watching the bodies burn as the sun sets.

The fire has nearly died down before Quirin finally turns to look at me. "Okay, Alpha. I'll go with you."

I smile down at him. "I'm glad you made that decision. It's late. Why don't we get some food and get a shower? You and your mother can pack up anything you want to bring with you. We'll head out first thing in the morning."

He turns and goes inside without another word, his mother watching him. "Will you be joining us as well?" Farrah asks her.

"I go where my son goes," she says.

It's not a restful night's sleep, the scent of death and rotting flesh remains in all of our noses, but in the morning, we pack up the car and head back to our pack.

I look in the rearview mirror at Quirin as he stares at his pack lands while we drive away. I have five years to make a difference in this young man. Five years to change his mind about going after Alpha Warren. Because nothing good can come from a heart filled with hatred.

Chapter 91: Preparing for War

Yara

The pack has been preparing for war. I insisted on completing physicals on all of our pack's warriors to ensure that they were healthy and able to fight. It also worked out that two warriors who didn't know found out that they were pregnant and are now required to remain in the pack. Apparently, all the celebrating that we've been doing means more pups in our pack. As long as it doesn't cause problems with mate bonds, I'm thrilled.

When Harold returns with his warriors, I'm excited to see Savannah again.

"Savannah!" I say, rushing to hug her when I see her. I see that Warren has followed her over to the pack hospital, and I know it's because he loves seeing me happy. It's not like Savannah doesn't know her way to the hospital.

"It's good to see you, Luna! Although, I wish it was under better circumstances," she says, hugging me tightly.

"How are you?" I ask her, looking over at my mate and giving him a big, happy smile. The one I know he's been waiting for. He winks at me and turns to go back to work.

"I'm good, Luna. I'm pregnant," she says excitedly.

I squeal, hugging her again.

"I understand that you are, too?" she says.

"Yes! And while you're here, I'd love for you to do an ultrasound on me. It's not easy trying to do it to yourself."

"Tell me! I'll do yours if you'll do mine," she says.

"Deal!"

She says hello to everyone, spending a few minutes asking them questions about themselves and how they are doing. She meets Katie's new pup, and as I watch her, I can see that she's grown into her role as Beta. She's a great leader, taking time to speak with everyone and giving them individual attention before turning to the next person. She's a natural, which I guess makes sense since she's mated to a Beta.

"Alright, let's get down to business. Tell me what we've got here," she says.

Noelle and I walk her through our plan for how we want the hospital to run. Since we know that we'll have a lot of injuries, we're keeping our operating side as is and stocking each room. Then we've opened up the other side for lesser injuries, setting up cots so that the warriors have a place to rest other than the floor while they are waiting for their turn to be seen.

"You, me, Noelle, and either Piper or Anna, whoever you choose, will be in the operating rooms. Anything you can't handle, I get. Katie will be in the safe room because she has a newborn, but Erica agreed that Katie could watch her pups, and she'll be here to help triage."

"Piper, are you strong enough to work in the OR?" Savannah asks her.

"Yes, Beta. My voice is still raspy, but finding my mate has helped me get stronger, faster."

"I can't believe everything I've missed," she says, shaking her head. "Okay, Piper, you'll be with me."

"Anna, that means you and Erica will be running triage for everyone coming in and then treating less critical injuries. I want the two of you to work together today to make sure you know where everything is and that you have everything you need ready to go and in place. Savannah, you, me, and Noelle will be assessing your pack's warriors today."

"I've already started the assessment, Luna. Before we left, I had to tell several of our warriors that they were sitting this one out. We're not as strong as this pack is yet, but we're getting there," she tells me.

"That's okay. We'll see what we've got."

It's a long day, one that is long for everyone. Warren, Harold, Charlie, and Franklin are working with the warriors, going over their battle plans and how they intend to attack Brady and his pack. They will each take a group and attack the pack on four sides, blowing the bombs and booby-traps and then destroying Brady and his pack.

I only had to tell three of Harold's warriors that they were not strong enough to fight. They weren't happy about it, but Savannah insisted. As their Beta female, they listened and calmed down.

Haynes and Laney will remain in the pack to make sure the warriors get through quickly and that the pack remains safe. Because we will have more warriors in our pack, Harold brought Henry and Farrah here as well. Farrah wants to fight, but so far, I think Harold has convinced her to stay.

After everyone was assessed, Savannah and I got the ultrasound machine and went into a room. I did hers first, excited to see her pup.

"How far along are you?" I ask her.

"A week, maybe, possibly two. I'm not sure."

"We may not be able to tell the gender yet, then," I say to her, putting the gel on her stomach before putting the wand against her still-flat stomach.

"That's okay. Franklin is just excited to see his pup. Like I said, I've done the best I can, but it's not easy trying to find your pup and lying flat enough to get a good image."

"And then trying to get a picture of them. Anna is great, but she's not as experienced as you are, and I think it was her first time using the ultrasound machine. Not having any pups of her own, I don't think she knew what to look for."

I move the wand around as we both watch the monitor. When I see the thumping of a heart, I stop. "There we are. Do you want a video so Franklin can hear his pup? I thought Warren and Arric were going to melt right there when we heard ours," I tell her.

"I would love that," she says, and something in her tone makes me look at her.

"Savannah?"

"Are you scared, Luna? Are you worried that they won't come back?" she whispers as tears well in her eyes.

I reach out and take her hand. It's always a possibility. Always.

"Our mates are strong. Our alliance is strong. There will be injuries, absolutely. But you know my rules. No one dies in my hospital. And since everyone is coming here, no one dies. I think I'd better make that announcement tomorrow. Your warriors don't know that, but they need to understand that no matter what happens to them, they live. That includes our mates, too. So, no. I'm not worried about them dying. Our mates are smart, powerful men. They've been planning all day while we've been preparing. Those that I've pulled out of the battle weren't strong enough to survive. The group that's going is," I tell her.

She takes a deep breath, letting it out. "And this?" I say, indicating the video with audio that I'm creating. "This will make sure that your mate returns to you. He has too much to live for. He did before when it was just the two of you, but now, he has even more to live for."

"Thanks, Luna," she says.

We switch places, and I get on the table. "Alright, Luna, let's see if you're having a boy or a girl."

When she starts moving the wand over my stomach, she frowns, tilting her head. "Savannah?"

I'm trying to follow what she's doing, but she's moving fast.

"Hold on," she says and walks out of the room.

She's back a moment later, strapping a heart monitor to my stomach. When she turns it on, I hear my baby's heartbeat. But then I frown.

"Savannah?" I ask, wondering if she's hearing what I'm hearing.

She smiles at me before taking pictures and giving me the information that I want.

When we finally leave the hospital, it's late. We're both quiet, deep in our own thoughts about telling our mates about their pups.

When we walk in, I can hear the sound of loud talking coming from the dining hall. There's an excited energy about that pack. Everyone knows that tomorrow, we go to war.

When we walk in, Savannah goes straight to Franklin. But I stand in the doorway, watching my mate as he talks to our pack members.

He's going to be so excited.

As if he heard me, his head snaps up to mine and he smiles that gorgeous smile of his.

He stands and walks over to me, wrapping an arm around me and stroking my cheek.

"I could use some good news," he says. I must have spoken out loud again. "So, did you find out? Are we having a boy or a girl?"

The room around us goes quiet, and I wrap my arms around my mate's neck. "You, my Alpha, have very powerful sperm."

"I was working hard to give my Luna what she wanted."

"And you did it very well because I'm not just carrying one. I'm carrying two of your pups."

I smile as I watch the shock register on my mate's face as our pack erupts into cheers around us.

Chapter 92: Our Luna

Warren

Two? Did she say two pups?

I hear the sounds of the pack cheering around us, but I'm focused on my mate's beautiful face and her smug smile.

"We're having twins?"

"Mhmm," she answers, her fingers running through my hair and sending shivers all over my body.

"Boys? Girls? One of each?" I ask.

"One of each. But don't think that gets you out of pup duty for the rest of your life. You promised to give me as many as I wanted," she says, grinning up at me.

"I always keep my promises," I growl. It's a happy, possessive growl as I lean in and take her mouth in a dominant kiss, pouring all of my love for this incredible woman into it.

'How many pack members do we have to threaten to keep their sons away from our little girl,' Arric growls, already feeling possessive of his pups.

'She'll have her brother to keep them away,' I say as an image of Henry watching Harold enters my mind. Only this time, it's MY son, and he's watching ME and learning to be a good Alpha from me.

I deepen the kiss even more, not caring who sees me showing my love and gratitude to Yara. She's given me everything that I've ever wanted in life and so much more.

469

When she begins to moan softly, I pull back and gaze down at her.

"Thank you."

She chuckles, her eyes still glazed from my kiss. "You did it."

"We did it," I say to her. I continue looking at her as I raise my voice. "Bradley?"

"Yes, Alpha?" He was already on the list to stay behind. Yara didn't clear him for battle, but even if she had, he's become her Luna guard. I just haven't made it official yet, waiting for him to heal completely.

"You know your job is to protect your Luna while we're gone?"

"Yes, Alpha."

"Now you are protecting her and my pups. Pick two other warriors. I want two of you on guard duty at all times, rotating so you can get sleep."

"Yes, Alpha," he says.

"Warren, you need every warrior you can take," Yara begins.

I kiss her, stopping her argument before pulling back and looking down at her stomach. "When's the last time you ate?"

When she has to think about it, I pull her to the table where I was sitting. "Let me get you some food," I tell her.

I thought you were eating for two, but now I know you're eating for three. I'm going to have to make sure you eat even more than I was planning. I'll have to make sure you get small meals multiple times a day.

"When did he start mumbling to himself?" I hear my mate ask.

"Not until he met you, Luna," my warriors chuckle. I hear the pack congratulating her and me as I pass them, but I'm focused on feeding my pups. I need to double everything that I was planning. Two cribs, two changing tables, two bassinets, two...

I turn, and Yara is there, taking my face in her hands. "My love, you have so many things to worry about right now. This can wait. Your pups won't be here for several more months. I wanted to give you the happy news before you go to war tomorrow so you know that you have multiple reasons to return home to me. My life is better with you in it. You need to focus on tomorrow, and after that, we'll work on preparing for our twins," she says, her mind and her thoughts calm and orderly, just like they are when she's in the hospital.

"I was getting ahead of myself, wasn't I?" I ask her, leaning my forehead against hers.

"Just a little. I'm glad you're excited. I am, too. Let's deal with Brady and the war, then we can live happily ever after."

I pull her to me again. "It will be a very happily ever after."

"With you in my life, I have no doubt that it will be."

I give her a quick kiss, letting her calm settle into my mind. She's right. I have other things I need to focus on before I can give all of my time and attention to my mate and our pups.

"You still need to eat," I tell her.

"Agreed. If you'll get me some food, I need to address the group before they call it a night," she says.

I get a bit of everything that is being served tonight, listening as my mate addresses the warriors.

"May I have your attention, please?" she says, and the room goes quiet.

"We already heard about the twins, Luna," someone says, making everyone laugh.

"Yes. That is wonderful news. But I wanted to address Alpha Harold's warriors specifically. Most of you don't know me, and your Beta female reminded me today that you may not know the rules of my hospital. Well, there's just one rule, really, but you all need to know that I'm absolutely serious about my one rule."

I finish getting her food and turn, watching this woman who has changed so much in the short amount of time that she's been here. I remember the first time I stood with her in front of the pack. She was so shy and timid.

'She was born to be a Luna. OUR Luna, the mother of OUR pups,' Arric purrs proudly. I see her gaze flicker to me, and I know she can hear him purring proudly at her. She fights her smile and refocuses on the room.

"You can ask any of my warriors, you can ask your Beta female, but I'm telling you now, my rule, the one absolute requirement that I have in my hospital, is that you don't die. I don't care how bad you are when you come through those doors. If your heart is still beating when you cross that threshold, you live. Period. There will be all sorts of hell to pay if you try to die on me. No one, and I mean no one, dies in my hospital. Are we clear, warriors?"

There's a lot of mumbled 'Yes, Lunas' as they all look around at each other as if they don't believe her.

"I said, are we clear warriors?" she barks at them like a damn drill sergeant.

'She's magnificent,' Arric purrs, the sound getting louder. She glances at us again, but her focus remains on the group this time.

"Yes, Luna!" they all say, much more forcefully this time.

"Good. Like I said, if you don't believe me, ask any of my warriors," she says, turning to me.

"Trust me, she means it," our warriors say as I lead her back to our table.

I can hear our warriors telling Harold's warriors stories about Yara in the pack hospital. Her telling Charlie that she'd drag him out of the Moon Goddess' realm is still a favorite among them.

"Why is my mate purring at me," she asks as she starts to eat.

"My mate is so beautiful, so sexy, so strong. Why shouldn't I purr proudly that she's mine?"

Chapter 93: Attack

Warren

After dinner, I take her upstairs so we can celebrate properly. I don't spend the hours that I want to with my mate, but when I return, I'll make it up to her.

I'm up before dawn the next morning. Arric and I are ready for battle. I shower quickly, letting my mate sleep in. I know that soon enough, she'll be overwhelmed in the hospital.

When I get out of the shower, she's sitting up in bed. The sheet is lying across her lap, but her breasts are bare for my view. Any other morning, I'd be crawling back into bed.

"Why don't you go back to sleep, baby? We'll be sending warriors back to you soon enough," I tell her.

She shakes her head. "I'm coming down to see everyone off. I want them to know that I love them, and I'm here if and when they are brought back."

I go to her, kissing her deeply, drawing strength for what I have to do today. I know it's a possibility that we'll lose warriors. I hate it, hate it even more than I used to because our pack has become so tight-knit. But this is war, and I've had to mentally brace myself to lose some of the good men and women that are in our pack.

She gets dressed quickly, and we walk downstairs hand-in-hand. Harold and I decided to take the trucks loaded with tree stumps. We spent a good portion of yesterday dividing them into the four trucks that will lead the warriors into the battle. With the trucks, we can at least get some of our more injured pack members back quickly so Yara has a chance to save them. But the first line of attack will be us dumping these tree stumps onto Brady's borders to spring his traps and blow his explosives.

Since I'm full of nervous energy, I have a couple of warriors get in the truck to drive it. I'm going to let Arric run. We'll have a few minutes to get into place, and once all four of us are ready, we'll attack.

As I make final preparations, I watch as mates, lovers, and pups who are remaining in the pack say goodbye to their loved ones. Yara, Noelle, Haynes, and Laney are going around talking to all of the warriors, making sure they are ready and giving them a final pep talk. Maybe I'm biased, but Yara's words seem to settle the warriors more than anyone's.

Over on Harold's side, I see Savannah, Farrah, and Henry doing much the same. Henry really wanted to go, but Harold explained that if anything happened to him, he needed to be ready to take over the pack. Part of me feels good knowing that my mate is growing my heir. If anything happens to me ...

'Nothing better happen to you, my mate. Don't think I won't drag your sorry ass out of the Moon Goddess' realm. You don't get to leave me. Not now, not ever,' my mate's passionate voice commands me in our mind link.

I look up and see her watching me. I smile and nod. She'd do it, too, I have no doubt.

'You're damn right I would. And then I'd kick your ass all over these pack lands for thinking you could leave me,' she growls before going back to speaking to our warriors.

"Is your mate threatening you, too?" Charlie asks, walking over.

"She sure is," I say, watching her proudly as the warriors begin moving to their assigned trucks.

I look at my Beta, my best friend. "We all come home, Charlie."

"You know I never want to let you down, Alpha," he says.

"Then, let's do this," I say, and as he jogs back over to the truck of warriors that he's leading, I look over at Harold and then at Franklin, getting their nods that they're ready. I strip down and shift, suddenly feeling my mate's arms come around Arric's neck.

"I love you, my mate. Your pups and I will be here when you get back. Take care of my mates," she whispers in my ear.

Arric turns and licks her face. Her arms tighten before she lets us go, standing up and stepping back with other pack members who are staying behind. As Arric takes off, he lifts his head to the sky, howling to his mate. Others begin doing the same, and soon enough, the forest is filled with the sounds of mates calling to each other.

We push hard for about an hour before we stop at the identified meeting area. From here, our trucks will separate, and we'll all get into position.

I shift back, and the nervous, excited energy in the group is palpable.

"Everyone," I say, raising my hand to get their attention. "We've learned from Thomas and Quinton's packs that not everyone wants to fight. We don't kill pups, and we don't kill innocents. If they don't fight against us, leave them be. We'll deal with them when the battle is over. If they attack you, kill them."

"Excuse me, Alpha, what if it's a pup that attacks us?" a warrior asks.

"Put them down, but don't kill them. Alpha Harold and I will deal with them."

I answer a few more questions, and Harold does as well. Then, we divide into four groups and head to our locations. This time, I'm in the truck. I have Harold, Charlie, and Franklin on a conference call.

We begin to hear Brady's patrols sounding the alarm as they spot us coming in. Good. That will make it easier for us to know who to fight. Hopefully, his omegas and pups will go into the safe rooms and stay there during the battle.

When I'm in position, I let the group know.

"Ready," Franklin says.

"Ready," Charlie says a moment later.

Harold had the farthest to drive, going around the other side of the pack. When he finally says that he's in position, I hang up and get out of the truck. I howl the howl of attack, hearing the sounds go up all around Brady's pack.

Then I leap into the bed of the truck, grab a tree trunk, and toss it onto the edge of Brady's pack, where I can smell the metallic scent of his traps. The moment it hits the ground, it blows, sending slivers of wood chips everywhere.

I duck, feeling some find their way into my body, but nothing that will cause more than discomfort. Then the bombs start going off all around the pack lands. As soon as our truck bed is empty, I shift and howl.

Time for Brady to die.

Chapter 94: Carson

Yara

We only had a couple of hours before the injured started coming in. The first thing I realized is that every single one of them has splinters all over them. Because they blew the bombs with wood, they've all been hit with various sizes and amounts of debris.

"Make sure you get every piece of wood out of them. If you don't, they'll become infected. Warriors, you need to let my team know if you feel pain somewhere so we can get all these wood pieces out of you. If we don't and you get an infection, I'll pull you from duty until you're healed."

"Yes, Luna," they say with varying degrees of strength in their voice.

Savannah and I begin doing triage, and I take the worst ones while she takes the ones that she can handle.

The first group that comes in have large pieces of trees that punctured through them. I'm guessing others did as well, but this group couldn't rip these pieces out without causing more damage to their bodies. I take the one with a large piece of wood in the thigh, and Savannah takes the one with wood through the shoulder. Both warriors will be down for a while.

While I work, Noelle begins cleaning out the other wood pieces. I've just gotten the large piece of wood out of this warrior's leg when I hear a commotion in the front of the hospital.

"LUNA!"

I look at Noelle. "Stitch him up and come find me," I say, rushing from the room.

When I rush out, one of the warriors is screaming in pain. Several warriors are holding him as Anna pushes a gurney to them. As soon as he's on the gurney, I see the problem. He must have stepped on a bomb. One of his legs from the knee down is missing, and what's left of the bone is sticking out. Someone, thankfully, put a tourniquet just above his knee so he didn't bleed out.

"Just let me die, Luna," he says, and when I get to him, I see that it's Carson.

"You know the rules of my hospital, Carson," I say, looking over his injury quickly.

"What can I do?" Anna asks.

"Go take over for Noelle, finish stitching up that warrior, and let her come help me."

"Luna, I can help you," Savannah says, rushing out.

I look at Anna, who quickly looks behind her and assesses the next most critical injury we have.

"We can keep the others stable, Luna."

"Let's go," I say to Savannah. She rushes ahead of me, holding the door as I push Carson into the room.

"Luna, please. I'm a warrior. A warrior needs both legs. Just let me die," he says. I can tell that he truly wants this. He wants to die.

"Now you listen to me, Carson! First of all, you're more than a warrior. You're a mate, and you're going to be a father. You need to think about Eva and your pup. What happens if you die? You're marked and mated now. If you die, she'll feel it, and what if that kills your pup? Is that what you want?" I ask while Savannah gets an IV into him.

I take his face in my hands, forcing him to look at me. "And second, you can be a warrior with one leg. You are still an amazing fighter, Carson. When you come out of this, and I said when, Carson, not if. When you come out of this, we'll talk to Warren about what we can do. There are prosthetics for you and your wolf that we can look into. You are NOT dying in my hospital. Do you hear me?"

When his eyes start to close, I lift my hand, telling Savannah to hold off on putting him under completely.

"Do you hear me, Carson?" I growl right next to his ear.

"Yes, Luna," he murmurs.

"Good man. Make your Luna proud," I say, then nod to Savannah.

This surgery took hours. Eventually, Noelle switched out with Savannah so she could continue to take the others who came in with critical injuries. I had to remove the broken bone and the knee, but I was able to salvage the rest of his leg.

"How long will it take for him to heal, Luna?" Noelle asks.

"That depends on him. Let's keep him sedated overnight and let his body and his wolf rest. Then we'll see how he's doing tomorrow."

"Yes, Luna."

I step out of the room, mentally preparing myself to take the next person who needs assistance, but instead, I get Eva.

"Luna! How is he? Is he going to survive?" she asks.

I pull her aside. "I'm going to be honest with you, Eva. He lost part of one of his legs, and he wanted to die."

"But no one dies in your hospital," she says, her voice desperate.

"That's right. That's what I told him. I also told him that he has a mate and a pup on the way, so dying isn't really an option for him. He has a long recovery ahead of him, Eva. You need to know that. But a lot of that will be mental. His role in the pack will change, but I'll be talking to Warren about what we can do to keep him on in some sort of warrior capacity. I mentioned prosthetics to him, but we can talk about that more once he's awake. I'm keeping him sedated overnight so that he can rest, and his wolf can heal."

"Can I stay with him?" she asks me.

"Of course. If anything changes, find one of us, but he's stable right now."

I open the door and let her in as Noelle finishes stitching some of his smaller injuries from the wood chips.

I watch Eva square her shoulders and walk over to Carson. "Now you listen to me, Carson Row. You don't get to leave me ..."

I smile and step out of the room. I have no idea if our minds or wolves can hear their mates when they're unconscious, but I believe that they at least know that they're there. Having Eva beside him will help him to heal faster.

When I turn back, Savannah is stepping out of another room. "How's it going?" I ask her.

"They've obviously moved past the borders of Alpha Brady's pack because the injuries we're getting now are slash marks and bite wounds. They're all still coming in with splinters and wood chips in their bodies, but those aren't the injuries that we have to worry about now."

When I get back to the waiting room, I see that they have stations set up for warriors to have their splinters and wood pieces removed from their bodies while they wait to be treated. Henry, Laney, and some of our other warriors who were forced to stay behind are helping to pull the wood out of these warriors. I quickly look them over, realizing that Anna and Erica have already triaged this group because their injuries aren't critical.

When I move into the room where the others are waiting to be treated, I see that the entire room is full. With only Erica and Anna able to assist, treatment is slow. I check in with Erica and start with the most critical injuries, beginning to stitch them up. Soon, Noelle, Savannah, and Piper join us, and we begin to move much more quickly through the warriors.

"Luna, you need to eat," Bradley says to me.

I feel exhausted. I have no idea how long we've been at this, but I know that I can't stop, not until Warren and the others return home. I know that they are still fighting.

Bradley hands me a wrap, and I step aside to eat it quickly. "Have you heard anything?" I ask him.

Bradley grins viciously. "Yeah. I heard they found Dr. Stephens."

Chapter 95: Brady's Demise

Warren

As expected, we ended up having to send a large group of warriors back as soon as we blew the bombs. I'd heard Carson screaming in my head and told some of my warriors with minimal injuries to get him to Yara. I have to hope that my mate can work the miracles she always seems to, and because I know she'll do everything she can, I remain focused on the battle.

It's been long enough that Brady's warriors are healed from the last time they attacked my pack, but Franklin and Harold's men severely decimated their numbers. Even with the number of wolves that we're having to send back to the pack, we're still outnumbering them. Add to that, we have two Alphas and two Betas leading this attack on four fronts, and it doesn't take Arric long to get to the packhouse. I send half of the warriors with me to help the others and prepare to enter the packhouse. With Brady, you never know what types of traps he's set.

'Franklin and I have Alpha Brady. Do you want us to kill him?' Charlie asks.

'No. Keep him contained if you can. If you can't, kill him. But I'd rather make it official in front of whoever is left from his pack when we're done here,' I tell him.

While I'm talking to Charlie, Harold and his group come running up from where they entered the pack lands.

He shifts and looks at me. "I told Franklin to keep Alpha Brady alive for now."

"I said the same to Charlie."

He nods, and we both enter the packhouse carefully. Both of our noses are in the air, sniffing for metal.

"Spread out, stay alert," I say. The words have just left my mouth when I take a step, and I hear the click of a trap releasing. I yank my leg back, barely getting out of the way before the spike shoots up in front of me high enough that I catch it in the air. I turn, holding it out to the others who are behind me and Harold.

"Stay alert!" I say again. We carefully make our way inside, periodically hearing the sound of a trap releasing. I hear one of my warriors scream, and I send him back to the pack. Yara or Savannah will have to get the spike out of his foot.

I've just about decided that I've figured out the pattern for the traps when I begin hearing pack members calling out that they've found the safe rooms.

"Harold, have you figured out the pattern?" I ask him, looking across to where he's making his way through the packhouse, clearing this first floor with me.

"I think so. It's like a chess board and the squares where the knight could move," he says.

"Yes. Two straight ahead and one to the right or left and then again from that position."

"Exactly."

I look around and start grabbing things that are heavy enough to spring the traps as Harold starts doing the same. They stop several steps from the safe rooms.

"How many?" I ask.

"We have two over here, Alpha, and I believe that we have two over there," one of my warriors says.

I turn and see Harold approach those safe rooms.

"Get them open," I say. "Remember the rules!"

"Yes, Alpha," the warriors say as they start breaking down the doors.

I hear someone come in behind us, dragging someone with them, and turn to see Charlie and Franklin toss Brady inside the packhouse. He screams until he realizes that the traps have already been sprung.

"Damn, I'd say you squeal like a girl, but the girls I know would have my balls if I insulted them like that," Franklin says to Brady.

"Your mate definitely would," Charlie says, stepping in and looking around.

"The warriors?" I ask.

"Dead or being run down," Charlie says just as we hear another explosion. I tense, waiting for a tether to snap or the sound of a warrior in pain. When I don't, I look at Harold, and he's giving me the same look that I'm giving him. I look down at Brady.

"Sounds like you lost another one," I tell him.

He growls at me as I hear the metal of the safe room door behind me begin to give way. I know the moment they break through because the scent of fear is pungent.

I turn and walk to the door, waiting for my warriors to finish ripping it apart. When they do, they step back.

"My name is Alpha Warren. Your Alpha is defeated, and your warriors are dead."

I can hear the sounds of keening and crying, so I know that some of the women in this safe room have warrior mates who were killed.

"If you attack us, we will kill you. If you come quietly, you'll be allowed to live and join my pack or Alpha Harold's or go rogue."

I hear Harold giving a similar speech to the ones in the safe room across from me.

"Come out of the safe room and go sit outside the packhouse," I tell them.

I have a couple of warriors follow them to make sure that none of them leave. They'll have the opportunity, but not before they see their Alpha beheaded.

My warriors have just started ripping down the door of the second safe room on this side when I hear one of my warriors calling out to me.

"Alpha, lookie who we have here," he says, his tone spiteful.

I turn just in time to see one of my warriors tossing Dr. Stephens across the floor.

"Oh, Alpha. I'm so thankful you finally found me! Alpha Brady kidnapped me ..." Dr. Stephens says.

"The fuck you say?" Brady demands from his own spot on the floor. "You sniveling little twit. I should have killed you like Quinton said. You're not even a good doctor."

"Don't listen to him! He's just trying to get me in trouble!" Dr. Stephens says.

I walk over to him and crouch down in front of him.

"Charlie?" I call out.

"Yes, Alpha?"

"Do we put our prisoners in safe rooms?" I ask. I notice the room around me has gone quiet. Well, until Brady starts laughing.

"No, Alpha. They stay in our cells."

"Interesting," I say, looking at Dr. Stephens. "I see you're still putting your own safety ahead of the pack's by hiding in a safe room during a battle. I can't believe I never realized what a coward you are. I didn't just upgrade to a better doctor; I got one who actually has courage and cares about her pack."

He sneers at me as he opens his mouth.

"Say one thing about my mate, and I'll rip your tongue out," I say with deadly calm. He may be a coward, but he knows I mean what I say, and he snaps his teeth together.

"You let a lot of my pack members, good pack members, die because you betrayed me and our pack." I stand and smile down at him.

"What are you going to do to me?" he asks, and I can smell his fear.

"I'm not going to do anything to you. I'm going to let the pack have you," I say, smiling maliciously as I hear my pack members growling around us.

"He comes home with us. Everyone he hurt should get a turn at him," I tell my warriors.

"Yes, Alpha!" my warriors say excitedly.

I turn and see that most of the omegas and young or pregnant mothers are outside.

"Let's deal with Brady. I'm ready to go home," I say.

As I walk over to him, his laughter at Dr. Stephens cuts off.

"Quinton will kill you if you touch me," he snarls. Now it's my turn to laugh.

"I guess you didn't hear. Quinton is dead. Thomas is dead. You are all that is left of an alliance that hurt my pack and Alpha Harold's over and over again. You can walk, or we can drag you," I say as Harold comes to stand beside me. We agreed that we would stand side by side again when we executed Brady.

He stands, looking around and spitting on the ground where Dr. Stephens is cowering. "I'm an Alpha, and I'll go out as an Alpha. You, however, will have a coward's death."

He turns and strides outside, Harold and I following behind him. This time, I allow Harold to lead the execution. Brady hurt both of our packs equally, and I've killed Thomas and Quinton.

"On your knees, Alpha," Harold says to him when we're standing in front of what's left of his pack.

Harold goes through the list of his crimes and then asks him if he has anything to say.

"I hope her pussy was worth all of this death," he growls, looking at me.

"Since she's carrying my twins in her belly, she's strengthened my pack and made me happier than I ever thought possible; I'm going to say that my warriors and I agree that my mate was worth more than you, Quinton, Thomas, and all of your packs combined," I tell him.

My warriors howl their agreement, and Harold raises his arm.

"Alpha Brady, for your crimes, I sentence you to death," he says, and in one hard swipe, he separates Brady's head from his body.

Chapter 96: Luna's Approval

Yara

The flow of warriors coming into the hospital finally starts to slow down. When we get one warrior with a spike through his foot, he tells us that they've breached the packhouse and the battle is winding down. I've periodically felt Warren's emotions, his pain, but nothing that my mate and his wolf can't handle.

Now that it's settling down, the fatigue of the day and night is starting to set in. But I know I won't be able to sleep until my mate is home and I've checked him over.

I'm still working with the warrior who got the spike through his foot, holding his bones in place while his wolf starts the healing process, when I hear a commotion out in the front.

"They're back, Luna," Savannah says, coming into the room.

"Go, Noelle. Go check on Charlie. I'll be out as soon as I'm done here," I tell her. She and Savannah rush out of the room.

"You should go too, Luna," the warrior says.

"I will, once the bones in your foot are back in place," I tell him, putting another one together and holding it while his wolf begins healing. Because this warrior isn't an Alpha, his healing is slower than Warren's. I push down my need to go see my mate, feeling him reaching out as he crosses our borders.

'I'll wait for you to finish,' he says in the mind link, and I relax a bit. I didn't realize I didn't want anyone else to treat my mate. I want to look him over and treat him myself. He's MY mate. Mine to treat, mine to protect, mine to love. He sounds exhausted, and I know once we're done here, we'll both need a shower and then some sleep.

When I finally finish setting the bones and stitching the warrior's foot, I tell him he can shower in the hospital shower. I also tell him that he has to keep his foot dry and he has to stay the night in the hospital. He starts to grumble, but when I give him a look, he stops.

"Yes, Luna."

"Good man. Katie will be on duty since the rest of us have been working non-stop. Give her any problems, and you will answer to me."

"I won't cause any problems, Luna."

I nod and head out of the room. The noise level in the waiting room is much louder than usual, but the energy is much more positive. I step into the room, looking around at mates who are helping their warriors pull splinters out of their bodies, talking and caressing each other, happy to be back together.

I search the room, finding Warren leaning against the wall, watching me intently. There's a hunger in his eyes, and I re-evaluate our plans before we go to bed.

"Alpha, it appears to be your turn," I say to him, pointing to a chair near me.

I watch as he strolls toward me, all Alpha – tall, strong, and confident. I feel my insides clench with desire for this man and watch as a smile spreads across his face as he feels my body's reaction to him.

"Something on your mind?" he purrs against my ear as he passes me and turns to sit in front of me.

"Yeah. I'm wondering how one man gets so many pieces of wood stuck in his body. You look like you let Arric roll around in wood chips," I say, beginning to assess which of the splinters that he has are the worst. I can't help my own little smirk at teasing my mate.

He growls as I carefully run my fingers through his hair, finding some pieces stuck in his scalp.

"I had no idea that the thought of Arric rolling around in wood chips could make you smell this delicious," he says, still purring at me. His hands begin to stroke up and down my hips, as he watches me.

"It's good to know that you don't have any serious injuries," I say to him.

"I have this incredible mate who has made me and my pack stronger. Arric is easily able to heal me because my mate is so amazing."

I look down at him, and the hunger in his eyes from before is even more intense. Because I know we're going to be here a while longer, and I need him to focus on something other than me so I can treat him without being distracted, I ask him about the battle.

We have a lot of omegas and some warriors that we brought back with us," he says. "Haynes and Laney are getting them set up in the packhouse."

"Do we have room for them?" I ask, frowning.

"No, but for tonight, they can sleep in sleeping bags or on cots. Tomorrow, Harold and I are going to talk to them about their choices. A couple of warriors chose to go rogue, taking their small children with them," he says, and his voice is now strained.

"You gave them the choice?" I ask him.

He nods. I know he hates the idea of pups, especially, being vulnerable out in the wild.

"Then there's nothing that you can do, my mate. You didn't kill them. You offered them a pack, a place to live ..."

"But we killed their mates," he interrupts me.

"And their mates have killed some of our warrior's and omega's mates, too. I don't want to sound callous, and you know I hate death, but that's the price of war. You lose people that you love. Speaking of which, I heard you found Dr. Stephens."

"We did. One guess where he was hiding," he says, and this time, there's a hardness in his voice.

"A safe room," I say, knowing I'm right. I was appalled when I heard that this is where he spent his time during a battle.

"That's correct."

When I look at him again, he's watching me. "Did you kill him?"

"No. Not yet. I'm going to let the pack have him," he says, watching me closely.

I step back and frown. "What does that mean?"

He pulls me to him again, holding onto my hips. "He let our pack members die, Yara. He's worse than Brady, Thomas, or Quinton. I'd put him up there with Simon because he betrayed his own pack. He let friends and family members die when he could have saved them. And he did it intentionally."

I stay quiet, watching him. I can tell that whatever he's planning, I won't like it. But I can also tell through the bond that he feels very strongly about this. So, whatever he's decided to do with Dr. Stephens, I'll have to turn away and let it happen. He's right. Dr. Stephens did betray his pack. I wasn't part of the pack back then, but I am now, and I don't see how he could have done what he did. I love this pack with all of my heart. I could never betray them.

"He's currently in our cells. I'm going to let him out and he'll have the choice to stand by as they tear him apart or run and hope that he can get away."

"He's not strong enough to get away," I say.

"No, he's not. But when you're facing your own horrible death, sometimes you grasp onto the only hope that you have of surviving."

I think about that, think about the pain that Dr. Stephens caused this pack, not just in allowing pack members to die but also in how he treated the pack members who were injured.

"That will be a much slower death for him," I say, knowing how much the pack hates him and how they'll taunt him, possibly even letting him think that he's escaped them before dragging him back and letting him try to run again. It's a cruel death, one that turns my stomach. But I have to remember that someone like Dr. Stephens isn't any better than someone like Simon. I allowed the pack to torment and torture Simon for days.

"I'll find something else to do while they hunt him," I say.

"Thank you," he says, and I look at him.

"I didn't know you were asking me for permission."

"If you were absolutely against it, I would have executed him. But he doesn't deserve an honorable death."

"No, he doesn't."

He runs his hands up and down my hips again. "You're the heart of this pack for a reason. All of us, every one of us, wants to please you, our Luna. So, if you're really against it, they'll understand."

I look up and see my pack and Harold's pack members watching me. It would be hypocritical of me to tell them not to hurt Dr. Stephens when I had no problem with them hurting Simon. Simon hurt me, but Dr. Stephens hurt them.

"Let's not get used to torturing prisoners," I say to the group.

"Yes, Luna," they all respond. Warren glances at our pack behind him, smiling.

I have him move around as I slowly get the splinters out of his body. "What about Brady?"

"Dead," he says.

"So, that's it then? Our enemies have all been defeated?"

"Yes, our enemies have all been defeated. For now. It's always a possibility that others will come and take their place, but for now, I think we can relax and begin to enjoy our lives."

I smile, looking at our pack members again.

"I think we should celebrate, don't you?" I ask.

The group cheers in agreement and after making sure that everyone was treated and safely settled for the night, Warren and I finally had a chance to go to our room.

Our celebration started before we left the shower and continued for several hours after that before both of us fell into an exhausted but happy sleep.

Chapter 97: Choices

Warren

After making love to my mate for hours and sleeping off the exhaustion of the battle, I wake up feeling fantastic. While I slept, Arric healed what was left of my wounds. My mate is safe, happy, and pregnant with my pups, and all that's left is Dr. Stephens, who is currently residing in my cells.

There's one more thing that I need to take care of before I deal with Dr. Stephens, and that's Carson. Yara told me that he wanted to die when he came in. I understand his fear. Not having a place in a pack is a terrible feeling for pack members. While we get ready this morning, Yara and I talk about the options and how we can possibly keep him running patrols. She explained to me about prosthetics and that it will take modifications on our part and his, but once he's used to wearing one and his wolf gets used to wearing one, they can continue to remain in their warrior status and help defend the pack.

Before that, we need to say goodbye to our allies and send them off.

When we get downstairs, the feeling is still festive and happy, and for the first time in my life, relaxed. I look around, just enjoying the feeling in the pack. I notice that it's contagious and Harold's pack is looking more relaxed and jovial this morning as well. I also notice that Harold and Farrah are sitting close together. He has a very possessive look as he watches her, and her look at him is very loving. If I were to guess, I'd say the risk of losing Harold in the battle yesterday made Farrah face the reality of life without him.

I get my mate and I some food, then join her at the table with Harold, Farrah, and Henry.

"Good morning," I say, putting a plate of food in front of Yara before sitting beside her.

"It's a very good morning," Harold says, and I'm confident now that Farrah has agreed to let him mark her. I glance at her neck, seeing that it still has her previous marks only. When she catches my look and blushes, I know I'm right. Harold wraps his arm around her, kissing the side of her head. If I were him, I'd want to wait until I was home and could take my time, too. Good for him.

"Will this feeling in the pack continue?" Henry says, looking around.

"I hope so. I think that will depend on how we run our packs and whether any new enemies present themselves to us. But, I know for me, this is the first time in my life that my pack has felt this good, and I intend to do everything in my power to make sure this feeling continues."

"I would agree. I'm older than you are, Warren, and it's the first time I've felt this feeling in my pack," he says, looking at me. "Thank you for being the catalyst that made these changes in my pack and my life."

"It wasn't me; it was all Yara," I say, and she laughs.

"I don't think so," she says, smiling up at me.

"Everything in my life changed the moment you entered it," I say.

"I think it's the partnership. You both bring something special to this pack, something that is needed. Together, you make a very powerful force and bring the cohesiveness that the pack needs. I've watched you, both of you, and your interactions with the pack. They respond to both of you as their leaders. You have strong ranked members, and that helps, but it's the two of you that are leading your pack into this next phase of life," Farrah says.

"I'm hopeful that our pack will have that as well, very soon," Harold says, grinning at his mate, who blushes again.

After breakfast, Yara, Charlie, Noelle, Haynes, Laney, and I walk Harold and his pack outside, seeing them off. Before he leaves, I pull Harold aside.

"I hope all goes well with your marking and mating," I tell him.

He looks past me to where Farrah is talking to Yara and Savannah.

"She told me she didn't want to lose another man that she loves in this lifetime. She said life's too short to waste it on hate or regrets, and it's about time she started living for love again." His voice gets thick as he talks, and I know he'll be a great mate to her.

"Giving the pack their heart makes all the difference in the world. We, as Alphas, can only do so much. It's why they're our soulmates. They give us everything that we were lacking in ourselves and bring the pack everything that we're not able to give them."

"It's been so long for me that I'd forgotten. But seeing you and Yara and how the pack responds to both of you has reminded me of just how important a Luna, the right Luna, is for a pack."

"Let's talk soon. Maybe we can start having pack gatherings, and eventually, I'd like to talk to Quirin if he'll listen," I tell him.

He nods. "I have my work cut out for me there, but I'm hoping that Henry can help with that. They are only a year apart. Hopefully, between the two of us, we can help him let go of his hate."

"Let me know what I can do. I'm always willing to speak to him whenever he's ready."

"I'll let you know."

We say our goodbyes, and I pull Yara in for a hug. "Ready to go speak to Carson?"

"Let's do it."

We head over to the pack hospital, and Yara leads me to Carson's room. He's awake, but the toll of losing his leg is evident on his face. Eva is here, and it looks like she hasn't slept.

"Warrior Carson," I say as Yara goes to his medical file and looks over his status before beginning to look over his injuries.

"Hello, Alpha," he says.

I turn to Eva. "Warrior Eva, you look exhausted. You're carrying a pup, and as a father-to-be, I can tell you that I don't like seeing those dark circles under your eyes," I say to her.

Yara looks up from Carson's leg to look at Eva. "When's the last time you slept?"

She shrugs. "I've slept some."

"When's the last time you ate?" Yara continues.

Eva looks around. "What time is it?"

"Go get some food, warrior," I say to her.

She shakes her head. "I want to hear what you have to say," she says.

"Go get some food, Eva," Carson says to her.

"No! If you're getting kicked out of this pack, then I'm going with you," she says adamantly.

"Why would he be getting kicked out of the pack?" I ask them.

Carson gestures to his leg as if it's obvious.

"Carson, we talked about this before I operated on you. I know you were in a lot of pain, but I told you there are options," Yara says.

"What kind of options?" Eva asks.

Yara goes on to discuss prosthetics, one for Carson and one for his wolf.

"It will take getting used to by both of you," Yara says, addressing Carson and Kane, his wolf. She goes on to explain that once he's completely healed, he'll have to be fitted in both forms, and then he'll have to practice in both forms, but that she expects that he'll still be able to run patrols and fight.

"It will be different. It won't feel like it does now, and you'll have to get used to the change in how your bodies move, but there's no reason you can't continue to be a warrior for this pack," Yara tells him.

Carson looks from her to me. I raise an eyebrow at him.

"You don't actually think I'm going to argue with my mate, do you? I've said many times that she's in charge of this hospital. If she says it can be done, it can be done. The hardest part, it sounds like, is you accepting that things will be different and being willing to put in the time and effort to adjust to those changes."

He looks from me to Eva's hopeful face and back to Yara. "You really think I can maintain my warrior status?"

"That will be up to you. But you're a fighter, a good one from everything I've heard about you. If you work to make this adjustment, you and Kane, then yes, I have no doubt that you can maintain your warrior status."

I watch him fight the tears that well in his eyes. His pregnant mate has no such ability, and she begins to cry. "Please say you'll try this, Carson. Please."

He looks at her, and his eyes soften. "Of course I will. No one wants to disappoint our Luna, and if she says I can do it, then I'm damn sure going to do it."

"That's the spirit. I certainly don't like being disappointed," Yara says. She says it casually, but I know that her words will ensure that Carson recovers and figures out how to live his life a bit differently.

"Now, Eva, it's time for you to eat and get some sleep," Yara says to her. "Carson, you need to stay another night, and I'll check on you tomorrow. Kane's not strong enough yet to have really started healing you. But if Eva spends some time here ..."

"I'm not leaving," Eva insists.

"Then eat and sleep so I don't have to kick you out of my hospital," Yara says firmly.

"Yes, Luna," Eva says.

"Can she sleep in bed with me?" Carson asks.

"If you can find a comfortable way to sleep, I have no issues with it. Just eat first, or you'll start getting nauseous, Eva."

Carson gives Eva a look and I'm guessing that she's already either vomited or has been feeling nauseous.

"Alright, when you're better, we'll set up a schedule for you to practice sparring one-on-one with me, Charlie, Haynes, or Laney until you get used to your new leg and how it works," I tell him.

"Thank you, Alpha. And thank you, Luna. You really are something special. This pack is lucky to have you," he says, and Eva agrees.

When we walk out of the room, I pull my mate to me.

"Carson's right. You're the most special woman in the world, and you're all mine."

Chapter 98: Letting Go

Anna

When the pack came back after attacking Alpha Brady's pack, they brought Dr. Stephens with them.

Dr. Stephens – the man I have despised ever since I started working in the hospital. All of us, the nurses, knew that he was hurting our pack, but there was very little we could do about it. At the time, we were in a constant state of war. We could barely keep the pack going in between battles, and Dr. Stephens had been part of that problem.

We'd all turned to Savannah. She was younger than Erika and Katie, but she had more medical experience. Without any conscious discussion about it, we had all deferred to her when we questioned Dr. Stephens' methods. Goddess knows, you never questioned him to his face. He'd berate you in front of anyone and everyone in the room. He was a horrible man for so many reasons.

As I stare at the man who is currently on his knees in front of Alpha Warren, I remember the day I lost the man that I'm pretty sure was my mate. I was almost eighteen. I had actually volunteered to work in the hospital because I felt drawn to him, and, as a warrior, he spent more time in the pack hospital than he did in the packhouse, just like most of them did. Back then, the packhouse was a place where warriors slept for a couple of hours before going back out to battle.

Theodore, or Teddy as he'd asked me to call him, had been a young, handsome warrior. I made sure that every time he came in, that I was there to treat him.

"The best part of coming into this hospital is seeing your pretty face," he'd say when he'd come in. I'd always blush, and he'd always stroke his fingers over my cheek and smile in a way that made me think that he felt the same way I did.

"How old are you, Anna?" he'd asked once.

"Seventeen."

"How long before you turn eighteen?"

"A couple of months."

"Hmmm, maybe in a couple of months, we can spend some time together outside of this hospital. Would you like that?" he'd asked me.

Back then, I didn't recognize the possessive look in his eyes. Now, I'm old enough, and I've seen it enough in our pack that I know what it was. He wanted me. Whether he already felt the pull of the mate bond or he'd just set his sights on me, I'll never know. But I knew that I wanted him, too.

He was one of the ones that got an infection that Dr. Stephens didn't treat. I'd had to stand by and watch as Teddy came into the hospital weaker and weaker each time. The brightness, the light in his eyes that I had fallen in love with, eventually dimmed. He'd still tell me that the best part of coming to the hospital was seeing my pretty face, but the smile no longer reached his eyes.

And then the day came when he hadn't returned to the hospital. I'd been busy; we were always busy in the hospital, but I kept looking for him. He never returned from that battle. I'd stood outside while we once again lit pyres for our dead, and this time, I grieved for the man who would never be mine. It was the day before my eighteenth birthday.

I stood by the pyres as they burned. The warriors, exhausted and overwhelmed with frustration and pain at losing more friends and family, didn't stay long. Alpha Warren and Beta Charlie stayed longer, and the desperation coming from both of them was palpable. We were being killed off too quickly, and our doctor wasn't doing anything about it.

I'd stayed out there longer than almost anyone else, crying for the man that I had fallen in love with. One other man was out there with me. When he turned to go inside, he was startled to see me.

"Anna? What are you doing out here? Did you lose someone, too?" he asked. I know I've seen him in the pack hospital, but I don't immediately remember his name. He'd only recently turned eighteen and started fighting, so he hasn't come in as often as the others.

"I did. I lost the man I think was my mate. I would have known for sure tomorrow. What about you? Who did you lose?"

"My brother. He was a good warrior. But there's only so much that can be done with all this fighting. None of us has time to heal properly."

"Who was your brother?" If he was a good warrior, I'm sure I knew him.

"Theodore."

I turned and looked at him. "Teddy is your brother?"

He had nodded and tried to smile, but instead, his lips had trembled, and he'd pressed them tightly together to keep from crying.

"He was the only family I had left. He was a good brother. He sure did like you. He thought ... well, I guess it doesn't matter now."

"He thought what?" I asked.

He'd looked at me sadly. "He thought you were his mate. He told me he couldn't wait until you were eighteen so he would know for sure."

"I thought so, too," I'd said, looking back at the burning pyres. "What's your name?" I'd asked, realizing I didn't know.

"Bennett. But you can call me Benny."

That night, Benny and I had forged a friendship through our combined sorrow and loss. I'd made a point of making sure that when he came into the hospital it was Savannah who saw him and treated him. I wasn't going to lose another friend, and eventually, he and I had become lovers. At first, it felt like a betrayal to Teddy, but I realized I couldn't go my whole life wishing he'd return. He won't. And if he loved me, like I'm pretty sure he did, he wouldn't want me to be sad and alone. Part of me hoped that he'd be happy that it was his brother that I'd given myself to, the only man I've ever been with.

Benny was one of the warriors whose wolf had gone quiet and was dying a slow death when Luna Yara arrived in our pack. He was just one of the many lives that she saved, and I'm so thankful to her for that.

Now, as I listen to Alpha Warren giving his verdict to Dr. Stephens, I feel Benny's hand slide into mine. I turn and look at him, and I see that same possessiveness in his eyes that I saw in his brother's so long ago.

I somehow understand what he's trying to tell me without words. This, Dr. Stephen's death, will close the loop on his brother's death. Teddy's murderer, because that's what Dr. Stephen's is, will die for his sins. I know what Benny wants. He's been asking me for months to make it official between us. Knowing that Dr. Stephens will die today, it feels right. It feels like I can finally let Teddy go.

I nod, letting him know that I'm ready to take him as my chosen mate. He smiles a smile that is very much like his brother's, and I blush. He strokes his fingers over my cheek, getting that same possessive look that Teddy used to get. I wonder if this is Teddy's way of letting me know that he's okay with my decision. I hope he is.

When Alpha Warren steps back, the pack, almost as one, steps forward to attack. As expected, Dr. Stephens takes off running. I don't need to kill him, but I want one good swipe at him for letting all those good warriors die while we, the nurses, tried everything in our power to save them.

The pack leaps, immediately giving chase. Benny and some other strong warriors get to him first, tackling him to the ground. Benny holds him while some of the weaker wolves and I catch up, taking our opportunity to swipe our claws through his body.

When they release him, he begins to run again, and once again, the pack gives chase. I let others have their turn. No one said it out loud, but we all know that our Luna doesn't like the idea of us tormenting Dr. Stephens for a long time, and we will respect her wishes.

It still takes us hours, but without our Luna, we'd have made him suffer like this for days. I was glad when Katie came out and poured alcohol on his open wounds. "That's for our warriors, you asshole," she'd yelled and kicked him in his stomach.

I'd stayed and watched. Everyone wanted to give Dr. Stephens a piece of the pain that he had inflicted on so many. It was Haynes who finally shifted and, holding Dr. Stephens, looked around.

"Anyone not get their chance at him?" he asks. Dr. Stephens' wolf hasn't been able to keep up with the assault the pack had given him, and his open, bloody gashes and bite marks are bleeding, making him weak. His wolf had forced his shift back to his human form hours ago.

When no one steps forward, Gamma Haynes pulls Dr. Stephens' head back. "You deserve so much more than you're getting. But we, this pack, love our Luna more than we hate you. We never want to disappoint her, and while she agreed to allow this, we know it's hard for her. You can thank her, the one you scoffed at when she first arrived, for your easy death."

Dr. Stephens screams, but it only lasts a moment before Haynes extends his claws and removes his head from his body.

When we shift back, Benny turns, walking straight toward me. There's a hunger, a desire that I've never seen in his eyes before. He wraps his arms around me, taking my mouth in a possessive, dominant kiss. I wrap my arms and legs around him as he carries me inside.

When we get to his room, he closes the door and finally pulls away from the kiss.

"Time to make you mine," he growls.

"Yes, Bennett. Make me yours," I say.

I send up a silent promise to Teddy that I will be a good mate to his brother, and I feel like something tight inside me, something I've been holding on to finally lets go, allowing me to give myself freely to Benny, to be and have the kind of mate we both deserve.

Chapter 99: Settled

Warren

It's been several months since we killed Brady and Dr. Stephens. It took a while, but the pack has settled into what I guess is a more normal routine. We spar, we run patrols, Charlie and I run the pack, Yara and Noelle run the hospital, and Haynes and Laney train and manage the warriors.

Now that life has settled down, our pack is having a baby boom. I'm pretty sure every one of my mated she-wolves is pregnant, and some who aren't mated are pregnant as well. Yara and I talked about that, and we've agreed that if both parents are fine with remaining unmated, they can. The ones who don't agree have to speak to both of us so we can come to a resolution. Thankfully, now that we're having pack gatherings with Alpha Harold and his pack, there are fewer unmated adult men and women in our pack.

Today, Yara is in the pack hospital making last-minute preparations before our twins come. I'm watching Charlie and Haynes working with Carson. It's been a long, grueling road for him. He's struggled a lot with frustration and anger. It made things between him and Eva strained during her pregnancy, and she ended up giving birth to their daughter a week earlier than planned.

Yara said it was okay and that their baby was healthy, but that made Carson think through his actions. He had taken a break and worked to get his and his wolf's, Kane's, frustrations under control. Since then, Kane has been able to start running patrols. He can't run a full schedule yet, but he's getting stronger and running farther every day.

"Come on, Carson, you're better than this," Laney says, coaching him through the training. He's able to hold his own now in a one-on-one situation, so they've started pushing him in a two-on-one battle. As I've watched, I've seen the frustration from before starting to come back. Charlie and Haynes are able to tag him one after the other. When he spins, his prosthetic leg doesn't move like his leg used to, and he snarls in frustration.

"Carson ..." Laney begins, but I hold up my hand and step in, walking over to him. He is panting with his frustration. I step in front of him and hold his gaze.

"Carson, first rule of battle, when your head isn't in the fight, you lose. Your head isn't in this battle. Your head is thinking about what you can't do and what your leg doesn't do anymore. Kane, tell me I'm wrong," I say, talking to both Carson and his wolf.

When I don't get a response from either of them, I nod. "Take a break, get your head in the fight. You're smarter than this, a better fighter than this. You can do this."

I go back to where I was standing and watch as Carson puts his hands on his hips until he catches his breath. Then I watch as he paces, knowing that Carson and Kane are talking, trying to get their head back where it should be – in the battle.

When he finally stops pacing and nods that he's ready, Laney gives the go-ahead, and Charlie and Haynes go at him again. This time, he does better. He still has a long road to recovery, but Charlie and Haynes aren't able to tag him as quickly as they had been before.

"Yes, Carson!" Laney encourages him.

I watch for a little bit longer, and then I get a mind link from Noelle.

'Alpha, I think you need to come to the pack hospital.'

I turn and begin walking as I respond. 'What's going on? Is everything alright? Is Yara alright?'

'I'm pretty sure she's in labor, Alpha, but she's not listening to any of us.'

'I'm on my way,' I say, and begin jogging quickly over to the hospital. I expected our twins to come early. They're large, and it's common for twins to come before their due date. I know Yara is feeling the pressure of being away from the hospital for a couple of weeks while we adjust to our little ones, but she can't stop our pups from coming if that's what's happening.

When I walk in the door of the hospital, I can hear my mate mumbling.

"A couple more days. Just a couple more days."

When I see her, she's bent over a counter, her forehead resting on her hand as she rubs her stomach. I come up behind her and put my hands on her stomach.

"I don't think you have a couple more days, my love. Our pups are coming, and no matter how much you're in charge of this hospital, you can't control when your body is ready. Let's get you into a room."

She growls at me, an uncharacteristic response from my mate. "Who told you?"

Rather than answer her, I scoop her into my arms and begin carrying her. Noelle points to a room.

"I think the more important question, Yara, is why didn't I hear it from you?" I ask her, unperturbed by her anger.

She huffs. "I don't have time for this today."

"Then let's see if you're really in labor. I'm going to guess that if you thought there was any chance that you weren't, you'd have checked. Since you haven't, I'm betting my twins are coming, and my mate is going to have to accept that," I say, laying her down on the bed.

"Warren, there's still so much to do ..."

I take her face in my hands as Noelle and Piper come in and begin getting things set up. "You're right, Yara; there is a lot for you to do. Delivering pups is no easy task, and you have two to deliver. Stop worrying about the hospital. If the others need anything, they can ask you. You're not going anywhere. You just won't be working for a couple of weeks," I tell her, keeping my voice calm even though I feel anything but.

My pups are coming. My pups are coming!!

"I'm here!" a breathless and very pregnant Savannah says, pushing through the door. From just outside the room, I see Franklin. He must have driven her over here.

Yara growls again. "They called you, too?"

"Oh, quit your snarling. I'm pregnant, too, and I feel like I have a fucking watermelon in my stomach. I don't need your attitude, Luna," Savannah says, and I have to fight really hard not to laugh out loud. I notice that both Noelle and Piper have to turn away so Yara doesn't see their smiles. Both of them are pregnant as well, but neither of them is as far along as Savannah.

"Just wait until it's your turn, and you're not ready for me to be there," Yara snaps.

Savannah gets in her face. "I'll try to have a better attitude than you do right now, Luna. Look at you, snapping at everyone around you. How very unbecoming of a Luna," Savannah says, giving it right back.

When the monitors start beeping, Savannah looks at them and then turns to Yara, raising an eyebrow. "How long were you going to wait, Luna? Until you were crowning? Let's get you undressed and into a gown."

Savannah turns and looks at me. "What are you smiling at, Alpha?" she grumbles.

"You make a damn good, Beta, Savannah."

"Thank you. My pack says the same," she says with a hint of a smile.

"What can I do to help?" I ask.

"Stay out of my way and help your mate to stay calm and breathe. We're going to be here for a while."

She wasn't wrong. It was well into the night when Savannah told Yara that she could start pushing. It was another hour after that before my first child, my son, was born. I got to look at him a moment while I was cutting the cord. He's beautiful, perfect.

While Piper went to clean him off, Yara had to start pushing again.

"Okay, Luna, we're almost done. You can do this," Savannah says.

I look at my mate. "Of course, she can. My mate is the most incredible woman I've ever met in my life. You've already given me a beautiful baby boy. Now you just have to deliver our daughter, and you're done, my love."

"I don't feel very incredible," she says. I can see and feel the exhaustion in her.

"But you are. You're almost there, and then we can hold our babies in our arms and begin the next phase of our lives together."

My daughter comes much faster than my son, thankfully, and I have a moment to see her and cut her cord before Noelle takes her to clean her off. I've just turned back when Piper returns with our son. She lays him in Yara's arms, and he immediately begins crying. I feel my own eyes burn with tears as I lean over, kissing the side of my mate's head and wrapping my arms around the two of them as Arric pushes forward, and we both look over our son.

"Did you decide on a name?" I ask her. We've narrowed down our list of names for both our son and daughter, but we hadn't actually decided. Yara said she wanted to see them first so we could decide which name fit them best.

She's just told me our son's name when Noelle brings over our daughter. "Alpha, do you want to hold your little girl?"

I take her in my arms, and for the first time in my life, I lose the battle with my tears. She's perfect. I wipe my tears from her chubby little cheeks, watching as her mouth turns toward my finger. Savannah helps Yara begin nursing our son, and when she's settled, she looks over at me. I haven't been able to tear my eyes away from my little girl. She started to fuss, but Arric was quick to begin purring at her, and it calmed her back to sleep.

"Have you decided on a name for her?" Yara asks me.

I tell her my choice, and after Yara has nursed both pups and fallen asleep, Noelle lets me know that the entire pack is in the waiting room, wanting to meet their Alpha heir and Alpha princess.

I carry my sleeping babies, one in each arm, out into the waiting room. It's the middle of the night, and many pack members are holding their own sleeping pups in their arms. When I step into the room, everyone goes quiet.

"Everyone, I'd like you to meet my pups, Alpha Connor and his sister, Alpha Kennedy."

Epilogue 1: Teaching Hospital

Yara

Five Years Later

If you had asked me six years ago what my life would look like now, I'm not sure I would have ever imagined this. My life is filled with love, happiness, work, school, the pack, and most importantly, family.

My mate is as perfect a father as I knew he would be. He LOVES being a father, and I love watching him with our pups. I never thought I could love that man more than I did. But seeing him being the incredible father that he is with our pups, I've just kept feeling the need to give him more. After the twins, we decided to wait a bit. Our original plan was to wait a few years while we adjusted to being parents to two babies. Warren wanted to focus on getting the pack financially stable and increasing the pack's income, and I wanted to focus on becoming a teaching hospital.

It took about six months of negotiation with the closest werewolf university and a lot of conversations with their board of directors on my knowledge and experience versus what they could teach in the university. In the end, they agreed to send five students to us for a month. At the end of the month, those students began excelling in their classes and begging to return, saying they'd learned more in that month than they had in two years at the university.

I'd let Warren take the lead on negotiating the fee that each student would have to pay to attend our teaching school. The university set up computers with video conference capability so that the students could continue to attend classes while in our pack.

The pack hospital extended to add an entire section for student housing, their own cafeteria, classrooms, and study areas. That part of the hospital is separated from the rest with a door that can be accessed to come and watch or participate in surgeries and other evaluations. Each semester, we've had more and more students attending our teaching school. We had to put a cap on the number of students that we could allow at one time, and now there's a waitlist to participate in our hospital.

As part of the changes to the hospital setup, we created two treatment rooms with windows so students can watch during the surgeries if they aren't participating. Since we still have sparring twice a day, we still have an indefinite number of injuries that need to be attended to, so there's never a shortage of patients coming through the door.

In addition, the pack has had a baby boom. I know, for myself, my mate and I couldn't wait three years. I wanted to give that man another child so desperately that we started trying again after only a year and a half. My mate, always wanting to give me what I want, got me pregnant right away, and our second son, Yorick, was born almost two years after the twins. The next time, we didn't wait as long, and our second daughter, Wendy, was born a year later.

I smile, looking down at my stomach, which is once again large with my mate's pup. This one will be another little girl. We've been back and forth with names. Since our boys look like Warren and our girls look like me, he's positive that this one will look like me as well, so he wants to give her a name close to mine. It's the first time we've chosen a name before our baby was delivered.

"Daddy's just positive that you're going to look like me, though, isn't he, Yana?" I say, speaking to my stomach. I've just stepped out of the shower to get ready to go to the hospital.

I hear the low, possessive growl of my mate behind me. I look up into the mirror in our bathroom and see Warren's dark eyes looking at me and my belly. He comes up behind me, sliding his hands over my large stomach.

"You look so fucking sexy with my pup in your belly," he says. And this is just one more reason why I love giving my mate pups. He can barely keep his hands off of me when I'm pregnant, especially when I'm pregnant with a little girl.

"Where are your other pups," I breathe as he pushes me forward and slides inside me. The intense pleasure of having my mate inside me has never gone away. If anything, I've become more desperate for him with time.

"Arric purred them back to sleep when we heard you getting out of the shower. Daddy needed some Mommy time."

"Daddy sure knows how to start Mommy's day off right," I say, watching my mate in the mirror as he brings me up and over and then again before finding his release deep inside me.

When he slides out of me, I stand up and he kisses my neck, sending shivers through my body.

"Are you sure you're done after this one?" he asks.

"I'm rethinking that," I say, making him chuckle.

"Let me know if and when you change your mind. I'm always happy to put another pup in you."

"Do we have room in the nursery for more?" I ask him.

"I'll build another one if I have to," he growls, nipping at my ear and making hot desire pool in my core again.

When our pack members started having pups, they ALL started having pups. Before the twins were born, Warren had to create a space for a nursery in the packhouse. He'd had to add on to that, extending the space when those pups started to get older and younger pups started being born. Now, we have a full-fledged nursery going every day.

Katie, who went to school to get her nursing degree along with Erica and Anna, decided she wanted to be closer to her pups, so she began working in the nursery full-time. It works because she's able to treat them for minor injuries or colds when needed, rather than their parents having to bring them to the hospital.

That doesn't mean that my hospital isn't still as busy as it always was. In some ways, it's busier. I may not have as many warriors coming into the hospital now, but I do have pups coming in every day for one reason or another. Thankfully, Noelle has been going to school to become a doctor, and Piper is going to school to be a physician's assistant, so they can help handle a lot of the needs that our pups have, especially things like annual physicals and minor injuries.

When Warren and I finish getting ready for the day, I see that the twins are up again. Warren swings Connor onto his shoulders before lifting Kennedy and Yorick.

"Ready for school?" he asks them excitedly.

"YEAH!" they all say.

I get Wendy, and we all head down to the nursery. Connor and Kennedy have started Kindergarten, but the others go to the nursery. Since my belly is huge, Warren carries Yorick to the nursery for me, and we drop him and Wendy off. I give them both kisses and hugs, then turn to my mate and twins.

"Say goodbye to Mommy," he says.

"Bye, Mommy," Kennedy says. I take her in my arms and give her a hug and kiss before looking up at Connor.

"Bye, Mommy," he says, leaning over to give me a kiss.

"Bye, Mommy," Warren growls, making the kids squeal as he kisses me.

Damn, my man is sexy.

"I'm glad you think so," he says, smiling at me. I never did stop mumbling out loud. It's a good thing my mate likes that little quirk.

I shake my head and hand Kennedy back to him before waving and turning to head to the hospital.

"What do we do when we're at school?" I hear Warren ask, just like he does every day.

"Listen to our teachers," Connor says before I step outside of the packhouse.

Yeah, my life is pretty perfect.

I get to the hospital and begin looking over our schedule for the day. Noelle, Piper, and Anna join me. All of them have their own pups. Noelle has three, and Piper and Anna have two each, although I'm pretty sure Anna is pregnant with her third one. They all tease me that I have so many pups. It's not my fault that I can't keep my hands off my sexy mate.

Our first warrior injury comes in soon after I arrive, and our day begins. It's late morning when the howl of alarm goes up.

"LUNA, INCOMING! Alpha Henry has Alpha Quirin. He's in bad shape!" the patrols say, just as I hear a horn honking and tires screeching to a stop outside.

"PREPARE FOR SURGERY!" I say to Noelle and Piper as Anna comes rushing up with a gurney. We push it outside as Henry opens the passenger door. The smell of blood is so strong that it makes my stomach turn. I swallow the bile in my throat and force myself to focus.

Henry picks up Quirin and lays him on the gurney. There's blood everywhere.

"What happened?" I ask as Anna pushes the gurney inside while I begin looking over Quirin.

"We were clearing out his pack lands. He turned eighteen, and he wants to retake his father's old lands. We were busy clearing the brush, and it was so tall. We were talking and not paying attention, and we flushed a mother bear out of her den. She came at me, and Quirin pushed me out of the way, taking the brunt of her attack. I was able to get her away from him, but ..."

But the bear left huge, gaping gashes on Quirin.

"Why isn't he healing?" I ask Henry.

"He has healed some. That bear nearly mauled him to death. He's only alive because of his wolf, but I think his wolf is fading," Henry says.

As we roll him into the room, I take his face in my hands. "Alpha Quirin! Alpha Quirin, can you hear me?" I say to him.

His eyes turn to look at me, but he doesn't respond. While Noelle and Piper get him hooked up and ready for surgery, I put my face close to his.

"I have one rule, Alpha. No one dies in my hospital. If you come in with a heartbeat, you walk out of here on your own two feet. Do you hear me, Alpha Quirin?" I ask him.

When he doesn't answer, I growl at him. I've never ever lost anyone in my hospital, and I don't intend to lose someone now.

"Do not think that I won't follow you into the Moon Goddess' realm and drag you sorry Alpha ass back down here, Quirin. Do you understand me? You do not die in my hospital. Tell me you hear me, and you understand," I growl.

"Yes, Luna," he says. His voice is barely a whisper, but he answers, and I'll take it.

I have no idea how long I'm in surgery. Quirin's body looked like it had been shredded. If his wolf healed him, I can't imagine what he looked like before Henry got him to me. Noelle and I had traded off, with me stitching up his organs that had been torn apart while she closed up the large gashes in his arms and legs. When we finally put in the last stitch, I drop my head, exhausted but pleased that Quirin's heart is still beating, and his pulse is steady.

I hear clapping nearby, and I look up. In the observation room, every student in our teaching hospital is watching. But I also see Warren, Harold, Farrah, Henry, Savannah, Franklin, and many others from their pack. Harold and Farrah had become something of parents to Quirin, especially after his mother passed away. I can see the concern on their faces, the same concern that I know would be on mine if this were my child.

I step out into the hallway, pulling off my gloves and scrubs as I go. My mate, always there when I need him, walks up to me and scoops me into his arms.

"I've got you, beautiful. You did a great job today. You saved that kid's life."

Harold, Farrah, and Henry all walk out of the observation room, thanking me and asking if they can stay with Quirin so he's not alone. I nod, knowing that having family nearby will help him and his wolf to heal.

"He'll need to stay for several days," I tell them.

"I'll make sure he doesn't fight you on that," Harold says before following Henry and Farrah into the room.

"Time for you to get some sleep, my love," Warren says, carrying me out of the hospital.

I'm asleep before we get to the packhouse.

Epilogue 2: Birthday

Quirin

One Year Later

"Come on, Quirin! You can punch harder than that," Henry, my best friend and the closest thing I have to a brother, says to me.

"It's your birthday, Henry. I don't want to make you cry before we celebrate your big day," I taunt.

Where Henry is a shining star of happiness, I'm a black cloud of anger. Being around him helps to keep the darkness at bay, but no one can remove the darkness that has consumed me since the day that I watched my father die.

I had planned my revenge on Alpha Warren for years and had intended to take everything that he loved from him. But all that changed a year ago when his mate saved my life. Not only had she saved my life, but she'd also insisted that I live. She, like Henry, has a bright golden light that shines around her. She'd taken my face in her hands and told me that I wasn't allowed to die. I had been ready to die, ready to give up the grief that I've held so deep in my heart, but she wouldn't allow it. How that woman saved my life is beyond me.

She had cared for me while I was in her hospital, and while I hate her mate, I can understand why my father wanted Luna Yara as a mate. He would have fallen in love with her. I know he would have because a part of me did as well.

After months of Alpha Harold asking me to let Alpha Warren tell me what really happened and why he'd killed my father, I'd sat quietly and listened to what the man had to say. Nothing that he said changed my feelings about him, though. It was Luna Yara who made a difference in me with her gentle kindness and loving soul.

While I call Henry my brother, I never could bring myself to call Alpha Harold father or dad. However, once my mother died, basically giving up on life because she could no longer be a Luna, I found myself drawn to Luna Farrah. She, like me, has suffered loss. She understands the darkness inside me more than Alpha Harold. They've both been wonderful role models for me, and while my father was a very different kind of leader than Alpha Harold, Harold has taught me a lot about what it takes to run a pack.

Before I turned eighteen, he'd pulled me aside and told me that he'd put the deed to my father's pack lands in his safe. He'd kept it safe for me, and when I'd turned eighteen, I'd returned to the place where my father had raised me. Henry had insisted on coming with me, wanting to make sure that I wasn't alone and probably to make sure that I didn't walk out of his life, never to return. I might have, except I really like the warm glow he brings to my life. And if I'm honest, I do love him like a brother. It's why I was willing to give my life to save his. That bear, the one that almost killed me, was going after him. I couldn't let that bear or anyone snuff out the life inside him. He's a good person, too good to die so young. But I'm not. I'm full of anger and hate.

When we'd walked into the packhouse, it was like déjà vu. All of my memories of growing up here had flooded back to me. I'd walked to my father's office and sat in the chair that was dusty and creaky from years of sitting idle.

Henry helped me go through everything, and the biggest shock of all was my father's finances. He'd made sure that I would be set for life. The pack was wealthy before he died, but since his death, even with no one managing the account, the money has multiplied. It was enough for me to begin cleaning up the packhouse and the pack lands. For what, I wasn't sure at the time, but I just knew that an Alpha needed a place to have his pack.

So, for the last year, minus the time that I was recovering, I've been cleaning out the packhouse and pack lands. That's when the rogues started to approach me. Moms with young pups needed a place to live. They were desperate and willing to do just about anything to have a secure place for themselves and their pups. There weren't a lot of them, but over the last year, my pack of one has grown to a pack of twenty-five. It's a start.

"Are you even trying, Quirin?" Henry goads me. He's a good fighter, but I'm better. The difference is that I don't mind hurting people; he does. However, I don't want to hurt him. There are very few people in this world that I care about, and Henry is at the top of that very short list.

Sometimes, I feel like I'm much older than he is, like the darkness in me has aged me somehow. And, since it is his birthday, I give him the gift of defeating me.

"YES!" he says, dancing around like a prize fighter where I'm lying on the ground.

"You're utterly ridiculous," I say, sitting up. "Come on. I need to shower before your party."

He puts his hand out and helps me up. As we walk in, Luna Farrah puts her hand on my arm. When Henry is a few steps away, she looks at me. "I saw what you did."

I shrug. "It's his birthday."

"Mmhmm," she says knowingly. I'm not sure how it is that this woman knows me better than my own mother did, but she does.

She turns and falls into step beside me. "How's the pack coming along?"

"It's getting there," I tell her.

"Am I ever going to get an invite to come visit?" she asks.

"I thought you knew you had an open invitation," I say, making her smile.

"Good to know. I'm going to take you up on that," she says, and I know she will.

The room I lived in for the five years I'd been in this pack was left untouched when I left. Luna Farrah said it was because she wanted me to know that I was always welcome to return and always had a place to stay if I needed it. This room feels more like home than my room in my own packhouse. Of course, that was my father's bedroom when he was alive. I moved my things into that room when I took over as Alpha.

When I finish getting ready, Henry's birthday party has already started. I take another look in the mirror, reminding myself that I can't kill Alpha Warren. Not only is he in an alliance with Alpha Harold and after tomorrow night, I'm sure he'll renew that with Henry, but I can't hurt Luna Yara that way, not after what she did for me.

I head downstairs, saying my hellos to Alpha Warren, Luna Yara, and the rest of their brood. The woman is pregnant again, and she's huge. I'm beginning to wonder if Alpha Warren is planning to breed her to death.

They have two boys who look just like their father and three girls. The two older ones look like Luna Yara, and the youngest looks like her father.

"Alpha Quirin, how are you doing?" Luna Yara asks me.

"I'm well, Luna, thank you," I say warmly.

"How's the pack coming along?" Alpha Warren asks.

"It's good, thanks," I say, with much more ice in my tone. "If you'll excuse me."

Without waiting for a response, I go find Henry, who is surrounded by friends. Unlike me, he has an abundance of them. I get a drink and stand with him, laughing at stupid jokes and smiling when it's appropriate. I'm bored out of my mind, but this is my brother's eighteenth birthday party, so I force myself to be nice and play along.

"So, you haven't smelled your mate yet, Alpha?" someone asks him.

"Nah. I guess she's not in this pack. Maybe Alpha Warren's pack, or who knows, maybe she's in Alpha Quirin's pack," he says, clinking his glass with mine.

"I doubt it," I say. I don't have any young females in my pack that don't have pups already.

The others turn to me, asking me about my pack. My short, cold answers quickly drive the conversation back to Henry, where it belongs.

When the cake comes out, everyone gathers around and sings Happy Birthday. I take the opportunity to duck outside, grabbing another drink before going to sit by myself.

I smell her before I see her. I'm not sure why her scent calls to me, maybe because of who her mother is, but either way, I know it's her.

"What are you doing out here by yourself, pup? You should be inside having cake with your family."

"I wanted to check on you, Alpha Quirin," Kennedy says, coming out of the shadows.

"Check on me?" I ask, raising an eyebrow at her. I take a sip of my drink and watch her over the edge of the glass.

"Mhmm. I've been watching you all night."

"Have you? And what did you see?" I ask. I'm not sure why I care, but I'm curious to know what this little pup thinks she saw.

She comes to sit down beside me. I take a deep breath of her citrus and mint scent. For such a young pup, her scent is very appealing.

"I saw you standing alone in a group of people. I saw you laughing, but the laughter didn't reach your eyes. I saw your jaw tighten or your fists clench when anyone directed a question to you," she says, making me pause. I'm unused to anyone noticing this much about me. Luna Farrah is the only one who has come close to seeing me like this young

520

pup has seen me. I don't like it. It makes me feel exposed, which is probably why my response is much harsher than it should be.

"You don't know what you're talking about."

"I know you don't like my father," she says.

"You're right about that. He killed my father, so no, I'll never like your father. Be glad you look like your mother, or I might hate you, too."

"Everyone says my mother is beautiful. If you think that I look like her, then you must think that I'm beautiful, too," she says, smiling up at me. Damn, she is beautiful, maybe even more than her mother.

"She's okay. I wouldn't call her beautiful," I say spitefully.

"Oh," Kennedy says, and I can tell I've hurt her feelings. Normally, I wouldn't care, but for some reason, I don't like hurting this little pup's feelings.

"You're prettier than your mother," I say quietly, and her face lights up. She's got that same glow about her, the one that Henry and Luna Yara have, the warm glow that I'm drawn to like a moth to a flame.

"Kennedy! There you are!" Luna Yara says, walking out. "Oh, Alpha Quirin. I hope Kennedy wasn't bothering you."

"She's fine," I say, watching as Kennedy goes to her mother and takes her hand.

"Kennedy, you shouldn't wander off like that. Your father and I didn't know where you were," Luna Yara says.

"I was safe with Alpha Quirin," she says confidently. Oh, little pup. You were definitely NOT safe with me.

"You should stay away from men like me, Kennedy. Men like me are no good for little pups like you," I tell her.

Instead of heeding my words, she pulls away from her mother and comes over and hugs me.

"I'm not afraid of you," she whispers in my ear.

I reach my arm around her, taking a deep breath of her scent. "You should be," I say quietly to her.

She pulls away and goes back to her mother.

"It was good seeing you, Alpha Quirin. If you need any medical assistance in your pack, please let me know. I'd be happy to come help you," she says.

"Looks like you're going to have your hands even more full than they are now, pretty soon."

"Mommy's having twins again," Kennedy says excitedly.

Yara smiles down at her daughter. "That is true, but the offer still stands. I know our pack is closer to yours than Alpha Harold's, so anytime you need anything ..."

"Thank you, Luna," I say, cutting her off. There's no way I'm asking a woman on the verge of having her second set of twins to come help me with anything.

"Well, we'll let you return to your peace and quiet. Come on, Kennedy," she says, leading her daughter away.

I watch and I'm pleasantly surprised when Kennedy turns and waves goodbye to me. I'm even more surprised when I feel the need to raise my hand and wave back.

**This story will continue in The Pack's Nemesis (Quirin's Story) later this year.

About the Author

C ooper has been a lover of paranormal romance since reading her first dragon book, Dragonflight, by Anne McCaffrey. Like most binge readers, she has been known to stay up until the early morning hours to finish a book that she can't put down. She strives to bring that same level of enjoyment and excitement to her readers.

You can follow Cooper's books and updates on Facebook at Cooper's Pack or on Instagram @coopersgreedyreaders.

Cooper lives in Florida with her husband and six dogs.